DAYLIGHT IN NIGHTCLUB INFERNO

CZECH FICTION FROM THE POST-KUNDERA GENERATION

Selections chosen by Elena Lappin

Catbird Press
A Garrigue Book

CATBIRD PRESS
16 Windsor Road, North Haven, CT 06473
800-360-2391; catbird@pipeline.com

Our books are distributed by Independent Publishers Group

ACKNOWLEDGMENTS: Catbird Press would like to acknowledge the direct help
of Michael Henry Heim as well as the ongoing training that Peter Kussi has
done with some of the translators whose work appears in this collection. We
would like to thank Maxim Biller for contributing the cover photograph, and
the many people who helped Elena Lappin in her quest to find the best new
work of the best young Czech writers.
Acknowledgments for permission to translate and include
the works in this anthology appear at the back of the book.

Library of Congress Cataloging-in-Publication Data

Daylight in nightclub inferno : Czech fiction from the post-Kundera generation /
edited and introduced by Elena Lappin. -- 1st ed.
"Anthology of English translations of short stories and novel excerpts written
by younger Czech writers ... since the Velvet Revolution..." --CIP info.
ISBN 0-945774-33-8 (trade pbk. : alk. paper)
1. Short stories, Czech--Translations into English. 2. Czech fiction--20th
century--Translations into English. I. Lappin, Elena.
PG5145.E8D39   1997
891.8'630108--dc20   96-43674 CIP

Publisher's Foreword

Catbird is proud to be publishing *Daylight in Nightclub Inferno*, the first English-language collection of fiction by the younger generations of Czech writers.

The older generation, consisting of such writers as Milan Kundera, Bohumil Hrabal, Josef Škvorecký, Václav Havel, Vladimír Páral, and Ivan Klima, has been better represented in English translation than the writers of any other small language. This generation reached its maturity as writers during the opening up of the Prague Spring in the mid-60s. They were published in English especially after the Soviet invasion of August 1968 and the Velvet Revolution of 1989. However, the younger Czech writers were ignored.

The situation is similar with North American translators. The generation that originally translated the older Czech writers — the Americans Peter Kussi, Michael Henry Heim, Jeanne Němcová, Vera Blackwell, and William Harkins; and the Canadians Paul Wilson and Káča Poláčková-Henley — have not yet given way to the new generation. Only very recently have some of the younger North American translators been given an opportunity to translate book-length works from Czech.

As the only American publisher specializing in Czech literature, we consider it our responsibility to introduce both the recent, post-Velvet Revolution work of younger Czech writers and the work of the younger American Czech-into-English translators. And since we have a Czech speaker on staff, who gained an apprenticeship in translation by working with some of the older-generation translators, we can also guarantee readers the same high quality prose they're used to getting from the more experienced translators.

Just the way CDs often have bonus tracks, this collection contains three bonus selections by excellent older-generation writers whose work has not appeared in English: Alexandr Kliment, Pavel Grym, and Marta Kadlečíková. It's hard to believe that this best-mined of generations still has such quality lodes left.

The ordering of the selections is intended primarily to give readers who actually try the read the book straight through a constantly changing experience — from dark surrealism to comic postmodernism, from realistic narrative to stylistic tour de force. We don't want the reader to get stuck in a long nightmare, in childhood or in the 90s. Also, longer pieces are separated by shorter palate clearers. The three older writers appear at the end of the collection (although some may want to read them first), and the work of the younger writers is framed by selections from the two most lionized — and different — of them, Jáchym Topol and Michal Viewegh.

As for the title of this collection, it is hard to tell from the writing which period is more infernal, the period of communism or the new period of growing capitalism. The daylight in the title comes not from the authors' visions of the world, but rather from the quality of their writing and from their ability to publish it freely at home (although no longer to so captive an audience).

I hope you will agree after reading this book that the younger generations — of Czech writers as well as American translators — also have enormous talent. Let us hope that their work will be published here without the benefit of any more invasions or revolutions.

CONTENTS

JÁCHYM TOPOL
from **Sister**
Translated by Alex Zucker

Chapter 6
"I Had a Dream."

Though Micka had for a while now been feverishly rubbing his hands together and transmitting the unmistakable byznys signal, we went on sitting in our club chairs and fine leather armchairs . . . the truth had spoken from the mouth of an innocent babe . . . David was sitting all crumpled up . . . the mountain boy positively reeked of mad city sadness . . . I felt an urge to uncork some of the Fiery and take myself a little vacation, Micka paced angrily around the room gnashing what few teeth he had, and Bohler browsed through his dog-eared old copy of *The Married Priest* . . . and then he slammed the book down and said firmly: Self-criticism! He was right, we could all feel it. It was obvious, even to Micka, that the time was right for self-destructive self-criticism and that the byznys day was down the drain.

It was only exceptionally that we engaged in self-criticism, only in the heavy-duty cases when we'd seriously crushed someone, not that we would ever violate the rules of our little profit-sharing contract, not at all, it's just that working within the confines of the market economy required us to engage in a few dirty tricks here and there. It wasn't like we cared about our victims, not by a long shot; when a guy gets under the wheel, it's because he just doesn't know how to use his power — that's his affair. We underwent self-criticism so as to be purer . . . more ardently prepared for the coming of the Messiah.

Self-criticism was an old bolshevik class invention, so they say, and murderer Mao, the teacher, developed it to perfection. We dusted it off so we could use it, not abuse it, in freedom. Bohler always began.

I had a dream, he said. I was just out walking around the old city of ours, shoes, pants, shirt and jacket, in my civvies, making the rounds of the bars and the old locales, and looking around for sinners, some infected whores I might possibly persuade to give up their disgusting ways. Keeping an eye out to snag some scamps and so on, you know me, guys. And I confess, my bosom was warmed with gratification and heinous pride, because the day before, I'd snagged three of the little gooners and herded them into an old garage and stomped their devil-dolls to pieces and baptized them. After some consideration I let them keep their weapons, they wouldn't get far without them, but I blessed all their little knifies and gun-guns, because after my persuading them into baptism and genuine contrition, they seemed to be on the right side. And the day before that, I sent a few hookers down the right path and also managed to heavily stigmatize one disgusting sinner who was battering his old kids . . . so now it'll be easy for Bog to recognize the fiend . . . and O my buddies, that same day I overcame stiff resistance from a band of revoltingly bloody butchers and took two blind old forsaken horses out of the slaughterhouse and set them free on the grass in back of our buildings . . . I confess, as I strolled along I had nothing but good feelings. Well . . . we all know how our first free president's beautiful new vision — namely, clean, quiet streets and nice, cozy little pubs, and all sorts of delightful little shops full of grub — is now becoming a reality all over the place, and how a lot of people are turning on to vitamins in the serenity of their families, and how a number of people have managed to move out from under the Castle up into the Castle, but we also know that the cellars are full. So I went by the skids and saw the people's wretchedness and vice and falsity, and met the sinners and their victims, hearts red with rage and hearts broken, and as I sauntered on down to the riverboat landing in the stench of the toxic Vltava, I was warmed with pride that I was on the right side . . . and that I was doing what I could to assist His coming . . and then outside one alehouse I saw a real wreck . . . a disgusting old guy in lice-infested rags . . . his face was completely ravaged by goose blotches, it looked like the skin was peeling off and running down his mug . . . he was shaking all up and down his filthy body from booze, or the lack of it . . . he was so disgusting that people stopped and laughed at him, he was exposed to ridicule and deepest contempt, he was totally under the wheel, and I mean real deep . . . he had on these filthy pants, all baggy and shit-stained . . . in a trembling voice he whimpered for change and little scamps threw mud and dirt clods, he took one smack in the kisser and didn't even feel it . . . I stopped alongside the freak and fished around in my pockets . . . I confess, I too felt contempt and ridicule. . . the guy was a clown . . . but just then he lifted up his filmy eyes . . . up till then he'd just stared at the ground, the way old panhandlers do . . . and I saw it was my father, my dad . . . and he recognized me, and he was so far gone he said: Michal, Michálek, get me outta here . . . he always used to say that when the moms sent me to bring him home from some dive where yet again he'd gambled away all his cash, and he'd be just sitting there, blitzed, in the corner, and the guys'd laugh at him and say . . . your angel's come for you, get up, Bohler . . . and I'd take him home, and when we got there he'd always find enough strength left to bang me up . . . piece of shit, I wanted to kill him . . . then I split . . . and left him with my mother, since she was the cow who went and married him . . . and anyway he and his booze tortured her to death before long . . . and now here he was right in front of me, the creep, and his eyes brightened up a little . . . but then he was gone, and he said: Give to the needy, young man . . . didn't know who I was anymore . . . but I did know . . . the dying cripple sensed someone standing there . . .

I noticed that greedy flash in his eyes, and I didn't give a damn about the people around us and said: Don't you know who I am? Don't you recognize me? Dad! And that ugly mug opened back up its eyes and said: Yeah you're my son Michael, sure I know you . . . I'm telling you, O my guys and pals, I had an awful urge to deck him on the spot for all he'd done, for what he'd done to himself . . . but suddenly there came pity, and I realized he was in there somewhere, there must've been something me and my dad had never talked about, maybe some sort of demon had decked him . . . something I didn't understand . . . and now he was really bad off, worse than a battered animal . . . and I was really afraid we'd never have a chance to talk . . . that it was too late . . . and it was, he didn't recognize me anymore . . . and so, my friends, I asked a couple of dopes from the crowd to wait with him while I ran off to find a doctor or whoever it is you go for in such situations . . . and I couldn't get anyone, and by the time I got back the old lush, my dad, was gone of course, and none of the good citizens were there either . . . and when I burst into that pub they probably thought I was nuts, nobody there knew him and nobody'd ever seen him. And that's it. I figure by this time he's gotta be dead. And I never did give him any change for a bottle . . .

Bohler concluded to the pack's friendly, vigilant grumbling. We held him by the shoulders, where the sources of pity are, and then gave them a thrashing, and despite our efforts to provide our companion with effective assistance he also took a slap here and there, and then his shoulders straightened back up and he was more or less all right.

Micka was next in line. I had a dream, he said. I was about ten, give or take, and I just happened to be playing out in the yard of our kultchured old-Prague family's old townhouse. And it just happened to be a weird day, the kind of day where the air's new and little guys get into weird moods and wanna try on worlds and try out their strength and see what it can do. I was poking around the old toolsheds and raspberry bushes, a little bit grouchy and a little bit antsy — they were no mystery to me anymore — and waiting and watching. Some force was pulling me, I dug around in the dirt awhile, tried to lift up a big rock and it was no go. I kicked around the cracked old pre-bolshevik pool, which our tenants — since actually it wasn't ours anymore and the house wasn't either — used for storing coal, and I dug passages through the coal. But somehow it wasn't any fun, I wanted to get to the surface, to something new. I bummed around here and there and tried to lift up the rock again. I wrestled with it, but it was no go and I fell down and banged my head. And I think it was at that very moment I was possessed by the Devil. As I picked myself up, a little bit dazed, I spotted a bird's nest up in the branches of a tree. It was full of featherless fledglings, cheeping and stretching their long bare throats out toward the mama raven, who was feeding them a worm. I'd never seen anything like it before, except in some pictures at school. It was new, it was interesting. I snuck over to the tree so as not to frighten the mama, but she spotted me, of course, and started raising an alarm and flying around the nest. I dunno why but she spooked me a little, I guess, and I grabbed a rake lying there in a heap of leaves on the ground. I wanted to get a better look at the cheepers, who'd just started squawking good, so I sort of tipped the nest a little and they started cheeping even more and wobbling their bare necks all funny; I could see their little mini beaks opening and closing. The mama raven was circling around my head and beating her wings. It was a bizarre feeling, I got goosebumps, all of a sudden I was their master. I could decide what happened to them next. They were so little and cute I got this totally burning urge to hold them in my palm and pet them and cuddle with them. But at the same time I was thrilled by the feeling that I could suddenly clench that friendly palm into a fist and squash them. It was both feelings at once. I still could have stopped it all, but no, I lifted the rake higher, bit by bit, and the nest started moving. I needed to know so bad what it would do and what all would happen. I guess I needed to know how my new power over living creatures worked. I didn't see it that way at the time, but I guess I needed to know how death works. And that it really exists. I could've stopped when the first one fell onto the ground. But no, I just went over to look at him up close, I touched him and I could feel his little heart pounding frantically underneath the down that covered his body. And that frenzy somehow got inside of me, or I got scared the mama raven would punish me somehow. She kept dive-bombing me, disappearing into the trees and then each time swooping a little bit closer to my face; her wings had skimmed me a few times already. I guess I was afraid she might somehow call the other ravens or my parents or I dunno . . . but I realized that whatever I wanted to do I had to do right then, and what it was, to this day, I still don't understand. I started smashing the nest with the rake, and the little birdies started dropping onto the ground, and then the nest split open. I think I let out a roar. When the nest fell, the babies started cheeping and wriggling weirdly all over the ground . . . suddenly they were disgusting, like worms or something, and I jumped on the nest and stomped. I stomped them into mush and then took the rake to the mama raven, who began wailing . . . don't anyone tell me birds don't cry, I heard it, anybody who says different . . . I warn you . . . and I chopped her with the rake, again and again, till she was just dragging herself over those children of hers . . . and then, O my brothers, then I pissed all over them . . . I was burning so much with excitement I just had to keep going somehow. I urinated on them, and I knew that what I was doing was really wicked, but it was also beautiful, bizarre . . and it wasn't over yet, because there I was peeing on the birdies and the mama raven and poking them now and then with my shoe, when all of a sudden I hear: Lukaš! Lukaš, what are you doing out there, who are you playing with? It was my mom and she was nearby and suddenly she could see it all . . . and suddenly we were facing each other, me with my fly unzipped and my mom . . . and the birds . . . and maybe if I'd collapsed, or at least started bawling, I might have broken it somehow . . . but I let out a dreadful yell, I was really scared she'd punish me, and I hated her for having caught me. I hit her in the mouth and screamed some swear words, she was totally bewildered and turned to make a fast getaway. But that made me fly even further off the handle, so I banged her too with the rake, and then again . . . she fell down, bleeding from her nose, and all at once it hit me. I fell down next to her and said: Mommy! It didn't hurt, it didn't hurt . . . but she pushed me away and walked off, tottering a little. I locked myself up in the shed and I was in there, I was just in there, I dunno how long, but long enough I guess, because by the time I came out again it was dark and the birds had been cleaned up. I noticed right away because the moon was shining. Somehow I slipped into the house, and the next day I stayed in bed with a fever. I wished real hard for it to be just a dream. But it wasn't. My folks never talked about it with me, just sent me to some psychiatrist fuck, who I told right off he could shove his cunt-sucking questions up his ass. But my mom never spoke to me again after that, except for the usual things like: do you want milk or tea, eat it up, bring me, show me, and stuff; she never talked to me again after that, never asked me about anything anymore, she wouldn't even . . . pat me in a friendly way, wouldn't touch me or anything; it was only then, really, that she untied the apron strings.

Micka concluded to the pack's friendly, vigilant grumbling. We touched him a little and patted him on the belly, above the stomach, around the stomach, and on the scruff of the neck, where the sources of malice are. But since the sources of perversion are as yet unknown to medicine, all over the rest of his body too, so he got a good working-over. I confess, he didn't get away without a few kicks in the nuts either. And then Micka took his seat, a little beat up, but more or less all right, and I was next in line.

I, however, to general consensus, ceded my spot to David. My buddies agreed, because even though Bohler handed out some fairly tough penances after our self-criticism sessions — for instance: 600 Our Fathers in a row or 1,000 push-ups or Go climb out on the roof and stay there! or Go and spin a Kalashnikov for the Castle Guard! — with our mountain boy he could usually wave them off, make do with two or three Our Fathers. And after the depravities we'd just heard, we were hoping he wouldn't let us down this time either.

I had a dream, said David. It was back home in the mountains, a blizzard swept snow around the Losín tribe's cabins, the trails were buried, so we couldn't go out hunting. Pa was waving a broadax around, but every so often he'd stop, stretch till his joints cracked, and say: A few poods a fresh raw meat, meat, meaty meat sure'd hit the spot 'bout now, ay ay-yi oy vay Maria! And he set to chopping up a beam. My younger brothers huddled on top of the stove while old Gramma told them tall tales. But the boys didn't pay much mind to the feats of old Choroš and gabbed away amongst themselves, and I heard them: A-yup, thim bloodily gristlin's, mm Godamercy! That'd be a fahn li'l lick now, Medor, wudn' it? Aw, don' go tellin' me no stories, 'd like ta eat ma own hand, Method, another one of my brothers, replied. My youngest brother, Benjamin, sat on the lap of my oldest brother, Abraham, and they gabbed away about the last bear we'd had before the storm, their mouths watering. Ma lit the Candlemas candle, because the cruel tempest that was burying our family's cottages had picked up in fury. I peeked over at my kind, honest ma, and she says: I kin tell ya'd go fer a hunk a that bloodsy bahr-meat, ya li'l critter, hoy! Could do mase'f, Davy boy, hoo! You see, buddies, wilderness was just a way of life for us, and not a day went by that one of old Losín's boys didn't bag a bear. We just weren't made for that kind of poverty in our clan! No, there wasn't any danger of us going hungry, we had sides of pork and veal hanging out in the pantry, ham old and new, all sorts of bolshevik meatballs, cauliflower, stacks of eggs and taters, a hidden pit of buckwheat here and there, sacks of oats, bushels of wheat, corn tall as a man, blindworms, sunflower seeds and oil with rice, dried fruit, millet, kabobs . . . it's just that we were short on vitamins. The storm wouldn't quit, and Ma was running low on candles. Old Gramma couldn't recall a winter like it ever, nothing like it even in the legends. It looked like the Losín clan might not even last through that godawful winter! And me, O friends and knights, I couldn't last anymore either! One night, when everyone in the cabin was asleep and my brothers were anxiously tossing and turning by the feet of my heavily slumbering parents, I quietly slipped into my li'l fur coat, slapped on my fox cap, gathered up Pa's old crossbow and a few arrows, and slipped my brother Abraham's hunting knife, the one he brought to country jamborees, right out of his boot. I took the sled out of the lean-to, loaded on the broadax, and untied Azorek, Pa's old bear-dog, who nuzzled up to me, eager to please. His eyes lit right up when I told him where we were going. He was a cross between a city cocker spaniel and a werewolf, and some of the younger bears died of fright just from laying eyes on him. We put the crossbow on the sled, hitched ourselves up to it, and shoved off. Into the tempest. You can believe me, guys and buddies, it was some awful Siberia. Luckily, though, we came on our first bear nest just a few meters back of the cabin. Azorek set right in digging furiously. I tried to draw the crossbow but soon determined that it was beyond my boyish strength. Then I got a salvational idea! With strong rope I lashed the crossbow to old Azorek's powerful digging legs and then sped downhill on the sled. I don't think I need to stress how tight I held on to that bowstring! Once it was taut, and Azorek, who kept on digging and digging and digging, began to bellow triumphantly, an old she-bear staggered sleepily out onto the snow . . . I let go of the bowstring and coasted off on the sled to a safe distance. The arrow whizzed between the slightly surprised Azorek's powerful werewolf legs and struck the bear right in her old heart! I clawed my way up the hill, sled and broadax prepared for portioning, and saw Azorek, who, as crazed as he was . . . saliva dripping from his jaws, his ragged red tongue flicking back and forth. . .

still held back, because he knew the meat was for all the Losíns! And I took pity on the good loyal beast. Now now, Azook, now the both of us's gonna git a litty bitty taste a that fine blood an' lard, snacky wacky, nummy num num! From all the excitement David fell into his old tongue and broke into tears.

We just sat there, stiff as statues, because self-criticism is sacrosanct and it is forbidden to interrupt . . . and as you probably realize by now, O buddies and pals, we went and . . . David beat his breast . . . we wolfed down that old honeysucker, every last bite . . . and I forgot all about my Ma and Pa's happiness . . . when they nibble on the snout and paws and slurp on the marrow . . . and my brothers', too . . . I ate that bear right up! And till the day old Azorek died, me and that werewolf never said a word to each other, not a holler, we were so estranged because we were ashamed! And, said David, trying to dry his eyes between sobs, and I stuffed myself so full that come dawn they had to lift me off Azook's back in order to get to the shed . . . and I'd lost the sled and Abraham's knife, and just like my associate Micka, back in his woeful childhood, I stretched out on the stove and lay there in a fever . . . and even though the next day, luckily, the sun came back out hey! hoy! and everyone was elated . . . and crazed . . . and my brothers raced out into the woods and hunted up dozens of bears, and Abraham didn't get mad at all about the knife, he had plenty more . . . David began to blubber and gush tears . . . and that night my brothers lugged the dead bears back and we gorged and gorged . . . and gorged . . . and the Losín tribe was saved and happy again, and I was never happy again, I couldn't look my family in the eye, and I left my tribe . . . and got lost in the stars and had to slay heaps of innocent wolves . . . and jaybirds . . . for food, and I roamed over nine mountain ranges and tripped over tree roots, and then I came down from the mountains . . . and got lost again and somehow I wound up in this city . . . and all you Knaahts a the Seekrit done found me, and me you, and . . . and the bear hunter once again broke into tears.

David concluded to the pack's friendly, vigilant grumbling, interrupted here and there by the friendly, joyous clamor of the members, and here and there and over here and over there we very gently patted David on the head, because even though it was the magic head of the great combiner, it was obvious to us what was at stake, because we were twisted, crooked swindlers of the Pearl and old raiders of sin and repentance, so we grinned affably at each other and yodeled manfully and congratulated one another that our Davey hadn't ended up frozen to death, but what courage that boy had, and at his age, imagine, guys, damnation, damnation . . . we nodded our heads and spit tobacco . . . and were glad our David could blubber over bullshit like this but didn't have to wail his heart out in bloody tears at those moments one glimpses the horrible wheels of the world . . . he doesn't see, we said conspiratorially among ourselves . . . that it's a wonder that mangy old beast Azor, we whispered, didn't take a chomp out of him, why, none of us'd get within five steps of that bad old grampa dog without a club, or better yet a good old AK-3, anyway it turned out all right, we congratulated each other, and Sharkey whispered kindheartedly to Bohler, two's enough, don't you think? meaning Our Fathers, and Bohler patronizingly nodded, like, sure mack, it's understood . . . and David sat blushing, but before long he was more or less all right, and I was next in line.

MICHAL VIEWEGH

from **Sightseers**

translated by Alex Zucker

Max's Personality Is Tragically Split!

Max had wanted to write during the afternoon siesta, but instead he masturbated twice.

His personality was tragically split.

If all Pamela had been was extremely dumb — which she positively undeniably was — he might have been nothing but a pleasant inspiration for Max's cherished word games, but she also happened to be extremely attractive, thereby making her also an agonizing inspiration for Max's — humiliating, though no less cherished — autoerotic games.

He ridiculed her in his mind frantically, for hours on end — and for hours on end he longed for her desperately.

Every one of her sentences, every one of her words, would under normal circumstances have represented for Max a setup for an easy and rewarding smash, but to his own amazement as well as to the growing disappointment of the spectators, he had failed to cash in on even one of them. Pamela's shallow cutesiness had afforded him plenty of perfect setups, but he couldn't put them away. His confidence as a player was dwindling as rapidly as his reputation with the fans — including, however paradoxical it sounds, Pamela — and dwindling along with it, as he himself knew all too well, was the probability that such a sorry smasher, such a drag, could ever hope to win the beautiful girl.

Yet he knew just as well that he simply couldn't be himself.

For had he made a genuine attempt to be once again dazzlingly ironic and disarmingly sincere, and had he struck any one of those countless bubbles of birdbrained banality with force and accuracy, the stark, and naturally for Pamela at best unpleasant, truth that deflation would undoubtedly have exposed, would have sealed off his imagined passage into her ample cleavage forever. If Max wanted to preserve any hope at all of one day being allowed to nibble on Pamela's sweet rosy nipples, he had to pretend, both to himself and to her, that she was clever and interesting.

Such a feat — Max realized — required the absolute negation of virtually everything he had ever read, written, or thought.

It meant total, absolute self-denial.

The thing is, those nipples of hers really were worth it!

Max Portrays Physical Desire

Max looked out the window: There was nobody down by the pool yet. He decided he would go outside and read. He ordered a coffee at the bar in the lobby and carefully carried it out to one of the tables with the blue-and-white umbrellas. He raised the chair back to the full upright position, sat down, and savored the quiet solitude of the siesta. He sipped the strong, excellent coffee, reading contentedly — but when after a while he raised his eyes, he spotted Pamela lugging an enormous, transparent, inflatable armchair over to the far side of the pool.

Thanks to the sunglasses, he was able to do a credible job of pretending he hadn't noticed her arrival; but while the black lenses were seemingly still trained on the pages of the open book, Max's eyes were following Pamela all the while. She placed the chair at the edge of the pool and went back to the nearest table, where she set down in succession her yellow artificial-straw purse, her short yellow skirt, and the upper half of her yellow bikini. She then took some bobby pins out of her purse, put them in her mouth, raised both hands behind her head, and coiled her hair into a bun, which she secured with the bobby pins. All of a sudden, she looked right at Max, but Max, heart pounding, kept a straight face and intently turned the page. Pamela began pretending she was impatient, or perhaps modest, and covered the few yards back to the pool in a great hurry.

Her swift stride along the hard tiles aroused in Max an almost painful physical desire.

But how to portray this literarily? he thought.

He had posed the same question in his previous novel: How to portray physical desire truthfully and convincingly — and yet avoid drooling pornography? One literary critic had publicly ridiculed Max's question, even quoting it in his extensive study as an exemplary illustration of Max's degeneratism, albeit — evidently in order to simplify his task somewhat — he omitted the question's second half in his quotation. "Well now, dear author, don't ask us; that's your concern and your craft. Give it a try, and we'll tell you what effect it had on us," he had advised Max sarcastically.

To this day, however, the above-mentioned question seemed entirely legitimate to Max. He was simply asking whether a writer could successfully, i.e., convincingly, transfer bodily matters to the plane of mere language without deviously and crassly employing the words and images that can be relied upon to elicit a physical reaction in every healthy reader. At the same time, he still believed that it was precisely by means of the author's seemingly mystified questioning that it was perhaps possible to suggest to the perceptive reader something of the magnitude and urgency of physical desire in an essentially refined manner.

So now, once again, he stood — or rather sat — before this problem: in front of him the painfully desirable, half-naked Pamela, behind him the obnoxious critic, with his demagogic half-truths.

Max looked over his shoulder to assure himself he wasn't mistaken. Yes, unfortunately, he was really there. He recognized him instantly — an older man with a straw hat on his head and a cigar in his mouth: Petr Fidelius.

"What would you say to a painter who, instead of showing you his painting, launched into a self-reflexive pontification on the difficulty of portraying this or that truthfully and convincingly?" Fidelius thundered at Max without warning.

Max wondered what gave this person the right to address him so impertinently.

"I don't recall asking you anything," Max said coolly, and he turned his back on him.

Pamela settled with difficulty into the inflatable chair; the pool's previously smooth surface rippled, and a slopping sound came from the drain at Max's feet.

The critic intently leaned toward Max.

"Do you feel that writers, more than any other artists, have the right to some sort of privileges?" he went on caustically.

"Leave me alone," Max said. "I'm on vacation."

If he had wanted, he could easily have had this idiot commit hara-kiri, shot him off to the moon, or chewed him up and swallowed him down as tonight's dinner (for that matter, he could have gotten rid of him entirely, with a single keystroke) — but something kept him from treating a living person like that.

He stood up in disgust, snatched up his book, and stamped back into the hotel.

"We ask you not to contemplate love, but to give us a vivid representation of it through the power of your fiction!" Fidelius called out, derisively puffing on his cigar.

Max peevishly waved his hand.

Back in his room, he rinsed off his burning face and frantically switched on his notebook.

Petr Fidelius laid down the magazine he was reading and surreptitiously examined the girl, whom he was suddenly alone with by the pool (he had to squint a little, as the ripples' flickering reflection on the surface multiplied the blinding rays of the intense afternoon sun): She half lay, half sat, head turned to the side and sunk back dreamily on the headrest of the silvery chair. The veins on her neck were taut. A few slender golden strands of hair had already come loose from the bunch. A few drops of water rested on her naked breasts. Petr Fidelius forced himself to avert his sight and tried to reimmerse himself in an article by Karel Hausenblas entitled "Imagery in Poláček's Narrative Prose." But before he had read even a full four lines, his gaze drifted back to the girl: She let her arms dangle over the soft, partially deflated armrests down into the warm water, and as she languidly, aimlessly paddled with her petite palms, her breasts duplicated this slow rhythm; her nipples were stiff and erect. Gusts of warm wind were drawing her chair closer and closer. The critic swallowed hard on his sticky saliva. He had the impression the watery map on the girl's baked brown belly was getting smaller right before his eyes. Her bent knees were open wide, and the dark fuzz of her vulva showed through the darkened yellow of her wet bikini bottoms; the wet material clung tightly to her crotch, faithfully outlining outer lips, inner lips, vaginal slit, perineum, and anus.

Petr Fidelius suddenly realized that at that particular moment he would have paid anything just to be able to place his mouth into that wet crotch and slurp it tenderly like the tastiest oyster on earth.

He quickly set the *Critical Gazette* down on his lap.

Max went out on the balcony.

"So what effect did that have on you?" he called down.

A Parable on the True Meaning of Literary Criticism

Jolana felt good with Max.

She warmed herself in the sun, ate the strawberries he had bought for her, and listened to him attentively. She didn't mind that he was speaking — obviously in an effort to avoid any further reference to last night — about almost nothing but literature, and about literary criticism in particular; she inferred correctly that Max was subconsciously using his troubles with literary critics as a pretentious counterbalance to his nighttime dolce vita — and she even got him back onto on the heated topic with the next question she asked. Max was pleased by her interest and began telling her about the critics in greater detail: One objects that Max's novel is almost too clever — while another says of the same novel that it is characterized by an utter absence of ideas. Another critic calls the novel a bare-chested love story — and another one goes and writes that Max doesn't have the courage to take risks.

"And that novel cost me my marriage!" Max shouted.

He was soon so carried away by his own monologue that he heatedly continued even while swimming in the sea. He talked on and on, with surprising passion, about the problems of the so-called autobiographical principle and writing in the first person — if he were to mechanically change the first person narration to third, he said, some critics would have to go back to square one and rewrite their reviews. That's why he has decided to write his forthcoming novel in the third person, though the writer character — whom he of course treats with a Fowlesian ironic detachment — bears his own distinctive traits, thereby supplying his appearance with the required credibility. Moreover, he does not, as alleged, assign his own experiences — with marriage, with friends, with parents, and with people in general — to his alter ego alone, but distributes them among several main characters; treading water, Max termed this the principle of hidden autobiography and added that he was extremely eager to read what all those songwriters, poets, and linguists, who for reasons unknown to him consider themselves literary critics, and who have lately displayed a touching concern for his healthy development as an artist, would say when the novel came out. They fault him, for instance, for pandering to readers. But they can go to hell for all Max cares. Ever since he began writing, he has wanted readers to understand his books and for them to be easy to read. That's why he tries to make his stories intelligible. And of course truthful and, whenever possible, witty. He says that's why he is always genuinely happy when his readers tell him or write to him that they liked his novel, that it fondly reminded them of their own life story, or that it made them laugh. For that, though, the critics brand him a superficial humorist who uses humor as a lubricant to ram his texts into the readers' heads — Max, however, would like to know if these critics have ever tried to spend just two hours, say, with someone who has absolutely no sense of humor. Or if they have been to a bookstore recently and tried to find a book that is witty, readable, and not insulting — naturally not for them, the educated Prague intellectuals, but for their father from the country, say, or their grandmother. Or if they have ever sat three hours in total silence interrupted only by timid coughing in a half-empty Theater Beyond the Gate. Max says he has. The cult of seriousness that rules the Czech Republic is totally incomprehensible to him — personally, he is convinced with all his being that there isn't a single reason why seriousness can't be just as idiotic as anything else. Take other books — it doesn't matter to most critics, he says, that they're clumsy, long-winded, descriptive, convoluted, unintelligible, unremarkable, and boring — just so long as they aren't at all humorous. According to the critics, Max is a typical representative of the middle — midbrow — culture created by the corruption of high culture.

Max is decidedly not high culture. All that Max is now he owes, according a man named Martin Les, only to the Czech nation's, or rather the Czech elite's, inadequate education. The undereducated cultural elite, Max screamed, spitting water, published all four of his previous books in several printings, undereducated jurors awarded him a prize, undereducated readers named his books their favorites in nationwide surveys, undereducated screenwriters, directors, and producers chose to make movies based on his novels and to adapt them for the stage, and thanks to the undereducated cultural elites of Germany, Holland, Hungary, France, England, the U.S., and Israel, both of his novels are now coming out in translation. Fortunately for Czech culture, Max commented sarcastically, there is still a sizeable *educated* national elite, which has laudably pointed out Max's absolute artistic inadequacy and called this whole unprecedented hoax by its true name. Max snorted furiously. Does Jolana want to know who this educated elite consists of? First and foremost, the aforementioned Martin Les — and then Lubomír Kasal, Jiři Dědeček, Pavel Mandys, Michael Špirit, and of course Jaromír Slomek, the biggest of the smallest Czech critics, whose lifelong critical achievement was the discovery of a spelling error on page one. And, finally, Petr Fidelius. Max was already spluttering with rage, but on mentioning this last critic — whose name, by the way, Jolana had never heard before in her life — he threw an outright fit. He was going so unbelievably fast Jolana could barely keep up. He thrashed the water wildly and screamed at the man as if he were there swimming in the sea with them: Max consistently referred to him as my dear critic, arrogantly used his first name, and cursed him out as the degenerate of all degenerates. At one point he got so fired up he failed to see an incoming wave and got so much salt water in his mouth that he nearly vomited. Jolana had to catch hold of his hand so he wouldn't drown from all the choking and gagging.

"Behold, a parable on the true meaning of literary criticism!" Max wheezed bitterly when he finally caught his breath.

What Hitchcock Told Truffaut

"You know what Hitchcock once told Truffaut?" Mrs. Košt'alova said to Max.

"No," Max said dejectedly.

"He said: 'I want you to know that whatever happens during your creative career, it has nothing to do with your talent.' You see? You can just tell those critics to go to hell."

"But I do," said Max. "I'm absolutely immune to them."

DANIELA FISCHEROVÁ

A Letter for President Eisenhower

Translated by Neil Bermel

Sometimes it seems that everything's pretend. That it's only a gesture that misses its mark. I am ten years old.

*

This was the year synthetic materials hit Prague. A new store, Plastik, appeared on Wenceslas Square and there were lines in front of it every day. Everything still amazed us: parkas, nylon bags, PVC statues.

One day my mother returned victoriously with plastic cutlery that looked like wood. The marvel was that wood wasn't wood, just like the statues' marble wasn't marble. This collective seizure would soon pass: within a year, the plasticware would land in the trash, but now we raised the strangely weightless knife up to the light; the knife tipped upwards like a finger pointing somewhere else and, marvelling, we fell under the spell of its artifice.

*

One morning Comrade Principal comes for me and for my best friend Hana. To the envy of all our classmates, she plucks us out of a quiz and brings us to her office. She doesn't say a word. Hana's dark ponytail trembles. She is perpetually alarmed, always more exemplary than me.

"Our school," the principal says curtly, "has decided to write to President Eisenhower."

She sits behind a large desk, wearing an army jacket: small, bent, and wrinkled. To my horror, I see that she is holding our notebooks. Hana's are much more attractive than mine. Hana has great handwriting. She gets to write for the bulletin board. Her handwriting is just like her: tiny, well-formed. Always the same, neat.

"The West," the principal continues, "is secretly preparing for war. They want to stab us in the back. But we won't let anyone take peace away from us!"

She picks up a composition I recognize, and fear makes my heart leap in my chest. It is my contribution to the Young Writers competition. It won second prize in the Prague 10 district. It is called "A Merry Christmas Party."

"You," the principal points her finger, "you will write the letter. And you: copy it over in your best handwriting. I want to see it before vacation. You have two weeks."

She opens the desk and spends a long time looking for something. She seems to have forgotten about us. I don't even dare utter a word. Suddenly she stands up and stares me straight in the eye.

"It's high time the truth be told!" she shouts as if from a deep sleep. The tips of my fingers go numb with excitement. The principal hands me an outline to work from.

*

I fly home, riding the crest of the moment. Outline, point one: greeting. Dear President Eisenhower! Outline, point four. The horrors of war. Like in Soviet films. Signature: We, the children of Czechoslovakia. And it was I who was given this historic task!

*

Fourth grade took something out of me. Just last year I swam through life like a fish through water. Now I'm a dry cork on the surface. I tread water and try to get down inside it. Life's every-day certainties are irrevocably gone.

Everything is just pretend. Since I can still faithfully imi-tate that loud, plump little girl I was not so long ago, no one has caught on yet. For example, everyone believes I love writing essays, but actually it bores me to death. My "Merry Christmas Party" was made up out of thin air. About thin-air kids doing thin-air things. In spite of this, everyone believes I'm going to be a writer. I'm sentenced to fiction for life.

It doesn't bother me. I play laboriously at playing. Sometimes I sense adults' fleeting anxiety that everything's already happened. I secretly hope for a "jolt," for some sort of catapult of transformation, as if I were a larva that ravenous inertia drives forth from the cocoon.

*

Is this my jolt? Presenting mankind's credentials in a letter? It's high time the truth be told! For ten days I write as if in a fever.

First I describe rivers of blood. I awaken the conscience of the American government. I speak with Eisenhower as an equal, but then behind all mankind's back I chew my pen. I cross out whole mountains of pages, I don't sleep, I fall exhausted beneath the steps of the White House. Hana's mother says the whole thing is pretty stupid. Hana, of course, repeats this to me.

Finally the letter is ready. It has the horrors of war, as depicted in films. It has many, many exclamation points. It has the sentence: "After all, I myself am still a child!" Hana com-plains that it's too long, but doesn't take a stand. Her copying is exemplary, without a single mistake.

*

That evening I come up with an excuse to go out, and I run over to Hana's. My authorial pride goads me on. I want to see that beautifully copied letter. I want to touch it before Eisenhower does. To weigh in my hands the paper confection in which my challenge to the White House will arrive.

Hana hesitantly lets me in. Usually we run right to her room, but today we stand in the hallway, shifting from foot to foot as if on a train. Suddenly I hear an explosion of laughter behind the wall and the voice of Hana's mother. She's reading my letter to her guests. "We children are still too weak, our hands cannot carry bombs," she quotes in a flat, cadaverous voice. That's how the TV comedian they call the Sad Man speaks. Hana doesn't laugh, but from her neat, perfidious face it's clear that she completely agrees with the antics behind the wall.

"My parents say the principal's crazy," she says defensively, and she looks straight at me with prim courage.

"You're the one who's crazy! Just wait till there's a war!"

I turn on my heel and trot down the dark hallway. Hana quietly closes the door, from which waves of laughter roll forth. Blind with humiliation, I vanish into the darkness.

*

For the three days till the end of the school year we don't speak to each other. On Friday, on the very brink of vacation, she stops me and says she can't be my friend anymore. Stunned, taken unawares, I say that I never asked her to. She says that there's no point in it. I say that I agree. Hana heads home with an even stride, trailing straight A's from her beribboned folders.

I flee into the coatroom and cry a little. It's my pride that hurts, not my heart. This year I have no heart. The principal sees me in front of the school and stops me with a stern gesture. She stares at me silently for a while, as if trying to remember who I might happen to be. Then she shakes her head with a strange horselike movement, strides off and, as she walks, says adamantly: "The letter's fine."

*

July is desolate. I wander listlessly around the garden with nothing to do. A dull film lies spread over everything; the summer fades under its protective coating like a cabinet under a plastic slipcover in a deserted room. I attempt to think about President Eisenhower, but since the incident with Hana a film has spread over him too. The cool gray days slide by.

On Sunday evening someone rings the bell. The superintendent's wife, Mrs. Zámský, runs to the gate. Boredom keeps me forever hanging out the window and so I see a burly old man come in. He has a cane and keeps coughing. Behind him walks a strongly built, dark-skinned girl. She furrows the ground with her dark, indifferent eyes, and scowls.

"Hello!" Mrs. Zámský shouts, and she waves at me. "We've brought you a friend! She's from Votice! Show yourself to the young lady, Sasha!"

*

The next day they put us together. It's wet, and we're wearing sweats and jackets. We hang around near the house. Sasha is glum.

"How old are you?" I ask.

"Just turned thirteen."

Even under the jacket I can see that she has breasts. She doesn't look at me. She doesn't look at anything. She just walks wherever she's headed, with a heavy, uninterested tread.

"Are you starting eighth grade?"

"No."

"Why not? If you're thirteen. . ."

We pass by the bench. Mr. Zámský lets out a guffaw. He slaps Sasha on the backside and for about the fifth time says:

"Thatta girl! And what a piece of girl she is, huh?"

Mr. Zámský gives me the jitters. His big head is

continually shaking. His tongue hangs out of his mouth and his eyes swim around as if bobbing in formaldehyde.

"Is that your uncle? Is he nice to you?"

Sasha just shrugs her shoulders. "He's nuts."

My feet are killing me. I'd like to go home. I have no idea what to say, but the footpath pulls me onward like a tugboat.

"What do you like to play?"

"You won't tell my aunt?"

I raise two fingers, wet with my saliva.

"Lovers," Sasha says. I'm dumbfounded.

"But . . . how?" I ask. It begins to rain again. Sasha looks around.

"Come over behind those trees," she whispers. We step into the cool, damp shadows. Rainwater drips down our necks. Sasha doesn't hesitate. She bends over and kisses me on the lips. Her mouth is smeared with baby oil.

"That's how," she says matter-of-factly. I guess that's all there is to it. We run out into the rain and then play rummy with Mrs. Zámský until evening.

*

And after that we're together all the time. We don't budge from the garden; we play uninterruptedly. At what? At being lovers. Sasha doesn't want to play anything else. How? It's simple. We walk through the birch trees hand in hand and give each other kisses. Do I like it? Not at all. I have just outgrown the cuddling phase and they won't get me back so quickly. Besides, there's something missing for me in this game, but I don't know what it is.

"And what are we called?"

"What is who called?"

"Ow, why'd you bite me?! I mean the lovers!"

Without names it just won't work. A name is always more than a body. Sasha licks a blade of grass, and concentrates on tickling my ear. I fidget uncomfortably.

"So are we going out with each other? And will we get married someday? And have children? Yes or no?"

Who knows. Sasha never asks things like that. The world around Sasha stands still. I have a Young Writers silver medal and I know full well that the world is a story, a finger pointing somewhere else: a direction.

"So let's make something up!"

"Why? I don't want to."

"If I make something up, will you play it with me?"

Sasha doesn't know. It's all the same to her. She stops tickling me and focuses her attention on squashing ants with her fingernail.

*

The next day I'm in the garden at eight. Furiously I stomp by the Zámskýs' ground-floor window. Sasha is sleeping and doesn't want to get up, but I'm stomping like a real live elephant.

I have a story! I couldn't fall asleep until two last night. A profusion of versions ran through my head. I'm as prolific as Adam in paradise. I am amazed how easy it is to create new worlds. Before sleep finally overtook me, I decided with solemn finality who Sasha and I really were.

At the window, Mr. Zámský is threatening me with his cane; he's angry that I'm making noise. Sasha yawns. She spends ages eating breakfast. Finally we're together behind the birch trees. Mumbling, I tell her her role. I know everything, absolutely everything! I (he) am called Mount Everest. Sasha (she) is Kilimanjaro.

*

There exist two famous mountain climbers. They bear the names of the mountains they have climbed. They have never in their lives met, but the world considers them fierce rivals. There is but one unconquered mountain left in all the world. It is the highest of them all and it has sent hundreds of climbers to their deaths. In the language of its country — Himalayan, I think — it is called the Mountain of Mountains.

Both decide to climb it. The whole world waits with baited breath to see who will be the first to raise the flag. The reporters are frantic, every transmitter is straining its ears. But a shock hits shortly before they set out.

At the foot of the Mountain, Everest discovers the amazing truth. The whole world thinks this is a battle of man against man. Only Kilimanjaro is not a man.

Sasha: It was only for your sake that I played this silly game. If you'd known I was a girl, you would never have competed with me.

Mount Everest (horrified): Kilimanjaro, I warn you — the Mountain of Mountains is the ends of the earth! At the summit there is nothing but sheer frost.

The ascent begins. Step by step the way grows harder. The sky is like a white abyss and the world is so tense it forgets to breathe. The most frightening part of the mountain draws near, the Wall of Death. No one, not even Sasha or I, foresees the truth.

*

From that day on, the game takes an unforeseen turn. At the end of the garden is a steep hill. The ground here is perpetually moist, covered with brushwood. So it becomes the Wall of Death. We press through the bushes on our bellies; a mountain hurricane rips us asunder, thorns catch on our sweatpants. The Young Writer has turned a fin-de-siècle stroll in the park into a military exercise.

Most of all, our love is now different. There's no more kissing, thank God. Love is no longer a perpetual dance in a circle. It's a contest, agony. It's a finger pointing straight up — direction! We crawl across the icy plain, exhausted. There is no thought of embraces, and anyway we are kept apart by layers of walrus skins. At these heights, a kiss without an oxygen mask spells death.

*

My parents are just thankful I'm playing and not lazing around the apartment with a bored expression on my face. Two or three times they invite Sasha over for a snack, but in the apartment she's glum again.

That evening my mother says that Sasha's a dim bulb.

"She's got breasts big enough to be nursing, but she keeps getting held back."

It doesn't make any sense to me. Sasha doesn't seem at all dim. On the contrary, she's fabulous. For example, she figured out how to freeze all by herself. I've never seen anyone freeze; I have nothing to compare it to, but she stiffens up like an icicle. She says I have to massage her with snow. Everest diligently rubs her with hands calloused by the fasteners of his coat, but Kilimanjaro does not wake up.

"Kiss me!" she hisses suddenly out of her unconsciousness, her eyelids still squeezed shut.

How do I know that the fateful moment has come? Like the snake-prince, I can even see in the dark. I know even what I don't know at all. With a single tug I rip off my oxygen mask. Everest falls head over heels in love.

The elderberry thicket encloses us. All around, the silence rumbles like a cracked bell, and the distant roar of avalanches gradually falls silent. Face to face with the sheer frost of death, Everest comes to know the terror of love. Practically without touching her, in a panic, he kisses the frozen girl. Sasha immediately opens her eyes, and — although she knows I don't like it — the cunning girl licks me all over.

One evening, there's a commotion downstairs. Sasha and I secretly peer through the window. Mrs. Zámský is chasing her brother around the kitchen; she swipes at him with a broom whenever she's close enough, while he cowers in horror against the wall and, with a shaking hand, parries with his cane.

"Shame on you, you pig!" she screams, and she swings the broom round her head. "I'll throw you right out! Go back to Votice, you pig! Bet they don't want you either, you swine!"

She throws a brush at him. Mr. Zámský bursts out of the door and makes his getaway. Sasha's eyes are shining.

"I know why my aunt's upset!" she whispers. She bites her fingers until red marks are left on them, brushes against me, and giggles with excitement.

*

By the end of the week, Sasha starts to revolt against me. We're all scratched up, we've broken our nails, and under our sweats our knees are thoroughly bruised. We've already climbed a slippery path along the Wall of Death, where the brushwood straggles to the ground. Sasha grumbles that she's lost interest.

I understand her. After all, we're always playing the same thing. What's more attractive in love than the starting line? I am perpetually rewinding the hands of our story back to zero. Sasha freezes, Everest stands over her. The circulation of his blood pauses, like an elevator. This helping of emotion is quite enough for me, but Sasha is muttering. She wants to know when we're going to get to the top.

The worst thing is that I don't know myself. The Young Writer is stuck in a creative crisis. I dragged us out to the ends of the earth, and for a week I've been holding us there like a customs official. Just short of the goal, my imagination has run dry. What awaits love at the summit of the Mountain of

Mountains?

I compress my feelings like a cylinder of gas. I cross out the kisses; we're fighting for every gasp of air. The mountain belches frost, I camp just shy of the summit and lack the courage for that last step.

"I'm not playing!" Sasha pouts. Spitefully, she sticks a thorn through my sweats. I beg her: just one more time. We both roll down to the fence and with a sense of relief I slip back under the starting line of love and once again I'm crawling along on my belly like a newt.

*

On Sunday, Sasha gets the flu. I can't go see her and I'm desperate. I thrash around the apartment like a Christmas carp in a trough, I talk back and cut people off and am so nasty that my mother ironically asks me:

"Do you love her so much you can't be apart for even a day?"

The question takes me by surprise. I don't love Sasha at all! It would never occur to me to love Sasha! Everest loves Kilimanjaro with the insanity of sheer frost, but it has nothing to do with Sasha and me. We are mere game pieces — a finger pointing somewhere else. We are only representatives, even if I don't know what of.

*

A dull excitement dogs me all day. I read a little, but made-up stories irritate me. I stuff myself with cookies. Finally, right before dinner, I get an idea for the next act of our game.

The exhausted Kilimanjaro is sleeping in the cliff grotto. Everest sets out for the summit. He stands right beneath it. One more step and he could leave his fingerprint upon the very apex of the world. The lofty vacuum turns his blood to foam. He is alone like no one anywhere ever. He sits down on a rocky protrusion and takes out a piece of stationery. Beloved Kilimanjaro!

The love letter is an utterly alien genre for me. Laboriously, I look for sentences to borrow, and cobble them together into something exceedingly odd. I don't believe what gets into my pen. What I understand perfectly as an inarticulate feeling is, when put into words, even thinner air than my Christmas Party.

Kilimanjaro! It's high time the truth be told. Until today I did not know what love was! . . . They call me to dinner, three times. Woodenly I stack line on line. I love you. Meanwhile, the spinach on my plate is getting cold. Till I die I will love only you. The fourth time around, they hound me to supper.

*

Then, to stay within the boundaries of the story, I figure out how we can correspond properly this far above sea level. With the help of some thin rope, of course! I run downstairs. Mrs. Zámský is in the kitchen with curlers in her hair. I'm hopping with impatience, I've explained it to her so many times! I'm even shouting a little. Mrs. Zámský wants to know why I don't just hand her the letter. With a speed borne of exasperation, I spill the whole thing again. Mrs. Zámský asks: And what kind of game is it? Finally she waves her hands at me and goes to wake Sasha up.

I stand on the balcony, tying the rope. Carefully I lower the letter. WRITE BACK IMMEDIATELY! Everest adds. I mope around upstairs, practicing my blandishments on the twilight. Hurrah! Sasha's hand sticks out from the rocky grotto. She attaches a note:

"My temperture's allmost normal. My aunts' going to the movies tomorow so if you want, come over."

*

40

As if to spite me, the heat today is like a frying pan. The sun pours through the closed windows. The basement apartment is oppressive and stifling. Mr. Zámský is sleeping in a chair in the garden, and Sasha is sitting on her bed in a rumpled nightgown.

"Do you still feel sick?"

"Uh-uh."

"Still have a temperature?"

"M-hm."

Suddenly I don't know what to say. I stand up and look around. Most of all I'd like to crawl right into the game, like a hand into a glove.

"So are we going to play? Like always?"

"Hey, could you bring me something to drink?"

"I'll bring it to you when we pretend."

"What do you mean, pretend? I'm dying of thirst!"

"So pretend like he's coming back to free her from the snow."

Everest brings her warm lemonade in a plastic glass; even Mrs. Zámský has had a plastic seizure, but she doesn't have a refrigerator. He finds Kilimanjaro asleep. No, she's frozen. Everest stands for a while, completely taken aback. Then he puts the glass aside and begins to massage the forearms of this victim of the Mountain.

"Kilimanjaro! Don't die!" he whispers — today he's not at all convincing.

The victim opens one eye slightly: "Got the drink?"

She gulps it down at once and wipes the spills off her nightgown.

"You know what you have to do!" she says, and freezes. Mount Everest is taking his time. It's not easy to introduce sheer frost into a hundred-degree zone. Sasha breathes aloud. The hairs on her neck glisten gold with sweat. Everest still cannot get into the game. Finally he leans over, perplexed. A dying arm grabs him around the throat. He didn't expect this; his legs slide out from under him and he topples right into the featherbed.

When it gets dark outside, Everest's first fear is that they will find him in the Zámskýs' bed in his sneakers. He jumps up and comes to attention like an army major. Mr. Zámský is squatting outside, tapping on the glass and snickering.

"Go jump in a lake, old man!" Sasha says irritably.

"What's he want with us?"

Sasha puts on an idiotic expression:

"Go for it, girls, that's right, do it!"

Then she tumbles back into the featherbed and snores. Mr. Zámský shuffles inside. He slaps me on my rear and sits down on the bed.

"Well, girls! Want to look at some pictures? Not a word to Mrs. Z.! She doesn't need to know everything, right girls?"

Sasha is snoring like a steam engine. And she's poking me in the back with her foot. The fever has unleashed her somehow. Mr. Zámský pulls out a tattered book.

"Come on, girls, let's have some fun together! After all, I saw you — you know how to have fun!"

Sasha leans forward and props her chin on his shoulder. Cardboard figures stand out on the page, a ballerina and a man holding a hat right below his belly. Strings hang down beneath them. Mr. Zámský winks at us. He pulls one of the strings and the ballerina raises her leg up high. It turns out she isn't wearing any panties.

"Whoa!" Sasha yelps, and she rips the book away from her uncle. She pulls the other string. The man jerks his arms backward.

"Give it back! Sasha!" Mr. Zámský shouts. Sasha jumps around the bed, the bed springs like a trampoline. In a panic, her uncle grabs the footboard.

"Get on over here!" Sasha calls to me. I waver, but she holds out her hand. I don't recognize her at all today. Hastily I kick off my shoes and climb over to her.

"Sasha! You little devil!" Mr. Zámský moans. He's afraid

to stand up and can barely hold onto the crossrail. I'm jumping as well. It's easier than keeping my balance. Suddenly a strange hotness enters me. Sasha jerks on the string, the man thrusts his naked belly against the ballerina, and we both yelp, "Wow!"

"You! Little girl! Make her give back the book!"

I'm choking in the stifling heat. I don't recognize either Sasha or myself. I jump and shriek with all my might, "Wow!"

Suddenly Sasha yelps, "Auntie's coming!" and quick as a flash throws the book behind the bed. Mr. Zámský is horribly frightened. As he shoots out of the room, he drops his cane, but leaves it lying on the ground and flees. I'm also horribly frightened; I've turned white as a sheet. Sasha laughs wildly and burrows into the featherbed up to her nose.

"No one's coming, don't worry. I just said that so he'd leave. Come crawl under the featherbed so he can't see us!"

She pulls out the book and blows off the dust. She nods at me and pats the place next to her.

"I'm still going to tell my aunt on him tonight!"

She sits up, takes off her nightgown, and spreads her legs apart. Carefully she examines the picture and then between her own thighs. Everest stands on the bed; he can't move, must be frozen.

"Come on already!" Sasha shrieks at me. The featherbed falls on us like an avalanche.

*

As I run up the steps, lightning flashes. It creates the impression that evening has arrived early today.

My parents aren't home, but there's a letter on the table. At first I overlook it. Only when I get out of the bathtub do I see that it's from Hana. I spend a long time rubbing my face with a handtowel. My hot skin itches as if an electric current were buzzing through the air.

43

The letter takes me by surprise; I had completely forgotten about Hana. I take out the folded pages and can barely focus on what I'm reading.

Two, three pages, an ordinary vacation letter. Swimming, the country house at Strakonice, colds, trips, mushroom picking. Do you already have your assignment done for September? Not me. Then I turn the page over.

"And I also wanted to write you and say how much it bothers me that we ended what was a beautiful friendship. Maybe you already have another friend, but I still love you and will love you till I die."

All of it in tiny, perfectly formed handwriting, good enough for the American government. Just outside the window, lightning flashes. Suddenly fear pins me to the wall. Scarcely an instant later, the thunder hits.

*

Sometimes it seems that everything's just a fiction. A substitute for something that doesn't exist. In spite of this, each life has its moments that stand for nothing but themselves. This is one of them.

Outside it's pouring. In bed, flashlight in hand, I'm writing a letter propped on my knees. I love Hana so awfully much that there is no room for wonder. I didn't know it this morning, but now the whole past serves only as the foundation for my love. In the feeble glow of the flashlight lines pour forth from me onto page after page.

I love you. Till I die I will love only you. The mountain hurricane carries me through the skies. A full five pages spill forth, foaming, over the margins of the paper.

When I finish writing, it is midnight. The house is asleep. I run along the balcony in the pouring rain and try to guess where Strakonice might be. Then I stand there in sheer triumph and transmit myself south-southwest. This is no fiction. This is no gesture. It is love itself. For it is high time the truth be told: what wouldn't I give to experience such love again!

*

In the morning, Sasha is allowed out into the garden again. For the first time she hangs around alone. I stay home reading. Sometimes I peer out under the curtains at her as she wanders along the paths. Only when I should be chopping carrots do I run out to see her.

"Hi. Were you sleeping?"

"No, why?"

"Cause you're later than usual."

"So?"

We sit, swinging our legs, on the edge of a basin full of wet branches. Sasha brushes lightly against my ankle.

"Are we going to play?"

"Play what?"

"The usual."

I don't respond. The sun makes a burning cap on my head. I twist my ankle around my other leg.

"I can't today."

"Why not?"

"I have a vacation assignment to do."

"An assignment? Over the summer?"

"Only the best students have to do them. Like me and my friend Hana."

Sasha loudly kicks at the basin wall. A yellow powder drifts down from a crack.

"We both write pretty well. We wrote to President Eisenhower together."

"So then will you come down?"

"And we also wrote to the American government. To make sure there isn't a war. My friend has the prettiest hand-writing in the whole class. And I have the best essays."

Sasha falls silent. Mr. Zámský comes trudging down the path. As soon as he spots us, he heads off somewhere else. At that moment a black spark of hatred flashes through me.

"Why do you keep kicking our wall?" I say. "You're going to wreck it!"

Sasha jumps down off the rim. Out of spite, I carefully pick up bits of gravel out of the grass, but she doesn't turn around. I have to go home for lunch anyway.

*

Sasha left Prague two days after this. We said good-bye casually. Mr. Zámský left with her. I never sent the letter to Hana. I carried it around with me for a few days and then left it in the pocket of my windbreaker.

As for the Mountain of Mountains, Mount Everest got the furthest, but even he never made it to the summit. His transmitter went dead. He must have wiped away the snow and then covered the frozen girl with his own body. Somewhere there the track was lost. No one ever conquered the Mountain of Mountains.

*

In September, Hana and I sit next to each other, but it's awkward and futile. The wheel of friendship doesn't spin up again. Fifth grade languidly and painlessly draws us apart.

One day, I'm rushing somewhere through the hallway at school. There's a bulletin board there for the class council. Suddenly something stops me in my tracks. "Dear President Eisenhower!" a tiny, familiar hand has written.

For a while I can't believe my eyes. Our letter has been in America for ages! After all, it was for President Eisenhower! Until finally the shock hits me and in a flash I understand it all.

That letter was never intended to be sent. There was no hope it would reach its addressee; it was just pretend. It too was

46

a gesture that missed its mark — a finger that might point somewhere, but somewhere it will never touch.

VAŠEK KOUBEK
Hell

translated by Caleb Crain

Mr. White is an average citizen. Not really happy, but on the other hand not so enlightened that he understands the extent of his unhappiness. Mr. White is a single young man. Right now he's staggering through the airport concourse and from the confused look on his face it's clear that he's no globetrotter. Foreigners request information about Tunis. Others about London. Still others are headed across the ocean. Mr. White is only flying to Brno. At his gate, a stewardess unexpectedly salutes him and wishes him a pleasant last flight. Last? Yes, it turns out the aged machine is flying today for the last time. The minibus starts moving and from the tower the air traffic controller gives a final wave. A band is playing in front of the airplane, and the pilot is personally shaking every passenger's hand. The staff are in a good mood and after uncorking some champagne they distribute as mementos little bottles of Becherovka printed with the word *LAST*. Mr. White reads his newspaper and pays no attention to the repeated attempts to start the engines. The vehicle finally starts; the plane still works. The onboard technician opens a floorboard and, after aiming a couple of blows into the heart of the machine, walks off satisfied. It's warm in the airplane. It's hot in the airplane. The passengers shed their clothes and the plane hesitates for a long time before it launches into motion.

"We're moving, we're moving!"

voices on the loudspeaker exult, and in no time they're cheering. The plane is taking off; the plane is flying. It hits the ground and rises again. One more valiant ricochet off the runway and the aged machine actually rises. The delight of the air crew quickly spreads to the other travelers. The airplane is undoubtedly in flight. It's made it. Even Mr. White's damaged seat is in motion. His head is stuck to the ceiling, while below, ham and eggs are being distributed. The plane finally reaches the clouds. Everything seems to be fine. It reaches its cruising altitude, stabilizes, and Mr. White's seat lowers into place. The stewardesses collect the empty trays. There's nothing left in front of Mr. White. His stomach growls in vain. The engines immediately stop. It's quiet; the passengers and the onboard technician are wary. Hungry Mr. White's strange growl repeats itself.

"We're falling,"

the stewardess states. White guiltily cleans his window with his handkerchief. His window falls out. For the horrified passengers, in such a tense situation, this crime is the last straw. As the plane falls, they demand that White be punished. He is asked to deplane immediately. White defends himself, but the stewardess insists. From the cockpit the captain's voice informs them that in a couple of minutes they will hit the ground. The plane is falling. The passengers hysterically chant for White to deplane. The situation is serious. A goose flies into the plane. No one sees it except White. The goose flutters and then turns into God. God smiles on him and the engines catch.

"We're rising!"

the loudspeaker announces. The technician is hugged by the passengers. Everyone is happy. The plane lands. The passengers get off. Mr. White is transformed. Put right. Mr. White is Christ. He exits the plane, but what is all around him is hell. Miserable people, dirt, smoke. Wreckage, noise, blood, drunks, thieves, wretches. Mr. White stops, raises his hands, and performs miracles. People gather; White distributes love. He bestows smiles. The people riot. They demand more. A mob. Panic. Mr. White is trampled. A procession carries Mr. White on a cross. They put him on an airplane. The vehicle rises. The people cry. The plane disappears. The people kneel. The plane is a cross in the sky. The people pray. The vehicle disappears among the stars. The people clap. The people dance. The people embrace. They are like Mr. White. They are the same as Mr. White. Not really happy, not really unhappy. Average. They flit through halls. They stand in line and they board questionable vehicles. An airport. Airplanes fly off in various directions.

TEREZA BOUČKOVÁ
Quail

translated by Caleb Crain

I.

Once there was a town. In this town a dairy, in this dairy a line, and in this line Hana falling down among empty bottles of milk.

Once there were some tiles. On the tiles Hana hears the ocean roaring in her temples. An unbuttoned blouse. A wet rag on her forehead; breathe deep, Hana, one, two, three.

Once there was a woman named Hana. And inside this Hana, a baby.

Once there lived a certain astrologist. He said: "You were born under the same constellation as Bach! Get away from her. Away from them. You'll lose your creativity!"

Once upon a time there was a man named Jiří. From Jiří the baby, the baby inside Hana, in the street, on the tiles that Jiří is walking across as he leaves them forever.

Johann Sebastian is playing the organ, the chorale *Von Gott will ich nicht lassen* (BWV 658). Hana, this was originally a secular love song. Its melody creates the impression of a joyful folksong. With its distinctive rhythmic motif, deliberately pursued throughout the course of the entire composition, this piece recalls Bach's chorales in the *Little Organ Book (Orgelbüchlein)*. Are you listening?

"And what am I supposed to do?" you yell at the astrologist.

No, that's not the astrologist's problem. The stars don't

lie. Jiří will always love you and your child, but understand, his music is worth more to him than life!

Hana was sobbing. She couldn't stand it all alone. She wanted to jump out the window, into the street, among the pedestrians, the men and women she saw squeezing each other's hands with amorous desire as they wheeled baby carriages together . . . She wanted to do it so bad, to jump, to kill herself. But from where? The highest window in their building was so damned low!

Hana couldn't stand it, she wanted so bad to live high up, to open a window and fly. And then a blunt pressure, pain.

And then again. And again. Dampness between her thighs. Bent over, she limped off to find her citizen's ID card. Soap and a washcloth, toothbrush and toothpaste. A comb. Three bras that fasten in front, a robe. Slippers (new, or at least clean). Five handkerchiefs. Writing paper and envelopes, some postage stamps. Some light reading.

Once there were some green tiles. There was a shirt yanked up. There was a wet rag on her forehead; breathe in deep, hold your breath, grab under your knees with your hands, pull them toward your chest, lay your chin on your breast and push with all your might, Hana, with all your might!

Now don't push, hang on, calm down, breathe like a doggy with his tongue hanging out, the little head mustn't shove through too suddenly or it'll cause undesirable rips and tears, Hana, I've got her now, sore and wrinkly, I've got her by the left hand and in the right I'm holding the tiny shoulders, the tiny body . . . it's a boy, a beautiful, healthy little boy!

Once there was a woman named Hana. And from this Hana, Jan.

The thirteenth invention in A minor (BWV 784), which

while constructed out of broken triads is nonetheless in the highest degree "singable art," was interrupted by the most beautiful music in the world: little Jan cried for the first time.

Jiří was staring. Now! Now one of the six Brandenburg concertos would sing out, now he would hear the St. John, or the epic-contemplative St. Matthew, Passion . . . Nothing. Not a note.

Jiří was staring at his month-old son and he couldn't summon up even an eighth note in his head. It unnerved him. He turned to Hana: "Since this isn't doing anything for me. . ."

"Because you don't live with him. If you were here, if you fed him and bathed him. . ."

Jiří fled the room in panic. He ran to the door. He desperately needed to escape this deafness, he yanked the door handle — and the door flew open.

When it finally clicked shut behind him, treble clefs chimed in his pocket, at the trolley stop basses rumbled, and in the trolley, oh god, in the trolley he heard the notes B-flat, A, C, and B-natural, the notes that in German musical notation are identified as *b, a, c,* and *h,* the notes Johann used as one of the themes of the final, unfinished fugue in his opus *The Art of the Fugue (Die Kunst der Fuge),* four notes and suddenly he felt fine, splendid. Baroque!

At his mother's house, although he was not allowed to play in her presence, he sat down at the piano and wrote: "I cannot see you for reasons that you wouldn't understand."

"I swear on my honor that immediately after the birth of our child I will voluntarily, cheerfully, and without hesitation divorce my husband. . ."

She gave him a copy of this document so he would be willing to agree to the birth of the child — the only child he would ever have — despite the astrologist's prediction.

"I hereby affirm that we slept together for the last time on. . . ," and he checked in his diary for the exact date, to be sure that from that day on he had nothing, absolutely nothing, to do with his wife.

"Damn, and what about the kid?" it occurred to the judge to ask.

Once upon a time, they assessed the kid at three hundred fifty crowns a month, and from that moment on they were divorced and the only thing they had in common were the green checks a certain Jiří filled out and a certain Hana cashed.

"Waaah!" was heard from the toddler's carrying bag before it left the courtroom, and the cry stung Jiří in the heart.

It was an absolutely disharmonious sound!

The year of our Lord 1969.

The traffic island in front of the Julius Fučík Park for Culture and Leisure. All three are waiting for the trolley.

Ex-mother-in-law: "You really did it to us; Hana is so unhappy."

His girlfriend: Doesn't know where to look.

Ex-son-in-law: "Yeah well, your little Hana behaved liked these Russians!"

Although the ex-mother-in-law has no way of knowing whether Jiří himself believes his answer, in 1969 a comparison like this is the foulest possible insult, and she raises her arm and slaps him.

At the same time, in a single gesture, she hails a passing taxi. She gets in and as in a movie disappears before the surprised hero has time to recover from his shock.

His girlfriend: Doesn't know where to look.

Hana is standing at the kitchen counter. She's mixing batter for sponge cake. The baby toddles at her feet. Her husband is resting peacefully next to her after a day at work. He's a wise man, he's a pianist, plumber, surgeon, whoever. In his field he's a professional!

Next to him, Hana has a feeling of security. She respects him. When she doesn't know how much further she can go, when things are hard for her, when she feels weak, whenever, the pianist, plumber, surgeon gently lays a hand on her head. And she feels the professional in his field protecting her.

Dream.

Reality: Hana stood at the kitchen counter grinding the ingredients for sponge cake. Little Jan sat between the legs of the table banging pot lids against himself.

"Dada, dada," he babbled contentedly. He still didn't know the word meant something.

"Where is he?" he asked a year later.

"He went away."

At a certain age this answer sufficed.

"When's Daddy coming back from that Vinohrady place?" he asked when he was four.

"First we have to find out where this Vinohrady actually is," she said after a pause, "in order to know how long the trip will take."

When Jan went to sleep that evening, she wrote Jiří to ask if he would come see them at least once every few months, so that Jan could have a concrete image of his father as a person.

Jiří, however, would feel bad denying the child his company if the child were to become accustomed to it. And there's not enough time, Hana, for Jiří to make more frequent visits. Since the exercise of his calling is not limited to regular working hours, he is in fact constantly at work; he has no free time at all. It might look as if he could act freely, since the only person he has to answer to is himself, but this is not true. You dragged him to court to force him to pay a thousand, instead of the original three hundred fifty, crowns per month, and if there's going to be anything left over for himself, he must work even more than he would have to otherwise. If, then, you want to know what he thinks you should say to Jan, and if the boy is as rational as you write that he is, it might go *un poco andante* and sound something like this:

"Dear Jan, I want the best for you, and so I went to court to force your daddy to pay me a thousand crowns a month. That's a lot of money, and Daddy has to work hard to earn it, along with the money he needs for himself. That's why he doesn't have time for us, and it's only me and Granny here with you . . ."

At the time, no one suspected that the trip from Vinohrady to Břevnov — from one Prague borough to another — would take twenty-three years.

The year of our lord 1974.
Prague subway, I. P. Pavlov Station. They are waiting for a train headed toward Muzeum.

Jiří walks onto the platform; he's waiting for a train going the opposite direction.

Hana: "Jan, do you want to see your daddy?"

A train rolls in, Jiří steps on board. Hana runs with Jan to his car. Now. They're standing face to face, Jiří and Jan. They stare at each other, they're so much alike! Now! Now Jiří calls out to his son, he steps toward him, takes him in his arms. . .

Now all the Brandenburg concertos sing out at once!
Nothing. Silence.

"Waaaah!" the train's honk echoes along the platform.
The son sticks his tongue out at his daddy.

He cared about her, and about Jan, too. He was intelligent, handsome, noble. When he worked, classical music stormed through his studio; he was an artist. He was for real.

"Couldn't Ivan Mládek be my father?" Jan had asked her

the night before. She had explained to him that it wasn't possible, and he had suggested the daddy of a schoolfriend instead.

You should try it, Hana, try having a man for yourself and for Jan!

He gave her a diamond ensemble, which she'd said the antique store in Uhelný Square was selling for a real bargain, that's all, in conversation she'd mentioned it and just like that, between two concertos, as if it were no big deal, during intermission she got it. He was big-hearted.

That night she went to him, earrings in her ears, necklace around her neck, she went to him, overwhelmed by this gift; he started to undress her, she let him undress her, he lost his head completely: "What breasts!" he cried in ecstasy. "You're beautiful, Hana," he said, flustered, "Hana, sweet Hana, my love, oh . . . ," he melted, on the brink of tears, and would probably have broken down sobbing if at that moment someone hadn't rung the doorbell. He realized he'd left the front door unlocked. He ran off.

When he returned, you were sitting there, Hana, fully clothed again.

"Why?" he asked, not understanding.

You shrugged your shoulders. "I can't, it's not working . . ."

He was intelligent, handsome, noble, big-hearted. He was the man she had dreamed of. Up until the moment he nearly fell to pieces in front of her out of mere love.

She just couldn't stand that sort of thing. That's life.

The year of our Lord 1975.

Národní Avenue, the sidewalk in front of the East German Cultural Center. All three walk up to her car.

First man: "Mrs. Exwhy?"

Second man: "Mrs. Whyex?"

The second man grabs the hand she's holding her keys in.

He also takes her handbag. Come with us.

Hana: "Where?"

Does she want to drive in their car or her own? They get into hers; after all, she's not going to leave it there. The second man sits behind the steering wheel.

First man: "Right now they're searching your house."

Hana: "Why?"

Ruzyně Prison. When the awful iron gate clangs shut behind Hana, the first man says:

"This gate doesn't open for people as easily as it closes on them."

Because of all the excitement, she got her period. She ran around the underground cell they'd locked her in, holding the one handkerchief she'd had with her, which she rinsed out in the hole in the middle of the cell floor provided for all her hygienic needs; she ran back and forth with it so it would dry faster, so she could use it again soon. She didn't know if it was day or night. She counted the seconds; a minute was endless. The light shone nonstop; someone was constantly watching her.

"Do you know why you're here? Oh really, you don't say."

Why did you go with them, Hana? As obedient as a sheep. Come with us — and off you go. Why didn't you grab the nearest lamp post and scream for help?

"If you tell us the truth, you can go home today."

You're an enemy of the people. When you hear the word *comrade,* everything in you clams up. You're on the other side. Treasonous element.

"So . . . what's the story with those books?"

Is it still day, or is it night already? She counted the seconds; the lightbulb shone nonstop; there was always someone's eyeball at the peephole in the door. It couldn't have been an accident that only freaks worked at the reception desk. They must have specially selected miserable creatures delivered with forceps.

The effect was perfect. A totally alien world. The cage was lowered.

Why did it happen? Where's my Jan?

"The state will see to that."

She sees him in an institutional jumpsuit . . . No! She mustn't picture him like that! She sees him sitting in an armchair, reading a book, his legs swinging. At four years old he'd already taught himself the letters off the typewriter.

"Mommy, what's this?"

"That's a *Q*. It makes a 'kw' sound, Jan," she explained.

"Aha, 'kw' like in 'ice kweam,'" he stated with satisfaction.

He doesn't have a father and now he doesn't have a mother either. Oh God! She wants to lose her mind, go crazy. Not know anything. Not think. Not remember. Be meat on bones, matter.

How many days has she been locked up here? How much do they know?

For my dear Hana

She sat at her table
she gobbled her mess-tin clean
I kicked her in the ass
and she fell in the latrine.

Once there was a cell with the number 216. In this cell a toilet behind a panel, a washbasin, Alenka: "I'm clean for a social parasite."

Soap, a toothbrush, and toothpaste. A comb. Every week, a book. The prisoners tore out the pages and rolled them into cigarettes. Every week, a book to smoke.

"What streets were you walking?"

Mama slapped Alenka so hard that the second blow landed her against the door frame.

There were narrow metal stools; there were calluses on

their buttocks; there were nights and days, days and nights.

"Shovel-guts! Come play shovel-guts, or I'll smack you."
There were group games. Slop in a tray, moldy bread, books.

"Books!"

No, Hana did not transport anything to the Soviet Union.
No, Hana did not carry any manuscripts out of the Soviet Union.
She knew absolutely nothing about it. She sent odds and ends to
her friends in Moscow, sugar cubes, Karlsbad wafer cookies . . .
Her friends in Moscow sent her an icon as a gift, a little picture
. . . She didn't know, really she'd never even heard the name of
the press that was publishing forbidden authors in Germany.
Someone was publishing them? Who was she affiliated with? She
didn't understand any of this . . .

Once there was a cell with the number 216. In this cell
Hana sat at her table. She gobbled her mess-tin clean.

"Cell 216 requests a supplemental allowance . . . ,"
Alenka shouted every day through the peephole in the cell door,
and from time to time two extra dumplings tumbled inside.

When it was time for Alenka to go to the court of
appeals, Hana had to stuff her into her civilian pants — which
wouldn't button.

"Say that from now on you'll always work," she was
giving Alenka a final piece of advice, and in Moscow Anna
Pavlovna was festively placing one light blue heart and one light
yellow spade on a tea saucer, "say that you want to live a decent
life and support yourself," and the honored guest carefully tossed
the heart and the spade into the tea and watched them as they
slowly lost their shapes, "that you've learned your lesson and you
want to improve," until all that was left was a mound in the
bottom of the cup. "And say thank you for everything,
constantly."

"Spasibo," Sergei Michailovich said when the hostess
offered him another cup.

They led Alenka off.

En route she got gum from someone. Chewing her gum and unappealingly bursting out of her clothes on all sides, Alenka stood before the court. She got another half year added to her sentence.

"At fourteen, Mama sent me to a home for juvies and that's where I learned to drink and shoot up," she told them, while Anna Pavlovna was pleasantly surprised to discover that in the sugar package from Hana each layer of cubes was separated by a sheet of tissue paper, "and now you're sending me to prison, and whatever I didn't learn from the juvies, I'll learn in prison!"

But the tissue paper wouldn't come unstuck; no sugar could come out. Anna Pavlovna turned the box upside down and gave it a good shake. Out fell *The Cancer Ward* by Aleksandr Solzhenitsyn.

As recently as yesterday they handed over a package from home with the sausage mangled and Mommy's Christmas cake broken in pieces, they frightened her with years and years in jail and even Siberia, and today . . . Today the investigator almost apologetically asked her, "But ma'am, why didn't you clear the icons with customs?"

Not a word about the books. And Hana had turned back into a "ma'am" again.

Her heart pounded. She was afraid it was easy to see how fast her heart was beating, that the investigator could tell just by looking at her what effect his question had had; all she had to do was not show him any feelings, no weakness he could take advantage of, and the cage would open . . . no, better if she didn't even allow herself to think about it, joy would run wild through her body . . . no, it was only a trick, a stratagem that had proven reliable thousands of times — to offer hope, and then strike it down!

Don't beat, heart, stay calm, don't feel joy. Don't believe them!

Hana couldn't stand it. She wanted to jump up and run home — already she's standing in the street in front of their home; she rings the doorbell. For a moment it's silent, she hears fumbling — it's perpetually dark in the entrance-hall — the door opens and behind it . . . oh, how horribly she envied the pregnant Gypsy woman they'd put in her cell for a night, for having her baby in her belly, for having him with her . . .

"Ma'am, please, why didn't you clear the icons with customs?"

Hana looked around her, uncomprehendingly. On the opposite wall, in a silver frame, hung a portrait of Josef Vissarionovich Stalin; it couldn't have been an accident; the effect was perfect. A cage.

Her heart grew quiet.

"I don't know," you said tamely. "Maybe it didn't occur to me."

The same year of our Lord.

Their street, their home, their door.

Hana rings the doorbell. For a moment it's silent, she hears fumbling — it's perpetually dark in the entrance-hall — the door opens and behind it . . . Jan!

He clasps his mother around the neck. He clutches her tight, he locks his arms and legs around her like a tick, he can't speak. He only breathes. He breathes against Hana's neck and holds on to her tight.

In the name of the republic she got a two-year suspended sentence and a fine. For failure to clear several icons with customs, eight weeks of detention plus a search of her home, during which they took the icons from her anyway.

And fifteen pounds.

In the name of the republic, Hana, be careful!

Because if the republic finds out what your friends in Moscow are using to sweeten their tea. . .

II.

Once there was a sofa. On the sofa, Hana in an unbuttoned blouse. A yanked-up skirt. Warm hands on your body, Hana, clasp your hands under your knees, pull them toward your chest . . . Hana, Hana!

A heel through the dust-cover. Undesirable rips and tears, lying on top of the rips Hana hears the ocean roaring in her temples. An unbuttoned blouse, a wet heat all over her body, you're breathing faster, one, two, three.

Once there was a woman named Hana. With this Hana, a pianist, plumber, surgeon. The stars don't lie. She loves her child, and she knows that Jan will never run into a strange uncle in gym shorts, in borrowed slippers, hem hem, a nervous, unfamiliar uncle wearing her robe.

Hana is going to come and go. She's going to make love in offices, hotels, in borrowed apartments. She's going to tear sofas if it comes to that. In this field she's a professional.

A line in the office of passports and visas to pick up the application form for an exit visa. A line for turning in correctly completed forms. So, early in the morning, ideally at about four, she's going to go get in line for a visa. She's going to pray that her turn comes before evening. A line for picking up permits, for transit visas.

In order for Jan to go to the seashore, in order for him to breathe freely through his perpetually stuffed nose at least once a year, Hana has to get through all these lines. In order to get through them, she needs the father's consent to travel abroad.

"Please tell me you've sent it in," she said to Jiří in a somewhat irritated tone of voice. She had asked him for it several times already; there wasn't much time left to get their papers in order.

"No," he answered decisively.

She tried to remain calm: "Then send it, please, as fast as possible, *prestissimo*!" She translated her message into musical terminology to make sure he understood.

"I'm not going to send it, period. I consulted a specialist — a stay at the seashore doesn't help allergies. The best thing is three thousand milligrams of vitamin C daily."

"That's good — you better take out a patent on that one," she wanted to snap at him and then slam down the phone. But they wouldn't allow Jan to go anywhere without Jiří's consent, Hana mustn't anger Jiří, she swallows her anger and in the most ordinary tone of voice possible she says, "He did get the stuffy nose from you, after all . . . And the consent form will only cost you four crowns . . . Why are you doing this to me?"

"To make sure there's a little something bothering you, too," he answered candidly, and the imprint of his ex-mother-in-law's palm burned on his face.

The year of our Lord 1979.

All three are hurrying down Jungmannova Street to the division of passports and visas of the Administrative Offices of the Police Department of the Capital City Prague and the Central Czech Region.

Jan: "Wow, Mommy, there's a new issue of *Bing*!"

Hana: "If you want to go to the seashore, then we can't stop . . ." She takes Jan's hand and leads him away from the display case full of magazines. Jan looks at Jiří: "They only cost twenty crowns — and there's a surprise inside every one . . ."

Jiří stops: "Buy it then."

He does not, however, take his wallet out of his pocket.

"Your father is a brave person, because even when everyone was repudiating everything, he didn't repudiate any of his positions or actions . . ."

Jan was asking about his father again. He liked it that he'd given him permission to buy *Bing.*

". . . except that he doesn't want to be with us, maybe out of laziness, or cowardice . . ."

"You just said he's brave . . ."

Hana didn't respond. Conversations like this irritated her. What was a mother supposed to say to her son about a father who didn't want to live with them?

"Is he brave or is he a coward?" Jan doggedly insisted.

Jiří didn't repudiate the memorial service for Jan Palach, the student protester who set himself on fire in 1969. But when she was in prison and things looked bad for her, he petitioned the court to lower the alimony he was paying, even though her mother implored him to wait until things cleared up . . . He didn't wait. And when she was out and she asked him for a loan to pay her fine, so that she wouldn't have to use the alimony she'd been setting aside for Jan, he said, "It's not an enormous amount of money."

No loan.

"So what is he?" Jan yelled at her from the piano.

"A paradox."

Jan was playing a couple of notes, which from time to time he accompanied with a broken chord. It sounded so peculiar, sad, pleading.

"What are you playing?" she asked.

"In music class we did some Bach — so I'm trying to play his name . . ."

Good God, Hana thought to herself.

"Did you come up with that yourself?" she asked.

She learned that Johann Sebastian Bach used the notes B-flat, A, C, and B-natural — notes that in German musical notation are identified as *b, a, c,* and *h* — as one of the themes in the final, unfinished fugue in his opus *The Art of the Fugue.*

"Do you know how to say it in German?" Jan couldn't wait for her to answer and immediately informed her: "*Die Kunst der Fuge.*"

Good God.

"And do you know how many children Bach had? Twenty!"

Good God.

"Where's the bed in this place?" Suddenly and wildly Oldřich thrust his hands between Hana's thighs.

"Oldřich?" she screeched in surprise and ran off.

For a while they chased each other through the kitchen, entrance-hall, and bathroom, until Oldřich's glasses fell off. His prescription was extremely strong; all she had to do was not hand them back to him.

She held the glasses behind her and said to herself, This is quite a racy situation. She was starting to enjoy it. She stopped running. Except for the kitchen, entrance-hall, and bathroom, there was a bed in every room. She didn't run. She deliberately made love to her friend's husband. In the bathroom. On top of the glasses.

Hana, the temples have broken off!

Luckily the glass wasn't cracked.

*

66

"I cook noodle soup for him, with homemade noodles, very substantial," Olga confided to Hana while she changed into her workpants. "They say it helps."

When neither soup, the Krkonoš Mountains, nor the ocean helped, Oldřich went for a medical exam. Anxious intellectual, the diagnosis read. The sperm are lazy; it would be hard to do anything about it. Maybe if they tried it somewhere high, at a great enough elevation above sea level . . .

"May I?" Olga slipped into Hana's galoshes. She had a vegetable patch in Hana's yard. No sooner did she leave with her seedlings to fetch her spade and trowel than Oldřich called:

"Come over!"

"But Olga's here, she's planting kohlrabi . . ."

"Exactly."

She came over.

They went on picnics in Hana's Fiat, where they fit quite snugly: Oldřich, Olga, Jakub, Olga's son from her first marriage, and Hana and Jan. They drove Hana's car to the picnics and in turn Olga made lunch for everyone.

The pot on the stove was already bubbling. Oldřich remembered that he needed to cart the synthesizer to the dancehall where he was supposed to play that night . . .

"Ask Hana," his wife advised.

They left, and she shouted after them down the stairs: "Come back right away, I've almost got dinner ready."

At the Malostranská Dancehall there was nothing to lean against. Except the synthesizer . . .

When they got back, Olga was setting the table. She turned to her husband: "Did you pay Hana?"

The year of our Lord 1980.

A sofa at the elevation above sea level of a third-floor apartment in Prague overlooking Letná Park. On the sofa, Hana in an unbuttoned blouse. Skirt who knows where. Oldřich beside her. He's trying to screw the temple back onto his glasses. Now. The nimblest of the lazy horde fulfills its biological mission. Now!

God help you, Hana.

She felt awful for days at a time. Really awful. Everything hurt, she was so tired any kind of activity was a great effort for her, she imagined the worst, oh God, let her live — until Jan finishes elementary school, until he reaches high school, at least until he can stand on his own feet a little . . . He plays the piano so well, he's so clever, curious. He doesn't have a father and now. . . After every meal she threw up. The final stage? But of what? No, she doesn't want to die! She's only thirty-eight years old!

Hana was sobbing. She couldn't stand it all alone. If she hadn't had Jan, she would have jumped out the window. She could hear an organ. But where? Johann Sebastian is playing the chorale *Von Gott will ich nicht lassen* (BWV 658). Hana, this was originally a secular love song. Its melody creates the impression of a joyful folksong. With its distinctive rhythmic motif, deliberately pursued throughout the course of the entire composition, this piece recalls Bach's chorales in the *Little Organ Book (Orgelbüchlein)*.

Are you listening?

This reminds me of something, Hana says to herself. But what?

Jesus Christ!

But they both assured her Oldřich was impotent!

Jesus Christ! But she's thirty-eight years old!

Have it. Don't have it. Have it. Don't have it. Have it. Don't have it. Don't tell. Tell. Don't tell. If you don't have it — tell? If you have it . . . Have it? Of course have it. She's thirty-eight years old. If she doesn't have a second child now, she'll never have one. Now.

They were having noodle soup with homemade noodles. The odor was already turning her stomach.

"Oldřich, don't gulp your soup while it's hot," Olga reminded her husband.

Hana stared at him; he stopped gulping.

It was making her sick. With all her might she tried to put another spoonful in her mouth. She felt like throwing up. She swallowed. She jumped up and ran to the bathroom. She only just made it.

She came out pale and weak. Face to face with Olga.

"Hana!" she cried out in amazement. "Are you in a fix?! Are you going to have a baby?! Hana, whose is it?"

There was no point in denying it. Yes, she was expecting. Whose was it? She couldn't say.

"Hana," Olga begged, "Hana, tell me . . . Hana," she confronted her and stared searchingly into her eyes: "I know! I know!" She turned toward the dining room: "Oldřich! OLD-ŘICH!"

Everything started to spin around Hana.

"Uh, what is it?" he asked guiltily and slowly walked toward her.

Breathe deeply, Hana told herself, one, two, three . . .

"Hana's expecting a baby!"

Astounded, he asked, "Whose is it?"

III.

Once there were some straps. Hands and legs tied down by these straps. Light. Green face masks. The murmur of water, rubber gloves. And pain and fear. IV drips above her head. Fear. Once there was a woman named Hana under anesthesia. There was a slice from hip to hip, there was hurrying, there was blood. Out of the blood, a son.

"I'm so happy I have a child! And that it's you I have it with!"

Oldřich came over to see her with a bouquet, a box of candy, and a ring.

"I'm going to marry you! And Jan too! I'm not Jiří! We'll be a family!"

He stole a glance at his watch. He noticed that she noticed and apologetically he said, "I'm at the dry cleaner's . . ."

Hana looked at his socks. They matched. She imagined Olga getting him ready to leave the house: "What do you have on? You can't wear those socks with that shirt!"

Oldřich goes off to change. When he puts on his shoes in the entrance-hall, his wife asks: "Oldřich, did you go number two today?"

"Yeah," he mumbles on his way out the door.

She wondered what would happen if he were to say he hadn't . . .

"Hana," he called out to her, "is something wrong? Are you in pain?"

She told him: "I'm not going to marry you."

"Why not?" he asked, and he switched his coat from one hand to the other. "I mean, you told me you were tired of acting as both the mommy and the daddy, that you don't want to do that anymore . . . ?"

"I don't."

The idea of pushing a baby carriage with a husband of her own no longer tormented her. Hana slept with Oldřich. Because he wanted to sleep with her, because she enjoyed it.

When she decided to have his child, she was very happy. She looked forward to the baby, she loved Filip long before she ever set eyes on him. She and Oldřich will be friends. They'll take care of their son together.

Be more specific, Hana.

Oldřich will come over. He'll play with Filip. He'll feed him, he'll change him . . .

And then?

He'll give him a bath.

And after that?

After that? What do you mean, after that? Oldřich will be Filip's dad! Oldřich is Filip's dad and he'll do what dads do with their sons . . . Oldřich will come over on his way to the dry cleaner's. He'll be in a rush. He'll leave, go home, to Olga. That's not going to bother you, Hana? Or are you going to be friends with her, too? It's about time for her to start the spring mulching . . .

"Hi, it's Oldřich." He phoned her one morning. "I just picked my mother up at the train station. I'm about to put her on the trolley . . . she'll be at your house in a bit."

Oh boy. Hana imagined the litany: she's splitting up the marriage. She's ruined Oldřich's life. She's going to use the child to blackmail him. And is it really his?

The doorbell rang.

She didn't hurry. She fumbled in the dark entrance-hall; for a long time she couldn't bring herself to turn the knob; she still hadn't opened the door when she heard:

"My courageous little lamb!"

*

71

I'm changing my habits, breaking off friendships, living differently now, for myself . . . she wrote to Olga right after that last visit. She was putting an end to a game that had slipped out of her control when she unexpectedly became pregnant. Olga called a few more times, but she couldn't find anything to say.

Oldřich brought things. Laundry, old newspapers.

He sat at the piano, put the baby on his lap, and plinked.

Plink, plink. After a while he returned the baby to the crib, rattled the rattle at him, and carted the things off. The laundry to the laundromat, the newspapers to the recycling center.

"Come back to see us again soon," she called to him as he walked down the street, and he called back: "The day after tomorrow I'm coming by with bottles . . ."

They're friends. When Olga went off to a health spa, they spent the weekend at his parents' house. All four, a genuine family. Oldřich isn't Jiří!

The year of our Lord nineteen hundred and . . .

Kitchen, counter, oven, table. On the table, Christmas candy. They've finished their coffee; they've eaten their fill.

Olga: Gets up to leave.

Mother-in-law: "Pretty baby, isn't he?"

Behind the glass on the kitchen counter, a picture of a child.

Olga looks: "Pretty."

She's stuffing her glasses into their case and the case into her purse when she hears:

"It's Oldřich's son."

It takes her a moment to understand the meaning of the words that have just been uttered. IT'S OLDŘICH'S SON. Pronoun, verb in contracted form, possessive case of proper noun, noun.

"With whom?" she asks icily.

Granny believes that right now she's giving Filip, the only grandson she will ever have, the loveliest Christmas present imaginable: a daddy forever.

At once happy and proud, she says: "Who else — with our Hana!"

The year of our Lord an hour later.
In the entrance-hall, darkness; in the darkness, a telephone.
On the telephone, a voice: "It's me."
Hana: "Are you coming over?"
Voice: "I'm turning tail, like Jiří."
It takes her a moment before she understands the meaning of the words that have just been uttered. I'M TURNING TAIL, LIKE JIŘÍ. Personal pronoun, present progressive tense verb in contracted form, noun. . . Hana recovers from the initial shock and says urgently, says desperately: "Don't do it, Oldřich! The longer you go without seeing us, the less you'll. . ."
Click.
". . . care for us," she finished saying to the deaf receiver.
Damn me, rings through her head, damn, damn, damn. . .
"Mommy. . ."
She didn't even notice when Jan came in, it's so dark in here, it's good that it's so dark in here . . .
". . . if I ever meet him on the subway, I'll snatch off his glasses and throw them on the tracks!"

The year of our Lord, the same year of our Lord, for the last time.
On the street, along the sidewalk, Hana pushes her baby carriage, 'tis the season to be jolly.
"You slut!"
In front of her, Olga.
Along the sidewalk, Hana pushes her baby carriage.
Olga: "You dare to come here with that brat?!"
Hana pushes her baby carriage.
"You slut! Slut! Slut! SLUT!"

IV.

Hana held the sheep's leg while the man injected
something into its hoof with a hypodermic. He was so adroit and
so taciturn! And when she saw him pull a calf out of a cow
during a complicated birth, saw him shove his arm into her up
to the shoulder and turn the calf around inside her and saw how
good he was at it! . . . Her love burst into blossom like a rose.

He would ride from Cheb on his motorcycle to see her.
She always waited somewhere near the border, and no sooner did
she prick up her ears than she heard his bike growling.

He led her to the off-limits zone near the border. Even
though it was her first time with a man, she tried, in vain, to
take care of the details. He broke the zipper on her linen pants.

She came back miserable. She was sure everyone could tell
just by looking at her. That she was pregnant.

And she was madly in love with him. He didn't show his
face again. The veterinarian didn't need an assistant anymore. The
agricultural work brigade was over. Her first lesson in what
people in love are up against was over.

Nobody could tell anything by looking at her. She wasn't
pregnant. Nobody could tell anything, even though the process
had already started: the process of emotional desiccation. Her first
spiritual abortion.

And her first actual abortion.

In her sophomore year at college she couldn't afford to
have a child. She was too young and Brno Repertory Theater's
Romeo, irresistibly lovely Romeo, didn't even suspect . . .

When she got her driver's license, she stole her father's car
out of the garage and drove off. She finished her joyride in the
Smíchov district, in front of the bus station. She hit a lamp post.
She broke her right hand. The doctor who treated her was a
surgeon named Masopust. Oh God, has anyone ever seen an ugly
or unmanly surgeon? At certain moments their eyes flash an
irresistible shade of violet . . . The flautist Jaroslav. They had

their first date at the Church of St. John on the Rock. They raced up the hill to see who'd get there first. Then at the bottom they washed their feet with seltzer water . . . She loved Jaroslav. His cagey humor impressed her. He claimed that the part of a woman's body that aroused him the most was the underside of the knee, which kind of looks like an *H*.

Just when she thought she had him in her clutches, he informed her that it was his destiny to marry a ballerina. Squint-eyed. Hana really wasn't anything of the sort.

He got married. To a ballerina, moderately squint-eyed. They had three sons; the third was born without a central brain. He told her this once in front of a post office where they ran into each other.

"What can't he do?" she asked.

"Think," he answered.

Now and then he called, more frequently as time passed. Now and then he stopped by. At Christmas he brought her three pencils from abroad. And the day Václav Havel was elected president. . .

Hana, you're getting ahead of your story . . .

That night she came home and found a message from her mother saying that Jaroslav had called twice. Let him wait, she said to herself, and didn't respond in any way.

Later she found out that he had died that night. Apparently he had a stroke. No one was home.

She remembered a night, it might have been four years ago, when he rang their doorbell. She remembered how, outside on the steps, the rain drizzled into his eyes. And at that moment she realized that he would always be a part of her life.

And then she ran into a friend, they were riding on the subway together, and suddenly he said in an off-hand way, "It's a mystery why that Jaroslav hanged himself."

Hana . . .

I was the last person he wanted to talk to! I'll never find out what he wanted from me!

Hana! . . . Where did you meet Leonel?

Pardon me? . . . Leonel? . . . At some conference. He walked like a predatory animal, short stiff hairs curled along his neck.

It all started during the dance, when he unambiguously pressed her against him . . .

They said good-bye in a hotel suite near Petřin Hill; he was returning home to Cuba. He walked her to her car. Since the trolley there ran on a raised strip down the middle of the street, she had to drive up to the next intersection in order to turn around and come back on the other side . . . After midnight there's not a living soul in that neighborhood. There was just one lone man, Leonel. She stopped the car and ran over to him, filled with intense emotions . . .

It's a shame there was no one around to watch this lovely scene . . .

Jan was five years younger and loved her too much. At night he would come hang on her doorknob his declarations of love, whose grammatical errors she would correct the next day in red pencil. She grew tired of him quickly and did something spineless, something she had only done a couple of times before. When he called, she said into the receiver without altering her voice:

"Hana isn't home."

With Petr. . .

. . . I got pregnant for the second time. He was Russian. He couldn't marry me; they wouldn't have given him permission. He himself asked me not to have it. He couldn't bear to know he had a child he couldn't take care of . . .

She got herself to the abortion on her own, and she got herself back on her own, too. And she stopped communicating. With her parents, who also wanted her to have the abortion. They didn't wish on her the fate of a single mother . . .

While they were still sleeping, she would get up and leave for work so that she wouldn't have to run into them. She would come back late at night and in the morning she would run away again.

She was typing something at work when he walked up to her and held out his hand:

"Jiří," he said.

She held out her hand and watched in surprise as he bowed and kissed her palm the old-fashioned way.

Eventually they were left alone. Eventually he escorted her home and the next day he called on her with a bouquet.

They were together constantly. At movies, at art galleries, at a theater she ran into a friend: "Are you going out with Jiří?" he asked.

"What a man — a dream."

She had work to do outside of Prague. She sat on the bus and he kept dashing on board to say heartfelt good-byes to her, making it impossible for the bus to drive off, and no sooner did she step into the hotel than the telephone rang, and it was him . . .

He had the thickest beard in the world.

They borrowed an apartment from a friend and started living together. She conceived.

"I'm afraid I won't be able to stand it," Jiří said, thinking about the child.

Hana wanted it. A lot. This time she needed to have the child.

"I'm afraid of your feminine nature . . . ," he told her one evening, and in the morning, when she was leaving for work in tears, in the morning he gave her a hug:

"Everything will be okay, you'll see. After all, I couldn't even make it to the movie theater without you."

She cheered up. She walked off in a happy mood: There was going to be a wedding.

In the afternoon he was waiting for her at the bus stop. As she approached she saw him signal to her, while she was still far off: No. I won't marry you.

She burst into loud sobs.

But there was a wedding: Bride and groom, two witnesses. His mother refused to take part; she refused to admit the wedding was happening or to admit Hana's existence. Jiří was getting married for the first time, in a church no less, and it — it was blasphemy!

Hana didn't invite her parents. Everything went forward civilly and unemotionally. Too unemotionally.

Her condition started to show, and Jiří became more and more anxious. He was afraid to tell his mother, because she would get very upset. But he was also afraid she would find out from someone else. Hana will go and tell her. He phoned his mother to say she was coming and accompanied Hana to the corner. There he waited, hidden in the doorway of a house.

En route Hana recalled their first meeting.

It was at some premiere; they were all sitting in a box at the theater.

Jiří stepped out for a minute.

"He leaves me all alone here like a dog . . . ," his mother complained loudly. Hana offered her a bag of sugar-coated chestnuts. She shoved them away brusquely: "I'd get constipated."

After the show Jiří mumbled: "I've got to walk her home, you know . . ."

And he was gone.

"If he's nice to his mother, he'll be nice to his wife," was Hana's grandmother's advice when Hana told her the story.

She rang the doorbell.

Mrs. Exwhy opened the door. Only then did Hana notice how alike they were: round face, reddish hair, almond eyes . . .

Mrs. Exwhy did not invite her in.

Hana walked into the entrance-hall anyway and shut the door behind her: "I came to tell you we're going to have a child."

The grandmother-to-be said evenly: "Well, that will cost money." And although she knew that she and Hana had the same last name, she said, "Don't drag me into it, miss."

"It'll be your grandson or granddaughter . . ."

"A child in this day and age? It's irresponsible. When I remember," she continued, shedding her diffidence, "how I complicated my life . . . How my friends would go out and I had to stay home with him . . . It's unforgivable!"

Jiří once confided to Hana that he had never heard his mother speak his name. Now she understood why.

The grandmother refused to recognize her own grandchild.

Several times, she imagined what she would do if Jiří were to call and say that his mother was ill and wished to see little Jan . . .

She wouldn't prevent it. After all she was a Christian.

And several times she imagined them sitting there across from each other on Christmas Eve, just the two of them, while a child of their own flesh and blood, who could make them so happy. . .

You're projecting your own emotions onto them. The fact is, a child doesn't make some people happy . . .

"Dear little quail." Instead of Jiří, a bouquet with a note was waiting for her in the apartment they'd borrowed. "Again I call on flowers to help me wish you a happy birthday and all the best along with it, and at the same time to break some terrible news: They called just now to say I have to leave for Dačice immediately. . ."

She sat in the living room all evening. Through the apartment wall came the sound of the neighbor's television; from time to time someone somewhere flushed.

The next day she drove her mother to visit her deathly ill grandmother in the hospital. She nearly ran Jiří over. He was crossing the street right in front of her car.

She was in her fifth month. There was no going back.

And would you have wanted to, Hana?

I was desperate!

There wasn't much left for the astrologist to spoil . . .

She lived in that apartment a while longer, and then she returned to her parents. Eventually her friends all got divorced as well . . . But from the start I pushed a baby carriage all alone! I felt so ashamed! How come, when a man abandons a woman and child, society doesn't. . .

Condemn him? Hana . . .

Hold him in somewhat less esteem.

Who would decide? The comrades on the citizens' committee?

I called him constantly. I wanted to know why he was leaving me like this . . .

The thirteenth invention in A minor (BWV 784) . . .

He never composed anything exceptional after that!

So there's justice after all?

He hung up the phone.

I wonder why ten years later you treated yourself to a second helping . . . ?

It was different.

The outcome was the same . . .

I never wanted to live with Oldřich. I didn't want to take him away from Olga.

You slept with your friend's husband.

I wasn't the one who chased him around the apartment!

You slept with your friend's husband.

Okay! I did! And her husband slept with me! . . . The strange thing is, their marriage actually became stronger. But I'm the slut. The slut with the brat.

You've got an inferiority complex toward her.

She may be his wife, but I'm the mother of his only child. And while she spends her whole life fighting like a lioness for her marriage rights, I'm a noncombatant. I don't really have anything to fight about.

Filip hasn't asked about his father?

He went to his grandparents' house during a school holiday; he slept under a photo of him: "That's your naughty father," his grandmother said, "but he's improving."

Once they even met. He was twelve. His father's foot was poking out from under the comforter on the opposite bed.

That's it?

Long before Oldřich got up, Filip had finished eating breakfast. Oldřich walked into the kitchen, and Granny introduced his son: "This is Filip."

They shook hands.

"How's school?" the father asked.

"I'm on vacation," the son answered.

Oldřich looked at his watch: "I have to be. . ."

Granny saved the situation. She asked her grandson to play something for his father. He sat down at the piano and plinked something out. Plink. Plink.

Oldřich was already standing in the doorway: "You should practice more," he told his son on his way out.

I got a postcard from Filip: "Mom, you amaze me."

I amaze myself.

If Jiří hadn't left me, I wouldn't have slept with Oldřich . . .

And if I hadn't slept with Oldřich . . .

V.

Once there was a town. In this town a street, in this street a car, and in this car a man opening the door for Hana.

It almost seemed like the good old days. She sat down next to him and realized how long it had been since she'd sat in the passenger seat — all she ever did was drive and drive and drive.

"Look out, red light!" she screamed at him at a traffic light, and she stamped down her right foot where the brake would have been if she'd been sitting on the driver's side.

They went for a walk. To a good restaurant for a good dinner.

And during dinner he announced that his marriage was just a formality. He was wearing a poorly washed shirt.

It didn't appeal to her at all when he said, with great emotion, that it had surely been far too long since anyone had held her in his arms . . .

He drove her home. And when he phoned the next day, she told him:

"Hana isn't home."

Vráž u Berouna, 1992–93

EWALD MURRER

The Mask

Translated by Julie Hansen

> It can happen
> that a person
> still alive
> turns into a demon.

(Ueda Akinari - *The Fingerless Eccentric:*
Tales of Moonlight and Rain)

I don't know how to make sense of what I witnessed. I don't know what this account will mean to you. The event I want to relate left me with a deep impression of oppressive horror. I realize that I was witness to a ritual whose symbolism seems to reflect primordial principles, and yet the principles of what, I am unable to describe. I am unable to analyze this occurrence. I was afraid to stay to the end, and therefore I don't know the point.

The experience was preceded by several other facts that may be important as well. Of course they, too, are shrouded by the murky fog in my memory. I am aware of only small fragments, which form the sketchy mosaic of this story.

I was wandering through some city, a large city to be more precise. It could have been any city. I walked along wide and narrow streets, among high-rise buildings, and a great number of lit advertisements assaulted me from all sides. The passing automobiles, like the passing pedestrians, threatened me. There was no refuge. Clearest in my memory is the sound of that place — a ceaseless and nearly unbearable din.

On some square I ran into two acquaintances, the sorcerer Blumfeld and Pablo de Sax. They were sitting on the curb and I didn't notice them at first — I wasn't expecting to find a friendly soul in that city. With alarm, they both told me about a woman who was supposedly looking for me. But both men warned me against meeting with her. Unable to say why, they just kept repeating over and over that it was dangerous. They suggested I hide in a building, because they thought I was vulnerable on the street. So trying to follow their advice, I searched for an unlocked building. Finding one wasn't easy, as almost all of them were locked. All the buildings looked empty inside, and their deserted silence was a harbinger of evil. I finally found one building whose entrance was illuminated by a piercing white light and whose door wasn't locked. I was surprised to find my own name on the doorbell. I hesitated for a moment, but the fear of the unknown woman was stronger than the fear of my own name unexpectedly appearing in a part of the world completely unknown to me, so I went in. The inside of the building looked like the office of a wealthy, prosperous company. It was furnished with thick purple rugs and heavy curtains of the same color, and a great number of mirrors and showy, expensive lamps. Various perfumes hung in the air, seeming to emanate from the bodies of attractive secretaries who were running briskly up and down the corridors, on missions that were unmistakably important. Through the labyrinth of corridors I unerringly arrived at a painted white door with a brass plate displaying my name. I was standing, therefore, at the door to my own *office*.

I went in and a strange world became still stranger. The room wasn't furnished like an office, but rather like a luxurious brothel. Still more peculiar was that the people in the room were Japanese. A man in glasses with gold frames sitting on a bamboo mat welcomed me with a bow and smile typical of his people. I also saw a young woman in a traditional kimono with ornaments in her hair. Then one of the secretaries I had seen in the corridors came in from a neighboring room. She was white, but she had the same ceremonious smile on her face as the Asians. For the first time in that city, someone who wasn't a foreigner like me and Blumfeld and de Sax, spoke to me. She said:

"This is really quite a nice boy!" And it was clear that the words were intended for the Japanese, even though she was facing me when she delivered them. Then the girl, who smelled of Rafael No. 1, seated me on a soft cushion in a corner and left me by myself.

The Japanese no longer paid any attention to me. They pushed aside a bamboo partition, behind which appeared a tall, narrow stool and, hanging on the wall behind it, a *mask*. Otherwise, that space was empty and coldly white. The Japanese woman sat down on the stool and the man positioned himself beside her. They meditated like that, motionless, for a while. Then the man took the *mask* down from the wall, and I broke out in a cold sweat, because I realized it was the skin of a human face — the face of an old Japanese woman — expertly removed and preserved. The man put this face on the woman. At that moment, without anyone having said anything, it was clear that the Japanese were husband and wife and that this macabre mask was the face of the woman's mother. The man ran his fingers over that horrifying face and smoothed it onto his wife's. His fingers ran faster and faster over the mask. The Japanese both laughed out loud during this procedure, but there was no joy in their laughter. They were in some kind of convulsive ecstasy.

Then, at the height of this torrent of laughter, the man jumped away from his wife and, mumbling some unintelligible phrases, ran into the neighboring room and abruptly locked himself in. At the same time, the padding of bare feet could be heard in the corridor. At the exact same moment, down to the second, that the Japanese man was locking the door, a female figure in a white flowing gown entered the room. She didn't have any skin on her face, so it had to be the woman's mother. Her horrifying appearance froze me to my pillow.

The figure approached the young Japanese woman from

behind, stretched out her hands, and stroked her hair with her fingers, which resembled the shiny black ornaments in her hair, the same kind the young woman wore. Suddenly, however, the stroking turned into furious scratching. The woman without a face opened up the skull of the young woman and stuck her own head into it, ultimately entering the daughter's body. After this occurrence, there was nothing strange about the young woman, she looked just as pretty as before. She turned her face toward me and stood up. She took several steps in the direction of my cushion. I cried out in horror and fled that place in great distress. I returned headfirst into my body, lying in my Prague apartment. Lízele, lying next to me, woke up and asked me why I was screaming. She said I had called out, "No, stop, that's enough!"

The next day, as I was looking through the mail, I found a postcard from Blumfeld, a reproduction of the Japanese print Lovers in Bed. *I should also emphasize that my correspondence with the sorcerer Blumfeld is rare: this postcard was the very first he'd ever sent me.*

MICHAL AJVAZ
from **The Other City**
Translated by Tatiana Firkušný and
Veronique Firkušný-Callegari

Chapter 8
The Pohořelec Bistro

Is it possible that we live in close proximity to a world
teeming with strange life, a world which perhaps has been here
since before our city existed and yet which we know nothing
about? The more I have thought about it, the more I have been
inclined to admit that it is very well possible, that it goes with
our way of life, with how we live within demarcated circles we're
afraid to leave. The dark music from the other side of the frontier
corrodes our order and fills us with anxiety; we fear the outlines
of forms we discern in dusky corners, we do not know whether
they are the broken, decomposing forms of our world or the
embryos of a new fauna that will one day turn cities into its
hunting grounds, the spearhead of an army of monsters that will
advance with stealthy deliberation on our homes. So we prefer
not to see the forms that originate on the other side and not to
hear the sounds that, at night, come from behind our walls; for
us, reality is only what has become rooted in our world, what
interacts with the other things and events of the few games we
keep monotonously repeating, whose interconnections we refer to
as cause, reason, sense. These games, which constitute the tissue
of our world, are no less strange or alarming than the nighttime
festivals of glass statues; and should someone be watching from

the other side, for example, through the gaps between the books in our library, he would probably experience the same disquieting amazement at the fascinating and oppressive ritualism that I experienced while watching the fish festival from the darkness of the arcade. "What amazing monsters!" he would whisper, peering at us anxiously and with dark admiration.

Yet the world into which we have locked ourselves is actually most confining; even within the space we consider our own, there are places beyond our power, dens settled by animals whose home is in the darkness beyond the frontier. We know the strange uneasiness that overcomes us when we encounter the hidden side of things and their inner hollows, which refuse to join in our games: when, while house-cleaning, we pull out an armoire and are suddenly looking at the ironically indifferent face of its back, which stares off down a dark hall reflected in its surface; when we unscrew the cover of a TV set and run our fingers along the tangle of wires; when we crawl under a bed to retrieve a pencil and suddenly find ourselves in a mysterious cave, its walls covered with magical, quivering balls of dust, a cave where something evil is slowly ripening, something which one quiet afternoon will crawl out into the daylight. What exists for us is only what has a part to play in our games: no wonder we know nothing about the world that extends beyond the edge of these games. We probably wouldn't even notice it if it were celebrating its festivals right in the midst of our daily bustle.

I was remembering how the linguist at the University Library insisted that what lives beyond the frontier is invisible to us, because the beings from those regions sate themselves at a different fountain of reason and thus elude our gaze. But I grew more and more convinced that this invisibility was more likely the result of how perfectly we have succeeded in mastering our gaze and keeping it on a short tether. The severity with which we restrict the roving of our eyes seems rather to indicate that we are aware of the fact that our gaze vaguely recognizes the monsters on the margins and that we fear it might encounter some familiar beasts and strike up a conversation that would recall an old friendship and a forgotten common language.

The next morning I set out for Pohořelec to see what the nighttime activities had left behind, but I encountered nothing to indicate that, mere hours ago, a chapel, a tent, and a ski lift had been standing there; I did not discover a single thing that would not be firmly planted in the conjoint daytime world. The small square was almost completely abandoned at this time of day; the tourists that would inundate it before long were still at breakfast in their hotels down in the center of the city. There blew a sharp, icy wind typical of elevated open spaces, abandoned cars with snow-encrusted roofs stood in frozen snowdrifts. The bistro with the large window was already open. I felt like having a cup of hot coffee and went in.

I found myself in a long, narrow room. Its front section was flooded with the gentle light that came through the window, which overlooked the snow-covered square; in the back, above the bar, dewy glasses and travel posters of beaches shone in the semidarkness. Two old ladies were seated facing each other across a small table; they obviously lived nearby and came here to drink their morning coffee. I sat down where I always do in cafés and bistros: by the glass windowpane, which offered up cold pictures, at a table across which an empty chair stared at me like a silent, understanding animal. I was looking out the window at the square when suddenly I heard above me a pleasant male voice asking me what I would have: the waiter had approached my table so silently that I had never even heard his footsteps. I turned my head and looked up into the inclined face of the waiter, who had positioned himself right next to my chair. I could see that this was the same man who had celebrated mass in the subterranean temple, the man who, in the TV van, had railed at the history professor, and the one before whom the guards had brought me last night because I didn't have a fish. So my flight on skis through the nighttime parks had been for naught, the pursuer could just wait for me in the comfort of the bistro sipping sweet, bright-colored liqueurs, and still I could not escape him. But the waiter-priest did not pounce on me, his polite expression never changed, his body, inclined forward in a servile stoop, never straightened. With some discomposure, I ordered coffee, and the waiter went off to the bar.

My coffee was brought by a slight lady in a dark dress; as she was placing her nickel-plated tray down on the table, the way her hands emerged from their long sleeves reminded me of little animals who have cautiously come out of their dens into daylight, ready to scurry back with lightning speed at the first suspicious rustle. I couldn't help asking her: "Does the waiter happen to like nighttime festivals?"

The cup on the tray, which the woman was still holding in her hands, rattled slightly. "He is my husband," she said, distressed. Glancing back to the bar and seeing the waiter disappear through the door into the kitchen, she said in a voice that betrayed a long-ripening anxiety: "Please tell me where you met my husband in the night." I asked her to sit down on the empty chair at my table, and I told her about the temple inside Petřín Hill, about the fish festival, and about the television sets on Kaprova Street. She turned her face toward the window and looked at the white square, where two tan poodles were chasing each other.

"I don't know what to do," she finally said. "My husband is a citizen of some unknown city. He has never told me about it, though we've been living together for twenty-six years. He has never admitted it to me, not even in the most intimate moments, and I myself have never asked. But I keep finding traces of the other city in the corners of our apartment and in the depths of the furniture: statuettes of gods with willful expressions, gadgets shaped like birds and turtles which buzz from time to time and flash the red bulbs set in their eyes; books printed in an unknown alphabet, with luminous, iridescent illustrations depicting temples in a virgin forest and tigers. When my husband goes out at night, I know he is going to some dark festival. I know nothing about his city. Is it a labyrinth of gold-panelled burrows, an endless palace spreading through the hidden spaces between apartments, a circle of yurts springing up in the plain at night, or a collective hallucination? I don't even know whether my husband is a king or a servant in his city, but I think he probably has an important position, because several times I've found copies of the other city's newspaper with his photograph in it. I have never been to the other city, although I feel it's nearby, within arm's reach, behind the wall. Sometimes, in the quiet of the night, I hear its voices, the distant murmur of its boulevards, the ringing of its bells, its promenade concerts. I think that somewhere behind the wall, in the unrecognized spaces of the building, there is some kind of concealed sea, sometimes one can hear the ships sounding their horns and the surf breaking against the rocks."

I sipped my coffee and listened to the sad tale. The first clusters of tourists appeared on the snow-covered sidewalk, several black cars with diplomatic license plates crossed the square and turned toward the Foreign Office. "All my life I longed to have a real home and, instead, I'm living in the vestibule of an incomprehensible temple, whose odors seep through the cracks in the furniture and permeate everything. There are moments when I loathe to touch even the most ordinary object; it seems to me that someone has just lent it to us for a while and that we use it for a completely different purpose than what it was intended for. I was hoping, especially after our daughter was born, that my husband would forget the other city, that in time his life would become rooted in our family life, that his place in the family would cease to be a role he acts out until he returns to his home behind the walls . . . But then I realized that the other city holds him with a pull that is stronger than any family cohesion. At last, I reconciled myself to loneliness and found consolation in having a daughter who, fortunately, has nothing to do with the other city. I know all about her life and I don't think it holds any dark corners. She's a good girl, she is studying Czech and physical education at the teacher's college and, when she has a minute, she comes here and helps us out . . . But lately I've been growing more anxious again: I feel that some strange conspiracy is brewing between my husband and my daughter, they are together almost all the time these days, always telling each other things. One day I caught my daughter looking at a book printed in the unknown alphabet. She might have just found it somewhere and opened it by chance. Maybe it's not possible for someone who was born into our world and has lived in it for twenty years to simply cross the border and become an inhabitant of a different space, but still, these days I can't sleep at night for fear. . ."

The kitchen door opened, and the waiter appeared in it carrying a tray with two dishes of omelets garnished with whipped cream. He headed straight for the old ladies, but I felt that in the doorway he had squinted for a split second in my direction. His wife immediately stopped talking and got up, turning her attention to a cheerful, noisy group of customers who were just entering the place. I sat in the bistro for a while longer, but she never addressed me again nor paid me any attention, not even when her husband was in the kitchen. The waiter kept passing by my table and apologizing for the bistro being so cold, because the central heating couldn't keep the place warm in such freezing weather. He made me have some sticky french horns, which he extolled as the house specialty. What faces are we going to make at each other when next we meet in the night? Down which roads, along which walls will he pursue me? What punishment will he sentence me to the next time the guards bring me before him?

I waved my check toward the far end of the room; that very moment the door opened and in burst a tanned girl with black, wavy hair, wearing a sporty, brightly colored snowsuit. Seeing a check in my hand, she called out: "I'll get it, Mom, you don't have to come." "Thanks, Klárka," answered a voice from the back. The girl took the check, spent a long time adding up my coffees and french horns, made a mistake and laughed at it, then finally managed to sort it out and place the check on my table. Beneath the column of figures on the sheet was a message written in big, slightly childish script: "If you want to learn something about the other city and see something unusual, come at 3 o'clock in the morning to the outer gallery on the bell tower of St. Nicholas in Malá Strana. The church will be open." I paid my check with an impassive expression, the girl thanked me cheerfully for the tip and ran off to her parents in the back. I went out and set off downhill toward the center of the city.

Chapter 9
In the Tower

Prior to three o'clock in the morning, I opened the door of St. Nicholas Church, walked through the dark nave, and climbed up a spiral staircase to the outer gallery of the belfry. The wind had swept the snow into high drifts along the wall, and on the stone balustrade there was also pristine snow. The Castle towered above me, the steep roofs of St. Vitus Cathedral shone pallidly and dreamily in the light of a blinding full moon. The sky was full of bright stars. Far below lay Malostranské Square, the dirty yellow light of fluorescent lamps spilling down its gentle slope. A taxi drove through the square and disappeared down Tomáš Street, then nothing else stirred.

After a while, the little gate to the staircase opened and the girl from the bistro appeared, wearing a bulky down jacket; her jacket was open, and a pearl necklace glinted on the black sweater she was wearing underneath. She leaned against the stone balustrade, the red lights of the Petřín Hill radio towers shone above her dark hair. "Is there going to be another festival down there?" I asked. The girl didn't answer, from the deep shadows under her eyebrows and her cheekbones I couldn't discern any expression.

"It was not for you that Darguz's holy body was torn apart by the tiger," she said, abruptly breaking the night's stillness with her hard voice full of scorn. "It was not for you that he wandered, feverish, through abandoned parks and stood on the glittering mosaic floor of the temple in long disputations with cunning priests, who tried to triumph over him by using syllogisms, their main premise being the burrows of blind subterranean horses, and by systematically distracting him when everyone was pointing at the troops of ten thousand brown mummies in shining golden armor that were marching past the open temple doors, stirring up dust from the road. Why are you sticking your nose into our affairs? Remember: he who crosses the frontier will become entangled in twisted wires protruding from objects you consider broken, but that have actually reverted to their true form, just as was engraved on the glass star that wanders among the constellations. Whoever wants to intrude on our city will never return, his features will disappear amidst the intertwining netting of cracks in old walls, his gestures will dissolve into the motions of bushes swaying in the wind. Don't think that your boldness could cause us any harm. But the fact that you have dared to penetrate into the border regions of our city is a desecration to the memory of those who, five thousand years ago, in the clearing of a primeval forest, with a cold flame in their eyes, knocked over the statue of the winged dog and then, as often happens, turned into something of winged dogs themselves. What do you hope to find here? Even if you did succeed in penetrating to the fountains in the inner courtyard of the royal palace and hearing their murmur, to which our philosophers listen so attentively, even if you were to walk through the halls of the palace library and heavy folio volumes, their dark pages blazing with fiery letters, were open before you, you wouldn't understand anything anyway. Clumsy and dull as you in that city of yours are, you have forgotten your primal tongue, and you think that what is spoken softly in this tongue is mute; all you see beyond the boundaries of your space is chaos, ruin, and decay. You are so busy and diligent, always building something, yet all your activity is but a frenzied search for a lost beginning, your buildings desperate attempts to recreate the golden temples and palaces, forms that remain darkly and persistently embedded in the depths of your memory — yet full of anxiety and revulsion, you avoid the only space in which you could encounter the living and authentic legacy of what you seek: the scorned margins. You don't sense that the terror which grips you on the fringes of your world is the beginning of the bliss of return, that finding your doom in the primeval forest on the margins is a glowing rebirth. If you were to sit down in the middle of a rubbish pile or in a dump outside the city and meditate on the shapes that bare themselves beneath the rotting, decomposing masks, it would bring you much closer to the secret goal of your journey than the confusingly revolving circle of all your plans and achievements."

I laughed. "Why do you keep saying 'you' and 'your city'? I know that you grew up in our world, just a year ago you probably didn't even know that the other city existed."

The girl moved closer to me and smiled. "I promised that you would see something unusual." Suddenly she pressed her body against my side, wrapped one arm around my neck from behind, placed the other on my shoulder, and turned me toward a bend behind which the gallery lay hidden in black shadow; through muffled laughter she whispered into my ear: "It's there, back there in the shadows. You have to go a little further, just a little." Leaning against me, she prodded me toward the dark side of the gallery, softly laughing to herself the whole time. Her chin propped on my shoulder, she said merrily: "Come on, don't tell me you're afraid? I thought you wanted to explore our city. It can't be helped, the tour begins in the tower."

Her soft laughter, the thick darkness beyond the bend in the gallery, and the feeling that something horrifying was lurking nearby, were making me truly anxious. Nevertheless, I disentangled myself from her embrace, pushed her away, and proceeded alone to the edge of the dark shadow. After all, she was right: I had set out on an expedition to explore the other city. Behind me I heard her soft laughter. I reached the line dividing the moonlit area from the impenetrable darkness. Something in the darkness rose up out of the snow and landed on me. A cold, heavy body without arms or legs pushed me down into the snow and lay on top of me, crushing me with its weight. Above me I saw the head of a shark with beady golden eyes, the moonlight on its gaping jaws revealing glinting white teeth. In vain did I try to get the shark off of me. He snapped at my shoulder, but I managed to jerk away from his teeth, so all he tore off was a piece of my collar. We grappled silently in the snow, the blinding moon shining into my eyes. The garret window in one of the houses below me lit up, and I could see some insomniac in his pajamas go to the kitchen and come back. I cried out for help, but no one except the shark and the evil girl could hear me. In a moment the light went out again.

The girl tiptoed closer to me, leaned over until her necklace lightly touched my forehead, and in a quiet, almost soothing voice told me: "All your life you've looked out at the world through cold glass panes, you loved the windows of cafés and trains, the glassed-in terraces of houses in the mountains. We know a lot about you. Behind glass you felt safe, so why did you leave your shelter, why did you set out on a journey into the jungle? Only rarely does a shark attack a customer in the Slavia Café. Why did you set out alone into an alien city where no one cares about you? The shark will now roll your bitten-off head around the tower gallery, and small children in our schools will learn about you in limericks and nursery rhymes."

The small gate opened and the waiter appeared; the girl

slowly straightened herself up and moved aside so he could see the status of the contest. The waiter smiled and nodded with satisfaction. The girl left me and walked over to her father who embraced her and kissed her on the cheek. I looked up and saw the silhouettes of their bodies huddled together against the starry sky. I swore that, should I by some miracle manage to get down from the tower, never again would I let the waiter talk me into buying his french horns. Then the waiter took his daughter by the hand and they both disappeared through the dark opening of the gateway. I remained alone with the shark on the gallery of the tower above the sleeping city.

We went on wrestling in the snow for a rather long time. I couldn't get the shark off of me, so I tried to at least prevent him from getting into a position from which he could take a bite. But my strength was gradually ebbing. The beast sensed it and reared up to make its final strike; the moment the shark raised its massive body and opened its jaws wide so that my head would fit, I gathered the last bits of my strength, jumped up, and pushed against it, whereupon the shark, in its precarious position, lost its balance and fell over the balustrade. Its body dropped through the darkness and was impaled on a tall metal cross held by one of the stone figures on the attic of St. Nicholas Church. I watched it thrashing about in its death throes, the contortions forcing its body further and further down onto the metal cross. After a while the movements stopped and the shark's limp body hung from the cross like a flag of the night. I staggered down the steps into the church, collapsed onto the cold floor at the foot of a column, and instantly fell asleep.

VAŠEK KOUBEK
The Bottle

translated by Caleb Crain

I had just arranged for a nap in the cast room and cleared off a
bed for myself when the admitting nurse squawked:

"Orderly, report to triage!"

"Oh great, one more beat-up drunk and I'm going to be on
duty all night."

Annoyed, I jumped into my tennis shoes.

A little old lady was sitting in the waiting room, cowering,
hunched up into herself, and she looked at my white coat
trustfully.

"Give her an EKG and then take her to radiology,"

the admitting nurse looked out her little window.

"Here's her chart."

"Take off your clothes,"

I took her to an exam room.

"What, me? Shouldn't you be the one to take my clothes off?"
the old lady surprised me.

"Does it hurt that bad?"

I stripped off her sweater.

"When I was young, various gentlemen took my clothes off,"
she said meaningfully.

"Oh really."

"They called me Poppy."

"Don't lie down, stay sitting up, or I can't manage,"
I fought with her buttons.

"Do you know Na Poříčí Street?"
she continued after a while.

"Of course."

"Well, that's where I lived between the wars."

"Lie down,"

I wiped under her breasts with a cotton swab.

"Only the very best paid me visits . . . and you'd be amazed what they would give for a sight like this."

"Don't breathe! Don't talk!"

I switched on the measuring device.

"Yow,"

she jerked.

The door opened and the admitting nurse added another form.

"Did you see this yet?"

she pointed at her National Health number.

I happened to notice her name.

"Oh, you're Ms. Poupětová; that's why they called you Poppy. Here you go, put this blanket over yourself and let's go to radiology."

Covered by an institutional blanket instead of her own clothes, the old woman lost her self-consciousness.

"Do you know what's wrong with me, doctor?"

"Grandma, I'm not a doctor, I only help out around here. Get up on the stretcher. Can you make it? Slowly!"

The old lady rolled onto the stretcher and groaned again. Her eyes grew a little sad.

"Do you want something to put under your head? It won't be anything serious, you'll see, Poppy."

The old lady shyly stretched out her hand.

"Could you give me my handbag? Please."

"Don't worry, nobody's ever lost anything here yet."

I pushed her along the long nighttime corridor.

At radiology I had to ring twice. They were probably asleep. By two in the morning, it's quiet around here most of the time.

"I was only in the hospital once, as a little girl,"

she suddenly interrupted our wait.

"Oh, really."

"I got fish hooks stuck in my fanny, heehee,"

she giggled coyly.

The X-ray table came up to the level of the stretcher and Ms. Poupětová rolled onto it.

"Take off her pants,"

the sleepy radiologist vanished into his booth.

My hands slid down along her soaking wet body.

"I wet myself, didn't I?"

she burst into tears.

"It's nothing; after all, it's only water, Grandma."

"Don't breathe!"

the radiologist ordered from behind glass, and the powerful instrument stopped above the old woman like a press.

"All done."

"I'll help you get her back on the stretcher, if you'll wipe this up for me here one more time."

the employee said measuredly.

We wheeled back into the twilight.

"What's your name?"

the old woman asked, back in the corridor.

"Vašek,"

I answered, and the way my name carried down the empty corridor nearly made me jump out of my skin.

"Here, Vašek,"

the lady reached into her handbag for ten crowns.

"No way, Grandma, don't do that."

"You don't even think I'm worth ten crowns anymore,"

she started up the waterworks again.

"I don't accept tips. I'm glad to be helping you, okay, Poppy?"

"Then at least buy your girlfriend some flowers with it,"

she raised her reddened eyes.

"But I don't even have a girlfriend."

We were approaching the triage station. The old woman pleadingly stretched out the hand with the ten crowns and her voice echoed so loud that to keep her quiet I quickly shoved the money in my pocket. The doctor looked over the lab results and examined the whites of the old lady's eyes.

"Get a room ready, we're going to operate — and you take her upstairs for me,"

he nodded at me.

We stopped in front of her room.

"If you have dentures, give them to me and I'll put them in a bag for you,"

and with a felt marker I wrote on the sack — *Poupětová 995302.*

In a blue gown and without teeth, her hair sprawling, Poppy turned into a miserable tangle.

"What's the big deal, Grandma? It's only your appendix. In the morning everything'll be fine. You'll see."

We rode the elevator and now I was talking instead of the old lady.

Until the clang of the elevator door put an end to my desperate attempt at conversation. Not until we were outside the operating room did the old lady speak up again.

"Václav, where are you going in the morning?"

"Maybe I'll go somewhere for a beer and then . . . I don't know yet."

"I'd like to have one too, with you — and some goulash to go with it, don't you think? Would you take me with you?"

"You know it, Poppy. You're great. And we'll drink those ten crowns together, at the U Brabanta pub. I mean, flowers are kind of silly, right."

"Do you drink rum, too?"

she asked sweetly.

"You know it."

"Give me your hand, please."

And Poppy squeezed my hand as hard as she could. The longest squeeze.

"Wait with her two more hours and then take her away," the doctor snapped her folder shut.

The nurse attached a tag to her leg and wrote the number *995302/2624.*

"We haven't had a number this high in a long time,"

she said indifferently and was about to disappear.

"Please, add the word *Poppy.*"

"But that's not allowed, that's against hospital procedure, isn't it? Well, if you want me to,"

and in large letters she wrote *POPPY.*

It was five and my shift was ending in two hours, not a living soul was stirring that morning and so I went to sit in the triage room.

"Václav, I've got something here,"

the admitting nurse broke in on my thoughts, and in her hand she held a bottle of rum.

"It was left here by that. . . ,"

she looked down at her records,

". . . Ms. Poupětová, for me to give to the one who wheeled her around last."

JIŘÍ KRATOCHVIL
The Story of King Candaules
Translated by Jonathan Bolton

for Zdeněk Kypr

Part 1
King Candaules

We are standing with our umbrellas open, waiting in front of the crematorium. More and more cars arrive, falling into place in the parking lot below the flower stand, and we quickly expand into a multitude of black umbrellas. In a moment, we'll all cram ourselves into the crematorium's hall, and yet I'm sure hardly anyone is here on account of the deceased.

I look in Svatava's direction. The umbrellas have thickened around her, stuck together in an impenetrable black mass. And yet . . . if anyone present tried to remember the moment when Svatava first appeared, when she quickly became what she is, they would be surprised to discover that until Ludvík introduced her into society (until he married her) she didn't exist for any of them. She emerged like the moon, at first covered by clouds, then flooding everything with its light. And we all foundered clumsily in that light, with the sepulchral appearance that only a moonlit landscape affords.

Svatava was undoubtedly beautiful, but the unearthly nature of her beauty, if I can call it that, was to a large extent

Ludvík's work. And I played a certain role in it myself. Since this is a story about beauty, I'd like to indulge in a short digression before I begin. A digression on genuine beauty, next to which Svatava is nothing but a provincial belle, the kind that hands out prizes to the winners of a town raffle.

But is this the way things really are? Or am I only trying to denigrate something that interfered too much with my life, until it became — thanks to the force of circumstance, unconscious symbolism, and myths that are always at hand — a near-trauma, a trauma I'm stubbornly resisting, but into whose center I'm being drawn farther and farther?

But even if things really are like this, my short digression is justified. In an abbreviated form, it characterizes what I want to talk about. And it precedes the story chronologically by just a few months, yet at the same time by a gulf of time. It reaches far away and, at the same time, comes quite close. And so it's exactly what I should begin with.

When, three years after graduating from the university, I managed to find a job at the psychiatric clinic of Saint Anna's Hospital, I was one of the first in Brno to try out group psychotherapy. Encouraged by Professor Hugo Široký, I also tried using some of the techniques of Morenian psychodrama to cure neuroses. I wasn't successful — as a mere psychologist among psychiatrists, I didn't have enough elbow room or authority for that — but I did gain a certain doubtful popularity. You might say I was something like a Paracelsus among Mendeleevs.

And while the Mendeleevs went to conferences, diligently published in the academic journals, and were long-standing, respectable priests in the Temple of Science, the doors of the Temple of Art opened a little for me. And in the middle of the sixties, the Temple of Art was the "atelier" of a certain popular cabaret actor.

Evžen's studio was in the attic of an apartment building on Obilní Square, and on Wednesday evenings everyone who was anyone (or, rather, wanted to be someone) in the Brno art world gathered there. It was a massive wooden rotunda that broke through the roof and rose above it like a tower with a cupola, looking from the outside like a nicely domed glans.

"It's my very own ivory tower," Evžen explained as we stood in front of the apartment building with our heads bent back. "With one difference: I've lined it with something far more ivory-like than ivory. You'll see."

Then we went up four floors in the elevator, and behind a steel door was an attic as roomy as the main hall of a train station. In the middle was the enormous cylinder of the rotunda, as noisy as a beehive. We stepped lightly through the concave door into half-darkness, where a cliquish herd of Brno actors, actresses, artists, and literati sat on pillows on the floor, glasses in their hands.

"Ladies and gentlemen, stop cupolating — I'm lighting up the cupola!" Someone protested, and Evžen waited patiently with his hand on the switch. And then it happened. Several floodlights went on, and the rotunda was immersed in a light so aggressive I had to close my eyes. And when I opened them a few seconds later, I saw the walls. They were papered all around with enormous photographs. Female nudes in several lascivious styles and obscene positions. But at a scale so much larger than life that these immeasurable intimate details — stretching from the floor up to top of the cupola — would have bewitched anyone straight away. In the harsh light of the floodlamps, they looked like gigantic mythical torsos, sunken continents, archetypal volcanic formations, the entrails of the gods, or absurdly large, sacred hieroglyphics.

"What's wrong?" asked Evžen with a smile. "Nothing," I said. Evžen turned off the floodlights. I stayed a while, then gave my apologies and disappeared, never to show my face there again.

I crossed the little park on Obilní, got onto the first tram that came, and rode who knows where. I had just suffered a minor shock. I had immediately recognized the girl on the walls all around. It was Jana, whom I had last seen eight years before.

We went to high school together on Antonínská Street, and during our last summer vacation (before college), we worked raking hay near Volary. It was the late fifties, we were seventeen, and the night before we returned home, we had a reprise of our graduation party. The local pub (in Svatý Kamen) was willing to rent us a room; all four graduating homerooms were there, Jana from C, me from D. We danced to the music of a small bakelite radio that stood on the bar. Inside it smelled of spilt beer, outside it stank of manure, and shooting stars rained through the sky. Everyone wanted to dance with Jana. I was able to talk with her only for a moment, but I managed to tell her that I urgently needed to speak with her and that I would wait for her outside. I waited more than an hour in the midst of the manure and the shooting stars, but she stood me up, and early the next morning the V3S trucks took us to the train station. She and I were in different train compartments, and we never saw each other again.

Jana was the most beautiful woman I'd ever met. All things considered, I was glad I was at least allowed to meet her.

After my visit to the "atelier," I began to investigate what had happened to Jana. And what I discovered is that Evžen had hunted her down while we were still in high school. A beauty like hers couldn't stay secret for long. While we looked up to her with unimaginative, boyish admiration, some serious skirt-chasers were already dancing around her, and the most successful of them all, the one with the best outflanking maneuvers, was fat little Evžen. And it was probably this meeting with him that sent Jana in a new direction, starting her on the path that ended with her suicide at the beginning of the sixties, when she was twenty. I don't presume to sit in judgment — these are all just guesses. At the time, a lot of people in Brno talked about it, but of course I never suspected that the sad protagonist of the story was Jana.

But I don't want to talk about that now. It was just supposed to be an introduction to my own narrative, which deals with the same theme.

That theme is Candaulism. Candaulism is a little-known

sexual deviation named after the mythical King Candaules. When King Candaules wanted to obtain a magic ring from the Greek Gyges, he offered him something of equal value: the chance to hide in the royal bedroom, make himself invisible with the magic ring, and thereby see the naked Queen Rhodopa, with whom Gyges (as the king well knew) was secretly in love. (How did it turn out? When Gyges saw the queen naked, his secret love changed into a violent passion; he disposed of the king and took possession of the queen and the throne.)

In modern psychiatry, many traumas, complexes, phobias, and even sexual deviations are given mythological names, to make it clear that they stretch far back into the history of humankind, into its collective memory and archetypes. The core remains the same, but everything else undergoes change, each era choosing its own forms, terms, and methods. And so Candaulists are those who have an irresistible urge to display their lovers naked to other men.

The room papered with gigantic photographs of Evžen's mythically beautiful lover, a room where people chat, drink, and wander about, surrounded on all sides by Jana's most intimate presence (her intimacy made eternal) — for me it's a modern version of the story of Queen Rhodopa. But I wouldn't say — and it's not important anyway — that Evžen was a Candaulist in the narrow sense of the term, a sexual deviant. I'm much more interested in the universal aspects of Candaulism: putting the most intimate things on display, as if nothing existed until we publicized it in ample, intimate detail.

But allow me to return to my own story.

Who was Svatava's husband, this Ludvík? Just a few years earlier, it would have been stupid to ask such a question in Brno. Ludvík was so popular during his studies at the university that a sort of Ludvík Fan Club was formed. He was a sought-after companion and was always around when something happened at the university — or, to be more exact, something remarkable always happened when Ludvík was around. Thanks to him, I first learned what a charismatic personality is: there was something elegantly majestic in his every move. People called him the Sun King (after Louis XIV, French for Ludvík), and wherever he went, he was accompanied by bands of happy girls, his current favorites. He became a symbol of youth, vitality, and nonconformity. On the other hand, he collaborated assiduously with university officials, helping to manipulate student opinion. He used his unlimited popularity to smooth over sources of friction between the university administration and the "manifold wildness" of the student body. Of course, he never realized that he was being manipulated, and would have categorically denied any such suggestion. Thanks to his ignorance, he lived in happy harmony with himself, and this was also the source of his charming, youthful vitality.

Several years after his graduation from the university, people still remembered him with enthusiasm, and Ludvík constantly gave them reminders. At regular intervals he sent long letters to the university, emphatically addressing the younger students. (My friends, so dear to my heart — he wrote — all of you who, in these days, are wandering for the first time through the halls of our dear alma mater, peopled to this day by the fauns and elves of our dreams. . .) At first, Ludvík's letters were published in shortened form in the university magazine; later, they were simply hung on the bulletin board in the main building.

Like everyone of his type, Ludvík was in reality a thoughtless and insensitive egotist, but unlike, say, Evžen, he had no real talent (his only talent was his personal charm) that could partially justify his egotism.

And when I think about him in terms of my profession, it occurs to me that he was a variation on what I would call the Fučík Complex: an idol of eternal youth, whose enormous ambitions were out of all proportion to his abilities. He had just one chance: to survive as an idol. But for that, he would have had to disappear forever, before it was too late. He did attempt suicide

— we'll get to that in a moment — but so clumsily that he ended up in my hands, the hands of a fashionable psychologist with a doubtful reputation. (And when he repeated the suicide attempt many years later, this time successfully, it was too late: he disappeared like a pebble thrown into the Lethe. But let's not get ahead of ourselves.)

So the end of Ludvík's glory began as soon as he graduated from the university, when he tried to collect his piece of the pie. At first, he quickly found a good position, thanks to his popularity, his connections and, in the end, certain "preferences from above." He started working in the House of Art, a museum and cultural center in Brno, with the prospect of becoming its director at some point in the future. It soon became clear, however, that his appointment had been an unfortunate one, for both the Sun King and the House of Art. But it was not at all easy to get rid of him. And that's how the first conflict arose between him and "the public interest." Ludvík took it badly; it surprised him quite a bit. He considered it an injustice, and he might even have been right: plenty of other incapable people retained their positions. A long series of such "injustices" was to follow.

It is a well-established custom to send suicides to the psychiatric clinic for a short convalescence. At the university, we had never really met each other properly (I was an insignificant student and he was a prima donna followed by a trail of admirers). Now we finally had time for one another. But I must add that he was no longer the same self-confident fellow who never let anyone get close to him and knew how to dazzle but not how to listen. Now he was a little more tame; the experience had thrown him for a loop, and he was undergoing a crisis that offered him the chance to open up to people and thus a chance for real self-understanding. It was an exceptional opportunity for Ludvík, and I wanted to take proper advantage of it, for his sake. He interested me, as does anyone who gets this chance to open up, and I was also curious to see what, deep down inside him, had been preserved and what had disappeared, temporarily or permanently — and whether the Sun King still thought, at least a little bit, that he was the center of the universe. In short, I was interested in the disintegration of this once dazzling idol, whose rise I had observed with a certain envy.

Among other things, I had always admired Ludvík's ability to react quickly and spontaneously. I myself am more clumsy, because I re-evaluate every situation several times over before I get moving. I become preoccupied with all the possible alternatives I have to choose from. And when I finally do choose, I'm tormented by the feeling that I've chosen badly. This may be a desirable trait for someone who has to evaluate, patiently and tolerantly, the deeds of others — for a psychologist, say — but in everyday life, unfortunately, it manifests itself as a troublesome clumsiness. Ludvík, on the contrary, always acted with an elegant impetuosity, which allowed him to excel where most people stiffen up and get stuck. He brought his ideas to fruition thoroughly and without delay, and since he didn't seem to weed out the good from the bad, he even acted on the truly lunatic ones. This worked surprisingly well at the university in the good old days, since the higher-ups generally took his ideas as a libation to his popularity, and we students simply relished them.

But now to the heart of the matter. What I want to tell about began with my own lunatic idea, my own absolutely exceptional and absolutely lunatic idea, and it began right here, in my cubbyhole of an office in Saint Anna's Hospital. I'll get to the cubbyhole later, but first, the idea.

When I was meeting with Ludvík at the hospital and our relationship was still determined by my role as therapist and his as patient, I was occupied with a thought, an idea that had something in common with my profession but was, above all, the sort of chicanery I have rarely indulged in because of the prudent clumsiness I've already talked about. Let me clarify things right away: the idea had already died away and had never been brought to fruition. I had merely attempted something, but as always I hadn't gotten very far, and now I was simply analyzing it — which is what I like to do best. I like best to wallow in ideas that I've never succeeded in carrying out, or better: that I've succeeded in never carrying out.

For years, for the most part theoretically, I've been intrigued by the phenomenon of mystification. What it is, from what human needs it arises, how it works, and what is achieved by it. Above all, I have tried to characterize mystification at the most general level. I think it's a game, one of the most consistent and hence one of the purest games, because in its sheer playfulness it touches the very essence of human identity. Mystification is, I maintain, a way of testing and proving identity. But if it is to have this exceptional capacity, it must remain a mere game, and there must be nothing purposeful or functional about it; it must not serve anything and must not result in any profit for the mystifier. Only then is there a chance that the mystifier will learn something essential from this game, will reach some kind of basic understanding. "In this sense," I joked, "mystification is both a means and a tool of basic research."

"Could you give me an example?" asked Ludvík.

"The time for examples will come," I agreed, "but today I'd like to stay on a more general level. A real mystifier is neither a crook nor a con man, because he does what he does purely for entertainment, without trying to get anything out of it. And as soon as you do something completely purposeless, while investing as much energy in it as you would in purposeful activity — and that is the essence of every game — you find yourself in a realm of blissful freedom. And mystification is the queen of all games, because it is the art of living. It extends the boundaries of play to the kingdom of reality."

This conversation took place in my cubbyhole, which had been formed by walling off a slightly bigger cubbyhole, the better half of which (containing the window and accessories like

111

electrical outlets) was occupied by a psychiatrist. It was, in other words, an unpleasant little cell with a light, desk, telephone, chair, and couch. Even so, Ludvík was grateful to me for giving him some place to sneak off to, because he shared his hospital bedroom, a cavern reminiscent of a monastery, with fourteen other patients, all of them good-for-nothing neurotics, psychopaths, and psychotics (at that time, for lack of space but also for other reasons, neurotics were thrown together with psychotics to form a blissfully meshuggenah mishmash). Once he asked me if I could "lend him my burrow for an hour or so." I told him we would have to synchronize it with the absence of my neighbor, the psychiatrist. But within a week it worked out: I lent Ludvík the key and asked him to stay on his toes and not let anyone see him.

And since I left the hospital before visiting hours, I didn't see Ludvík's girlfriend, but I had no doubt she was a lovely sight, the kind the Sun King had always treated himself to, in a wide assortment. When I got the key from Ludvík the next morning, I didn't have the chance to exchange a word with him, because the nurses were preparing the patient in the next bed for electroshock therapy, and the preparations alone (during the actual procedure the other patients were sent into the hall) were such a painful sight that they struck Ludvík dumb, as if he were some mythological creature.

But hardly had I entered my burrow when I noticed that the scent of perfume was in the air and that the couch had been moved. Well, I confess, I'd been expecting it. Since I couldn't rise to the ceiling and take a bird's-eye view of the room, I dropped down on all fours and inspected things from below. And my eyes had hardly adjusted to the gloom beneath the desk when I saw a tiny, indisputably metal object. I drew it out into the light of day: it was a steel-blue hairpin.

Have you ever tried, friends, to compose a woman's portrait from three details: a steel-blue hairpin, a subtle scent of perfume, and a slightly displaced couch? I managed it in a second. And I constructed an image of Ludvík's visitor so quickly and effectively that I squirmed with desire and envy.

And when I visited Ludvík, I was holding the hairpin in my fist.

"If you mean that bitch," he said bitterly, "she didn't even show up. 'Cause if you didn't know, when you fall into a shit-hole, no one gives a shit about you."

"Wait a second," I protested, but Ludvík insisted that he had played chess all afternoon with one of the (male) nurses, the one they call Ježíšek.

I went to Ježíšek and he confirmed it: no one had visited Ludvík.

"The guy's a demon," said Ježíšek. "Not only did I lose every game we played, but he answered all of my moves immediately, and when I asked him if he got bored waiting for me to move, he said he didn't care, because while he was waiting he went over some famous Parisian recipes in his mind. The guy's a chef?" Ježíšek asked.

"You said it yourself," I assured him. "He's a demon."

And I understood how insidious the imagination can be. How it can conjure up a whole reality based on mere anticipation (and a misleading suggestion)! Because now it became clear that the hairpin belonged to Věra, a teacher at the high school on Křenová Street, whom I'll call my fiancée for your amusement and because I'm in a good mood. The couch, of course, had not been moved, and my nose, the lech, had made up the perfume. Thus from my fiancée's lost hairpin grew, as if from a magic seed tossed to the ground, her rival: a woman for whom I promptly felt an awful craving that would hardly have been appropriate in polite society.

"And just as mystification is the queen of games," I continued my explanation the following day, "the queen of mystifications, the queen of queens if you will, is literary mystification. Of course I don't mean Hanka's counterfeits, those unfortunate forgeries of ancient Czech manuscripts, because that wasn't a game at all; it was a utilitarian affair, merely a literary swindle with a definite purpose: to show how dandy our nation is and what a rich culture and history we have."

I assumed this part of my lecture would especially awaken Ludvík's interest: I knew about his own literary efforts. Once he had published a couple poems in the university magazine, and Brno's radio station had broadcast some his commentaries. He wasn't successful with the literary magazines, even though, I have no doubt, he tried his hardest. But I was convinced that an illustration of literary mystification would capture his attention more than a general phenomenology of the term.

But you should see how well Ludvík knows how not to listen! When you weren't speaking explicitly about him, about his own rare and remarkable person (his royal majesty!), he always listened apathetically and distractedly, and even that took an effort. I could see in his eyes how quickly his attention faded and how his interest was promptly extinguished. Even though he was undergoing a deep personality crisis, as we say in our professional jargon, it was difficult to open him up to the world, and sometimes it seemed impossible.

Nevertheless, I have fond memories of those afternoons and evenings. At that time I had a special fancy for teas that a friend of mine brought me from all over the world, and since Ludvík was a snob, he deigned to drink them. I can still see that cubbyhole, cramped as a pressure cooker, where we took turns sitting on the chair and the couch, as if we were constantly exchanging the roles of psychoanalyst and patient, my tea paraphernalia spread out on the table, a set of foreign tins and cruets and colored glass containers. It was late summer and early autumn, the days were already getting shorter, and since I didn't have an electrical outlet in my half of the walled-off room, and the ceiling light was intensely annoying, my cubbyhole was lit by nothing but a propane-butane burner.

And so I told Ludvík about literary mystification, the queen of them all. I mentioned Robert David, the imaginary balladeer created by Vítězslav Nezval, and I also talked about the stir surrounding Minue Drouet, the eight-year-old poetic genius of France, whose poems, as it turned out, were written by her father. Nor did I forget Balzac's unknown masterpiece, the novel *The Dowries of the Merchant's Wife*, which Balzac himself patiently dictated from the other world to a Lyon medium over the course of one hundred and fourteen evenings in 1947. And naturally I spoke of how Guillaume Apollinaire assumed a woman's guise and, in 1908 and 1909, invented the lovable old-maid poet Louise Lalanne, bombarding respected literary magazines and literary salons with her poetic creations. And from there it was just a step to the pièce de résistance of my lecture — the literary mystification I myself had attempted.

Stretched out on my psychoanalyst's couch, Ludvík opened one eye, waved his eyelid at me like a fin, and then swam right back into his own libidinous dreams. So I was really just talking to the propane-butane burner, similar in its nakedness to the soul of the beautiful poetess I had dreamed about but never landed. In carrying out my mystification idea, I had to settle for a not-so-charming nurse from Neurology. Or rather — so as not to exaggerate again — it was just the opposite: I got the idea when our own little romance novel was reaching its climax, and at first it was just part of the romantic games I played with Vladěnka; then it separated itself off, hypertrophied, and began to live a life of its own. I wrote twenty erotic poems, love poetry in the style of a young woman, and sent them to several literary magazines under Vladěnka's name.

And here I hasten to add that I was always a diligent columnist. Not only did I write a popular column about the psychology of everyday life, but from time to time *Lidová demokracie* or *Svobodné slovo* would publish one of my art reviews, and if I could have gotten anywhere with *Rovnost*, I was willing to write versified news summaries for them. I didn't have any original style of my own, to be sure, but I was able to mirror faithfully the techniques of famous columnists of the past. It was a game I enjoyed, and I acquired a certain facility at it, so it wasn't a problem to produce twenty poems for my mystificatory purposes.

I'll let you in on another secret: I was sure of success, sure that the poems would awaken people's interest, and I also saw the situation from a psychologist's point of view: a confusion of the erotic subject! When a man writes love poetry from a woman's point of view, it's always very different, I maintain, from what a woman would have written. The poems are not only erotically more daring, more open, but they create a different, more potent atmosphere. For the uninitiated reader, they're something mysteriously unique, and they acquire a magical allure. That would be the ticket for a mediocre poet: a sex change and you're a genius overnight! Besides, such poems always contain a little bit of parody, and thus are not lacking in humor — something, you'll notice, that is completely foreign to love poetry written by women. And in the end this humor too becomes erotic, precisely because of its unique, unfeminine foreignness.

I knew all this ahead of time, before I sat down at my desk and sealed my twenty poems in an envelope. And what do you know: they printed fourteen of the twenty, a respectable performance when you consider that editors are constantly flooded by the work of beginning poets and poetesses. But I also knew that if another fourteen appeared in print (and originally I wanted to trump Apollinaire himself and conceive an entire book with Vladěnka), my fate would be sealed. For the nurse from Neurology would, as I realized before it was too late, take every further verse as proof of our deep spiritual affinity. By putting her name above my poems, Vladěnka was actually identifying with my thoughts, while I, each time I wrote one of those erotically inverted verses, was identifying in return with her femininity! It was something like an exchange of magic engagement rings. And that kind of magic was the last thing I needed. It was no longer a game, it was a trap. And I got out of it quickly, before the rooster crowed his last.

I ought to say that Ludvík listened to this last part with a certain interest, and even suggested that I let him see Vladěnka. And when an opportunity arose soon after (Vladěnka was playing Ring Around the Rosy with some paralyzed patients in the hospital courtyard), he praised me for making my escape. "If you're going to fall into a trap," he instructed me, his forefinger raised in warning, "make sure it's a really beautiful one — preferably a brunette."

It has stopped raining, and umbrellas are closing all around with dignified care. And I finally see Svatava, who has let down her long black hair in mourning, because Svatava knows what is appropriate. Not many human beings know so exactly what they want and what it involves. And to think that for a long time I suspected her of being merely Ludvík's puppet, without a will or even a fate of her own.

I should collect myself, concentrate, and approach her, as is expected of me. Of course, no one knows that Ludvík and I are united by a certain something, perhaps a conspiracy or an involuntary alliance, but everyone suspects that I belonged to the inner circle of Svatava and Ludvík's closest contacts. And Svatava, at least, is convinced that I was Ludvík's closest friend.

I close my umbrella, shake it off, and deliberately rock my round figure into motion. The pointed towers of the crematorium stretch ominously into the sky. I force my way through the black crowd toward Svatava.

Part 2
Queen Rhodopa

I remember — it was in the spring of 1967 — when a patriarch among English poets, hitherto neglected in Czechoslovakia, paid a visit to Prague. Let's call him Sir Edward, but I hasten to point out that his real name brings the birth of modern poetry to mind. Something fairly unusual happened. Czechoslovak Television provided Sir Edward with twenty minutes of live broadcasting, a sort of evening enclave or sacred space for the word, for subdued gestures and poetry, in which the elderly gentleman sat surrounded by professors from the English Department and overseers from the Ministry of Culture. And another unusual thing: Czech verse was represented not by a deserving poetic coryphaeus, but by Svatava.

Svatava had burst onto the Czech poetry scene so suddenly that it caused a rather large scandal in our small country. She was a completely new phenomenon in love poetry. If I may exaggerate just a bit, her poems set a whole hairy forest of masculine limbs a-trembling, and the gently rocking rhythm of her verses was the unmistakable rhythm of copulation. An authoritative Marxist literary critic, famous for his occasional fits of broad-mindedness, quickly spoke out in her defense in an article whose title paraphrased O'Neill's famous play: "Lusting Becomes Svatava." He noted that, from a dialectical point of view, her poetry was chaste and moralistic, and yet he found something in it that was rare in women's erotica: a sense of humor. He wrote that "while the majority of women's love poetry burns with pathos and drowns in sentimentality, Svatava scorns these feminine tactics; and if she does use them, it's always with a hint of parody, proving to us that a woman's lot, squeezed

118

in between her first menstruation and menopause, can be viewed with scintillating humor. Svatava is the first erotic woman clown of Czech literature!" And then Svatava published (quite rapidly for a Czech poet) two poetry collections, and her photograph — the unearthly visage of a priestess of Poetry, a lustful angel, an erotic Madonna, the first lady of Czech literature and Miss Ars Poetica — appeared everywhere, from the cover of the women's magazine *Vlasta* to the pages of the avant-garde monthly *Notebooks for a Young Literature*. So no one was surprised when Svatava was chosen to join the famous English poet in the television studio.

She stuck out among those professors and dried-up government officials like a vase of dewy roses among the shards of an old pot. And Sir Edward asked one of the translators of his poetry — he interrupted him just as the translator was explaining how difficult it was to find an adequate Czech equivalent for the Master's landscape metaphors, which grew out of a different language as well as an absolutely different type of landscape, seen as an image of the soul — he interrupted him forcefully and asked him to get up and change places with the beautiful Czech poetess, because he wanted to have her at his side. For even without having read a single one of her verses, he wasn't embarrassed to say her metaphors grew from the same spiritual landscape as his: "An old poet, gentlemen, is like an old dog, who can always smell out a beautiful pooch of poetry despite the barriers of language, time, and social system."

He was immediately obliged and, for the rest of the discussion, this patriarch of English poets looked at Svatava alone, answering every question as if she were the one who had posed it, even though she never said a word and persisted in a silence so piercing that its sacred fire burned continuously in the television studio like the eternal flame at a druid's altar.

Ludvík, on the other hand, posed a whole range of questions in her stead, and we should not overlook his presence in the studio. Because he didn't know English, he asked the translator who had changed places with Svatava to interpret for him. The translator, crushed by his banishment from the Master's side, was now transformed into a lump of wet clay and into Ludvík's personal interpreter. There is one question I won't forget till the day I die.

"Svatava would be interested," said Ludvík, "whether you know, Master, that the mysterious girl with the birthmark on her right hip, the heavenly concubine with whom You copulate in your dreams, whom You describe in the sixty-second sonnet of *Songs of Raspberries and Blackberries*, is in reality Svatava herself."

And Sir Edward gazed at Svatava the whole time Ludvík was asking his question, and he kept looking at her a moment after the question had been posed and translated. Only then did he answer, slowly and quietly: "Yes, I know. I recognized her at once."

I saw on the television how the puritanical overseers from the Ministry of Culture were suffering like dogs (they nearly dropped dead!), and later it was whispered in the corridors that, in punishment, they canceled the English professors' trip to see the homes of England's proletarian poets. And another thing, my friends: Sir Edward, of course, never wrote any sixty-second sonnet — he didn't even write a collection called *Songs of Raspberries and Blackberries*!

A selection of Svatava's poetry came out in England with amazing speed, and Sir Edward himself collaborated on the final translation. And Ludvík gave me the slender but comely volume, in which Svatava wrote me a cordial inscription.

Some time after we released Ludvík from the hospital, I learned that he was teaching at a nursing school, and it occurred to me that he had finally found a profession appropriate to his abilities and taste. I could well imagine him surrounded by admiring girls, overwhelming those silly geese from the countryside with his personal charisma the way a proud peacock shows off his tail, its large eye enchanting the girls until they shiver and quake like tender little rabbits. And pleased as I was that I had managed to fit so many animals — geese, a peacock, and tender rabbits — into just one thought, I amused myself for a while by expanding it further until a telephone call summoned me to the ward.

And then I forgot about Ludvík for some time. Until the wedding announcement arrived. I thought he must have made a rash decision — I hadn't expected it of him. And I was curious to see the woman who had managed to hook him.

It was clear at first sight that the bride had both style and charm, but I still didn't understand why Ludvík had decided to marry her. Ludvík's house in Řečkovice, a suburb north of Brno, was packed with wedding guests, including nearly the entire university from the days of the Sun King. I talked with lots of people I hadn't seen in years, but I found out what I really wanted to know only by pure coincidence, and from strangers.

Impelled by the call of nature, I slipped into the bathroom, only to find three dumb blondes sitting on the bathtub, rattling the ice in their glasses and completely wrapped up in their conversation. I understood immediately why they were hiding in the bathroom: there's a charming superstition that you shouldn't talk about the bride in the home of newlyweds, just as you shouldn't mention rope in the house of a hanged man.

"You mean you don't know," the first one was saying, "why he's marrying Svatava? She's a student of his from nursing school. She was supposed to become a nurse, but he discovered a poetic streak in her! He's marrying one of the highest hopes of Czech literature!"

"Incredible!" said the second, laughing. "So now Ludvík's interested in women's writing!"

But then the third one saw me in the doorway, started, and whistled a warning.

"Don't worry, ladies, I didn't hear a thing!" And I cheerfully waved goodbye and continued wandering through the labyrinth of the wedding reception.

Finally I bumped into Ludvík. He had some cheap bon mot ready to fend me off with: did I know why people die just once but get married as many as six times? But I wouldn't be dissuaded. "Listen, Ludvík, I heard you're marrying a poet? A nurse who writes poetry?" He hissed menacingly and reminded me that you're not supposed to talk about the bride in the house of a hanged man. "A newly married man, Ludvík," I corrected him. "Fine," he said, "please excuse me. It's a big wedding and I have responsibilities. I'll give you a call sometime and you can come for a visit. I don't forget my true friends, and I know that a person has fewer true friends than a cripple has fingers on one hand." He squeezed my elbow.

The wedding reception dragged on endlessly like a festive strand of snot. Finally, I wiped off my boogered-up jacket and wandered out into the night to catch the tram home.

Literature is my secret love, and I treat it like one: sometimes it's as if I'd completely forgotten it, but then I return with all the more passion. It had been a long time since I'd leafed through literary magazines and devoted myself to something other than the casuistry of neurotics and psychotics, but then I began, like a horse who's had the crop put to him, to make the rounds of newsstands and bookstores, dragging home armfuls of literary magazines and bestsellers, pouring them all out on the bed, and climbing in after them like an greedy lover.

And this time it was really worth it. I found plenty of poems by Ludvík's bride, and there was no mistaking it: they were all written according to my own recipe for mystification — except that they were a little overdone. Ludvík wasn't satisfied with a girl's typical romantic themes; he pushed them to the border of obscenity, where I would never have ventured. But I hadn't dared only because I would never have gotten away with it! I admired Ludvík for playing such a risky game. His metaphors were rather banal, but his adventurous use of erotic details gave them a visionary force. My idea had been malevolently magnified.

I was wondering how this offensive of obscenity had managed to break the barrier of puritanism, when the telephone rang. It was Ludvík, as he'd promised. He and Svatava were looking forward to seeing me, he said, and I shouldn't bring along a bottle because there was plenty left over from the wedding. "So come right away," he offered. "I'll be expecting you."

And as I rushed through that beautiful summer day by tram to Řečkovice, it never occurred to me that I was getting ready to cross "the border of a shadow."

A house naturally appears much different when it is crammed with the madness of a wedding reception than when the whole thing is at the disposal of just three people. At first I even had the feeling it would be just the two of us. And I was a little sorry, because I still remembered how Ludvík had promised on the telephone that "he and Svatava" were looking forward to seeing me. I wanted to look her over properly and up close, in a way that's never possible at a wedding.

"Don't take off your shoes," said Ludvík. "We're going out on the balcony." He grabbed two bottles by the neck and we went upstairs. There was a delightful little table on the balcony, an asinine gewgaw — imagine a table shaped like a giant tortoise shell, set for two.

Only here, on the balcony, did I realize how cleverly the house was situated. It was on a hill, its front facing the suburbs, but its garden looking out on to a deep valley, through which ran a railroad track with trains crawling along it like tugboats. The garden was surrounded by a high, ivy-covered wall, so that the feeling of majestic privacy was complete. Even the July sun — it was the wonderful summer of 1966 — hung in the sky like a jewel flung there by a splendidly extravagant hand.

Ludvík, the perfect host, turned the tortoise's back into an epicurean buffet — which you had a hard time reaching, because the edges of the capacious shell kept you from sitting too close. Whenever I reached for a plate, the shell pressed into my stomach and held me at a distance. Until Ludvík showed me how it was done: he stood up, reached for a plate, and then sat down with it. I followed his example, but when I leaned over the tortoise's back, I could see across the other edge of the shell into the garden. And the jewel in the sky had its counterpart there!

Svatava was tanning herself on a folding chair right in front of the balcony. She lay on her back, and the only thing she was wearing was a green leaf on each eye. She was so dangerously close that I clearly saw the traces of amatory rituals, which intensified her beauty until it nearly drove me insane. I stayed stuck in that bent-over position until I realized with horror what I was doing. Ludvík, after all, must have known what I was looking at. I sat down again a little suddenly, but Ludvík was talking about something and seemed not to have noticed anything. This same situation kept repeating itself. Whenever I stood up for some more food and stayed there, bent over, for a moment, only to force myself to sit down with an effort of the will, Ludvík paid no attention at all, as if he didn't realize what was happening.

(But at that time I couldn't have suspected that this situation would be a model for our future conversations. In the weeks and months that followed, whenever I tried to speak with him about what really interested me, he paid no attention at all. When I brought up him, Svatava, or literary mystifications, he simply didn't hear me. He didn't react to the theme of mystification. Until I began to feel like a dog that keeps biting repeatedly into its trainer's padded sleeve.)

But back to the story. We sat there a long time. I didn't say a word; Ludvík chattered on about something, as only he knows how. I kept getting up to put aside an empty plate or pick up a full one. Then the sun dipped down to the horizon and I was quietly filled with Ludvík's delicacies. Whenever I made the slightest move, a warning pyramid inside me began to totter. I no longer dared stand up, let alone bend over.

Sitting there dully, I heard a door shutting and someone crossing the room to the balcony, and then I saw Svatava. I'm not sure, but I may have quietly cried out. Ludvík turned around, saw her as well, and smiled. He stood up and went over to her. She stood in the doorway, now in a dark evening dress, but still resting on her eyes, on her absolutely motionless face, were the two green leaves. Ludvík moved closer and carefully removed them.

Big brown eyes appeared, illusory, mysterious, mocking (the first erotic woman clown!), eyes that photographers would soon sow like a luxuriant exotic flora in the homes of readers everywhere. But let's not get ahead of ourselves. It's still July 1966 on the balcony of Ludvík's house in Řečkovice, and he is bringing out another chair; Svatava sits down at the tortoise shell, and then tea is served. In my honor, but also to my infinite suffering, because no one in Brno knows how to make tea, with the possible exception of me in my propane-butane den, behind whose paperboard wall an old psychiatrist dozes, snoring as loudly as the hammer in the city's clock tower.

Only as I was going home that beautiful summer evening (on the tram!) did I realize that Svatava in the nude was a bribe, consideration for my silence.

Things moved so fast that I hardly had time to get my bearings. Three months after the first poem appeared, Ludvík's poetry, published under Svatava's name, began to appear regularly in all the literary magazines. She was a bombshell: she exploded and I found her fragments everywhere. The first poetry collection appeared at the end of the year (in December 1966), quite rapidly for our country; the second came out in the spring of the following year (just before the patriarch of English poetry paid his visit).

The first one was called *The Faun of Marzipan* and it was a fortunate title, whether because of its similarity to *Fanfan Tulipan*, still a very popular film at the time, or because of the image of a gingerbread faun ("he thrusts his ginger hands through my dormer-window eyes and hunts me in my head as in a courtyard, until I loudly press myself against him").

Some of the verses were quite to my liking (for example, the poem, "In the rushes of the night there burns a golden tench"), but most of it was what I would call, without hesitation, sophisticated doggerel. Besides, in Czech, poetry writes itself! Tons of verses already written, the language's treasury of silver, gold, and platinum, quietly shiver behind every new line of poetry.

I was amused by the success of their little stunt, and I noted with satisfaction that they had simply confirmed my own invention and design. I was pleased that someone had adopted an idea I hadn't managed to carry out completely, so I could see how something I had only dreamed of would look in reality.

Ludvík improved on my instructions with three ideas of his own. I've already mentioned one: his daring erotic details. The second was his realization that every literary success needs a capable agent. And Ludvík himself was, of course, the most capable of all.

The ease with which he made connections, the insolence with which he penetrated into editorial offices and met influential people, his suggestive eloquence and dogged intrusiveness, his indisputable social graces and high-powered charisma — all of that now served to promote his own poetry. And so something that he could never have done as an author — because such unflinching promotion of one's own work has always been considered a sure sign of graphomania — now became quite natural: why, he was simply working in the service of his beautiful wife! And such service, the service of beauty and poetry, has always been considered a sign of chivalric refinement.

And, finally, the third idea: Svatava! A gorgeous woman and at the same time a poet — that's not something you see every day. As if the verses were a mysterious metamorphosis of that shining creature: the gold of her beauty was transformed into the gold of her poetic imagery.

But then it stopped being a game and turned into a question of Ludvík's own literary ambitions. He not only realized his conceited dreams, he outdid them several times over: his poems clambered up to the highest rung of the ladder of popularity, until no one had any doubts about their value! Finally he had once again become the center of the universe, albeit in hiding and incognito. And I realized that he felt something like a secretive medieval monk, an Anonymous Master.

On Friday morning, two days after my visit to the house in Řečkovice, I called Věra (the one I referred to earlier as my fiancée) and told her not to buy tickets for that evening, because another doctor had asked me to take over his shift. Each night a psychiatrist, psychologist, or neurologist stayed at the ward in case of an emergency.

There were no emergencies, but something strange did happen. I once again realized what a treacherous companion tea can be: once in a while it has the paradoxical effect of putting me to sleep instead of keeping me up. I hardly had time to look at my watch (it was a little before 6 p.m.), turn out the light, and find the couch in the darkness. A dream was waiting for me there.

I was walking through an unusual landscape when I finally realized that it wasn't a landscape at all, it was Evžen's atelier. It was so big that it stretched from one horizon to the other, and the gigantic photographs that papered the endless walls were submerged in the Milky Way above. But Svatava was in the photographs instead of Jana. And I understood: Svatava is Jana, Jana is Svatava. She was returning to me from our far-away high school days.

But then it was no longer Evžen's atelier. I recognized the village of Svatý Kamen near Volary, where we had worked raking hay the summer after graduation. And I saw the pub where we danced that last evening, in front of which I waited for Jana in the night. As I drew closer, I knew that this time she was standing there, this time she was waiting for me.

And suddenly there was a staircase inside a house and I was below and Jana above, and then a light came on, spreading out over the stairs like a carpet. I didn't see her, but I heard her breathing above me. And I felt an inexplicable fear.

I woke up in darkness, the kind of darkness that can exist only inside a windowless room.

I forced myself to get up, turn on the light, and open the door into the corridor. And then I sat down again — with the lights on and the door wide open — and smoked a cigarette. I felt like an ermine caught in a trap: I wouldn't sleep any more that night.

When you know you won't fall asleep, you shouldn't try to force it. I looked at my watch (it was one-thirty), walked around my burrow, and made another cup of tea, which worked normally this time and strengthened my wakefulness. I opened a drawer and pulled out a stack of magazines I hadn't yet read. Immediately I came across more of Ludvík's poems. He was as disgustingly fertile as a rabbit.

And the worst thing about it, I realized with horror, was how perfectly it worked — even in my case, even though I was in on the secret. Svatava's name above those poems was unbelievably effective. I took the erotic decorations in Ludvík's poems as if they really had been embroidered and crocheted by Svatava. So even though I knew that the erotic joke, "I dance like Salome, my feet on the ceiling, your head in my lap," had been hatched in Ludvík's head, I associated it with Svatava, and when I read the lines, "I was left on the beach of the night like a shell, filled with the murmuring of your blood," I pictured a close-up of Svatava's lips and the distinct line where they lightly touched. On reading "my well has shame in its depths, and I'm deeply ashamed of that shame," I missed Svatava terribly and yearned to hear the sound of her voice. I found Ludvík's business card in my wallet, picked up the telephone, and slowly began to dial; it wasn't until the last number that I realized what I was doing. I stopped short, put down the receiver, and sat there till morning, staring at the telephone like a real asshole.

It was Saturday morning. I went across the street for breakfast, brought back a tin of Portuguese sardines, and ate them up like a cute little girl, dropping them down my throat by the tail. Meanwhile I was thinking about what to do after breakfast. I wiped off my hands and picked up the telephone again. I dialed my fiancée's number, and when after a moment I heard Věra's sleepy voice, I informed her: "The Titanic has just set sail on its happy voyage," which was the password we had agreed on in case one of us decided to end the engagement. "Take it easy, so long," I added, and hung up without waiting for an answer.

And I became a family friend of Ludvík and Svatava's, practically an everyday part of their household, a meat grinder mounted permanently above the kitchen sink, their set of wedding china. Ludvík kept me close by so he could keep an eye on me. I was, after all, the only one who knew the secret of their mystification, and therefore the only one who posed a threat to them. Which suited me fine, because it allowed me to be near

Svatava, to sit at the same table as her, listen to her empty chatter, see her in the most varied circumstances and, in her ever rarer moments of peace and quiet, be the quiet companion of her marital siesta.

Until then, I may have secretly been counting on a reprise of that July afternoon on the balcony of their home in Řečkovice . . . But now, on the contrary, I noted the sharp contrast between the erotically stimulating poetry and Svatava's chastely subdued behavior. And it immediately occurred to me that even this contrast was actually just a refined form of coquetry, that I was witnessing what a pliant puppet Svatava was in Ludvík's hands, which was certainly why he had chosen her. Exactly — that was the reason! Svatava made a good puppet.

Important culture mavens, mercenary journalists, editors, and even the true celebrities of literary Brno were now regularly visiting Ludvík's wife. It soon became unimaginable for a first-rate writer, poet, playwright (or even painter, musician, director, or actor) to come to Brno without immediately undertaking a journey to Řečkovice, to the Tower of the Turtle-Dove, as the house began to be called in jest (Robinson Jeffers and his Hawk Tower were very popular at the time).

I was allowed to be a regular participant at these literary mixers, almost all of which took place in Svatava's spacious kitchen. This was another one of Ludvík's successful managerial ploys: the priestess of Poetry had to be presented to the world as a goddess of hearth and home, a domestic vestal virgin. Another provocative contrast. I don't know whom Ludvík consulted with respect to the appearance of this temple, but it must have been some sought-after expert: Svatava's kitchen turned up in an issue of the West German monthly *Schöner Wohnen*. And without renouncing its original function (Svatava really did cook in that kitchen), it also became a traditional salon for literary gourmets.

And hordes of literary gourmets stopped by. There were evenings when the kitchen (even though it really was quite spacious) couldn't hold all the guests, and they stood outside in the darkness of the garden, shifting carefully from one foot to another amidst Svatava's vegetable patches. Ludvík and his poetess would always appear in the kitchen door and smile kindly and nod into the many-voiced darkness, only the admiring muzzles of cigarettes shining back at them.

And here I would like to note once again that our story takes place safely in the middle of the sixties, when literature was the center of attention, new books by popular authors sold nearly as many copies as cookbooks (sic!), and a team of the most notable writers was respected nearly as much as a hockey or soccer team. On the other hand, despite the number of literary magazines, it was rather difficult to hold one's own in the midst of so much competition. And so it was all the more incomprehensible for me that Svatava's poetry didn't sink into oblivion along with all the other ephemera; it became more and more clear that she was a fixed star in the literary heavens. And yet it was always the same lines, the same old verses, the same incoherent style, limping metaphors, and compilations of others' poetry (among which only occasionally did something shine) that editors had sent back to Ludvík by return mail or had thrown right into the wastebasket. Now they nearly choked with praise, and considered it an honor to be his first readers.

One exceptional circumstance particularly entertained me in Ludvík's realization of my mystification idea. When I chose a partner for my game, the nurse from Neurology, I chose a hard-working, cultivated reader of poetry who knew whole paragraphs of Vančura's *Capricious Summer* by heart and even knew who Alfred Jarry and André Breton were. She began each day by copying an aphorism from Rochefoucauld, Jerzy Lec, or the satirist J. R. Pick into her datebook.

In contrast, Svatava didn't know a thing about literature, and in becoming the first lady of Czech literature she changed nothing of her former habits or interests. Of course, she eventually picked up a certain knowledge of literature, but with a charming indifference you could compare to the Archangel Gabriel's lack of interest in Einstein's theory of relativity. The joke was that much better, the mystification that much more complete! (If it was a joke at all, of course, and if it was nothing more than mystification!)

It was as if Svatava was a creature from some mysterious Island of Poetry, a creature who didn't understand human speech and spoke only the magic language of Poetry, and therefore always needed an interpreter. Visitors looked at Svatava, addressed her, and Ludvík, standing tactfully aside, answered in her place. This didn't surprise anybody, no one thought it unusual, and to me it was just another clever managerial ruse to make the poetess seem more unique. But in fact, someone simply had to speak for Svatava; otherwise it would have been a disaster.

Wooden country-style chairs with hearts carved in them (and eiderdown cushions for the comfort of the guests) and a tablecloth from the flatlands of Moravia on the wall above the kitchen table, with a poem Svatava had embroidered on it:

> Past the carved window frame
> into the embroidered darkness
> I look into the night as into a well
> and in the sky is mirrored
> muddy water black water
> and in this water sky
> and in this sky water
> and in the water sadness
> full of golden chaff

In the corner, a conspicuously inconspicuous desk with a vase of wildflowers and a picturesque arrangement of manuscript pages and notes. And I noticed that the manuscripts, just like the wildflowers, were changed regularly, and that the handwriting wasn't Ludvík's but was genuinely a woman's. I imagined that

Svatava's homework each day was to copy the typewritten manuscripts of Ludvík's latest poems into her own hand.

A grotto of words with the aroma of kitchen spices and a set of polished pans that threw hypnotizing flashes above Svatava's head, as in the church of a genuine goddess. And all depart singed by these flashes and intoxicated by the narcotic aroma of spices.

And all depart with a look of inspiration on their faces and a gift that — it's up to them alone — might stay with them for the rest of their lives.

Part 3
Gyges

And suddenly we began to move. Before I could get to Svatava, the black crowd, armed with umbrellas, set itself in motion and began to fill the crematorium's hall. And Ludvík was already waiting in his place in the open casket.

I had hardly sat down (in one of the middle rows) when Martin took the seat next to me. Martin is a young composer who is already being spoken of as the most significant representative of his generation. The first in a line of Svatava's lovers, the one who broke through the barrier of untouchability so carefully constructed by Ludvík and made it possible for the erotic strophes of those poems to begin working like an insect's pheromones, emitting far and wide the aroma of sex and the smell of Svatava's greed. But enough about that. A fantastic thought occurred to me: that the black crowd in the hall — except for me, of course — consisted exclusively of Svatava's lovers.

I don't remember anything from the ceremony, except that once Martin leaned over to me and noted in a whisper how awful the choice of music was, as if it were (in his words) the cremation of a butcher from the boondocks. It was clear to me that this was the work of Svatava, whose catastrophic taste was no longer under anyone's watchful eye.

After an oppressively long ceremony, everyone began to form a line. I had no choice but to join the line as well. Martin was in front of me and, because he's a lot taller than I am, I couldn't see past him. We moved slowly, swaying along the monstrous wall of the crematorium. The line bent at a right angle in front of the catafalque, and Svatava waited behind the coffin.

It was a hot day in July. The rain had been refreshing — that gorgeous summer of 1968 — but it was muggy inside, and of course the air conditioning was lousy as could be. I just looked at Martin's back until finally we drew near the catafalque, and Martin (like everyone else) bent over the coffin, remained standing a moment, as if surprised, and then went on. And then it happened. I saw Ludvík and I may have quietly cried out. He was lying on his back in a black suit, and two green leaves had been stuck to his eyes.

I stood there motionless until I realized where I was and what I was doing. By sheer force of will I made myself take a step and raise my head. And I saw the big, brown, illusory, mysterious, and — there was no mistaking it — mocking eyes of Svatava. I shook her hand like everyone else, but I couldn't get out a single word. I instantly understood that she didn't expect me to.

Her long black hair framed the unearthly beauty of her face; for a long time I had had no doubts about Svatava's beauty, but now I was ashamed as I had ever been, so much that it hurt, and Ludvík's-Svatava's verse flashed through my mind: "with greedy lips I call you, with my burning flesh, foaming royal scarlet. . ."

Slowly I left the hall. Outside, it had started raining again, a violent summer shower had begun. But even over the roar of the rain I seemed to hear the dead King Candaules, with green leaves on his eyes, noisily sliding into the crematorium ovens.

What had to happen happened. The more I went to that literary kitchen, the less I was able to resist her black magic. And although I'm a trained professional (as a psychologist I underwent schooling in suggestion and hypnosis at the Kratochvíl Clinic in Kroměříž), I wasn't sufficiently immune to the hypnotic glimmer of the kitchen pans and the suggestive aroma of Svatava's spices. It all confused me more and more. And although I was the one who had offered Ludvík the recipe for literary success, I no longer understood it myself.

How could undisputed experts consider such bad — well, let's say, mediocre — poetry to be first rate, and not only in the context of Czech literature? Was that trick of confusing erotic subjects, along with Svatava's consummate beauty and Ludvík's perfect management, really enough?

Would somebody tell me what happened to the hierarchy of values, how this pyramid of values, built up over centuries, was overturned by a few bullshit tricks? And what is literature, anyway? Am I wrong about its very essence — is my conviction that truthfulness is the mysterious core of literary talent just proof of my own foolish naiveté?

More than once I witnessed how well-versed literary experts — even real writers whose genuine purity was in harmony with the order of Poetry — came to the Tower of the Turtle-Dove to pay their respects to the poetess. I saw them spend long hours in their devotional exercises, speaking to Svatava even though she was deaf and dumb, and carrying on endless conversations, through Ludvík's intercession, with this idiot of Poetry.

And what if I'm attributing too much significance to literature? What if many more such shameless swindles and managerial tricks, to this day undiscovered, have made their way into the history of literature, without even having to rely on such sophisticated mystification? And what if these swindles aren't even undiscovered, if initiates have long known about them, and the whole history of literature is just an infinite chain of hoaxes and dirty tricks, "a universal history of infamy"? And what if all any arrogant scribbler needs is a cunning agent and tenacious ambition? And what if literary worth is merely manufactured, and woe to those who bet on talent?

I admit (if you'll bear with me a moment longer) that this thought preoccupied me all week long, and my confusion merely increased. Such a discovery, if it is a discovery, can be tested and verified only with respect to the most significant authors and incontrovertible values.

I moved with the certainty and eagerness of a bloodhound. What if — it immediately occurred to me — a skillful Jewish manager, as Max Brod undoubtedly was, had turned a diligent graphomaniac into a dish to feed mythmaking literary theorists? With this in mind — full of repugnance all the while for such a sacrilegious idea — I leafed through Kafka's *The Castle*. I once again read the pages I knew so intimately, and sometimes I was immediately engrossed in Kafka's anxious world, but other times I ascertained with horror that I might be right.

I didn't stop at Kafka, but went on to test anything and everything. Of course, I chose above all my own literary loves, the idols after whom I had, to a great degree, modeled my intellectual world during various phases of my life.

My confusion and embarrassment assumed agonizing proportions.

The Romantic poet Karel Mácha seemed to me sometimes a singer of metaphysical hymns about the abyss of human existence, at other times an ecstatic loudmouth choking on the emptiness of his own thoughts. Vladimír Holan was at times a Prometheus mining boulders of light from a burning Universe, and at times a psychotic prophet like countless others who pass through my hands here at the nuthouse. In one long paragraph Faulkner seemed to embody all the world's harrowing oppositions, but when I read the same paragraph just a few moments later, it was nothing but a chaotic heap of spasmodic inconsistencies and affectations, not worth wasting time on. Proust at first enchanted me with his magical mirrors of memory, then got on my nerves and bored me to death. And Ginsberg, with his breathless meter, set my soul singing — and then buried me with his homo hysteria.

And I could go on. Why hadn't I noticed it earlier? And I should emphasize, if it's not already clear, that I could read the same book by the same author, the same paragraph, even the same line, once as something original and essential, initiating me into the strictest secrets of the universe — and then, when I tried again, I found myself looking with disgust at a hodgepodge of banalities and incomprehensible squeals.

In those hectic hours and days I lost forever my beautiful, innocent relationship with literature, as well as the certainty that there exists a border dividing the genuine and true from the literary swindle, from vain scribblers and confidence men. I realized I knew nothing about literature, and that was the only thing I was allowed to know.

We got a new patient, a seventeen-year-old schizophrenic, whose schizophrenic attacks culminated in his locking himself in his room and refusing to see anyone. When they brought him to us by force, hundreds of scraps of paper were found in his room, and on each was written the same word: "Now!" along with a number. The numbers varied, as did the writing (from carefully stylized lettering to hasty, sloppy notes), but the word remained the same.

Schizophrenics try desperately to get a footing in space and time, to find a fixed point to rest on, from which they can defy chaos. I guessed that the numbers next to the word "Now!" were those points in space-time, hours and minutes: 16,20 and 8,32 and 9,11 and 10,48 and 21,26 and so on. In the end, the scraps of paper covered every minute of the day; every minute was the decisive one (the "Now!"), and with each minute everything started and ended again and again. In such numbers, they negated one another. In the end, each and none of the scattered moments was the decisive one, and time thus stopped in its inflexible interchangeability.

I tried speaking to this patient about it, and was surprised when he called the unreality of his reality a "game." "Whatever I do," he explained to me, "no matter how hard I try, I never have a feeling of reality. It's always just a game." "Do you mean a mystification?" I asked. And this time he looked at me in surprise. "You put it very nicely," he praised me. "Everything is really just a mystification."

Once when I was sitting in the Tower of the Turtle-Dove, already a little bored, Ludvík took me aside and, with the pompous gravity that accompanied all of his proposals, offered to help me out if I wanted to make a go at being a writer, a poet, or even, God forbid, a playwright. "Just look around," he said, waving his hand dismissively, "everyone who's anyone shows up here. All I have to do is put in a good word for you."

And then he talked a while about what he called "his menagerie." "That's the editor of *Rovnost*, who tries to make it big by latching on to famous authors, Mikulášek, Skácel, and now Svatava. And here's another one like him. People without any talent of their own, and because they can't even recognize talent in other people, someone has to tell them who is a 'safe bet,' a 'mark,' in their lingo. And here," Ludvík pointed to another level of the hierarchy, spread out picturesquely beneath a shelf full of onion-motif bowls, which were hard to find at the time, "here are the ones who call the shots and decide who the 'marks' are. Real talent can appear only with their kind permission. They don't have to latch on to anyone, because they're already established. But there's only one difference between the two types: the first ones are as impudent as houseflies, and the second as horseflies."

I thought a lot about Ludvík. His offhand comments were certainly meant as a virtuoso display of his ability to see through people — to observe intelligently, and to present his observations quickly and correctly. But unfortunately, he lost this detachment as soon as he had to evaluate himself. Here his judgment failed miserably.

Ludvík confidently dominated most social situations. He was a born schemer, and I soon realized that the one thing he enjoyed most was plotting: thinking up gossip and slander, spreading them around, feeding the flames, and then watching as the fire consumed human relationships, rapidly crippling them and turning them into ugly piles of ash. And so, when I refused his offer to promote me as a writer — it was clearly meant as another bribe to keep me quiet, we know what about — he began to make ominous threats, and I had no doubt that he could make my life unpleasant with his intrigues, until I couldn't take any more.

But if it's not the case that I simply envy him — not only his fortunate spontaneity but maybe even his unfortunate insensitivity to others and his lack of self-criticism, because these qualities, although they occasionally cause him difficulties, usually carve out plenty of elbow room for him — and if I'm just an unexceptional little creature in this human preserve, then Ludvík is certainly something vigorous, with a sleek coat of fur. And in the end, isn't this story about envy as well? He shamelessly stole my idea, feasted on it like a boar, and now he was charitably sweeping me crumbs from the table.

And so I don't even understand myself anymore. Or the story of which I'm the self-appointed narrator. It's no longer clear to me where its center is, or whether everything I'm so stubbornly concentrating my attention on isn't just incidental, compensatory, gratuitous.

And I began to reconsider Svatava as well. She was definitely beautiful, but a crucial component of her beauty was the fact that she was the author of extremely popular collections of poetry. She wouldn't have been so beautiful if she hadn't written love poetry, and vice versa. The two things spurred each other on. Her beauty shone through her poetry, and her erotic metaphors lit up her beauty like constellations in the night sky.

I would compare them (poetry and beauty) to two mirrors set with their foci directly opposite one another. A glimmer, reflected back and forth to infinity, grows into a conflagration.

And this conflagration consumed the doubts I once expressed about her (a provincial beauty handing out prizes at a town raffle), and I no longer doubted Svatava, but just as a repressed trauma looks for, and eventually finds, a different, more general form, I now doubted beauty itself. The very idea of beauty, if you like.

As you see, I found myself in Plato's cave of ideas. And on the walls of the cave, in the glimmer of the dancing flames, something was reflected in ample, intimate detail. And I recognized Jana, my long-gone platonic love, Evžen's little whore. And on and on.

We had hardly released Miloš (the seventeen-year-old schizophrenic) to spend a Sunday at home (on "psycho's leave") when he committed suicide. There are as many sorts of demonstrative suicide attempts as there are cats in a cathouse, but when someone jumps from a sixth-floor balcony to the pavement below, he is usually dead serious.

And I'm not even sure if Miloš really was a schizophrenic. Of course, he exhibited some of the classic symptoms, but that's not so important. In the end, what do we know about schizophrenia? Few people have sought truth and truthfulness more desperately. He let everything else slide and pursued that alone. You may object, of course, but if you'd known him, your objections would soon disappear (which is not, of course, any argument against them).

"Do you think we'll ever learn the truth about the fifties and all that?" a friend once asked me, a pathologist-idealist with whom I sometimes went for a drink at the soda fountain across the street from the hospital.

I shook my head decisively. "Not at all. In my opinion, it's just another swindle. When they realized that people were no longer buying it, they gave us socialism with a human face. But socialism has just one face: the one you wipe with toilet paper."

"For God's sake, quiet down," the pathologist-idealist pleaded.

Since time immemorial, people have had only four ways of searching for the truth: religion, philosophy, art, and literature, or on their own, with stubborn truthfulness. I never had a strong enough stomach for religion; I never managed to work through philosophy; and I'm not stubborn enough to search on my own. That left only art and literature. And just because literature meant so much to me, I never dared start up anything with it, never dared trespass on its sacred territory. If I really had literary talent, I would devote my whole life to it without hesitation, without the slightest doubt that it was the most valuable and worthy thing I could do. But in literature there's nothing worse than cultivated mediocrity. Or so I had believed until then.

"Tell me, but tell me the truth," Miloš whispered to me

during our one long conversation, "tell me: if you found out that everything, absolutely everything, was just one big mystification, would you draw the necessary conclusions?" I tried to explain to him that the question was poorly phrased. "Then ask it the right way," he suggested, and waited.

He took advantage of the fact that he was home alone, and he jumped from a sixth-floor balcony. On Veveří Street. I was told he was hastily covered with newspapers, because no one was willing to use a sheet or a blanket, until they came for him.

To my surprise, I realized that I was taking it worse than anything else. Even though I knew Miloš only from his diagnosis, anamnesis, and a single long conversation. And even though I know that a clinical psychologist's career is dotted with as many suicides as the emperor's portrait is with flyspecks. I was furious at the world, which since time began has played into the hands of clever swindlers, heartless dunces, and every manner of shithead.

They say it happens sooner or later to every psycho-therapist. Just an occupational hazard, nothing more. But although I repeated this to myself over and over and then over again, it doesn't help and didn't solve anything. Maybe it's also because of the time that it happened. Either way, I didn't know what to do. I needed to do something that would either confirm or overturn everything, once and for all. A deed that determined everything, once and for all (and was, therefore, absurd).

If what I've said up to now about Ludvík's "menagerie" has given you the impression that the literary salon in the Tower of the Turtle-Dove was open to anyone who happened by, it's high time to note that it wasn't like that at all (or perhaps only for a short time at the beginning, before the Tower of the Turtle-Dove became a household word). Ludvík very quickly established unwritten but universally respected rules. Only someone with an invitation, or whom one of the regular guests brought along the first time, was permitted in.

So when a distant acquaintance asked me to take him along as a guest (or even someone I had never seen before, who now came to me with the intention of using me as a carrier, by means of which they could easily slip inside, like an infection), I always remembered that Ludvík had told me to check out every guest with him ahead of time. Out of distaste for such a procedure, I preferred to reject everyone outright.

But I decided to make an exception in Martin's case, even though it was clear to me that Ludvík would not be very pleased to see him.

Martin was a young composer who was already being spoken of as the most significant representative of his generation, and who was, in addition, gifted with rugged good looks — the gifts of the gods tend to be unevenly distributed.

Martin had set Svatava's poem, "Moons Fall Asleep in My Womb," to music for a girls' choir, and had overseen its dignified performance, in the company of several of his other remarkable new compositions, in a concert at a cultural center in Brno. When he greeted Svatava and Ludvík there, he was expecting to get an invitation to the Tower of the Turtle-Dove. And if it weren't for me, he would still be waiting.

Ludvík, on principle, did not invite young, handsome, and truly talented authors (it was bad enough that he couldn't keep them away on their occasional visits from Prague and other international metropolises). He filled his "menagerie" with freaks, semi-freaks, and quarter-freaks, or at least people who weren't too good-looking. It wasn't merely because Svatava's beauty shone all the more brilliantly against such a background, but also, as I quickly figured out, because he actually wasn't all that sure of Svatava. And so I decided not to check out Martin's visit with him beforehand.

When I first brought Martin along (in April 1968), I

watched with amusement as he sat modestly and inconspicuously amidst the glitter of kitchen pans, soup ladles, and polished cupboards, his eyes glued to Svatava. And when someone sat or stood right in front of him and blocked his view of Svatava's enchanting countenance, as happened a few times during the evening, he stood up decisively and shifted his chair, with its little carved hearts, to another place, where he would once again have a good view of the poetess.

And I understood that this young genius, over whose favors two distinguished Brno actresses had recently brawled (biting and scratching), was hopelessly in love with Svatava. That fascinating contradiction between tantalizing erotic poetry and vestal inaccessibility, that glow of obscenity surrounded by the chaste ramparts of the kitchen, that provocative beauty and discouraging indifference, all of that awakened in him a mad desire that paradoxically cast him into a woeful immobility. And Martin, used to having girls' breasts drop freshly cooked onto his plate, could only stare hungrily.

I was sure that he wouldn't come back. He wasn't one of those genius-martyr types, like Beethoven.

But he surprised me, the stubborn ram. He decided, now that he had been introduced and initiated, to put down roots.

Svatava
for Marina Tsvetaeva

A splinter of light
under a nail of darkness
the night gathers its ravens
a rose-carafe of underworld water

a song of which we only hear
the turning of the score
a storm of which we only see
the scale of the barometer
the ash of cities that never burned down

a longing of which we only hear
the beating of others' wings
a pain of which we only see
the tumbrels of someone's dreams
a love we know only from television clips

and then Somewhere-something
slashes open the belly like a harpoon
and the Ocean is flooded with our blood

When I came home from the crematorium that day, I still didn't understand anything. Several weeks had to pass before I finally figured out that what I had seen there — what must have been for everyone else a mere ritual eccentricity, the likes of which they were used to from the Tower of the Turtle-Dove — was in reality a signal, Svatava's signal, meant only for me!

And then I acted quickly and decisively.

I knew that now, after Ludvík's death, Svatava had no choice but to be silent forever. And as the only one who was in on the secret, I could look on with pleasure.

In the last months of Ludvík's life, something strange had happened. Svatava was a puppet that revolted. She rejected the role that Ludvík had assigned her, slipped free, and began to live her own life. I decided to put everything back in order. This would be my condition.

So, above all, enough of the angel of lascivious dreams! Now that she had a name, I could take the liberty of turning her into an author of strictly religious poetry, and I would justify the conversion that preceded this profound inner change as the result of a cathartic cleansing after Ludvík's death. And I began by composing a long, hymn-like elegy to Ludvík, inspired by Ginsberg's famous poem *Kaddish*.

I told Svatava I would be visiting her. And one August evening, a month after Ludvík's suicide, I armed myself with my elegy and a small velvet box (the kind you usually put a ring in), and set out for Řečkovice.

The house was unbelievably dark and quiet. The buzzer

sounded, unlocking the door.

And suddenly I stood at the bottom of a staircase. And a light came on, spreading out over the stairs like a carpet. I below, Svatava above. I didn't see her, but I thought I heard her breathing. And then it occurred to me that I already knew this scene, that I had lived through it once before.

But of course I understood the cause of such a peculiar situation. When a person unexpectedly reaches a goal he has been moving toward for a long time, when this motion wasn't always clear and the goal wasn't always conscious or admitted, he finds himself in a somewhat dream-like situation. This could be put otherwise. I was happy, and happiness is always irrational. I had finally thrown off the burden of torturous doubt that had been plaguing me for months.

And then I did what I had carefully planned out and prepared for ahead of time. I pulled the velvet box (the kind you usually put a ring in) out of my breast pocket, took out two green leaves, moistened them, and stuck them to my eyes. And this was my reply to Svatava, to show I had understood her signal.

The leaves on my eyes, I began to climb the stairs, gropingly, slowly, blindly. But then, with a loud click, a signpost in my body snapped up, buoying me and guiding me reliably. I went up slowly, lightly, solemnly. I was approaching Svatava, and I knew, I knew with certainty, that for the rest of my life and forever I would remember this evening and this night (August 20, 1968).

Written in August 1990

ALEXANDRA BERKOVÁ

from The Sorrows of Devoted Scoundrel

Translated by Jonathan Bolton

. . . in the beginning there is nothing — force fields — whirlwinds and waves — look, smoke: Is there a right angle here anywhere?

There are two little monkeys in the photograph: they hug each other tightly, convulsively, and gaze into the lens with big, questioning eyes. Underneath is written: Two frustrated baby monkeys . . .

— and humanity, confused, still sings . . .

it could, incidentally, be phrased otherwise:

once upon a time everyone lived in paradise happy as a kitten —

— they rolled around in the soft grass and nothing was lacking: they hunted for beechnuts, warmed themselves in the sun, cuddled up together, nibbled each other's limbs and intertwined them, wrestling playfully —

and the sun rose and set, and divine energy changed from one form into another —

and another and another and so on . . .

and all living creatures devoted themselves to this flow of forms as birds devote themselves to the air and fish to the waters —

and one creature ate another — and everything was good —

and things went on this way for a thousand years and a

thousand thousand years —

and the Supreme One said to his most devoted angel, who was licking His toes at the time: Go jump in a lake, you scoundrel, you bore me!

— and something rumbled inside devoted Scoundrel —

he immediately turned black, like any culprit —

and understanding nothing, he stole off into a corner to quiver;

and for him water is no longer water, grass grass, night night, or day day —

everything has rolled up into writhing anguish: petrifying — paralyzing — suffocating — it's raining in his eyes, his stomach is full of snakes, in his heart there is only cold and darkness and a silence without an echo, as he moans without a sound:

break, my heart, let me lie in the dust —

flow out, my eyes, onto that dust —

leave my body, my black soul, and don't come back; the sun shines equally on everyone, only over me is there a cloud, for the umbilical cord of His love has throbbed its last, and there is nothing else to nourish me, since I am no longer allowed to roll in the grass at His feet . . . !

. . . ugh, Scoundrel, Scoundrel,

as long as the God of Water ruled the waters and the God of Wind the winds,

as long as the God of Grass dwelt in the grasses and the sun warmed everyone equally, the world was at ease —

— but tell me, Scoundrel, what was it for?

How will you, not knowing darkness, recognize light?

How will you, not knowing evil, recognize good? Well?

You won't recognize them — you don't know them. Because you're an idiot.

Come on, Scoundrel, you don't even want to recognize them — admit it!

It was enough for you to roll in the grass at His feet . . . but that isn't enough for Him. For Him it's too little. He requires more. He wants to see some movement — change — growth — results;

And He will help you grow, He has chosen you! He wants you to be perfect, because He loves you, Scoundrel — understand? That's why, in His infinite kindness, He will let you undergo much persecution: He will hound you through grief and misery and agony; He will drive you from your mother's lap right into a whirlwind of wrath — so that you can overcome it, so that you will be better! — Isn't that great? He will visit you with suffering and pain and tears and blood and sweat . . .

— aren't you delighted? Well, Scoundrel?

. . . ugh — you writhe in the mud instead of offering thanks, you moldy fool!

. . . ah, I like that — when the juice flows out of a wounded soul as if it were a hewn tree — after all, only a wounded oyster bears a pearl, and only a wounded beehive gives forth propolis . . . that's why I love art. A lot. It's therapeutic — and besides, it's not as boring as life . . .

Paralyzed by despair, devoted Scoundrel sobs silently, calling to the lord who has abandoned him —

— but the Supreme One doesn't answer. He's not keeping watch over that moldy fool, who doesn't know the value of His goodwill — He's not even anywhere nearby: He must have gone away. Somewhere else. He must have work to do. Something more important — and He has left Scoundrel alone.

And all the beasts devour each other in peace, and go on reproducing, and the sun shines equally on them all — except Scoundrel. He has burrowed down into the ground so he won't be so alone . . .

And always, when it gets dark and all the beasts, happy in

their ignorance, lie down to sleep, God, unburied, stands quietly next to Scoundrel's bed of clay . . .

. . . you take life too seriously. You just can't take things so seriously . . .

Don't try and tell me that. I don't understand it, and it bugs the shit out of me that I don't understand it. But I'll tell you something: intelligent people think everybody else is intelligent, too, that you can learn how to be intelligent, that anyone can do it. But that's not the way it is, that's just what intelligent people think!

Scoundrel might bury God every day — but God returns to him: every night.

He sees everything and doesn't help.

. . . who are you to judge me? You Conceited Old Man? You Drill Sergeant? You Fart of the Absolute?! You electrical discharge!! You gaseous substance!! Don't pretend to be asleep! I'll find another God, if you're going to be so cruel!

. . . listen here, young man, calm down — none of us has it easy. Look at water, for example: so many obstacles in its way, and how hard it tries . . . or this tiny little ant here: he's built himself a path — and hey, whoops! — where'd it go? it's been destroyed! and he has to build a new one, poor little guy — idiot — there, you see: he doesn't complain. He plugs away and plugs away . . . So don't you complain either, and plug away. We can put this world into some kind of shape with or without you, you got that?

. . . Thou shalt have no other Gods before Me . . . !!!

This is how we pray to Scoundrel:
Devoted Scoundrel,
our brother!
Thou, who have been chosen to writhe in anguish instead of us,

Thou, repudiated for our sake, suffering for us, infinitely striving for us,

forgive us our depravity, in which, inexperienced, we persist,

as we forgive ourselves, wretched and weak —

— but that's just the way we are — what do you want from us — our prince!

sun of our days!

intercede for us!

just look at us: our women get more and more pregnant,

our children want even more expensive toys, our mouths are greedy for feed, and our bodies have no strength

ugh, oy vay, sun of ours!

salvation!

intercede for us!

somehow you'll work things out with the Supreme One —

why, you have a way with him —

none of us could manage —

to talk our way out of it —

the way you can —

redeemer!

intercede for us!

You're my only friend, you bastard! I mean, you're all I have in the world . . . ! Look at me. See? I'm crying! I'm actually crying . . . ! When I realize how terribly lonely I am . . . and helpless . . . and weak . . . how I can't ever seem to resist sin: I keep resisting and resisting — and suddenly I look up and see I've given in again . . .

what can you do . . . plenty of other guys have resisted and resisted — and in the end given in . . .

what can I say — you know best of all . . .

intercede for us!

here's a buffalo leg and a few raisins — that ought to be enough for today. I haven't been all that bad this quarter . . .

there wasn't even any reason . . .

or anyone to join me. . .

you know how it is. . .

sometimes it's awful. . .

When I realize how lonely I am, I actually cry and feel like a drink. . .

intercede for us!

well? is it a deal? Can I count on you?

Thanks!!

I knew you were a pal!

amen

They say the Heavenly Virgin was discovered by the mailman while he was searching for his hat. He was working his way through some bushes — when suddenly there was a marvelous light — and there was the Heavenly Virgin, sitting in a cherry tree. He called the police right away; they shot at her — but they just couldn't seem to hit her: she kept flying to another tree. So they called on the villagers for help — to cut down the trees. Our people are lazy — but once they're paid properly — besides, we were curious what would happen when the last tree fell: would the Virgin just sit there in the air? or would she fall to the grass? we could catch her and put her in a cage — what kind of feed do you think she eats? we could breed her . . . but with what? . . . we have to figure all that out: if she's edible, and so on . . . if she can reproduce all by herself, and if she's edible and a little intoxicating, we could export her. . .

. . . when all the cherry trees were cut down, the Virgin turned into a white dove and flew away.

And suddenly we all realized we'd liked her: how good and kind and wise she was, how she loved us all and how the mailman had tricked us. . .

We cried bitter tears and asked for forgiveness, but no one ever saw the Heavenly Virgin again. . .

She was declared a saint, and the mailman was burned in a ceremony on the village square, which was named after her.

— too many unburied dead are hanging around our settlements; they're always giving us reproachful looks, crawling into our beds, getting underfoot, eating off our tables, interrupting us, babbling on about everything . . . maybe no one ever said a proper good-bye to them?

— that's why they introduced public confession, that's the only reason. . .

Scoundrel is setting off on a journey: he's been banished; okay. There was probably a good reason for it . . . Maybe he really is — bad, otherwise none of it would make sense . . . but he'll turn things around: as a matter of fact, they made it quite clear it was expected of him. And he'll manage: he'll go out into the world and show them he's good for something. That he knows how to try, how to grind and grind away until he destroys himself. That he knows how to sacrifice himself. That he can renounce himself for the sake of others. Completely. Forever. Until they say: Scoundrel, you're okay. Come join us unbanished ones.

Yes: that's how it will be. Of course — he has to try. In the end, it's not so bad: after all, he has his rags and his staff. If he's lucky, he may find a small bowl. . .

— We're a wretched society, it's true — look at how many sick people have been beaten to death by our merciless Samaritans —

why, we're waiting for Scoundrel, any day now —

meanwhile we change the rules of grammar, and are healed by the more sensitive among us: we bleed the sap out of them and we pry out their pearls with knives; we help ourselves whenever possible: a gardener, after all, tortures roses when, with his knife, he forces them to bloom; listen to the beautiful moaning of this wretch — and when I really hurt him: ooooooh. . . !

Of course, we throw the pearls back into the sea, so they'll remain rare, and we kill off the most beautiful girls, foreigner;

153

how else could we go on loving them?

And abused children make such wonderful poets! — this one, for example: he's a capable bard; his mother never hugged him, his father drove him out — would you like to blind him?

Scoundrel set off, not knowing where, but the landscape seemed friendly to him: the high, rosy grass wrapped itself around his ankles, catching hold of his shroud with tiny fingers; all three suns sailed slowly to the west — and the green moon rose above them with a quiet whirr. A bluish zephyr carried sand dunes to the north, and a shiny silver insect, sailing through the whirlwinds, buzzed its evening songs. The green sea too was getting ready to go to sleep: with a rumble it began to turn itself water side down, until its white seashells faced the sky — a sky both black and low, because it was full of stars, as skies, if they're splendid, tend to be.

. . . and everything was there, yes, everything was there: steep hills whose tops were illuminated by the rising sun — their greenery a silky silver — and between them, far down below, valleys: green-black — black-green — deep, cool, and dark; yes, everything was there: the tops of hills, the sky, dark clouds — space — light and shade — the sky's open embrace — God: yes.

. . . everything all around is beautiful — but Scoundrel doesn't see it: he's just left paradise and stepped into the appalling landscape of humans. . .

In a village a woman ran out of her house, loudly lamenting:

oh, help me, foreigner, you've traveled through many lands and seen many things, surely you can tell me what to do! I have a husband and he doesn't want to die! I would kill him myself, but I fear the wrath of God. And he torments me and torments me and I'm so tired. . .

He's been getting ready for it all his life: the clothing for when he's in his coffin, the memorial speeches, the music, the banquet, the flowers and wreaths — he ordered everything in advance and paid for it, and all he talked about was what it would be like, the preacher, the hired mourners, the requiem mass, whether he'll look nice in his coffin — he sold the fields and the house and frittered away our daughter's dowry — but he says: I can have plenty of daughters — hah! — but I'll only die once! — and now he just doesn't want to die —

— the doctor tried reasoning with him, the priest tried reasoning with him, even the gravedigger — and I say to him, what are you afraid of? Why, you've done everything you could to prepare, you fed yourself the best food in the house, groomed, cleaned, and powdered yourself, covered yourself with perfumes to drown the smell of sweat, tanned yourself, exercised, had yourself massaged — you have nothing to be ashamed of, you'll be a beautiful corpse, the handsomest one in the graveyard!

And he says no, he has to think it over, and he whines and wants me to bring him something, take something away, scratch his back, turn the featherbeds, take him to the bathroom, give him something to drink and take away the bedpan, he won't walk, doesn't want to strain himself, at most he'll let himself be carted around in a wheelbarrow, around the square or the garden so he can see everything he's leaving behind, but otherwise he's conserving his energy, after all he's been dying long as I've known him, and that's a mighty long time, but now that he has the chance, he's suddenly been overcome by weakness and begun to get frightened —

— he wants me to be tender, though he never was to me, and to take care of him, though he never took care of our children, and to have sympathy for him, though he never had sympathy for his aging parents. He wants everything for himself —

— and the only thing he liked was his tomcat: for years that animal just rolled around in front of the hearth, slept in the same bed as him, and ate from the same plate — my husband caught mice for him and brought them to him every morning and evening —

— but now the cat's gone and died, and it's like my

husband's thread's been cut — so I say to him: you've got no more spirit since that cat died — and your body doesn't want to go on living without the cat, so why don't you finally get a move on?

But he says no, it's not so bad — and he hangs on to the world as stubbornly as mildew — he has his hair curled and his ugly face made up and his ass-hairs dyed — and I sleep in the barn, with a sack for a blanket and nothing to eat — and now he wants me to love him — where am I supposed to find any love for him?

Scoundrel didn't know. He was looking himself. From the house came a droning voice, drawn out and mournful like the sound of a trombone: Mo-o-ther, don't let them ta-a-ke me to the ho-spi-tal, they'll kill me there, do-o-on't leave me alo-o-one. . .

The woman ran back into the house to tell her husband a bedtime story.

In another city there lived a woman with large, imploring eyes: her punishment in life was being born a woman, as everyone knew. She lived with a weak, pale, languid man who was balding, had sweaty palms, and respected her immensely: he prayed to her and wrote her poems, kissed her hand, gazed at her longingly when she wasn't looking — but as soon as she raised her eyes, he turned away. This fellow was very happy to have her: he bought her all kinds of gifts and the best food and bragged to everyone about his wonderful, beautiful wife. At home, he would sit three meters away from her so as to adore her better. But when she spoke to him, he immediately pulled back, and whenever she showed him affection, he rudely brushed her off and locked himself in his room, sobbing and moaning loudly about how she tormented him, how she understood nothing of the depth of his feelings . . . and when the woman then withdrew into herself, avoiding him, there he was, bringing her presents and paying her compliments, loudly praising her — and when she reached out her hand to him, he ran. He was also in the habit of approaching her bed at night, behaving affectionately and telling her of his great desire and love, praising her body, and describing everything he would like to do with her on that very bed, if she would only let him — in this and many other ways he would tempt her, driving her crazy until she yearned to give herself to him, her soul and body on fire, aching with excitement and longing — then he would get up and walk away. The woman often begged him, crying, to let her leave him, and he was always shocked: What was she talking about? Why, everything was going so well: look, in the spring I brought you that beautiful scarf from the fair, and last fall I had those two pairs of shoes resoled — and this is how you show your thanks? And he swore to her on his knees, if only she wouldn't leave him, he loved her so much, he would die without her, could she stand having that on her conscience?

— and so it went, day after day, night after night, on and on for many years — and no one knew what terrible things the woman had done to deserve such suffering; and when people passed her house, they walked on tiptoe, even during the day.

The woman was pale and shook like an aspen, there was a deep sadness in her eyes, and her unfulfilled desire blazed forth like flames to a distance of several miles, so there was a pleasant warmth all around and remarkable, heavily scented, pastel flowers grew up around her house, and whoever passed by could not help being moved and felt a sudden need to hug somebody. And so lovers, when they wanted to intensify their love, came to spend the night in that garden, and couples who had been married for many years walked by, seeking to revive their weary desire. And they called it The House of Bitter Love.

Such a peculiar world, thought Scoundrel, as he set up camp nearby. A man sat down next to him and said: I'm an endearing fellow and I'm going to tell you my story. I was born in a small village where people do nothing but work. My mother told me: people are swine. If you want to do something besides work all your life, give everyone a handsome smile and greet them politely. And because I wanted to do something besides work all my life, I gave everyone a handsome smile and greeted them politely. And people, those swine, smiled back at me and said, oh, isn't he nice, let me borrow him, let me pet him — and people were always sitting me on their laps and rooting around in my hair or in my underwear, and I held on and gave everyone a handsome smile. I was the darling of aunties and teachers and aldermen's wives; of inspectors, policemen, councillors, and older schoolboys. My classmates envied me, soldiers gave me medals, cooks gave me extra dumplings and girls secret signs — and I gave everyone a handsome smile. I was too endearing to support myself by working: I became a Darling. My last master — I think he fixed elevators or something before he became a judge — always used to sit in his armchair after an execution and devise instructions for future generations. Not even his dog liked him. When he was thinking, it got dark around his head and he gave off a terrible stench. I wrote down everything, as duty required; for example: "The world is guilty and is going to pay . . . ," pretty fitting, eh? Or this: ". . . I like to punish colored people — they are so endlessly stupid!! What, do they think they're beyond good and evil . . . ?? . . . how inhuman!!"

And then, this is a little more — personal . . . : "Listen, idiot," — that was a kind of term of endearment, he called me that sometimes — anyway — "listen to what I tell you: — today I saw another dead animal, dead for some time, the way I like them — but — " and he said this with amazement — "but its gray color had been skillfully concealed with red aniline dye, its greasiness covered with sawdust, and its stench hidden by the scent of tar — it was pretty hard on my stomach . . . and I relieved myself in the bathtub: it's so — liberating . . ." A beautiful confession, don't you think? Ugh, his addiction to fresh salami, the endearing fellow sighed, and he closed his notebook —

Scoundrel looked at him questioningly.

I just wanted to point out that I don't know anything!! Is

that clear? I didn't see anything, didn't hear anything! Yes, a lot of bad things happened, yes, supposedly he committed a lot of evil deeds, yes, people talk about it a lot, but I didn't have anything to do with the old man's crimes, understand? So kindly leave me alone for once, okay??? — smile at me like I smile at you — and leave me alone! damn it, leave me alone!!!!

The man pounded his cane in the glowing ash.

And what happened to him — to the old man? asked Scoundrel.

What? — nothing — he kicked the bucket, naturally — Fuck it — I've had enough of it, damn it!! why didn't all of you smile too, damn it? you were all supposed to smile, damn it! — All I can say is, fuck your proper upbringing. . . !!

The man flung his cane into the fire and walked away — thereby rendering Scoundrel's world even more peculiar.

JÁCHYM TOPOL
from **Sister**
Translated by Alex Zucker

Chapter 2
What Made My Heart; We Ran.
The Objects. Back Then in the Sewer. Conspiracy.

And then one gloomy post-bolshevik day I stood in the street and I was alone and nothing will ever sear that day out of my memory. I had a memorable appointment with Micka at the Tchibo café and we laid the cornerstone of the Organization.

Nothing will sear out the Sewer days either, because that was what made my heart. Zigzagging through the streets and testing the weight of the buildings you carried on your back, and you can ask your mirror: Tell me who's the fairest one of all? and the mirror is silent for a moment and it's eerie and you draw on that moment for the tension in your movement, and then the mirror's just an object and:

a broken mirror is cut-up snapshots, I look at myself and it would be nice to write my way into the third person, but no, says Potok: I'd lived in various apartments and packs, and one cheery street-walking day, when they released me from the wicked old city insane asylum, I got a social service key and a dump. There wasn't exactly any family I could stay with. For a certain period of time I couldn't take any hostility or any kindness. Gasworks Street, that's where I lay down and filled my closet with disguises. Canina was still in my dreams.

There were boyfriends and girlfriends and conspiracies, you'd grin and say yep and nope, hah, and wink . . . there was Bohler and Micka and Čáp and Cepková and Elsa the Lion and others, each in his or her own circles, which sometimes intersected under the combined pressure . . . and there were objects surviving with spirit stored up inside them, they're generated in the war against death, shit and fear, and they are often the matter in which images, sounds and speech — and that's written speech too, so savage, so humble — originate, they grow in there with the other ingredients, often in obscurity. And just by the way and like there was nothing at all going on, there were people here walking the streets who knew how to make these charged objects. Some of them were artists at surviving even at the cost of self-destruction. Some of them lived in the Pearl. I wanted to learn. I was hungry. Most of the rest of the population was too slow for me, or even dangerous, the grayness of sour time had gotten them, but I full-throatedly wished good luck to all, contempt is best left for oneself.

No charged object ever stopped water or tanks, brought a dearest girlfriend back, or chased away a single wicked wrinkle, they just lapped up time; that's enough sometimes. I ate them up like bread, putting them into my tongue.

Coincidentally, I use the tongue of Slavs, of Czechs, of slaves, of once upon a time German and Russian slaves, and it's a dog's tongue. A clever dog knows how to survive and what price to pay for it. He knows when to cringe and when to dodge and when to bite, he has it in his tongue. It's a tongue that should have been destroyed, and its time has yet to come; it never will. Invented by versifiers, spoken by coachmen and maids. And this is in it too, it evolved its own loops and holes and the savagery of a serpent's child. It's a tongue that often had to be spoken in whispers. It's soft and cruel and has a few good old words of love, it's an agile and speedy tongue, I believe, and always going on. Not even the Avars could get this tongue of mine, not burning borders, not tanks, not even the most revolting of human types: cowardly teachers; cash in a shrinking world is what will get it. But I still have time, as Totilla the barbarian once said in his wicked time, before his battle had begun. Before they got him.

As soon as we had dispensed with our childhood, me and Bohler, the theologian, began doing deals with the Poles. There were times in my youth I wanted to be a Pole. I watched from beneath a rock. There wasn't much time, I watched like a primitive. On account of the avalanches. I liked the simple things best; the trick was to make up your mind fast. The Indians were already dead. The Poles were pounding cops. Praying. Vodka. Romantics always and in all things, but standing up. So great was the hatred of the Ghoul and so strong the feeling of humiliation, there were times you could dream of your own murder.

Another one of the overlapping shards of glass, a snapshot: Čáp, white with anger, reads a statement in which our fathers and grandfathers appeal to us to abandon the protest because they might start shooting.

Hey, this is insane, says Čáp, they've all gone off to their cottages! So what, if they stayed they'd just get locked up anyway, I said knowingly. Yeah, but that's the point! It's all right for folks to dance around and under the billy clubs when they know these guys are in the slammer. But at their cottages!

So Čáp accepted the responsibility that was lying in the streets and organized his own juveniles. I was the first to sign his manifesto because his vision of a kingdom was the wildest one around. Hey . . . nothing works, but you have to try . . . our Polish brothers have the Church, ours have been destroyed . . . hey! What, oh sure, I nodded, right absolutely . . . like Blake used to say, either create your own system or be enslaved by another man's. Bohler appears again in the shards of broken mirror: Take that watch from Tokštajn, we'll hawk it to the Poles, and toss in some ideological diversion. The bazaar naturally was illegal . . . those Czech morons, they really piss the shit out of me, Bohler declared, smiling at the Polish bandits, I mean can't those Bohos see that at least these guys are men, I mean their families could starve, so they trade, what else can they do, they don't foster the disgusting sin of whimpering . . . they steal . . . the Poles have always bled and battled, Bohler said dreamily, the Polish nation is the Christ of crazy Eastern Europe, he blasphemed . . . the Polish bandits had finished unloading their cars full of carpets smuggled from Kazakhstan and one of them strode through the setting sun, a carpet thrown over his shoulders, hence the vision . . . and who is that gentleman hanging there . . . the one with his arms spread wide like an airplane?

The older and wiser ones who said: don't go, they might shoot, were losing us, and if it hadn't gone so fast later, Čáp's juveniles would have been lost . . . he himself was getting skinnier every day, his curly hair fluttering, his eyes shining . . . we'll pass it out to 'em after the prayer! I said in church . . . out of the question! Čáp protested, just the opposite, let it interrupt, dammit! . . . I mean half of 'em can't even hear the words anyway . . . he had a point, we handed out the flyers with the Czech lion on it, the one tearing his chains, the Christians snatched them up and gaped in horror, stuck the flyers under their coats, in their bags and purses . . . one older guy told me "thank you" and in his eyes was a smile, a joyful one, he knew that there was a time for war and a time for prayer, and that they merge . . . a single sister shook my hand . . . she was smiling too . . . we're off to Ignác's, said Čáp, and we maneuvered through the passageways and carriageways quickly and agilely, with glances left and right and eyes in the back of our heads, quickly and quietly, with that good old catholick joy for life . . . Čáp's teachings were becoming increasingly attractive, because he knew that the war against communism must lead also to the liberation of ants and all living creatures, that no one must harm the helpless and the young, and that whoever does must accept the punishment . . . only his vision of a kingdom was a kingdom not of this world. And I was all the more amazed later, because those juveniles of Čáp's . . .

they were the most jaded bunch I ever had the honor to meet —
hardcore cynics, at times extraordinarily reckless . . . at the age
when we were still youths struggling with school, they were already running away from it, saying to hell with all that . . . back
when we were still tearing down a flag here and there and on the
sly, they were learning to dance under the billy clubs . . . some
were really young . . . kids practically . . . and the experience
with insane asylums and prison cells that we had, first from those
ten years older than us and then ourselves . . . we in turn passed
on to them, only they were tougher . . . at the age when we were
collecting stamps, they were collecting tear gas cartridges off the
cobblestones and having fun doing it . . . and they had the Polish
model too . . . and their tongue sped up with their movement
over the cobblestones . . . sometimes our eyes glowed with fire
. . . the machines of the enemy thundered in the air and under
ground, but we had a vision.

Everybody knows, after all . . . that back then in today's
central woman, Europe, there's nothing but dogs, they wiped out
the wolves, the only thing left in that preserve you could devote
yourself to was illegal shamanism, and just here and there and
once in a while, for a fleeting moment, do a dance and possess
the strength of a warrior, a mortal prepared to die.

There was beating in the streets, it was ready and waiting,
but the people with vision went back for it again and again
because it was the realest thing they had left.

Čáp threw cobblestones at a personnel carrier on Železná
Street and his juveniles were thrilled . . . because the kingdom
won't come all by itself, it stands to reason. It was movement, it
was new. How many people accepted the movement didn't
matter, all it takes is one rotten tooth in a loyal healthy set to
give the Ghoul at least a headache . . .

And nobody in this country, with that shrewdly manipulated picture in their stupid heads of the Poles as the hungry
pathetic enemy, had a clue . . . and nobody across the border in
Poland had a clue about those Czech Popeyes . . . none of them

had a clue about our insanity . . . none of them monitored us from a satellite or eavesdropped from the airshaft on the scarred language of our cooperatives, that sped-up cityspeak . . . and whether sitting in their cottages or in the slammer, none of them had a clue what the conspiracy was really about . . . all the scattered gangs of the urban underground were preparing themselves for an important assignment, rushing to design the final blueprint for the soul . . . auguring from their own dread-filled intestines, tensely watching the quaking skies . . . secretly going for the future's throat and conspiring to nothing less than a murder . . . namely: the conclusive and brutal assassination of Josef Vissarionovich Švejk.

HALINA PAWLOWSKÁ

from **Thank You for Each New Morning**

Translated by Lisa Ryoko Wakamiya

We are in the sky. The landscape beneath us. Hills and mountains. Grass, forests. Everything is lush, immaculate, clear. Everything quivers in the sharp, clean, limpid air. Blue sky, golden sun, green earth. Everything is full of its own secrets. Even this highway, narrow and potholed and vacant, leads somewhere far away, all the way to the horizon. . .

Chapter One

Oh! I went drinking on Monday and drank away forty cows

I hated Oskar Káhler. He came over to our place all the time and roared awfully and swore. My father didn't swear, wore gym shorts with legs down to his galoshes—they didn't have briefs then—and had he not maintained a proper level of decency in society (he absolutely hated the popular expression for it), he probably would have hanged himself. Like his Latin professor at *Gymnasium*, who did just that in front of his entire class. Well, first thing that afternoon he didn't hang himself, he drowned. Everything human — going to the bathroom, making love and bearing children — seemed "vulgar" to my dad. Distasteful! He had a positive attitude to food and food alone. He was from a village, and there wealth was determined by who had what in his cellar. Consequently, in the little pantry in our one-room apartment near the National Theater, we would have pepper sausages that cost thirty-five crowns a kilo and salt pork and a smoked pork flank and once in a while a side of pork smeared with garlic and cooked in paprika. This my father made himself, and afterward the whole apartment would be filled with its aroma.

Oskar Káhler was fat and his daughter Romka didn't hear well. In contrast, his son Lesyk played the oboe rather decently and showed off at our Ukrainian "melanky" which always took place before Christmas. I didn't like going to them because then I too had to show off, show everyone how pretty I was and how like my father, and recite Ukrainian poems in a soft voice. One was about a gypsy stealing some cucumbers, but a farmer catches him red-handed and has him locked up, and in the end the gypsy gets the better of him. The next poem was by my father. It was about his beautiful homeland, where the mountains don't have sharp peaks and are covered with succulent grass, where the sun shines even on the moss, the forest smells sweetly of resin, and there are bears, which, though dangerous, are good-hearted "kings of nature," as opposed to the wolves, which think nothing of furtively attacking you. Oskar Káhler always referred obscenely to something that belonged to my father's past. It mostly had to do with women. I was particularly sensitive to this. My father with those long gym shorts could never have had anything to do with anyone but my mother. But even with her I was convinced he didn't have anything to do. All they had was me. Oskar Káhler came over to our place for parties. Doctor Vakula, Mr. Shutko and Mr. Sushko, Mykhal Petrenko and Slavek Demianenko, Stefan Bora, Mr. Oleksa, and Vasyl Maldulian came too. Oskar shouted more than any of them and smoked. My father also smoked and sang, my mother anxiously brought sausages and salt pork to the table, and I crawled behind the couch. They always pulled the couch a few feet away from the window for me, and in there I "played house." There I kept Miss

Olena, who I got the moment I was born, and told her how I hated Oskar Káhler. Once he said to Father, "You know, Anna Nikarakivna has a beautiful crotch!" I began to hate Anna Nikarakivna and the word "crotch." My mother cried that time. Oskar also said, "He's a cabinet-maker. You let your son be a cabinet-maker!" I didn't understand which son he was talking about, as I was an only child!

We moved to a bigger apartment, one with two rooms. That's about when it started. It was the time when people began buying summer houses and cars and Mother started to blame Father for us being poor. I didn't think of us as poor: people didn't go to their summer houses every week and not everyone had a car.

Then he bought me an English raincoat like the one all the other students in the special language class had, and when I picked out shoes at Italia that cost 450 crowns, I eventually got them.

There were parties at our house all the time. But on a smaller scale. Only when it was father's name day or his birthday. Once, I think when he turned sixty (my father was always very old), the guests didn't want to get drunk; they wanted to go home sober at around midnight. Father locked the door and shouted that they weren't "guests" at all, they were "nobodies," and he wouldn't let them go!

He didn't let them go, and Doctor Vakula, Mykhal Petrenko, Stefan Bora, Mr. Oleksa, and Vasyl Maldulian went and sat down again. Mother was traumatized by all this. Father complained to her that his nephew Vasyl Maldulian had touched her leg under the table, then he threw his glass at the television set, but missed and pretended everything was fine; then he challenged nephew Vasyl to a chess tournament, and broke his nose.

Nephew Vasyl stood in the hallway and repeated over and

over, "Something's wrong with my nose. I can see it now! I see my own nose!" It was completely lopsided. (Somewhat to the right.) So father grabbed his leather jacket, which he'd worn on a train during the war; in one compartment they mistook him for a Jew and spoke to him in Yiddish, and in another compartment for a Gestapo agent and addressed him in German.

Father didn't like Germans or Jews, except for Oskar Káhler, who was a Ukrainian Jew of German descent, and was very bothered once when someone called out to me on the street — "Sarah!" I had and still have his long nose, you see.

Daddy went to the emergency room in his leather jacket with nephew Vasyl so they could straighten his nose out, and in the meantime Oskar continued to pester my mother at home.

Mother found this unpleasant, and she giggled and turned away and Oskar said something about "chops" (from that moment on I've hated the word "chops" and can tolerate it only in connection with pork chops and aspic), and he said, "Věrka, you're a saint!"

The way I dealt with my attitude toward Oskar Káhler was that whenever it got close to a name day or birthday I cried hysterically, locked myself in the bathroom, and refused to come out even though Father pleaded with me, beseeched me, and threatened to use his braided red leather whip on me. Finally Father gave in, brought the television set with the big screen over to the small room we'd partitioned off the kitchen, pulled the curtain across the glass door, brought me some salt pork and sausages, and promised me that he and Mother would pretend I wasn't home. He also promised to close the door to the "big" room, so there would be no chance of Oskar's piercing voice penetrating the two doors between us.

When Oskar went from "chops" to "boobs" I left the room. I was shaking inwardly and screamed at him to get out! Out!

He was so surprised I was home, he actually got up and left.

Without a word, my mother began cleaning up the cigarette butts and remnants of salt pork, sausage, and peppered pork flank. Then she said, "That cost us four hundred crowns and Daddy behaved horribly. The older he gets, the more he shows off and the more he acts like a dictator!"

"Hm," I said. "Things will only get worse."

Things only got worse. Father showed off more than ever and was always lecturing someone. But not me. On the contrary. I had absolute freedom. Father lectured everyone in matters of law (because he had never finished studying it) and Subcarpathian Rus, the part of Ukraine that used to be part of Czechoslovakia. How it looked then and how it looks now, even though he hadn't been there in over thirty years.

He wrote fewer poems, but rewrote them constantly on his typewriter. He was retired and had time on his hands.

Also, Oskar Káhler died and his hard of hearing Romka never returned from Switzerland. That's when it started. . .

Chapter Two
Oh! I went drinking on Tuesday and drank away forty oxen

It was 1968. Our class went on strike and painted the benches canary yellow. It was a pastel color, we destroyed it with our ball-point pens, and I went home covered with canary-yellow droplets. Another day we stayed after school and played a game of Truth. I didn't have anything to hide, but I forfeited, and as my "punishment" I had to kiss Michal Šipka. He was short, good-looking, and dim-witted. (Now he's a doctor, a gynecologist, and at the class reunion twenty years later he was suddenly tall, fat, and . . . dim-witted.)

When we left the mountains in the summer of 1968, I was afraid the soldiers would eat my cat. In Prague we saw neither tanks nor troop transports, nothing . . . Calmly, we took a taxi — looking left and right, my cat in my lap — home.

We opened a window — after being away for a month — and stepped back. Right in our house, in our living room, we found the barrel of a tank. The Embassy of the People's Republic of Bulgaria was across the street, and the soldiers were aiming straight at us. They lived there in this tank until the middle of winter. My father would dim the lights and draw the green curtain tight, then make a narrow opening, get out his telescope, and watch them. How they shaved, kept themselves occupied, slept . . .

He was retired and had time on his hands. He stopped having "parties," because he'd fallen out with everybody, and on name days and birthdays only Aunt Olina and her husband Honza came over. They would bring Father's brother, Uncle Stepan, but he was over eighty, showed off even more than my father, lectured more, was more of a dictator, and drank more too.

Whenever he went past his limit he would pee in his pants a little, which made his daughter, Aunt Olyna, who was really my cousin, terribly embarrassed . . .

Yes. That's when it started. Mykhal, Vasyl, Fedyo, Vasylina, Petro, and Anna would all come. Mykhal was over seventy and had a pointed nose and wore a leather jacket. Maybe the very one in which my father got mistaken for a German and a Jew during the war. Mykhal had azure-blue eyes.

Vasyl (he was really Vasyl the First, because he was ten years older than his brother, my father, who was also Vasyl. My father didn't take well to being second — Vasyl the Second —

and he gave himself the nickname Bumblebee. Vasyl Bumblebee) also had blue eyes, as did Anna and Vasylina. I have them too, but they're not so old-looking or pure and innocent, nor are they so blue that they remind one of the sky. Like in Daddy's poems — a blue sky with only the rolling green hills touching it. Blue eyes, which are directly associated with breathing freely.

Though in those days we couldn't breathe very freely.

I took English in school because I had a knack for languages and was convinced that I knew all there was to know about German. But I mainly took it because Martin Duba was in the English class a level higher.

I fell in love with him while harvesting hops. I was over at an uncle of a friend's place and we were helping Martin gather hops and toss the hop-cones into a barrel when he smiled at me and said, "You have a very pretty name and pretty eyes. . ." He was a clever one. Another classmate was in love with him too: Pavla, who I highly respected because she was an outsider and painted beautifully and was intelligent, and I subconsciously thought that if I also loved Duba, then I'd have the same powers, the same intellectual superiority as my artistically gifted classmate.

I tried to look at Duba in a way that would make him understand that it wasn't just my eyes that were beautiful, but everything.

On evenings when it smelled like hops, Lenka and I would role-play together in bed. She was Him — Duba — and I was Me. In the dark I was more beautiful, more clever, more desirable. . .

Lenka spoke as Him and I spoke as Me. We said caressing, erotic things, which I've never heard again since, and we were completely aroused, though we didn't know what that meant.

A day with Duba. Reality, conversations, and glances, it

was all a pale reflection, props. In fact, all along I subconsciously waited for evening, for night, when Lenka would be Him and talk wittily and awkwardly stroke my breasts.

I got eighty points out of a hundred on my English exam, but the principal didn't recommend me for the special English class even though it had kids who got less than fifty points. She justified her action to my mother by saying that one's performance depended not only on one's score and intelligence but also on one's social status. The social status of my supremely apolitical family was evidently such that I was unfit to study English in the special class for eight hours a week and would have to accept four hours in the normal class.

I started to attend the "normal" class and was glad because the "special" class was all children of ministers and ambassadors who had had years of school abroad and spoke English so well that it was hard for even our rather competent teacher to understand them.

Martin Duba started to go steady with Renata the Yugoslav, who was about four years older than him. He carried her purse and bought her berry-flavored drinks at the dairy bar. It made my heart break.

The same thing must have happened to one of Uncle Vasyl's sons — Danylo. Uncle Vasyl came to see us with Mykhal, Petro, Vasylina, and Anna to have fun, to chat, to forget. . .

His only son, Danylo, in the army somewhere far off in Siberia where it was over fifty degrees below and you could openly drink pure alcohol, had fallen in love with a married woman. He lived with her for a while, but when her husband came back she let him go. And he went. Into the forest. Into the woods. And he didn't come out. They found him after several days, but he never spoke again.

He was sent home to Vasyl, and when no one was

watching, Danylo would go out to the meadows where it smelled sweetly of the kind of resin you can chew, up to the mountains, which are wider than they are high and where the grass is green and succulent.

Vasyl the Second, more than ten years younger — Vasyl the Bumblebee — my father, showed Vasyl the First the small pantry full of salt pork, peppered pork flank, and a side of pork smeared with garlic, and had Mother bake a chicken. In Ukraine they only boil chickens. That was how he showed Vasyl the First how sumptuously we live here!

Uncle Mykhal asked about prices and salaries, Vasylina and Anna picked out cashmere scarves, and Uncle Vasyl the First remained silent like his son Danylo, then went back home and immediately died.

In those times it didn't do to be naive. One day Mr. Šindelář went to the principal to complain about an elementary school girl — Daša. Petite, fastidious, with straight-As and dark hair woven into braids. Whenever they took a picture of our class, Daša sat next to me. We held our heads — both with long hair — close together, as if we were trying to protect each other from something. Daša probably had an inkling of what it was. She was a believer, and her father was a Protestant minister.

The Evangelical Brethren in the U.S. constantly sent her family small sums of financial support, which in our circumstances came to dizzying sums, and Daša was the best-dressed girl in the class. She had super-modern dacron skirts and nylon sweaters in the softest pastel colors.

Jealous Janka was Mr. Šindelář's daughter. Her mother (who had gigantic feet and wore men's shoes) took her to Štvanice at five in the morning for ice skating. I went there too.

My mother had a gray cloth coat with a big collar. My father hated it because it reminded him of bat wings. Mrs. Šindelář wore a tiger skin coat.

Skating went pretty well for jealous Janka. She always came in second, right behind the coach's daughter. I came in last. Mother decided she wouldn't come to skating lessons with me anymore. Once, in the midst of a spin with my leg raised, I triumphantly crashed straight into the wall; this gave her something to laugh about for several years.

Our family, taking after father, had rather sensitive noses. Daddy's bled every morning, nephew Vasyl's consistently veered to the right, and after my skating accident mine had a little bump up on the bridge that never went away.

After Mr. Šindelář left, the principal called me and Lenka in. Lenka was the only one in the class from a working-class background. Her mother was a gardener and her father was a butcher, who after his apprenticeship worked in a mine for three months or so. My father knew him and liked him because, during the war, at the butcher shop on Národní Boulevard, he would give him a pig's head without asking for a ration ticket.

The principal asked us what we thought of Mr. Šindelář. We thought he was a fool, and when we returned to class we let everyone know right away. Then we decided to prove to the principal that our classmates' western clothes didn't have a negative influence on us.

The phone rang all evening and our parents didn't interfere, even though they didn't know whether they should fear or admire the solidarity of our class. My father recalled that he even knew Mr. Šindelář. In the distant past Mr. Šindelář was a doctor who recommended people for invalid's pensions. My father didn't get one then and was convinced Mr. Šindelář was a "political swine." He told us to be careful around him.

The next day we all went to school in dark blue Pioneer skirts, Pioneer blouses, and red Pioneer kerchiefs. (I was granted permission to take the Pioneer pledge later than everyone else. The chair of the group, who had so decreed, was Lenka (father-butcher, mother-gardener) of all people, who had pretended to be *my* Martin Duba and who was known for having an ugly chipped tooth and unusually bad skin. I had pretty teeth and clear skin and when we were ten Lenka maintained that if you're a pretty child you'll be an ugly adult and vice versa. And once, I said that playing blind man's buff was stupid and then I actually said that the whole Pioneer organization was stupid because what did we play at every Pioneer meeting but blind man's buff. With the result that about three years later, me and the dropout Ekol ended up standing alone beneath the flag at the Lenin Museum and I threw up on account of nerves.)

To this day we don't know whether our teacher felt the same way about Mr. Šindelář as my father or whether it was a coincidence. In any case, she showed up in a blue skirt and white blouse too, only instead of a kercheif she wore a black scarf around her neck.

Janka Šindelářová, who was wearing tight yellow trousers that her father had brought home with him from a meeting in Italy and a mohair sweater that shed and made me sneeze, didn't make it past the main recess. Her father managed to get to school by the end of the day. This was more serious than mere fashion.

Mr. Šindelář ideologically assailed the principal and demanded that Daša be expelled from the school immediately. He expressed disapproval and a lack of understanding — how could it be possible for a girl whose father is a Protestant minister to get into the special class for intensive language study?

The principal had only two months left until retirement (and until the end of school for that matter), so Daša finished out the year with intensive language study.

The night after we received our report cards, someone wrote, "The principal is an ass!" all over the sidewalk in front of the school. It took us an hour to stamp it out.

So my father was right about Mr. Šindelář.

He was also right about how horribly fat Vasylina, the daughter of skinny Mykhal, who was almost ninety and whose eyes were so blue he saw hardly anything with them, spoke Ukrainian.

Vasylina rang the doorbell, flung herself at my father, mother, and me, and no sooner had we managed to greet her than she gave us all wet kisses. Father assumed an uncertain, but slightly haughty expression, and in her horrible Ukrainian Vasylina said, "Uncle, I still have one more suitcase." You should have heard the word she used for suitcase!

Father pushed Vasylina out of the door and locked it. Only when he fell asleep was Mother able to let her in. Crying the whole time, the fat foreign girl had attracted the attention of the entire building and a neighbor had even given her something to eat.

When I was still in school, Father taught me a simple lesson about the Ukrainian language. I recited it all the time and still do: "The Czech word for notebook is *sešit*, the Ukrainian word is *zoshit* and the Russian is *tetrad'*. Now, which language does Ukrainian resemble more?"

The Czech word for suitcase is *kufr*, the Ukrainian word is *kufor*, and the Russian word is *chemodan*. And Vasylina arrived with a "*chumaidan*"! Eventually Father acquiesced, read Vasylina all his poems, and pointed out the magnificence and the musical qualities of their native language. Vasylina, fifty and overweight due to her bad health, merely sat politely, piously nodding her approval, then timidly said, "I know, Uncle. Kufor! Kufor!" and Daddy finally rewarded her with oranges for her children and also bought four cashmere scarves, each of which had a different colored border.

I was friends with Lesyk Kähler. He was much younger than Romka from Switzerland, who occasionally sent a glimpse of a vacation in Spain, Italy, or Yugoslavia and gave birth to successful-in-the-west but nevertheless slightly deaf children. Lesyk didn't play the oboe anymore. His father Oskar got on his nerves almost as much as he did on mine, but at the funeral Lesyk turned to me and said, "I never liked him, but now that he's dead, it's so weird, really weird. . ."

Lesyk collected foreign records. Romka sent them to him from abroad and they brought him into contact with strange people. Black-marketeers. Only in those days they didn't put them into prison or make movies about them. But one day a fair-haired friend of Lesyk's had about thirty thousand in western currency, and the next he had nothing but eyes so black and blue that Lesyk had to lead him through the streets.

Lesyk was short and his hair began thinning when he was seventeen. He didn't have much on the top of his head, but he let it grow long on the sides.

He taught me to enjoy songs I was too young to remember from childhood — songs with titles like "Shoes Against Love" and "When the Evening Stars Rise Over Český Raj. . ."

Lesyk managed to persuade Romka and her mother to buy him a worn-out Mini Cooper and we took it on our outings, listening to those songs and projecting ourselves into them.

Lesyk had a girlfriend named Jindra who he was embarrassed to introduce to me because she wasn't particularly pretty and wore gray, store-bought clothes, but when he finally did I approved of her because she was so nice.

She spoke in a soft voice and loved animals and children.

I had two turtles at home, and I liked tall Honza, who was in the class ahead of me. He had long, wavy hair, and I had just read a biography of Shelley and decided that Honza was a full-fledged "Ariel."

At the pub Honza poured me a beer and I began to urge him on. He let me to some extent. That "to some extent" was important. I was innocent and was terrified of remaining so. "I love him, He's the one!" I said to myself sagely.

He didn't love me, but when I took him to a play in which they talked about nothing but "that," forced him to come home with me to the little room off the kitchen remodeled for me in earth tones, everything in natural wood with a bed all made and waiting, and nestled up to him and said bluntly, "Well, Honza? Well?" he relieved me of my innocence. Then he fell asleep, exhausted.

When my parents returned from their visit to nephew Vasyl, Mother got hysterical and told me to send him home. I didn't want to. I wanted him to lie in my bed for a while longer, in my room, in our apartment . . . I wanted to have the feeling for a while longer that he was *mine!*

Mother pounced on Father. "Well say something to her! Tell her to throw him out! Have her throw him out! Throw him out!"

But Father's mind was elsewhere. He was arguing with Poljana, nephew Vasyl's daughter (who had studied journalism and had Communist leanings) about Marx, Stalin, and contemporary politics and shaking in exasperation over her left-wing naiveté.

The only thing that bothered Father about Honza was that when Honza left our house to go home, he would see Father lying on the couch in the foyer. My father slept in the foyer, you see. As far as I can remember, he never slept in the same bed with my mother. He could never bear any intimacy! He always said that he suffered from chronic insomnia and kept the light on all night and that he didn't want to disturb us. And since we first lived in a one-room apartment and then in a two-room apartment, and the kitchen (with its wicker chair) was my room, Father really did disturb us. He snored irregularly but vigorously!

Honza left early in the morning. But first he went to wash his hands and face. My father had easily solved his couch problem in the foyer by lying in the bathtub amidst the steam that rose out of the water. He was wearing striped swimming trunks and holding a book of poems by Taras Shevchenko in his hand. (It had just come out and he had bought it at the Soviet bookshop.) The dye from the cover, with a Ukrainian embroidery motif, trickled down father's forearms in red streams and made horrific circles on the hot surface.

Shocked, Honza said good morning, and my father (thrilled at having mastered a difficult situation) said affably in his most discreet voice, which retained only a trace of accent, "Are you hungry? There's plenty of peppered sausage in the pantry!"

The time came when people began to join the Socialist Youth League. Inconspicuously. One after the other. I didn't particularly care, as this was the time they were wearing anoraks with colored stitching and I still didn't have one. Finally I saw one that I liked. I bought the saleswoman some coffee and asked her to wait until I came back with my mother. It was raining hard, and my devoted mother was in the staff room comforting a colleague whose daughter had been killed in the mountains. Her colleague was in tears: the mountain climbers had brought her back her daughter's knapsack from the Tatras — only her knapsack. Mother hurriedly borrowed some money from her and I dragged her to The House of Fashion.

The jacket was medium gray, and I had it for precisely one evening.

At about nine, my eighty-seven-year-old Uncle Stepan came over, his lips red with wine. He wanted to clarify just what had happened in 1933 at the site where he and my father had a timber business. I brought in my jacket. "It cost six hundred!" I boasted.

Uncle Stepan, who had hair like milk and a profile so aristocratic he could have been a model, walked up to me and tore the jacket out of my hand. For a while he just stood there, then he took a pair of scissors from the sewing table and cut.

And cut. And cut again. He cut the jacket into narrow strips and I watched in horror as the plastic fluff and paper wadding came puffing out of my elegant purchase.

By the time he got to the sleeves, he could go no farther. His lips had gone white, the red wine purple, and he said to me, "I wore mine in Siberia for twelve years!"

"And he didn't pay a thing for it!" my father added.

The newly elected chair of the youth league, whose father was one of the most important editors of *Rudé právo*, was speaking over the school's public address system. She was so shapeless, so ugly, so utterly without sex appeal, that the only time she could feel like a woman was when she was reprimanding her attractive classmates. Her deputy was a curly-haired boy, whose father's name, during the troubled years, was written on walls as a traitor to the nation.

When his turn came, he called upon all of the new members to pick up their ID's immediately.

Everyone in our class stood up. Everyone except Lenka (father-butcher, mother-gardener), Eva Boušková, and me. Eva was upset.

"When did you register? When? I didn't know. No one said anything to me! I must have been out sick that day!"

The rest of the students headed toward the door in a disorganized cluster, somehow maintaining a dignified silence. Lenka and I threw uncomprehending glances at one another before class and then we agreed that we were going to act heroically. Every good hero stands alone. Against the crowd.

Or that's what we thought, and we sat there nobly for a tension-filled moment, while Eva Boušková screeched, "Maybe they'll still take me!" and ran out after the crowd.

Meanwhile, the old, honest, and rather boring Latin teacher sat up on the podium, and as he watched the young people filing out for their ID's, said sadly, "I wanted to test that

Boušková. She is weak!"

Marika came to visit with her daughter Anna. Marika worked at a dormitory for railroad personnel and brought us several new government bedsheets as a gift. Her daughter, the forty-year-old Anna, brought souvenirs that were supposed to remind her uncle, my father, of his homeland.

She brought wild strawberries made of pink paper that were attached with wire to wood chips, and a wooden hawk, which when you put a battery in him, would open his eyes and glow.

Father threw the hawk at Anna. The wings broke off, and when I picked them up I discovered that the glowing hawk was even collapsible.

Finally Marika and Anna unpacked something sensible: ten bottles of genuine Ukrainian wheat vodka. Father went off to get some glasses. He asked them to tell him about his native country. His brother Petro had gone off to see friends and was found dead twenty kilometers away in a quarry.

"I see," said my father, expressing neither astonishment nor sorrow.

"If only we all ended that way!"

It was summer. I was friends with my artistically-gifted classmate Pavla. We drew figures ad nauseam using colored markers that the Evangelical Brethren had sent to Daša from America. We spent our vacation together at my aunt's place by the river, in a small cottage that reminded us of our scouting days and where our legendary collapsible hawk fit in perfectly. Our eyes shone in the night because there was no electricity and we read *Eugene Onegin* and told each other that when someone loves someone else, he must love forever, because what else could become of that invested energy, that colossal quantity of strength that is a requirement for love? Is it everywhere around us? Is the air permeated with it and does it fill each of us with its potential for love?

Pavla didn't feel much love around her. After the invasion her mother was no longer allowed to work as a historian and became a cleaning lady, complete with plastic pail and rubber gloves. Her father didn't wait to be thrown out of his job; he had himself certified as eligible for retirement by a well-known doctor and spent all his time writing philosophical treatises on literature. Pavla knew that their phone was bugged.

Honza didn't love me. I looked all over for him in the pubs of Malá Strana. I was embarrassed to go in because the men would always look up at me because my breasts were big for my body.

Once I bought a white hat and put on a plum-blue jacket with huge, red leatherette flowers instead of buttons, and I walked into a smoke-filled beer hall and said to Honza, "I'm not here for you, and I'm not here by accident; I'm looking for my *brother*!"

"You have a brother?!" Honza asked, surprised, since he'd been coming to my little room, which I'd redecorated in red, for two years now.

"Hm," I said coolly. "His name is. . ." I was stuck. "Orest."

I should have known. Honza was ashamed of me.

My parents belonged to the social stratum that may be called the destitute intelligentsia. In any case, because my father was from a large country where the barns were full but there was no education, only sound peasant wisdom (which apparently suggested to my grandfather and grandmother that in these changing times their gifted children should devote themselves to their studies), he attached terribly high value to secondary and higher education. He had aspirations, but his aspirations went no further than a diploma. He didn't wish for a career or material gain.

In the eyes of my father all teachers were unfeminine and stupid. And so he pressured my mother, who was a teacher, into getting a degree in law. She never practiced it, but whenever he introduced her, Father emphasized her title.

We had no money, which caused my mother no end of suffering. Only then did she make references to her education and point out how embarassing it was when she — *a lawyer* — had to borrow two hundred crowns from her colleagues. Daddy didn't like to hear about money. If he had it, he spent it; if he didn't, he borrowed.

The only thing that mattered was that there were sausages and salt pork in the pantry and a bottle of something or other.

In our time of need, he knew he could get things from the Ukrainians who came to us. And he did.

All the Vasyls and Marikas and cousin Mykhal and little Anna too, they all could obtain letters of invitation from my father only if they brought vodka.

Father paid them for it. Probably about ten crowns less than a bottle cost here.

Anna placed six bottles on the cracked kitchen table, which had been painted over with white latex three times.

"Here you are, Uncle," she said meekly.

With a very stern face, which indicated that this was serious business, Father placed three hundred seventy crowns on the table.

Anna pulled out one more bottle.

"And this one is a gift from me!"

Father opened the bottle on the spot and proceeded to drink with Anna until morning.

I was always unhappy in love. With Honza. It was so painful. I followed each of his movements, his eyes. . . He didn't care about me, but my love was so strong that it occasionally overpowered him. Sometimes he made love to me and I would tell Lenka and Pavla and Daša even the smallest details.

Once I irritated Lenka so much that she forced me to draw up a contract. She browned the edges of a piece of heavy paper over a fire, and I had to sign in blood that I wouldn't mention Honza more than ten times a day.

It didn't work. I was so full of passion, longing, and pain that I ceased to be myself, I existed purely through Honza's words, gestures, eyes. . .

I wrote bitter, poetic and at the same time cynical verses, and my father patiently typed them up, making plenty of punctuation errors. Then he added the date to each poem and put them in the black folders that made up his files.

Once we went to Zbraslav for fruit. My mother wanted to make preserves, and someone with a good heart, perhaps the father of one of the students she tutored in Czech, let her take home whatever she picked.

We picked greengages and regular plums and "butter" pears and we had baskets full of fragrant and overripe fruit and my father's old khaki knapsack (the one he wore in the year 1933 when he opened the timber business with Uncle Stepan. After three days they went broke, for three days they didn't eat, and then they went home. To Ukraine.). Now with the knapsack full of green plums, yellow plums, and butter pears he was on his way home to Prague. It was hot. The Sunday bus was packed and after a while juice began to leak out. It streamed down his back onto his trousers and made his shirt sticky. Wasps and bees swarmed around him and no one could chase them away because our hands were full of free fruit.

At last we were home. Mother couldn't find her keys. She had to put everything down on the doorstep and rummage through the fruit.

Once inside, father stooped and threw off his knapsack.

"Why are you throwing it around?" Mother asked.

Daddy, sweet and sticky, just looked at her for a while.

Then he started jumping on the knapsack. For about ten minutes he jumped up and down on it defiantly.

Then he jumped up and down just as energetically on all the baskets.

That winter we had no compote, only jam.

Though retired, Father worked part-time at a cafeteria called The Lamb. He drew beer from the tap and made sure everyone got full measure, and he would bring home his tips in the lid of a shoe box. It was full of ten-heller coins, five-heller coins, one-crown notes, two-crown notes, and occasionally even a five-crown note. It was very useful to me. I went to a small wine-cellar in Bethlehem Square several times a week. The manager was a tiny old Jew, and his tall wife worked in the kitchen. A liter of wine cost twenty-six crowns. All of my girlfriends went there. Lesyk and his friends from the technical school went there too. We were a fun-loving gang and the little old Jew liked me a lot (yes, me in particular!).

Once I went to see Father at the cafeteria and I watched him pour beer and count money awkwardly, hurriedly, uncertainly, making unbecoming faces. You could see right away that he'd never been a bartender or a waiter.

One day a cleaning woman came up to him and and said, "I could die of thirst today, Doc!" Doc! Well, my father, who didn't have a doctorate, beamed, and what is more, he gave the sly, loud-mouth cleaning woman, who called everyone who wore glasses "Doc," a small beer for nothing.

When we were walking along Spálena after his shift, he told me how people steal at that cafeteria, how they cheat the customers on the salads and eat the leftovers. He also told me that he definitely had over two hundred in his box, and gave me fifty crowns right then.

I was about to go to the wine-cellar on Bethlehem Square,

but who should be coming in our direction but the manager, the little old Jew. He smiled broadly. I had never seen him smile before. In the wine-cellar he was always prim, proper, and glum. I was startled. I was afraid my father would think it strange that an old man would smile at an eighteen-year-old like that.

We were just about to pass him when my father suddenly stopped, and the old Jew did too. And they embraced.

He had once owned a big hotel in the east of our old republic. It was called the Užhorod, after a town in Transcarpathia, and it had real silverware and red plush upholstery.

Evil tongues claimed (several years later, the Jew died and the wine-cellar on Bethlehem Square was turned into an unfriendly restaurant where mostly Germans ate) that the Užhorod was not a hotel. That it was a house of ill-repute.

My father was a frequent guest there.

My collection of love-related outcries won first place in the "Young Socialist Poet" competition. Inconceivably, the Olympic runner Emil Zátopek handed me my diploma. He asked me what the most important thing in life is. I argued for various things. Happiness, love, satisfaction at work. . .

Zátopek kept shaking his head. I cleared my throat. "Life," I said. Emil Zátopek smiled in agreement and shook my hand.

Honza didn't even look at me. Lenka and I secretly took his keys out of his jacket in the school coatroom and broke into his apartment.

We knew that he and his parents had gone to their summer house. We bought red wine and I followed Honza's tracks through that beautiful, large apartment near the Prague Castle. I rummaged through his drawers and saw his old toy car and soldiers, and found a love letter.

"Why don't you even look at me?" it said, as if I had

written it. "None of the others around me is the least bit worthy of you. Love, Rébi."

It was about two o'clock in the morning and I unscrupulously called all of Honza's friends. "Who is Rébi?" I asked, holding my nose to alter my voice.

No one wanted to tell me.

But I figured it out. At the bottom of Honza's dresser lay a photograph of the fiery Yugoslav girl who had lured Martin Duba away from me. On the back of the photograph was the inscription: "Forever yours — Rébi."

Lenka tried to cheer me up. She pulled on some high boots she'd found in a closet, cracked a horse whip in the air, and shouted, "Yipee, the best of life is yet to come! Yipee!"

The neighbors were soon knocking on the walls; then they rang the doorbell, but we wouldn't open up and then we did and who should we see but Mr. Šindelář, who lived in the apartment next door, and he stared at us and we at him and in the end I burst into tears and Mr. Šindelář took us to his apartment and his wife with the colossal feet in men's slippers made us coffee. Then Mr. Šindelář went back to Honza's apartment with us and we put it in order and Mr. Šindelář took the keys we'd stolen from Honza's pocket and promised he'd return them and say he'd found them in the entrance to the building.

His jealous daughter Janka had gone to her aunt's in Germany to practice her German, which we'd studied together at school. And she stayed.

I brought up figure skating in the children's ice revue and Mrs. Šindelářová showed us some color pictures. We roared with laughter because Janka had on a costume. A cow's tail stuck out from under her little figure skating skirt.

Towards morning we walked home singing, "Janka was a cow and is a cow to this daaaay!"

And once in a while I vengefully added, "And that Rébi, she's a cow too!"

To which Lenka said soothingly, "You bet she is."

About a year later I wrote a story about that night and won the "Young Socialist Prose Writer" competition.

I signed up to take journalism.

At the exam I whispered the answers to the black-haired boy next to me, and then I wrote a two-hour essay on the theme: "Why I Want To Be a Journalist."

I wrote a number of pages and still had time left to read them over to myself. Suddenly I felt faint.

"Do you think this is enough?" the black-haired boy next to me asked, showing me one miserable page on which I immediately saw a howler.

"I think so," I said, and at the end of my essay I wrote, "And that's why I don't want to be a journalist!"

Marika came to visit with her daughter-in-law, who, like me, was named Olga, and who looked like me and was the same age. All her front teeth were metal, not gold, and their bottom halves were oddly enough covered with silver. She spoke no Ukrainian, only Russian, and complained about how they spent all their time standing in lines and if she hadn't had two pigs at home her family wouldn't have had anything to eat. Her nineteen-year-old hands were rough and almost black, and she had an occasional silver hair.

She was wearing a track suit, with a skirt over it, and rubber boots. Father refused to go out with her and Marika. I didn't go either.

I went on a work brigade for two weeks with father and Doctor Vakula. We pumped and measured water as seasonal workers for the Geodesic Institute.

I brought a suitcase full of Prague Spring literature, and only occasionally, rarely, did I peek at my Russian textbook because I had exams coming up.

"The dictatorship of the proletariat," I babbled as I devoured Aškenazy and Pick and Kundera, and my father played chess with Doctor Vakula.

He and my father were old, and I sometimes heard them arguing.

"You're white!"

"No. *You're* white!"

"You're mistaken, dear Doctor. *I* am black. I'm always black."

Both of them snored and I had to stuff cotton into my ears and put on a close-fitting rubber swimming cap as well.

We came back. Marika and her daughter-in-law were about to leave. They had the most ordinary front-hall runners around their necks. My mother had the largest one.

Father didn't help anyone. "The next time you come, wear more decent clothing!" he said nastily.

The Ukrainians bowed fearfully, and Marika's daughter-in-law was afraid to say goodbye in Russian.

"Do mushrooms still grow there at our place?" Father asked.

"They do, they do!" the Ukrainians said, bowing enthusiastically, and Father said condescendingly, "You could have brought some! And not this stuff!" pointing to the bakelite lantern with its varicolored tulips.

From that time on we always had a canvas sack full of dried mushrooms hanging in the pantry. They were light brown, cut into halves, and had a piquant aroma.

DANIELA HODROVÁ

from **Perun's Day**

translated by Tatiana Firkušný and
Veronique Firkušný-Callegari

Miss John

Up until now, she has only seen the church tower from the
ground, when Mother or, later, Jacob took her for walks, or else
from her bedroom window. And now she is to conquer it, the
way mountain climbers conquer alpine summits. She is not in a
wheelchair, she is walking, the way she used to. They are scaling
a ramp — Father Slabý, behind him Miss John, and behind her
two Portuguese men who, like her, wish to go up into the tower.
The architect, Plečnik, had the strange idea of building not a
stairway, but rather a peculiar, narrow ramp reminiscent of the
bridges suspended from ropes that span gorges and sway beneath
pilgrims' footsteps. An uneasy and vertiginous sensation is
enhanced by a noticeably flimsy railing, which could scarcely
serve as support; the two Portuguese obviously share her feeling.
Miss John does not understand their words, spoken in low voices,
but every time she looks back, their facial expressions confirm her
suspicions. Father Slabý alone does not seem to be experiencing
the slightest anxiety. He proceeds with unshakeable resolve,
walking nonchalantly up the middle of the ramp, in contrast to
the three of them, who are trying to stay as far away as possible
from the abyss that deepens with every step; from time to time

At last they find themselves level with the clock. But what a surprise it is for Miss John to discover that, although its face is at least twice the size of the one on Old Town Square, the clockwork is no bigger than a carry-on suitcase. Father Slabý points to the clock. In his gesture there is pride as well as respect for the clockmaker's work. Miss John realizes that the time on the clock is nonsensical — five minutes to eight. She knows with utmost certainty that their meeting with Father Slabý was for a quarter to four. The ascent, even at the slowest possible pace, could not have taken as long as that. The time on her watch, incidentally, is five past four. Is the tower perhaps ruled by a different time — by the time of the Great Clockmaker?

The two Portuguese do not seem to have noticed the strange chronological phenomenon. When Miss John stops for a moment to catch her breath, they pass her. Apparently they can't wait to see the view of a city that is said to have something in common with Lisbon. Miss John is now climbing with great difficulty, as if at this altitude the air were getting thinner. Or is it her illness flaring up again? Just short of the tower's summit, every step becomes extremely difficult for her; she does not understand how the Portuguese men could have completed the last leg of the ascent with so much ease. Is it because, unlike her, they are not carrying within them the experience of a different time? Finally even Miss John is standing on the uppermost landing of the tower. She can see the two Portuguese walking from one window to another, looking down at the city, their expressions surprisingly indifferent: the view does not seem to have enthralled them. At that moment the sound of flapping wings fills the air. Miss John stares in amazement. A bird of prey, a falcon or an eagle, alights on Father Slabý's arm and pecks some bread crumbs out of his hand. Father Slabý is looking at the bird with a kind and appreciative smile. The raptor seems to belong here, too.

Miss John can see the city below — Vyšehrad, Hradchin Castle, the red cupolas of Karlov. From this vantage point the new television tower appears incredibly close. She also takes a look at the building she lives in. It seems different somehow. It takes her a moment to realize that there is no falcon or eagle sitting on top of the gable. Father Slabý motions to a small seat hung on ropes. She could bet her life that it is a seat from a merry-go-round, or a child's swing, just like the one she used to swing on at her friend Luke's. Father Slabý couldn't possibly be expecting them to swing on it? Surprisingly, the two Portuguese don't seem taken aback by the father's mad idea, they are as excited as children. One of them is already getting into the swing, Father Slabý fastens him in, and then the seat begins to descend into the deep gullet of the tower. Father Slabý is turning a crank that Miss John did not notice before, perhaps because she was so engrossed in looking at the city. Shortly the swing re-emerges and the other Portuguese gets in. Finally it is her turn. No sooner does she get into the seat than all her fear, surprisingly, vanishes. The swing sways slightly as it is lowered, but keeps descending very steadily.

The descent is completed, Miss John's feet touch the ground. She wants to wait for Father Slabý to lower himself (who would turn the crank though?), but the swing remains on the ground, its four ropes softly vibrating. Miss John walks out of the church. The Portuguese men are standing around in front of it in lively conversation, perhaps about the city that reminded them of Lisbon. As Miss John shakes their hands to say goodbye, they introduce themselves to her: Fernando Pessoa, Álvaro de Campos. The time on the tower clock is now ten past four, just like on her watch.

Miss Matthew

Every time the streetcar goes through Klárov, past the Malostranská subway station, Miss Matthew checks to see whether the portrait, actually a double, man-bird portrait is still there. It is, it hasn't been painted over yet, although the sun-rays have faded it a bit. Rain might wash it away, but there has been a period of drought, for many long weeks not a single drop has fallen upon the city. The preacher sees, even in this, a sign that the end is nigh.

As the streetcar travels along the tree-lined avenue, past the Belvedere, toward Hradchin Castle, Miss Matthew thinks she has caught a glimpse of Mr. Hořínek through the trees whose branches occasionally lash the streetcar windows, she recognizes him by his wide-brimmed hat. Mr. Hořínek is heading for the Castle. And then suddenly Miss Matthew remembers that there's a full moon today, it's the day crazy people keep streaming into the Office of the President; surely by now a whole crowd has gathered in the courtyard in front of the entrance. By evening the Heart, as the mailbox for letters addressed to the President is called, will be overflowing. What a day this will be once again, oh, what a day!

As Miss Matthew passes the castle sentry, one guard sticks out his tongue at her. Have the guards gone crazy today, too? She was not mistaken. Scores of people have already gathered in front of the entrance to the Office. She thinks she recognizes the father of the murdered girl among them, he has been here once before, and the Doll Lady is already waiting there too, her coat bulging over her stomach. Some greet Miss Matthew respectfully, but she tries to pass through quickly as possible, preferring not to look right or left lest the many-headed dragon, looked at askance, should pounce upon her and devour her.

The guard who lets her in and then quickly locks the door behind her is shaking his head: What's going on today? — There's a full moon, Miss Matthew explains. A discontented murmur, becoming progressively louder, is heard from outside, the dragon is growing impatient. Today the President will have to enter the Castle through the underground tunnel, Miss Matthew muses. Hopefully he has been warned about the full moon, Mrs. Kriseová surely keeps track of it. Miss Matthew, due to a kind of sixth sense, can always tell the exact moment the President is coming through the tunnel into the Castle. The sound of the approaching car cannot be heard from her office, but suddenly something in the atmosphere changes, the air begins to vibrate like a taut string, and she knows he has arrived. She imagines him getting out of the car in his slightly clumsy way, walking down the carpet to Plečnik's elevator (this elevator is strange — circular in design), going up in the elevator. . .

The moment is now, the air around her has begun to vibrate. He came through the tunnel, so Mrs. Kriseová had warned him, thank heavens. At the same moment, the noise in the courtyard becomes twice as loud, as if the many-headed animal has somehow guessed it has been deceived. And then, as the guard lets them in, they begin to enter, one after the other, the plaintiffs and the petitioners, some of them are content to put their letters into the Heart, for others that's not enough, they clamor to see the President. And now the Doll Lady has run in pulling a doll out from under her coat in which she carries it around, she wants to show the President her baby. As soon as Miss Matthew has seen her out, the father of the murdered girl grabs at her sleeve, gesticulating wildly, nobody's going to tell him it wasn't the President's fault, she got killed by someone he gave amnesty to, someone who stabbed her thirty-three times, let the President pay him a million for the life of his daughter. With great effort, Miss Matthew manages to convince the father of the murdered girl that his request must be submitted in writing. And then Mr. Hořínek strides up to the counter, ceremoniously doffing his hat; almost with relief, Miss Matthew listens to the tidings he brings to the Castle on a regular basis. Among the crazy lot, he is her favorite. He, too, wants to go straight to the

President with his ominous tidings, as if the President didn't hear enough of them from his advisors; but when Miss Matthew explains that the President is not here today, Mr. Hořínek just nods his head as usual and slowly departs. And when she calls after him, telling him he's forgotten his hat, and then hands it to him over the counter, Mr. Hořínek fixes her with a sad, knowing look.

Miss Mark

Miss Mark went to see Miss Gregor. Miss Gregor lives on one of the highest floors of an apartment house in Prague's North Town high-rise complex. She is still quite confused by the visit, she doesn't know what to think about the whole thing; wasn't it just yesterday that she ran into Miss Malátová, the gym teacher, who told her Miss Gregor was dead, that she had died of cancer two months ago, that she had heard it from Miss Gregor's mother? But Miss Gregor cannot be dead, because Miss Mark has just visited her; most likely the teacher mistook Miss Gregor's mother for the mother of someone else from their class. Miss Mark is trying to think whom the teacher may have mistaken Miss Gregor for. Miss Luke? Miss Paul? Or Miss Matthew? But not long ago she had caught a glimpse of Miss Matthew among the spectators in Wenceslas Square, it was certainly her, although for some reason Miss Matthew had pretended not to see her.

And while mentally going through the list of her one-time classmates at the Perun Street school, wondering which one may have passed away, she suddenly realizes that she left her handbag in Miss Gregor's apartment. To her amazement she now sees that the building actually consists of several structures in various styles, something she had not noticed before; the structures are stacked one on top of another, in no apparent order, some of them are repeated on a smaller scale. Somewhere up there lives

Miss Gregor. She could get over losing the handbag, but it's a snakeskin one; she got it from Lorenzo, Lorenzo was an Italian she used to go with. There are two ways to get up to where Miss Gregor lives. At first Miss Mark chooses the one that seems shorter. It is shorter but, on the other hand, very steep and rickety. The staircase consists of volumes of some international encyclopedia, the books are piled up in such a way that there are only very narrow surfaces left to step on, barely big enough for one's toes. The incline of the staircase is practically vertical. Miss Mark climbs up the first few book-steps, she can feel them shifting under her feet, the encyclopedic staircase is in danger of collapsing. It is clear that she will have to go back and take the longer route.

And now it becomes apparent that the building is in fact a labyrinth. Miss Mark passes through various halls and rooms, one of them reminds her of the Green Room in the Palace of Culture, where they had their tenth class reunion. She also passes through various alcoves from which corridors rise in all directions. Some of these lead into what seem to be airshafts ending in hinged skylights, one can see the dark blue sky above them. She retraces her steps over and over, but in the meantime the rooms have changed, they look different from the way they had when she left them moments ago. Once again she ends up in an airshaft, the only way out is through the men's room; passing through here earlier, she hadn't noticed the white urinals along the wall. She slips past a man who stands there urinating slowly and with great concentration, the man turns his head but continues urinating, undisturbed. He looks vaguely familiar, maybe he is one of her countless lovers. She resumes her ascent, and once more the corridors, the walls of which are covered with repetitions of the letter E scrawled in red ink, turn into dead-end passages. And here Miss Mark finally realizes that she will never succeed in getting back to Miss Gregor, the snakeskin handbag is irrevocably lost. She walks out into the daylight. She seems to have come out on the opposite side of the building, or maybe while she was inside, the whole structure changed. From here the building looks like a giant sailing ship. Her gaze slips to the ground: in a pool at her feet (it must have rained while she was inside) lies her handbag. Could Miss Gregor have tossed it out the window? Yet it's also possible that she has had it on her the whole time, hidden under her coat, and that it has now slipped out. As she wipes the handbag off with her handkerchief a letter begins to emerge from the black-and-white snakeskin pattern — E.

What could this E mean? The realization strikes her like a bolt of lightning: E as in être. At one time Miss Mark used to tutor Miss Gregor in French. In those days Miss Gregor lived in Vinohradská Street, in the corner building, where now there is a night club in the basement. Miss Gregor simply could not manage to learn how to conjugate the verb être — to be — even though they went over it again and again. And, for all Miss Mark knows, she never did learn it. Suddenly it dawns on her that Malátová, the schoolteacher, was not mistaken, Miss Gregor did die — she died because Miss Mark hadn't taught her how to conjugate the verb être, not even in the present, let alone in the future tense.

Miss Luke

—Luke! Luke! Who could be calling her by her last name, who could be running after her? She turns around almost unwillingly, as if sensing that turning around might fundamentally change her life. But she has no choice; even if she didn't look, Miss Matthew would catch up to her anyway. Miss Luke recognizes her, although they haven't seen each other in years. They used to be classmates at the Perun Street school. There was a time that Miss Matthew visited Miss Luke almost every day, but once they were out of elementary school they lost track of each other. Miss Matthew had in fact stopped visiting Miss Luke even before that, because of the accident. Miss Matthew liked to swing on Miss Luke's swing, Miss Luke even suspected her of coming just because of the swing. One day Miss Matthew got herself swinging so fast, she flew out of the swing and landed on her head. Blood was running down onto her bright green sweater. Miss Luke visited her at the Karlov hospital, she remembers the huge room divided by a glass panel. There was a row of beds in which children of both sexes, from the youngest to those who were practically grown up, lay side by side. Miss Matthew's head was encased in a helmet of bandages. When she saw Miss Luke, she turned to the wall. She never visited Miss Luke again.

Now they are facing each other, Miss Matthew slightly out of breath from running after Miss Luke. She seems to be genuinely glad to see her, she must have forgiven her for having fallen off her swing, most likely she has forgotten about it. But Miss Luke hasn't forgotten it, and running into Miss Matthew like this seems odd to her; it's been barely a week since she brought the old swing out of the pantry, she swings on it every morning now. —Is your last name still Luke? Miss Matthew is scrutinizing Miss Luke from head to toe. Miss Luke nods. She, too, is scrutinizing Miss Matthew, and she finds her greatly changed. Where is the shy creature who used to stand in the doorway, begging to be allowed to swing a little? She even feels a sense of superiority emanating from her that was never there before. At one time Miss Luke longed to bear Pablo's Spanish family name, but Pablo turned out to be married and ended up returning to Barcelona, leaving Miss Luke with a Czech last name in Prague. Miss Matthew isn't married yet either, but soon perhaps. . .

With these words, it seems to Miss Luke that her classmate lights up, she must be very much in love. Miss Matthew begins to tell Miss Luke that some time ago she ran into their classmate Miss Paul, and no, she isn't married yet either, but she's seeing somebody, although he may turn out not to be the right man. They could all get together if Miss Luke wanted. Then Miss Matthew tells Miss Luke about the Prophecy, and is especially glad to be able to talk about it to her, to her old friend. It is certainly no coincidence that they have all been running into one another. The other day she saw Miss Mark and now she has run into Miss Luke. —There will be no death, says Miss Matthew. There won't? thinks Miss Luke with bitterness. What good is it when death has already come and taken her and Pablo's child? And Miss Matthew invites Miss Luke to come along with her, it isn't far, just a little way down the hill. And Miss Luke goes, without much deliberation, although she fears that the resurrection Miss Matthew is raving about with such enthusiasm will not affect her child, but what if it does. And maybe she goes with Miss Matthew because just today she has again caught a glimpse of the dazzling hall, its walls studded with precious stones. It occurs to her that perhaps Miss Matthew has already seen the hall but kept it to herself, that this was why she always longed to swing so much. And it was why she pushed off so powerfully once that the swing flipped over and she fell out: because she wanted to stay in the dazzling hall.

The streets of the Žižkov quarter, through which Miss Matthew is leading Miss Luke, strike her as being totally unfamiliar; maybe she has never set foot in them, though they are actually not far from Lucemburská Street, where she has lived since childhood. Does she promise not to disclose to anyone the place Miss Matthew is leading her to? Also she mustn't reveal that they know each other, they'll say they met in the street, it's best that way. Stumbling alongside Miss Matthew, Miss Luke nods in agreement, she won't say a thing, though this request seems odd to her. Miss Matthew doesn't stop talking, she is spewing a torrent of words at her, words that don't seem to be coming out of her own head, yet Miss Luke keeps listening with curiosity. She wonders: can this really be Matthew, the meek little sheep? When Miss Matthew stops talking for a moment to catch her breath, Miss Luke says: Do you remember the swing that used to hang in our doorway? No sooner does she utter the words than she realizes she shouldn't have mentioned the swing; Miss Matthew suddenly curls up and becomes the poor little sheep again, a trickle of blood runs down her cheek, onto her white woolen sweater

Miss John

The fuzzy black dog comes right up to her bed. She asks him: What do you want here? —*Nada*, he says. Miss John freezes. A talking dog? A human turned into an animal? What does *nada* mean? She gets up and steps over to the window. The church is still lit up, so it can't be all that late. Or did they forget to turn the floodlights off today? Up in the tower, where the cross sticking up from the green apple of the Earth points to the heavens, she seems to see some shadows moving. It occurs to her that perhaps Father Slabý has climbed up to the roof and is feeding her building's bird of prey.

The animal grows restless and begins to growl. Maybe there's someone out in the hallway, neighbors returning from the theater. No, the dog seems to notice the activity up in the tower; when Miss John turns back to the window, he gives a sharp bark. Two human figures are moving about up there, now Miss John can see them distinctly. They are standing on either side of the apple, like two heralds, the apple with its cross now appears like a gem on top of a huge escutcheon. The dog begins to tremble, its fur stands straight up. Miss John asks him what's wrong, but he has lost the power of human speech.

When she looks out again, she can see the apple moving, inching slowly along to the edge of the tower, then keeling over, for a moment the cross gets into a horizontal position, the apple teeters, then finally topples, and comes hurtling down from the tower. Miss John covers her ears but, surprisingly, there is no deafening crash, the apple lands on the roof of the nave softly and soundlessly, like a balloon, bounces up and down a few times and, the cross having broken off somewhere along the way, rolls down in front of the church.

What kind of prophecy lies hidden in this nocturnal scene? Is it perhaps an image of the world's destruction at the end of the millenium after which Christ's kingdom on earth shall come, as proclaimed by Jehovah's Witnesses? They have visited her several times, but she has never let them in. The wolf shall dwell with the lamb and there shall be no death, nor wailing nor sorrow either, nor shall there be suffering, for everything that has been shall have passed. Suddenly she has an idea. She starts going through her *Dictionary of Symbol*s, Jacob brought it to her years ago from Southern France. She was not mistaken. A circle topped with a cross is the sign of the world and of life, as well as the sign of an intellectual soul, of the spirit liberating itself from matter. If the cross is turned to point downwards, it becomes the sign of an instinctive soul, of the spirit's fall into matter. Is this perhaps the beginning of a new cathabasis — the descent into matter and death — for mankind, for this city, for Miss John? And who were those two up in the tower? The twins from the cosmological myth, symbols of morning and evening, of equilibrium, but also of — equivocation? And suddenly Miss John understands. It was the two Portuguese, of course. That's why they went up into the tower with Father Slabý the other day, they were not interested in a view of the city at all. They are the ones who threw down the apple, in order to wake the city up from its sleep. And that's why they sent her the dog. After all, it spoke their language, it said *nada* — nothing.

PAVEL BRYCZ

Dance on the Square

Translated by Julie Hansen

It was a bang-up funeral. The likes of which the little town of Teplá at Mariánské Lázně had never seen before. My brother was being laid to rest. Martin Besmertnych, 1969-1992. My name is Andrej Besmertnych . . . Forgive me for crying.

I had just started living with Leona when my brother did it. Leona was a little brunette with firm breasts and cherry nipples. When you bit into them you could be sure you would strike pits. During lovemaking she would sigh beautifully *ohhhh* and call out "*mmmmore*" — never just "more" — sometimes it sounded like "*mmmmoooore.*" Those long sounds were important. You don't know nothin' if you don't know that. In short, she was like a cancerous growth to me. Since I couldn't tell her this, I told her I LOVED her.

My brother didn't know I was living with Leona, and so every other day he would call me at Klára's. I have only the best things to say about Klára . . . But I won't.

Klára had an answering machine, so as soon as she had returned from her vacation in Geneva, where her husband-to-be introduced her to his parents, his motor boat, and the Red Cross, she brought me a cassette at Leona's. Klára and Leona can't stand each other, so Klára threw on her fanciest rags from Switzerland in order to put Leona to shame. But Leona had just been trying on a black Italian dress by Foletti for my brother's funeral, so the contest at the door was a draw. Cats. Tigresses. Girlfriends of mine.

"I've got some messages for you from Martin, one whole side of the cassette . . . Maybe he had something important to tell you."

"Airhead," Leona mumbled with hostility.

I stood beside Leona, facing Klára in nothing but my underwear, and looked on mournfully. Maybe I looked ridiculous, but I'm not ashamed in front of my girlfriends.

"Has something happened?" Klára noticed my sadder-than-sad eyes.

"Martin's dead. He set himself on fire in the bathtub," Leona shouted at Klára. It seemed like too much information to me. I took the cassette from Klára's hand and went to another room. I wanted some peace and quiet. My underwear was cutting into my behind. So what, I didn't care. I'm not ashamed of anything in front of my girlfriends.

Once in the room, I put the Sony cassette into a Japanese tape player. I think Leona got it from her parents for graduation. She taught me how to turn it on, record music, and play cassettes. Graduating is good for something, at least. I love all of those people who were so foolish, they enrolled in school in order to learn something, who were born to live, even though, from the very outset, their parents were against it. Once a crazy sculptor, a friend of my brother's, was sculpting his parents for the town park. He wanted to depict them standing before the abortion committee. He started with the committee and it turned out well. Lifelike. Just the committee. He began boozing as soon as he'd finished it, and when people asked him why he didn't sculpt his parents, he said on one occasion that it didn't interest him, another time that he couldn't remember his parents and couldn't get a model, and the third time he just gave up and died. Now no one will ever sculpt his parents, but the abortion committee stands as one in the park. Fortunately, those who aren't in the know won't recognize them as the abortion committee.

My brother spoke to me from the Japanese tape recorder graduation present. He told me several things which are worth recounting and which I won't comment on. It would only make me more depressed:

"Andrej, Andrej, when are you ever gonna be home? Are you avoiding me? I bet you're with someone else. All I have to say is that I liked Klára. Really. You looked good together, and besides, I was used to her. Listen, Andrej, I really hate talking to the phone. This is stupid. . ." A pause, and then my brother went right on talking. As it was, between those two monologues, he had to live through a night and day of despair without me.

"Do you remember, Andrej, our conversation at the botanical garden by the lake with Victoria lilies? I asked about women and you answered: I don't trust women. Then how come you get along with them so well? I wondered, and you said, Maybe for precisely that reason. . ."

I didn't want to interrupt my brother, but this upset me. I jumped up from the sofa and pressed the black stop button. I felt terrible. I always say we're only human. Both my brother and I are swimming in the world, each in his own way. And we don't know how to swim.

I recalled our childhood. From the depths of my mind I hauled up a sunken Titanic. It was heavy as my heart, but suddenly there we were: Martin and Andrej, two boys with strawberry-blond hair. We sat facing each other in a bathtub filled with water that was cooling down; we were pushing each other with our knees and reaching out with our little wet nail-bitten fingers for each other's wieners. We were five years old. I was circumcised at birth.

We played with matches. We tried to set water on fire. Trying to set water on fire would fascinate us over and over again.

Actually, our childhood is linked with fire throughout. We were pyromaniacs. Little mammoth hunters. Danger was every-where except in flames. We longed for fire and clapped for joy whenever we got to light a cigarette for our mother. The first poem Martin gave me to read, after coming over and declaring himself a writer, was about childhood and fire. He came over on his twentieth birthday, and not knowing how to inform Mother that he had left the university, he sighed in his quiet voice: "I'm a writer. With immense courage I write down on paper things I don't have the courage to live." Then he couldn't speak anymore and burst into tears. That's just the way my brother was. The poem he wrote is lying among my things in one of Leona's drawers, and moves a lot. It's short, like my brother's life:

> In childhood
> fires light
> night's darkness

People bullied him because of his pure nature. Our father started it by humiliating him and treating him like a girl. I think father was perverse. But Martin was too pure even to be a girl. He cried when he was supposed to, and laughed ingenuously. He never learned the ropes. He never learned to tell the truth only when it was convenient. He told it so much it was pathetic. When he was challenged by a teacher to say why he didn't like him, he said, bless his heart, that the teacher shouldn't look at the girls in such a peculiar way. That caused a big fuss. The teacher invited one of our parents to school. Father wouldn't pass up the opportunity, and so those two perverts talked shamelessly about Martin right in front of the frightened boy. Father referred to Martin as HE and kept repeating: "Fortunately I still have one son left. Fortunately I still have one son left."

I don't know why he bragged about me, considering that at an early age I had created the ideal hypocritical mask for myself. Father always wanted something from me and I learned to fulfill his wishes in such a way that, with time, I was able to predict what he would want. It all rested on a single banality. Father was an advocate of strength. Whenever my brother and I got into trouble, he would call us and thunder, "Choose for yourselves! Either I give you a thrashing, or else you don't go skiing during winter vacation." I knew what he wanted to hear. I said, "I'd rather you thrash me, Dad." I didn't come out with it just like that — I muttered it through clenched teeth. As if there were some kind of horrific struggle of motives going on inside me. It wasn't true. Father softened up because I could take a blow like a man. It didn't even come to a thrashing, and naturally I got to go skiing. Martin burst into tears, wouldn't utter a word, got a licking, and wasn't allowed to go skiing. I missed him horribly . . . And so I learned to live without him and his truth.

When my brother was eleven and in the sixth grade, he came and told me that he couldn't stand the other kids at school anymore. I understood this. A person like my brother had to be alone everywhere he went. Education is dangerous in that wolves run with wolves. Martin's classmates were growing up to be little Nebeskýs (that was the name of the teacher who looked at the girls), little Nováks, Besmertnychs, Dušeks — all just like our parents.

So I made the most foolish decision of my life. I was twelve and decided to flunk into my brother's class in order to protect him. That boycott was a blast! Overnight I turned from a first into a fifth. Finally I had to stop going to school altogether, because the spineless schoolmasters would have gladly let me slide by, probably out of nostalgia for my past record. I think it was the first crazy thing I did out of love. I realized much later, from similar situations, that's what it was. From the sixth grade on through high school I played the diver so that Martin could walk on water. I won girls and friends, so that all these people would accept Martin, too. And they did. Always as my brother.

Several years ago I read some reflections by the sculptor who made the sculptures in our town park. I have adopted one of his thoughts as my own: "Love? It's only for the strong . . . It's for Hitler." Thus spoke and wrote the man who died before sculpting his parents.

Leona came into the room. I could feel her gaze on me, and it wasn't something I wanted to feel. Leona stepped up to the large mirror and looked at herself, at the way the narrow black skirt clung appealingly to her gorgeous little ass. Leona has a backside like an onion. I always cry when I cut into her.

"Undress," I yelled and immediately began taking her clothes off. In front of the mirror, I pressed against her from behind. I don't know from whom or on what occasion she got that mirror. Nor do I want to know.

"You're crazy, we have to go to the funeral," Leona whispered into my ear. She only wanted to stick her pink tongue into it, anyway.

As soon as we had finished and Leona reached for her mourning clothes, I said, "Don't you get dressed. I don't want you at the funeral."

Leona gasped and, still smelling of our love, ran into the bedroom, slammed the door, and shouted, "Bastard."

I grasped the sex manual that I got for winning the pole vault in high school, and threw it at the bedroom door.

"You spoiled the afterplay, which, according to what it says here, my dear, is tactless! It's my funeral," I muttered to myself and for the last time I pressed PLAY on the Japanese tape recorder.

> "If you're not here
> I'll die
> if you're here
> we'll die together
> don't go. . .

". . . I'm on the edge here, Andrej. Remember the philosophy of my friend the sculptor, who made those hideous people in the park? Once he told me that after all the words, books, learned wise men, after all the scientists, philosophers, artists, and politicians this planet has hosted, there remained for him a single, categorical imperative which was given to him not by any Kant from Königsberg, but by a swarthy Brazilian guy talking into a French television camera in a TV documentary about Carnival in Rio: 'I don't have enough dough to shine my boots, so I sold my boots. I don't have any food. I don't think about women. What can I do when sleep won't come? At such a moment, as in the days of my childhood, my old dad appears and says: 'Go and dance on the town square.' Dance on the square! You know, Andrej, maybe I'm headed for heaven, but before I get there, heaven will have disappeared."

Those were my brother's last words to me. The tape ended, and I put on the suit I'd worn to dancing lessons. That suit from when I was sixteen still fit me well. I tied my tie in the bathroom on the train. It had a mirror.

When I came into the compartment with my tie tied, a weird girl was sitting there. Completely different from my mother and from all the girls I'd met before. She was an albino, completely without pigment — white hair, white skin. She wore large, completely dark glasses and a purple turtleneck, so it was obvious she had no breasts. Boyish breasts. I thought of my brother.

Just so you understand, Martin wasn't any faggot. He admitted to me that he had slept with a man once or twice, but that man was the sculptor from our town. If you had known those two and how desperately lonely they were, you would forgive them in an instant. Martin didn't do well with girls, and he didn't do it with anyone other than the sculptor. It wasn't out of love, but could a saint find joy in such a thing?

And yet he loved, like a swallow who won't survive if her companion leaves her. He loved with a love that belongs to fire, and therefore would have led him all the way to hell!

In the winter, five months before his *autodafé* in the bathtub, my brother came out of his voluntary exile in the town of Teplá. We went to the sauna. In the sweat room I said to Martin: "You're circumcised?" I was stunned.

And Martin answered cheerfully: "I wanted to be like you, Andrej."

This seemed rather dubious to me, and I mused over what kind of clinic he had it done in. Strange thoughts were racing through my head, and Martin looked at me. It was 230 degrees in the sauna, and the sweat was streaming off us. There was no one there but the two of us, and Martin, my brother Martin, said to me, "Andrej, I'm not your brother, I'm your sister. . ."

I know it might sound laughable, but I didn't feel like laughing at the time.

"Martin. . . ," I gulped.

"I know what the sculptor wrote and how you adopted his thought as your own. I understand you both, how well I understand you, and yet . . . love and Hitler is an intellectual joke as far as I'm concerned. An excuse. I LOVE YOU!!! I LOVE YOU, ANDREJ. I FEEL IT, JUST AS I SAY IT!!! I love you LIKE A WOMAN, like no woman has ever loved you before! You don't trust women! Trust me!"

If you don't want to read any further because this is about love, skip a few lines, send me some potato seedlings so I can take up another trade, or else give it to children to read. Children understand everything. They will understand that I was infinitely aroused by the sight of my unhappy, naked brother, and so we left the sauna and went home.

While I was repeating to myself that I trust my brother (and if I had had a walkman I would have played his messages from the grave, but I didn't), I looked deeply into the dark glasses of my compartment mate. I still couldn't find her eyes, though.

As if she had read my mind, she said, "Are you wondering why I have such dark glasses? You see, I'm not blind, but for me the sun's one giant atomic bomb. You don't feel anything with those blue eyes of yours, but it would burn my eyes out."

"I didn't know the sun was so cruel," I joked ineptly, but

then I immediately added: "Thanks for alerting me to the danger posed by the sun. Thanks."

I would have liked to chat longer with that colorless girl, but the train came to the Teplá stop and I had to get off. I waved at her from the platform. She had long ago disappeared from sight but I still had her stuck in my head. Just like my brother.

I arrived at house number eight, where I met up with Martin's landlady and our mother.

"Your father didn't come. He left a message saying he has only one son," my mother said weakly. She must have cried the whole night through.

"It's good he no longer lives with you, Mom," I answered, and I kissed her on the forehead. "Neither do you anymore," Mother countered reproachfully.

I turned to the landlady and said, "Let's go."

Not only were all of the Besmertnychs Ruthenians, they felt Ruthenian, too. And so it wasn't a coincidence that we managed to arrange an Orthodox service for Martin. A sloshed priest came up from Karlovy Vary. He swore like a sailor, prayed in Old Church Slavonic, and out of his carelessness with a candle a curtain in the funeral hall caught fire. When my brother was finally deep in the ground and Mother and the landlady were preparing the funeral dinner, I telephoned Leona. Leona is an incredibly smart girl, she's studying science. I wanted desperately to find out what the deal was with albinos and the sun and what was up with the girl's eyes.

After Leona had figured out that I didn't want to make up with her, but was really only interested in the albino question, she blurted out: "Well, why not, Andrej, you go together like two peas in a pod. A red-eyed, pigmentless albino will live to be about twenty, and your love is just as ephemeral."

I hung up. Talking on the phone about the mortality of other people is not my idea of fun. Maybe it was stupid of me to hang up on Leona like that. I'm not ashamed of anything at all in front of my girlfriends.

I could hear excited voices coming from the kitchen. I couldn't make out the words. Suddenly Mother flung open the door to the room, pale and upright as an altar candle, and exclaimed, "The cemetery's on fire, Andrej."

My memory keeps meeting up with everything unbelievable in life. The cemetery was on fire and Mother told me, "The firemen are already on their way. All of Teplá is there. Who would believe such a thing, a fire in a cemetery?!"

While speaking these words, she turned toward a little girl, an angelic, blond-haired creature in a white dress, who pattered into the room.

"Little Věrka ran here to tell us." Mother stroked the blond's head. It was touching.

Someday in the future I will learn how six-year-old Věrka lost her father, and I will always, whenever I think of her, try over and over to be as tender as my mother.

Věrka's father was the police officer at the emergency desk. When the telephone in his office rang shrilly, it always meant the death knell was tolling for someone. Once he lifted the receiver and the cheerful voice of his daughter addressed him, "Hello, Daddy."

"Haven't I told you, sweetheart, that you can't call me at this number?" he scolded her.

"Only people who need help can call this number, right?"

"Yes."

"But Daddy, Mommy and that husband of hers want to take me away to Antarctica. . ."

"You're mixing things up, it's to America, your mommy's husband has work there!"

"Is it closer than Antarctica, Daddy?"

"Closer, my darling, of course it's closer. But please hang up, I have to work."

"Dad? Will you come visit me in Antarctica?"

"Of course I will," the police officer answered, and then he hung up the receiver.

Someday in the future I will learn of this fragile fate, as well, and because of it I will forget two or three Jewish anecdotes. The unbelievable will shake hands with my memory. But today I don't know anything. I see the girl who came to inform my mother and me that, in the cemetery where he rests, my brother's heart was burning once again.

My mother and I, together with the landlady and blond Věrka, walked to the cemetery again. There were lots of people there. They were looking at my little brother's grave almost piously. (There hadn't been so many of them the first time.) All the flowers and wreaths had been reduced to ashes, and the fire had even ignited the cemetery's chestnut trees. The air smelled of burning, and I realized that for the first time ever I was standing in a cemetery that had been deserted by doves and pigeons. Ever since childhood, cemeteries have been linked in my mind with the cooing of doves. A peculiar change. My brother is dead and childhood has ended.

We returned to the funeral dinner. We ate silently and slowly. Mother had set a place for Martin. She had made stuffed beef rolls with rice — Martin's favorite dish. As a child he could eat it till he keeled over. He wouldn't even touch the food if he were alive today. He had been a vegetarian for a year already. The landlady left after the meal, and so Mother and I were alone. Neither of us dared to clear Martin's plate from the table. Thoughts ran through my head. I wished for my brother's sake that death would not end everything, that it would even *hurt*, but that something would remain, and that he would once again meet the sculptor — his friend and philosopher. Mother turned on the radio. World news. We didn't even hear it. I cried. Tears glistening like gemstones rolled down my face. Maybe it wasn't manly, but I cried. I'm not ashamed of anything in front of my mother.

Five years from now, if eleven-year-old Věrka returns home from Antarctica, and if she still understands Czech, she'll be able to read a story about love by Andrej-Martin Besmertnych. I, a twenty-nine-year-old man, will write it — if I don't first commit suicide in a manner worthy of my brother. The story will tell of love for a girl without pigment, and I would like to warn all great people of the possible dangers of the sun. And if all those fabulous people have enough will and joy, we will meet on the town square — to dance, as best we know how. . .

"DANCE ON THE SQUARE!" Martin and the sculptor call to me from far away. I obey them.

"WHAT ELSE AM I SUPPOSED TO DO?!"

PAVEL ŘEZNÍČEK
from **Animals**

translated by Malynne Sternstein and Jason Pontius

I

Kadavý hesitantly opened the door of the Weathervane and cautiously looked around. The place was full. A cloud of bluish smoke lolled about the ceiling, and for a second it was impossible to see through, for it fell from ceiling to floor like a military blanket. In a coat, by the fireplace, sat an old man. He was smoking a cigar, a Camarillo. This made Kadavý's entrance easier: The old man was certainly somewhat ragged, and his jacket was held together with two gigantic safety pins, yet he gave the impression of a biologist or physiologist or something better (maybe he *had* been a biologist or a physiologist once, but who knew if he had even gotten his degree), and this helped Kadavý with his decision: the Camarillo and the biologist/physiologist would certainly not go into a questionable tavern. He entered, removed his hat, and said hello. The tavern owner responded affably. The old man by the fireplace drew on the Camarillo and smiled. Kadavý turned to him and asked: "Is this seat free?"

"Why yes." The old man smiled. "Of course. Sit down." He cleared a place for Kadavý on a stool by the fireplace and again drew on the cigar. Kadavý sat down next to him, still in his coat; he had forgotten to take it off, pleasantly surprised by the kind reception. He sat there in his winter coat, his hat in his lap, and scrutinized the old man. He was somehow familiar. He looked like the old gardener Geburtstag. When he was a boy, he

215

and his friends used to climb the fence and steal the old man's radishes. No, no, it couldn't be, Geburtstag was already pretty old when he had chased them off with a stick, he could have been seventy, which would make him around a hundred today. And this old man looked more like seventy-five. It was definitely not Geburtstag, so it had to be someone else. Could it be Řehoř, who worked his pole so beautifully on the ferry? It could have been the ferryman, because when he used to ferry Kadavý he was fifty, so he could easily be seventy-five today. The owner interrupted his contemplation. In a kindly voice he asked what Kadavý would like.

"Give me the beef soup," Kadavý said with a smile. The manager smiled and said that he was glad to be of service. "Will there be anything else, sir?" He showed his healthy white teeth.

"Perhaps you would be so kind as to recommend something," said Kadavý.

"Well, sir, we don't have a large selection," replied the smiling manager of the tavern, "but there's rabbit in cream sauce, leg of venison, and deer goulash. You know, the market is in town today, so there's all the game your heart desires. The food here is of course first-class."

"Well, give me the rabbit in cream sauce," said Kadavý, smiling again. The old man next to him nodded in agreement, as if to indicate that Kadavý had made the right choice. The manager bowed and drifted off to the kitchen to place the order. The old man nodded and sang something to himself. Kadavý tried in vain to figure out where he might know him from. Could it be Ambrož, the driving instructor? It could be, he had the high forehead of a thinker, his noble white hair flowed around his ears, and his velvet coat, though held together with safety pins, indicated that he had once traveled in high society.

The old man suddenly leaned over to Kadavý and whispered into his ear: "Every state or action is unequivocally delimited by the totality of its conditions: the law of causality (like causes—like consequences) is thus transformed into a law of conditionality: like conditions find "expression" (*Ausdruck*) in like phenomena, unlike conditions in unlike phenomena." He drew again on the cigar.

Kadavý shuddered and said nothing. The old man likewise said nothing. He finished the cigar and tossed the butt onto a bench. Kadavý stared ahead blankly.

The manager broke the silence by bringing the beef soup. "Your soup is coming, young man," he called from a distance.

Kadavý shuddered. He hated to be called "young man," for he was no young man, he was already past fifty; though he lived like a bachelor and was contented, he hated the phrase "young man." However, he didn't want to spoil the prevailing good cheer, so he kept quiet. The soup did, indeed, come. Steam rose from the bowl, smelling of tamarisks beneath the stars of some exotic land; Kadavý felt an unchristian hunger. The manager stood before Kadavý and looked around with embarrassment.

"You see, we don't have tables, everyone eats off his knees, that's just how it's done . . ."

"But I have my hat on my knees," Kadavý replied sadly, looking the manager in the eye.

"Put the plate on your hat; that way, the grease won't soak through onto your knees," advised the manager.

"But the hat is new," protested Kadavý.

"Well, if the hat is dearer to you than your pants, do as you like," growled the manager, and the smile vanished from his face like a snowstorm suddenly bombarded with X-rays. The old man beside him grew somehow serious. It was as if the room had suddenly darkened. A few barflies surrounded him menacingly, their hands in their pockets and cigarettes in the corners of their mouths. Kadavý took the bowl of soup from the hands of the manager and placed it without protest on top of the new hat on his knees. In his winter coat, which he had forgotten to take off, he was vigorously sweating. But suddenly it was as if the room

217

had lit up. The stones fell from everyone's hearts. The kind smile returned to the manager's face, and he announced he would return in a moment with the rabbit in cream sauce. The locals took their hands out of their pockets and returned to their cards. Kadavý ate his soup on his hat (he had to admit, it was quite good) and did not dare look up. It seemed that he could hear the old man's cunning laughter. But perhaps it only seemed that way. The old man looked so dispassionate! In all likelihood, he was a philosopher. Philosophers are dispassionate. Philosophers are free. Philosophers have no master. Cunning is not the master of philosophers. Kadavý continued to eat the soup, looking neither right nor left. The old man beside him began to chuckle unpleasantly. So it was cunning after all. Some philosophers are cunning . . . for Kadavý this was a new discovery.

"You know, Occam's razor would work best for this," noted the old man, producing a doll out of somewhere.

"Occam's razor?" sighed Kadavý, and the spoon fell from his hand. "Yes," said the old man, "if you knew Occam's work 'Tractatum de imperatorum et pontificum potestate' or 'Summa totius logicae,' you would know that it is useless to do with much calculation that which can be done with little. That is Occam's razor . . ." said the old man, trying to close the blinking doll's eyes.

Kadavý stood and set his bowl on the mantle. "Excuse me, something's not agreeing with me, I'll be right back."

"Of course, of course," said the old man, still pushing on the doll's eyes.

Kadavý spent a few moments in the bathroom. When he felt a little better, he headed back to his soup . . . but what was this? . . . he couldn't believe his eyes . . . the old philosopher was actually spitting into his bowl of soup, which he had left sitting on the mantle; then, with gusto, he stirred the spittle with the hand of the doll with the blinking eyes. He probably wanted to keep a clean conscience: he washed his hands just like Pontius Pilate.

Kadavý was stupefied; he looked like the bastard child of Lot's wife, or like a dried-up crow's beak. The old man hadn't noticed Kadavý; with gusto he now stuck the entire doll into the bowl and stirred the soup with it as if it were a spoon. He spat again into the bowl, stirred it in with his own finger, and composed himself.

Kadavý hesitantly walked over to the fireplace and picked up his bowl. The old man acted as if he didn't see him and again became preoccupied with pushing on the doll's dripping eyes. Kadavý sat down and placed the bowl on his knees. Again he looked around forlornly, as if, with his eyes, asking for help.

"What's the matter, you don't like it?" asked the old man sweetly. "I suppose not very much. Just eat it, it's healthy — and nutritious. And don't forget the hat," he added.

"Excuse me?" asked Kadavý. He didn't understand what the soup had to do with the hat.

"Don't forget the hat, that's my advice," the old man said sweetly once again, stroking the doll's dripping head. He had already succeeded in closing its eyes.

"The hat . . . why?" asked Kadavý again, not comprehending.

"Our tavern manager doesn't like to be opposed," the old man growled angrily. "He already told you to eat the soup on your hat, didn't he?"

"But this hat was new, and now look at it," Kadavý protested feebly (indeed feebly, because he had suddenly become afraid of the old man and in general of the entire tavern).

"New, not new," growled the old man, "here we're not accustomed to this sort of blither-blather. So put it on the hat, or do we have to help you?" wheezed the philosopher, turning blue.

The manager appeared behind them: "Is there a problem, gentlemen?" he asked.

"This bum doesn't want to eat on his hat as you directed, Mr. Záruba," the old man complained, choking with the effort.

"But, but, Mr. —"

"Kadavý," Kadavý introduced himself quickly. The manager growled out of the corner of his mouth, "Záruba," and continued: "Now, Mr. Kadavý, our guests listen, they don't make speeches. Will you eat on the hat or not, I am asking you for the last time. . ."

"But of course, why not? I'm happy to comply," stammered Kadavý, "but this man. . ."

"This is Mr. Max Verworn, the founder of condition-ism," the manager Záruba said, deferentially introducing the old man.

"Every state or action is identical with the totality of its conditions, from which it follows that scientific knowledge of an object is equivalent to the knowledge of all its conditions," said the old man, bowing. This was the second proposition of conditionism, and old Verworn was thoroughly proud of it.

"This Verworn spat into my soup, and on top of that he even stirred it in with his finger," Kadavý complained, his voice shaking. Then he pulled out a handkerchief big as a carter's canvas, and blew his nose.

"What?" the old man said defensively. "I would never be capable of such a base act. It seems, sir, that you are overstating things somewhat. For such a lie you deserve to be punished. I have never in my life stirred anybody's anything with my finger, as sure as my name is Max Verworn."

"Mr. Verworn is right," echoed a bearded regular who was sitting some distance away, incessantly chewing his lip. He was heavy-set and freckle-faced, wore a white miller's jacket and clutched a heron feather in his hand. It wasn't clear why he had the feather (perhaps for the same purpose as those Roman emperors: when they had overeaten and wanted to make room for still more, they tickled their throats with a feather and disgorged all).

"It's true, Mr. Verworn didn't stir Mr. Kadavý's soup

with his finger, but with the doll's hand. I saw it clearly, I'm not blind, or sick in the head either," the fellow continued. "Mr. Verworn is a respectable old man, and he would never descend so far as to put a hand in someone's soup."

"But after all, gentlemen, as you must see," Kadavý whispered, "if Mr. Verworn was stirring something in my soup, then he therefore must have spit into it . . ."

"A little spittle is no big deal," opined Záruba. "The thing is, you have to eat the soup, otherwise you will give us the impression that our establishment is not to your taste. And we know how to deal with such people."

In confirmation of his words, a small circle of locals encircled Kadavý. They had gaudy red scarves around their necks, cigarettes in the corners of their mouths, and hands in their pockets. None of them had shaved in at least ten days, a friendly-looking bunch. Kadavý looked faintheartedly around him.

"And so, the hat . . . what about the hat?" Verworn needled him maliciously.

"Yes, what about the hat?" asked the barflies, dragging on their cigarettes.

"The hat . . . will you put the hat on your knees?" the manager asked icily. The barflies dragged again on their cigarettes. Old Max Verworn took a cigar out of his chest pocket and nervously lit it.

Again Kadavý looked apprehensively around him.

"So, will you put the hat on your knees, or not? Will you put the plate on the hat, or not?" hissed Verworn.

Kadavý was looking around him like a trapped animal. There was no crevice for him to slip through. The locals had formed a barricade of malodorous bodies. Escape was completely impossible; of this Kadavý was quite sure.

The manager was pale as the wall. Max Verworn smiled cunningly and sucked his cigar.

Suddenly Kadavý saw before his eyes a bloody curtain,

and everything turned red. He jumped up and shouted,
"I will never put my hat on my knees! Never!"

*   *   *

IV

Smoke rose from the open windows, and on a stretcher the
paramedics were carrying a body, covered with a white sheet,
through the open gates. An old, corpulent lady was being led
from the building. She was wringing her hands, and between her
individual sobs it was possible to make out the sentence, "Dr.
Římský hanged himself . . . Dr. Římský hanged himself. . ."
Indeed: the body on the stretcher beneath the white sheet
belonged to Dr. Římský, the well-known philanthropist and
benefactor of the poor. Alarmed pedestrians stopped and crossed
themselves. Dr. Římský, who wouldn't hurt a chicken . . . could
he have done harm to himself? No, it wasn't possible, this was
surely some ugly dream from which the townspeople would soon
awaken and see once more the plump, red-faced man waddling
about the city in his usual duck-walk checking up on patients.

"He wouldn't hurt a chicken, but himself . . . yes. Ah,
such is life . . ." commented some old man in a velvet hat. "Even
so, even so, it's a sad thing," said the schoolteacher Fermanová,
looking at the doleful spectacle.

The assistants (for there was no longer any need for
paramedics) in black coats, crows, carried the stretcher to a black
car and slammed the rear doors. They hopped in the front and

the car sped off. The old woman, who turned out to be the housekeeper of the deceased Dr. Římský, threw up her hands and fainted. A few compassionate people picked her up from the ground. "The doctor hanged himself . . ." she whispered when she came to. "The doctor is no more."

"It happens to all of us," said Fermanová compassionately.

"But not in this way, madam," the housekeeper lamented. "The doctor could have lived among us for another twenty years," she sobbed.

"And you don't know what got into his head?" asked the schoolteacher, an old bony, bespectacled owl, for whom scandalous gossip was the most beautiful thing in the world.

The housekeeper hung her head. Then she looked around and whispered: "I would tell you, but I'm not sure that I can."

"Don't be shy, Mrs. Vavřínová, you are among friends," the eager Fermanová whispered. The housekeeper hesitated. She did not want to show her cards . . . She knew what she knew. If she told, people wouldn't believe her; but it was all true.

The crowd dispersed slowly. The black car carrying Dr. Římský disappeared into the distance. Smoke still rose from the windows of the doctor's apartment. It was ash-blue, but there were no flickers of flame, so there was no worry of fire. The schoolteacher looked at the housekeeper with curiosity. The latter looked around and whispered to the teacher: "The doctor was hung by animals!"

Fermanová rolled her eyes and said to herself, "The woman is out of her head. It's no surprise, such a tragedy . . . she was the doctor's housekeeper for twenty years. Římský was a bachelor . . . now she's babbling, because she doesn't know what will become of her. . ." But this wasn't what she said aloud: "Yes, Mrs. Vavřínová, the doctor was hanged by animals," she said to Mrs. Vavřínová in correct Czech, and she stroked the poor housekeeper's face.

The housekeeper only trembled and said, "Madame schoolteacher, you surely think that I am mad. Yes, the doctor was hanged by animals. I saw it with my own eyes, and I must insist that it is true . . ."

A terrible thunderclap rang out, as if to confirm the validity of her assertion; the schoolteacher looked around and saw a ten-year-old boy who had just popped a paper bag. So much for the thunderclap. And so much for the assertion of the crazy housekeeper that the doctor was hanged by animals.

The housekeeper leaned over to the schoolteacher and again whispered: "The doctor was hanged by animals; it is true. The doctor created them, and then they turned on him. I told him to give it up, but he didn't want to listen."

Fermanová rolled her eyes again. Well, that's the living end. Dr. Římský created the animals, and in the end they hanged him. The poor, poor housekeeper; perhaps she ought to call an ambulance.

But suddenly her eyes popped out of her head. The smoke from the windows of the doctor's laboratory had ceased, and a giraffe with sparkling eyes was poking its head out. Around its neck it wore a dazzlingly white scarf and on its head a *chapeau-claque*. The schoolteacher crossed herself. Then the massive gates swung open, and out came a strange procession. At the front marched goats, completely green, with purple lips and golden horns. Before them rolled sheafs of incense, like bundles of sticks, and they gave off a most pleasant scent. Then came a fox and a lynx. In their paws they held a sexton's candle-snuffing pole and they were laughing their heads off. The schoolteacher crossed herself again. After the fox and the lynx came a steer. He was eating a canary cage: he didn't seem very interested in the canary, he liked the taste of the wire better. After him waddled two giraffes. They had long overcoats the color of salt and pepper, and gave off the characteristic odor of a Hamburg café. They were blue all over, like the beaches of the Azores. In their muzzles they held a Hamburg café.

The animals left the building by twos, arm in arm, as if on some sort of field trip. At the same time, the schoolteacher lifted a finger to remind the animals not to make so much noise. But the animals only turned their hairy and downy heads with scorn, and each pair spit at the teacher. Her blood froze. Such blatant impudence left her completely numb. In some of the animals she seemed to recognize former pupils and certain townspeople . . . no, it wasn't possible that the pharmacist was in the form of a fox or a lynx, or the teacher a goat, the furrier a chicken . . . he would have taken the form of something shaggier, something with fur, not a feathered chicken . . .

And the procession of animals continued. It seemed that it would never end. Green parakeets, blue ferrets, red echidnas, marble-white baboons. It seemed to Fermanová that she recognized herself in the heap of severed hooves and paws which a gilded anteater was carrying . . . no, it wasn't her, it was only the paws and eyeglasses of an anteater. Then there was a terrible crash on the stairway. The animals had dislodged a kitchen cabinet. The animals had dislodged the laboratory fixtures. A few feathered rowdies dragged the custodian, an eighty-three-year-old man named Sádecký, out of the building by his hair. He was so rattled by all this that he didn't even struggle. The animals knocked him around just as they had the cabinet, and all Sádecký did was let out a few soft groans. From his lips came a bloody foam. "You'll kill him!" shouted the schoolteacher. There was nothing she could do. Some furry skunks grabbed her too by the hair and dragged her along the pavement. Pedestrians stopped and crossed themselves. The animals marched on slowly and majestically, not taking notice of anybody. The feathered and furry menials dragged Sádecký and Fermanová by the hair at the end of the bizarre procession. Struck dumb with horror, neither of them uttered a sound. They made the occasional rattling noise, or sighed, but they didn't put up any sort of fight.

The schoolteacher suddenly realized that the animals were dragging them out of town, to hang them as they had Dr. Římský. The procession continued its menacing journey with pomp and circumstance. From time to time the gilded anteater sounded a bugle, the marble-white baboon clanged cymbals. The fox and lynx constantly giggled about something. The one-eyed steer looked for his other eye. But it had already been lost long before in some mousetrap, when it had wandered away from the steer's eye-socket and set out on its own path through the world. Well, for an eye to play the mouse doesn't pay! The steer had sworn that he would find that lost mousetrap which had deprived him of his eye, and then life would be sweet again. The trap peeked out from a corner and craved the other eye. But the steer didn't know this yet. The trap joined the line of animals, considering itself one of them. And yet, in their midst, it caught a few of them; it was something of an amorous union, the mice and trap forming a single object, a single legal entity. . .

And the animals marched through the town. Ahead of them rolled some plates. Nobody knew why. Not the animals, not even the plates themselves, were completely sure. The animals tried to push the plates aside, but the plates pushed back. Increasing their pace, the animals chased after the plates; they'd show them. The plates started to stampede. The marble baboon crashed the cymbals in a frenzy. The plates became alarmed and began to go even faster. The animals too became alarmed and ran like mad. However, no one let go of Sádecký or Fermanová. Dragged by the hair, they felt as if their souls were slowly leaving them.

"This is base, vulgar murder," the teacher managed to shout, and then she fainted. Nobody heard her, nobody paid any attention; they were too busy chasing after the plates. The gilded anteater blew on the bugle. The kitchen cabinet, which they had dragged with them, roared as if being eaten alive: "Cagliostro, Cagliostro, where are your veins that I might drink? Cagliostro, give me your consumption." But consumption was sitting on the anteater's bugle and blowing into it along with the strange gilded animal. The anteater sometimes inflated the consumption, and then the sound of the horn was especially blaring. When the consumption saw that everyone was racing after the plates, it jumped down from the bugle. The cabinet slammed itself down and refused to be dragged any further. In the blink of an eye, all the feathered and furry rowdies threw themselves upon it and clawed it to pieces. When Sádecký saw this, he didn't say a word. Almost all his hair had been pulled out, and pieces of skin had peeled away from his head. The plates raced on. Then suddenly they stopped short. The animals, who had not expected this, tumbled past them. The entire monstrous procession crashed into the dust. The plates laughed boisterously. Then they began to trample the animals. They jumped all over them with obvious pleasure. They were plate-sadists. The animals could only struggle feebly and groan. The gilded anteater blew the bugle furiously. The marble-white baboon broke the cymbals apart out of sorrow and covered his ugly face. The consumption joined in on the side of the plates; it skipped with obvious delight from muzzle to muzzle, stomping on their loathsome snouts.

Sádecký and Fermanová lay unconscious beneath the mass of animals; fortunately, they couldn't see or hear. And the plates stomped and stomped until nothing was left of the animals' bodies but a bloody tangle. But then a few of the boldest animals shook off their stupefaction and began to jump all over the plates. The plates let out a cowardly squeal and did not defend themselves. The roles had been reversed. The animals trampled the plates until all that was left was a bloody kasha. The gilded anteater blew victoriously into the bugle. The marble-white baboon regretted having broken his cymbals apart. He uncovered his ugly face and stomped on the plates until porcelain feathers flew. Then a couple of the plates lost their intestines — this was not at all a pretty sight, so the animals stopped. They sat on the ground and licked their wounds. The baboon found one of the cymbals and licked it. The other cymbal kicked him in the ass. It was a touching picture, something like the return of the Prodigal Son. The consumption began to dissemble and change sides again, supporting the animals. Fortunately, they hadn't noticed its treason.

The mass of stomped-upon, disgraced animals stirred: it began to undulate, to swarm, to roll about. Then it came apart. At the bottom, as if in a crater, lay the custodian Sádecký and the schoolteacher Fermanová. The animals looked them over inquisitively. The plates, all bloody and trampled, weren't interested. But the animals were interested in what they were going to do with the captives or, better yet, prisoners, as the echidna put it. The marble-white baboon kept licking the cymbal. The gilded anteater blew into the bugle. The consumption scratched the back of its head. What to do with the prisoners, this was completely clear.

"We hanged Dr. Římský, we'll hang these two as well," pronounced the iguana, who had occasionally styled himself a specialist in Roman law. The anteater blew the horn in agreement. The marble-white baboon struck the cymbal against his head. Fermanová and Sádecký fainted.

They had been born under a bad sign. So it goes. . .

MICHAL VIEWEGH

from **Sightseers**

translated by Alex Zucker

How Did Max Ever Get the Idea of Writing a Novel That Takes Place Entirely on a Sightseeing Tour?

Max couldn't remember anymore exactly when he first got the idea of writing a novel that takes place entirely on a sightseeing tour to a foreign country — it was 1993, probably sometime in the spring, or maybe it was summer. While even he himself wasn't able to give a straightforward answer to the question of why he had chosen precisely this topic, he had begun to be attracted to it more and more. Whenever he imagined the protagonists of his next book, God knows why but he saw them boarding charter buses, having a smoke at highway rest stops, or unpacking suitcases in hotel rooms. He spent long evenings jotting down all kinds of compositional ideas, outlines of prospective scenes — and more and more often he found that they were exclusively scenes on a bus or a beach, and that all of the invented characters he had been making the necessary notes on were without exception participants in a fictitious sightseeing tour. At this point he knew he would in fact write his sightseeing novel, regardless of whether or not he could sufficiently convincingly explain his initial obsession.

There was, however, a certain logic to it: above all, he had always enjoyed traveling. After Czechoslovakia's borders had finally opened in late 1989, he spent the next two years enthusiastically undertaking every one of the then virtually obligatory, exhausting bus tours to Passau, Vienna, Venice, Paris, and London; later he also visited Italy, Slovenia, Denmark, Finland, Israel, and even one of the small islands in the Caribbean. Although all of these were more or less nothing but banal sightseeing excursions, Max's travels represented for him an unusually adventurous, remarkable, and enjoyable variation from his otherwise quite settled, unenjoyable, and basically unremarkable life. He had spent the last three years shut away either in a publishing house office or at home in front of his computer, and so it sometimes seemed to him that if he had experienced anything even halfway noteworthy in the past few years, it was on these tours.

Ignác was the first person to whom Max confided his intention to write a novel with the working title *Sightseers*.

"A novel about people on a sightseeing tour, you say?" Ignác remarked thoughtfully. "All right then, dear Marco Polo. But — forgive me my asking, Dr. Holub, Poet-Traveler — why?"

After all, Max was definitely not, and never had been, what one would call a traveler, Ignác objected. Wouldn't Max's travel experiences seem rather run-of-the-mill compared to the experiences of all those countless adventurers who routinely hitchhike across the U.S. or roam around the Far East? After all, Max was a mere rank-and-file tourist who — like many of us — had been on a couple excursions to Paris and the Adriatic since the revolution.

"First of all, of course it's not going to be a travelogue," Max contended, "and secondly, look at how I live now. Shut up alone at home writing for days on end. And if I do get out in the evening with anyone, it's almost always disgusting literary types like you. Poets. Deviants. So when do I get a chance to meet any normal, healthy, ordinary human beings I could write about? Only on two occasions," Max answered himself: "When the mailwoman brings me a registered letter, or else on a tour. The only people I know at all are sightseers."

"And the mailwoman," Ignác reminded him. "Why don't you write *Woman with a Mailbag*?"

Underneath Max's exaggeration was a grain of truth. Just in the last four years he had undertaken a total of fifteen different trips on which he had met countless people: bus drivers, tour guides, children and their parents, married and unmarried couples, teenagers, successful and unsuccessful entrepreneurs, students, retirees.

One politician and his family.

Two young homosexual men.

A man with a videocamera, whose marriage fell apart during a sightseeing trip to Copenhagen.

A courteous roadworker and his wonderful family.

Another man, who gratified himself during night stops on the way to Italy (he always pretended to be urinating but secretly watched the women who didn't dare go too deep into the dark, feces-filled woods and meekly relieved themselves behind the not exactly mighty trunks of the nearest spruce trees).

A man with an inflamed red complexion, who spent the entire day in Vienna patiently holding up his dead-drunk father.

A kind, hard-of-hearing retired lady, who died on the bus coming back from Italy.

A married couple in Paris whose two children had years ago burned to death.

A cheerful obese lady from Teplice who for nearly an hour stood having her portrait done by a street artist in Venice — with Gérard Depardieu at her side.

Another lady who confided everything terrible about her life to Max over coffee at the Hotel Kriváň, only to say with a guilty smile: "But I must be keeping you. . ."

And the Slovak trucker and his little boy at a rest stop near the French border. They sat on little folding stools on hot, dusty asphalt in the shade behind the truck, the father warming up some food on a propane stove. The sun was too high for the shadow cast by the truck body to cover them completely.

"When are we going to see Mommy?" the son asked.

"Don't talk to me about Mommy!" the father snapped.

And dozens of others.

Some trips and sightseers Max had only heard about.

The Guy Across the Aisle

Last fall Max got together with a former college class-mate of his at Gany's Café. She had gotten married two weeks earlier, so Max expected her to talk about the wedding and her husband. They had barely taken their seats, however, when she said she had to tell him about her vacation in Spain.

At first Max couldn't understand why she attached so much importance to the trip.

"And sitting across the aisle from me was this nondescript, sheepish guy, a bit over thirty," Max's classmate recounted. "Your typical pushover. Besides that, he seemed old and just not of any interest to me: puffy, sleep-deprived eyes, rumpled hair, face full of pimples — you can imagine what a crazy bus trip it is. In short, I wasn't interested in him at all."

She brushed her hair off her forehead. The waiter came to take away the empty glasses and asked if they wanted more wine.

"Yes, thanks," said Max.

"He had a spot on his fly."

"The waiter?" said Max. "Or the guy?"

"The guy," she said with a smile. "One night at some piss stop he turned to me and asked something — where we were, or how long we would be stopped, some stupid thing, I can't remember exactly what. All I know is he had a little wet stain on his fly. — Sorry about the details, but I want you to see it as

232

much as possible the same way I did at the time."

"It's okay," said Max. "Go on."

He recalled that at that exact moment she threw up her arms.

"Actually, that's it. You see: I wasn't interested in him. I found him repulsive," she said.

She laughed:

"And two days later on account of that guy I stayed up all night smoking and — for the first time in my life — writing poems."

Max didn't say anything.

"Tours, yep. . ." Max's classmate said. "We got married a month after we got back."

Max's surprise was indescribable.

"Great story," he finally praised her.

"Oh yeah, but can you figure it out?" Max's classmate urgently appealed. "I can't."

The Person Next to Jolana

Jolana was sitting in front of her parents.

The seat by the window was still free, and Jolana was trying to guess which of the sightseers standing outside would be her neighbor — in view of her motion sickness she definitely would have chosen some nice old lady. A nurse would have been ideal. Unfortunately, though, her neighbor turned out to be a man of about forty. Conspicuously tanned. And — Jolana inwardly grimaced — with a chain around his neck, of course. Cheap, shoddy blue jeans, tacky black shoes, and a synthetic yellow T-shirt. A third-class playboy, Jolana thought scornfully. His smile, however, slightly contradicted her preceding categorization: it came across as distinctly shy.

"Izvineetyeh," the man said apologetically.

So he's Russian, Jolana realized with surprise. She made room for him to slip by her. She noticed many scrapes on his ravaged hands. A broken nail. Those hands disgusted her a little. She peeked discreetly at his clothes, but they were clean. Except for his fly — though she may have just been imagining it — which seemed to have a little stain on it. She silently drew air into her nose, but he didn't seem to smell. The smile on his face now gave way to a serious expression, almost deliberately dignified.

Jolana by and large welcomed the fact that her neighbor was a foreigner. At least she wouldn't have to engage in any obligatory conversation. Nevertheless, she made a tentative attempt to recall what was left of her high school Russian: to her astonishment, she couldn't recall a single useful phrase; all her memory could offer her was an often-parodied excerpt from a Soviet officer's 1st of May speech — and then the opening of Tatiana's letter to Onegin, which Jolana had once had to learn by heart: "Ya k vam pishu, chevo zhe bolye, shto ya magu yeshcho skazat. Tepyer, ya znayu, v vashei volye menya prezrenyem nakazat," she summoned up after a while.

What a conversation opener that would be, she thought with amusement. Imagine the look on that Russkie's face!

She smiled at him cordially:

"Do you speak English?"

He shook his head and shrugged helplessly.

"I no speak Czech good," he said.

He smiled again apologetically.

"Nichevo. Ya tozhe uzheh zabyla rusky yazyk," Jolana said cheerfully.

She felt a certain superiority over this man, and that comforted her. If she wasn't at all embarrassed to speak in front of him, she might not be so embarrassed to vomit in front of him.

A Girl Who Literally Loves Her Work

Oskar showed up ten minutes before the scheduled departure; most of the sightseers were already sitting primly in their seats.

"I was starting to get anxious," the tour guide said with mock reproach, and she beamed at him. Oskar shrugged diffidently and scanned the bus for Ignác and Max; he headed over to them and with visible relief seated himself in the free seat next to Ignác.

"Sorry," Ignác turned to Max. "We are joined forever by a love of John Lennon's music, distrust for people over thirty, and faith in a more just societal arrangement."

Max's neighbor laughed. It sounded unforced.

"Right," said Max. "In short, you believe that one day there will be peace. So why shouldn't you sit together?"

"And we also believe that all you need is love," said Ignác with an infectious smile.

Oskar smiled too, and with the expression of someone who owns a Honda Accord and hasn't ridden a bus in six years he took a look around, slightly awed. The guide cleared her throat and introduced herself. She then told them that her friends call her Pamela and she invited all the sightseers to call her that too.

"All right, Pamela," Ignác said loudly.

Pamela smiled amiably at him, but then immediately became serious as she told them that this was only her second tour, but in spite of her brief experience she could now say that she literally loved her work. She then glanced down at her notes and expressed her belief that in the course of their week-long sojourn, breathing in invigorating sea air and ancient Italian history at every step, the voyagers would expand their spiritual horizons. Next, she informed them that during the bus ride the drivers would be selling filtered coffee, Bonita multivitamin drink, and beer — as well as Becherovka and Fernet for more discriminating drinkers.

"According to the latest medical research, each person should drink roughly two liters of fluids daily," she read from her notes. "The feeling of thirst, however, is not necessarily crucial. In hot weather the daily fluid intake may be increased to as much as three liters, but any greater volume of fluids places an excessive burden on the kidneys."

Ignác turned to Max and looked at him quizzically.

Max laughed.

Pamela meanwhile had moved on from the matter of drinking regimes to the matter of bus seats.

"Your seat has several adjustable positions," she continued reading. "You will find the control lever on the outer side under each seat. To adjust the position, pull up vertically."

While some of the passengers patted around under their seats, others — including Max, Oskar, and Ignác — fixed the tender young tour guide with thoughtful looks.

"Naturally, our bus is equipped with air-conditioning," Pamela continued. "So you can turn it on yourself if you get hot."

"Where's the lever, Pamela?" Ignác called out.

A few of the passengers laughed.

"Ignác," Oskar admonished him gently.

Pamela smiled, wished all the sightseers a pleasant journey, and at last put down the microphone. Max, Ignác, and Oskar pulled out the newspapers they'd bought and made themselves comfortable, assuming they had at least two uninter-rupted hours ahead of them before the bus stopped in České Budějovice. But to their great surprise, the onboard PA came right back on again.

They looked up in annoyance.

"We are just passing the Smetana Theater," Pamela announced to all the passengers. "And now we are driving by the famous National Museum!"

Ignác closed his paper.

"What?" he called out loudly. "What was that?"

"The National Museum," Pamela kindly repeated for him, and she glanced at her notes. "As many of you may know, this neorenaissance structure by architect Josef Schulz was completed in 1885."

The passengers gazed in dismay across the highway at the museum.

"On the right is the renowned monument of St. Václav by Josef Václav Myslbek," Pamela solemnly went on.

"When was it completed?" Ignác shouted.

"Myslbek completed the statue in the years 1912 to 1913," Pamela smiled triumphantly.

"I could use a Fernet," Ignác immediately retorted. "Large!" he called out to the driver.

Oskar sighed.

"Make that two," Jolana's father called out.

Jolana sighed.

Ignác looked approvingly at her father.

"Meeting people who literally love their work," he cheerfully explained to Jolana, "can sometimes be a considerable burden on the human kidneys."

JÁCHYM TOPOL
from **Angel**
translated by Alex Zucker

Lord of the Slab

Machata reached for the broom. He hadn't had any fun like this for a long time, and the bitch deserved it. He'd had an eye on her for a while now.

When it wasn't him in the store but Helena, the gypsy women came in twos and threes, chattering, strutting, and showing off their flamboyant blouses, sweaters, and jeans until Helena's eyes nearly popped from their sockets. Meantime their hands were deftly slinking along the counter shoving cigarettes, lighters, pens, and magazines, whatever they could get their hands on, into purses and under skirts. Helena was astounded by how unbelievably cheap their goods were, and she was so incredibly naive she'd listen and haggle with them every time. That was before. Now she probably wouldn't even talk to them. And they never sold her another thing.

Machata kicked the shop door shut, grabbed the broom, and pummeled the terrified woman on the head, the shoulders, the back, as she hopped about in the corner.

That'll teach you, you black gooch, you thieving bitch, he wheezed as he pummeled her. The gypsy cowered in the corner, covered her face with her hands, and begged him to stop. Machata, the hulk, was red in the face with exertion, arms and legs full of strength. And he was enjoying it. Eventually he got tired though.

Outside it was already dusk, in fact it was after closing time. Nobody'll come now, he thought. But he quickly dismissed the arousing image that ignited for an instant in his head: pinning the skinny gypsy bitch to the floor and giving it to her good. He would have had to pull down the heavy iron shutter; should have thought of that sooner. Besides, even though he wasn't counting on any late shoppers showing up, the gypsy men might come looking for her. They wouldn't condone this as it was, but it's one thing to rough up a thief and another to stick it to her. And get every Bajza and Grundza in the area on his tail. He grabbed her by the hair, stood her up; she looked dazed. But the second he ran his paws over her breasts, she kneed him and ran out the door. He hadn't even gotten his fill of her.

He tried to overcome the pain, his fury at being humiliated completely frazzled his thoughts. He saw red and yellow circles before his eyes, not from pain, it was rage exploding inside him. He slammed his fist into the counter so hard it almost splintered. Just moments before he'd been afraid to try anything with her. But now he would have welcomed the whole horde of neighborhood gypsies coming to avenge her.

Once he'd had a similar seizure standing in front of a pub with a knife in his hand. But the guy he'd been waiting for had suddenly opened the window above him and dumped out a trash can on his head. The whole pub roared with laughter. Machata walked around the corner and rammed the jackknife into his thigh. To this day he has the scar. It's not the only one on his body.

He calmed down. Even before the sweat on him had dried. He surveyed his objects, his domain. It's a gold mine, he thought. It's a gold mine, having a store and apartment together, he told himself for the thousandth time. Nad'a was alone in the back, her doggy got himself tangled up in Machata's legs. Outta the way, ya nutty mutt . . . his anger had passed and, strangely, he kind of liked the pup. What're you starin' at, he snapped at

Nad'a, don't look at me like that, princess . . . he went to the fridge and as he bent down he thought, what if the girl forgot again to put the beer in to chill, he was totally rigid with rage, but the bottles were there. Meanwhile the girl cleared out of the apartment, took the dog. She did right, too. Machata needed to think a few things over in peace.

He quite liked this new era. Enterprising's for men, women oughta sit at home, was his favorite slogan. That's how he put it. He would have told it to the President or the Pope, the one Helena had over her bed. He would have shared it with all the astronauts, just in case any distant worlds were interested in his message. Now Helena was his biggest worry. Looked like that religion stuff had made her crazy. He'd hoped when he brought in Nad'a that it would mean less work for his wife at home and in the store, and that she would come back more into the world. Nad'a had taken on most of the work, sure, that's why they'd trained her. It'd come in handy for the girl one day. But Helena was still like a stranger.

Machata sipped his beer and studied the bottle for a while. Either Helena wouldn't be home or she'd spend all evening sitting in the corner with her junk, straightening and arranging the figurines and rugs this way and that. Or else she'd pray.

Not that Machata didn't tag one on Nad'a every so often, the girl was sometimes slow to get a move on. But he'd seen bruises on the little one's face again today. Helena just wasn't herself. And who knows where she went, some meeting with the brothers, she said. If he ever caught one of those brothers banging her, Machata snorted with amusement. Now *that* he couldn't imagine.

She was a fanatic, his old lady. But there was something about her he loved. Her curtness, directness. There was something about her he loved, something about her he needed, and now he was angry she wasn't there. They'd grown on each other over the years. And now he was even used to the changed

Helena. It hadn't bothered him when she got juiced every once in a while before. But then she changed in earnest.

At first he'd laid into her. We started the privating thing together, dammit — he pounded his fist on the table — and together we'll stick it out! Shit, it ain't easy. There's more important things, she said back, hissing through thin, clenched lips.

He had more respect for her every day, he had to admit. He couldn't just let go at her anymore. But strangely enough, he liked that. Some kind of power came from her, and if he, Machata, esteemed storekeeper Richard Machata, feared and respected in his territory, had searched deep within himself, he probably would have discovered a feeling that her endless praying somehow protected his store, his dealings and double-dealings. And some of his ventures were most definitely in need of higher protection.

He strolled through his apartment, proudly circling the piles of brushes, boxes, and sacks, a foundation for future riches. The apartment had been converted into a storeroom. Machata, you see, was building his new business dung-beetle style. The time for a proper warehouse would come later. And it'll be equipped with a state-of-the-art security system, Machata daydreamed. For now he had to make do on his own. And as for the warehouse . . . he had a plan. He was going to see the owner of the building that evening.

Meanwhile he had a thousand snow-white Alaska Candles stored in the bathtub. The closets were piled high with paint cans. Eight Superbus mountain bike frames sparkled in the living room. Sacks of spices, powdered dumplings, and crates of sardines stood carefully stacked around Machata's bed. A glass cabinet provided asylum to six hundred Pulp ketchup packets. Etc.

Machata was constantly digging through his property, acquired for the most part at street markets and from stands: recounting it, dusting it off, shuffling around the apartment through the stacks. He took a peek into Helena's room too. The

Pope wasn't hanging on the wall anymore, he noticed. The picture had disappeared. He didn't give a damn about religion, they didn't talk about it together. Not once since Helena had "converted," as she put it. Machata just accepted it. Like the fact that Kuder's boy now went to the Sokol club. It was just part of the new era.

As for himself, Machata was no longer a downtrodden super, an informer with busts on his record, a small-time tobacconist with an axe of debt hanging eternally over his head. Uh-uh, those were the old days. So Nellie prays, so? And what of it, gentlemen? All the others are alkies, whores, they're lazy, they're into cash, into clothes, they lie . . . Richard Machata, connoisseur of women, counted them off on his fingers. And the fact that she'd taken down the picture . . . Machata was proud the Pope was Czech. As proud as he was of Pilsner Urquell, Semtex, and Czech tennis. I mean, we, the Czechs . . . besides, Vlk — it's got kind of a fighting sound, manly. But the portrait was gone. The Devil only knew what was racing through Helena's mind now.

He went back to his beloved planning. The gradual transformation of the tobacco shop into a general store was his pride. With his own hands, on weekends and in his spare time, he had knocked out a wall, put in a doorway, and now the store was linked to the apartment. It was pretty practical. Not to mention that he and the girl who owned the building could calmly reach an agreement. Not to mention the luck of a girl like that getting the building, doesn't know beans about it, so at least a guy can get moving, he thought with satisfaction.

They entered the apartment through the store now the door to the hallway was walled over. At least that way they didn't have to come into contact with the lowlife in the building. Every night, Machata pulled down the barred iron shutter: My apartment is my castle, he'd say to himself. It was a brand-new type of double-layer security shutter, built like a drawbridge. He was the only one with a hook, had it custom-made. There in his castle he had his wife, his girl, his dog, and his goods. Between them and the street was a massive sheet of metal. At last they could sleep in peace. Even the pup felt trapped in there now.

Machata sensed more than heard that someone was in his store. In spite of his bear-sized frame, he slipped with unusual agility into the narrow hallway that led from the apartment to the store and snatched a crowbar off the table. He kept one just like it under the counter. He held it in his hand, ready to use it, or to serve the late customer in any other appropriate fashion. But he needn't have bothered.

What a pigsty, the caller muttered.

He crashed into crates and carts, into the canisters and cans that filled the store.

Lay off it, Machata told him, you'll be back, and gladly.

I'm expanding, he couldn't keep from boasting. Knock down this here — he waved his hand — smooth out this here, he showed the late guest, and then you'll see! I'll show you. All of you!

Yeh sure, yeh, minimart. Dime a dozen! You see the Australian's? The caller was referring to the new shop, a modern convenience store a few blocks away. The place and its owner had sucked about a liter of Machata's blood already.

Fuck that! It's a scam, a bubble, it'll pop like that. You got?

What's this here? the caller, a runt in a striped T-shirt and leather jacket, kicked one of the canisters.

Leave it, Machata reprimanded him. Benzol, don't go flicking a cig on it, my advice to you.

No shit, yeah? the little stud baited him. He pulled out a match, with one fluid motion struck it against the elegant black denim that covered his slightly scrawny lower half, and held the stick to one of the canisters. His earring sparkled in the flame.

You asshole, Machata snapped with unfeigned alarm, and the character blew out the match.

For you to see, said the little guy, and he tossed on the counter a wad of bills that seemed to appear by sleight of hand.

Machata counted the cash, then nodded solemnly, slipped two bills out of the pile, and slid them across to the kid. He didn't even move.

Alright, okay, the shopkeeper chuckled, and he added another two. Just testin', yeah?

And what if I delivered a few drops of this Benzol here to the Australian's place, huh? the character grinned, jokingly saluted, scooped up the cash, and staggered off.

Machata stood there. That had hit him hard. But he soon calmed down. Not that this goon wouldn't go and set the red rooster. And not that Machata wouldn't enjoy watching it flicker. But what about the character then? He would know, know enough to put the squeeze on. Steer clear of that guy, the dealmaker told himself.

He walked out, surveyed the street: cars whizzed by stinking in the stink. He spit on the sidewalk, stretched deliciously for a bit. This here was his turf. He followed the street down, his gaze gliding off toward the intersection; the sun was just setting. Its rays played over the shutter, a massive sheet of metal, the thing looked like a gridiron now.

Machata spit in his hands and grasped the hook with gusto. As he pulled down the bars, it looked like they were slicing the sun's glare, metal biting into flame. They're gonna hafta knock, my gals are, thought Machata, lord of the metal slab, least they'll learn to come home on time. He thought about Helen and Nad'a and the dog, comin' and goin' as they please, his girls. And when they come and start knocking on the iron wall, Helena energetically and a little bit angrily, Nad'a softly and intermittently, he'll gladly get up and go let them in. Now he had work. Shunk, went the metal, and kcchh, it scraped against the sidewalk.

ALEXANDR KLIMENT
Portrait of My Landscape
Translated by Andrée Collier

Walking across the Charles Bridge I had a good, utterly festive feeling. I hadn't had such a good feeling in a long time. I was happy to give myself up to this feeling. The Svatovítský Bell in the Prague Castle had just begun to ring out five in the afternoon. The princely, kingly, imperial voice of the bell spread down over the roofs of Malá Strana to the banks of the Vltava and settled on the dark-gray surface of the river. And it settled into me, sounding in me as well.

It was growing dark. Autumn, almost winter. A light fog rose. The year nineteen sixty-seven. In a few weeks, just before Christmas, I would be forty years old. Until recently, this realization had made me feel ill. But now I had the impression, as I had had years ago, that everything lay ahead of me. It wasn't just an impression. The fog felt pleasant.

I turned my face into the wind and the gentle tumult of rain, and I think that I was smiling, happy. Several people looked round at me. Perhaps even the heads of the statues turned to look at me. I wouldn't be surprised. We now have something to talk about, my dear old saints. Even cobblestones can sense when someone walks with a firm step, bearing within him a good decision. For such a person things go gently, well, festively.

It's simple. I will walk to the end of the bridge and across the Kampa, I will greet the wet profiles of the Braun statues in Vrtbov Gardens, and then I will say to Olga:

"Olga, here I am. I will go with you."

I ran down the steps to the Kampa. The curves of the baroque façades formed a harmonious ornament to my mood. The wind blew onto my shoulders the last leaves of locusts, lindens, and sycamores. A beige figure, who seemed to have stepped out of the stories of Jan Neruda, was lighting the gas lamps with the help of a bamboo pole. I watched for a moment. My city, which I will soon be leaving, has its little miracles, its everyday liturgy. For a moment I stood there piously, as if at a ceremony.

Behind the glass of a green, cast-iron lantern there hangs a circular white mantle, in which a gas flame flickers. You pull a little ring under the lamp and the gas spreads through the rim of the filament, the lantern lights up and quietly, musically hums. It sounds like the delicate, luminous register of an organ. Didn't I climb the lampposts of Malá Strana many times as a boy in order to light a gas lamp for myself? But always senselessly, because I lit the lamps during the day. In the evening they were already lit.

As senselessly as the world itself turns, the mill wheel here is propelled by the running Čertovka Canal. I listened for a moment to the water bubbling and sloshing through the wooden slats of the wheel. Once, long ago, there was a mill here. Now there is some kind of warehouse. In such a lovely place there could be a fine apartment house or a pleasant pub, but why get worked up over it.

I also stopped before the gate to the church of the Virgin Mary. This gothic church burned down in the Hussite Wars. Like all the others, it burned in vain. All that remained were two square stone towers and a gothic portal. The church was rebuilt in the baroque period with a fine, airy, spacious courtyard. Go inside! In this courtyard surrounded by the tall buildings of the Maltese Knights grow beds of hydrangea. A huge crown of pastel panicles is drenched by an ancient rain. Every year I've come here to pick bunches of autumn hydrangea. This year I forgot. I will pick one blossom now and bring it to Olga.

I used to pick hydrangea before the first autumn frost. The blossoms dry to the consistency of paper and will last all year in a vase without water. Many times, perhaps ten times, I picked them here with Jarmila. I was overwhelmed by the vitality of this sentimental memory of a time of love that is already behind me. But this is something I have to expect. Hydrangea bloom all over Europe. I'll take my memories with me.

The courtyard is carefully swept clean. An old woman whose age is impossible to guess takes care of the church and the courtyard. I remember this tiny, wretched, stooped woman from my childhood. She had a noble face. She swept here under the First, the so-called Bourgeois Republic, and she swept here during the war and the German occupation. After the war there were two or three years of problematic democracy and now we have had almost twenty years of the communist regime and still she smiles, like that time when I said:

"It's so nice how well you take care of the hydrangea here."

"All I did was plant them," she said. "These bushes are cared for by our dear Lord, who gives rain and sunshine. Come here next year and pick them again."

So I picked one blossom for Olga and said to myself: Olga, I'm picking this for you and I'm picking it now without the memory of Jarmila.

The muffled sound of piano music floated over from a nearby institution for the blind. They look, they watch through music, I thought to myself, and I went to Vrtbov Gardens with one hydrangea blossom in my hand.

Before ringing the bell at Olga's studio I greeted the Braun statues on the terrace. I was resolved. It was already nearly dark, but in the distance, in the mist lit up by the last glow of the sun, there was still a beautiful, unmistakable view of the Old Town's towers. There are supposedly a hundred of them.

One of the statues smiled at me. Was it only the statue that was smiling at me? Miladka was also smiling at me. The sharp little nose with the lovingly formed line of the chin reminded me of her face, and the statue's silhouette recalled her body, just as baroque. A stately, nicely curved body with delicate limbs and even more slender fingers. I will go say good-bye to Miladka at Prague's central train station. Olga is different, Olga is tall and slim — almost as tall as me.

Jarmila was small, tiny — but why am I saying this, that she was? Why am I telling myself she was tiny, like a toy? Jarmila still is. She is very much here, in this very city, only for me has she become the past, which I am beginning to forget, until I forget altogether. Not really altogether. There will remain several petrified gestures that have a primarily aesthetic meaning, and I will occasionally, gratefully return to them in the gallery of my memories.

I will have to say good-bye to Jarmila as well, calmly and cordially. I'm not running away, not fleeing anything, least of all myself and the shadows of my loves. I'm simply going abroad.

But I stood there a moment, motionless like one statue among the others, and shared with them their calm and their even calmer decisiveness: we statues will remain standing here and you will go. You'll go first across the terrace, then climb the several steps to the little garden house and ring at Olga's door. Everything will happen just as you imagine it.

The door opened. The light dazzled my eyes. Olga gave me her hand. In the blinding light, in the moment before I found her hand and pressed it, I suddenly saw Olga upside down. It's not insane or unbelievable. It's just that my heart stopped for a moment, and before I inhaled again, a luminous wave of warm air, permeated with the studio's scent of turpentine, poppyseed oil, and beeswax, took my expectant gaze and turned it upside down. Water thrummed in the gutter.

This is how love begins.

Suddenly you see things upside down, and both of you are changed forever.

My first glimpse of Olga was just as intense. It had, of course, its prelude. I'm exaggerating somewhat when I say prelude. Nothing happened. It was only the recording of a feeling of a landscape that a train was passing through. Once I wrote to you, Olga, that you are my landscape, my homeland.

Trains of that sort are no longer running — no longer wheezing and whistling and pouring out smoke. Here and there express trains powered by diesel or electricity whiz on by. I will take such a train to Paris with Olga.

We'll go just before Christmas. A day before or a day after my fortieth birthday. I hope that it will be snowing between Beroun and Zdice. I would enjoy that. I will be sitting across from Olga, by the window, but at the same time I will be standing on the snowy hillside over Knížkovice and I will be watching the train moving west into the distance. It will pierce my heart as it always does when I see a train passing through a landscape, although now, dear Olga, they are much more technologically advanced.

Something is leaving me and I am standing here in a snowy field. I am leaving and I see someone standing there in a field. I will leave something, someone behind. I am sad. I would like to go into the forest at Svata and further on, to Křivoklát. I'm happy there even on rainy evenings in autumn. Should I turn right around and go to the station?

But you needn't worry, Olga, my resolve is firm. I'm already sitting with you in your studio, and in a few weeks I'll be sitting with you in the Prague-Paris express. I hope we will be sitting by the window.

And I will also show you that I already have, thank God, all my papers together and in order. By the way, don't you think it's funny — and certainly in a few thousand years nobody will believe — that the journey from one European country to another could be such a huge problem, and for me a fateful decision?

I wasn't deciding between East and West. I was deciding between being alone or with Olga. It's a private matter. Nevertheless, I will have to cross the border between East and West, and I know that I will be entering another world. The Reds are everywhere, of course (I smiled), but somehow, from a geographical point of view, it can be said with certainty that from here back to the Pacific the world is decidedly red, and from here to the Atlantic the world is questionably white. The Lord God and several presidents have determined that this dividing line should, without nuance or nicety, run right along our fine, wooded border. But why get worked up over it.

People used to escape to the West over these wooded hills, sometimes getting shot in the process. Then they built a continuous barbed-wire fence and, as a result, very complicated ways of getting out had to be thought up. Now it is easier. The bureaucrats are somewhat tired and, with a little craftiness, it is possible to arrange everything quite easily. So, for example, I am going to Paris on the basis of a private invitation which certifies that I will be taken care of during my stay there. You cannot change Czech crowns for dollars outside of this country. These people know, of course, that I won't even so much as have breakfast at their place. It's a mere formality. The woman to whom I applied for a transit visa also understood the invitation as a formality. It was enough to show her the stamp on the envelope from France. She didn't even want to look at the letter. But the fact that I want to remain abroad is something that no one can know about — this wouldn't be viewed so liberally. If someone were to report me, they would throw me off the train at the border. Aside from Olga, no one knows about it.

Over the past twenty years I have often spoken, with many different friends, about emigration. It was one of the crowning themes of our eternal and hopeless conversations. Stay?

Go? Which is better? Which is worse? Lose one's home and gain freedom? And naturally we examined the question from the other side: what is freedom and where is home?

We were definitely not active opponents of the Czechoslovak communist regime or even of socialism in general. We just weren't communists, we weren't in the party, and for that reason our lives were more difficult. The practical and moral burdens of leading such lives in Czechoslovakia led many people to consider going abroad. For me such a step never seemed more than a topic of conversation. I simply didn't want to go anywhere else.

When Olga told me that she was going to stay abroad, I was sorry. At the same time, I was afraid that she wanted to talk with me about the principles involved in leaving, that she wasn't yet fully decided, and I didn't have any new ideas to add to that old theme. But Olga was firmly and unambiguously decided. If she had felt uncertain she never would have started to talk about it.

Olga painted with the same sort of absolute certainty and sovereignty. If I were a painter, I would first of all turn the picture over in my mind doubtfully and at length. Olga is different. There is nothing between her imagination and a patch of color except her beautiful artistic gestures. Not even a piece of paper. In the twenty years I have known her, I don't remember her once spoiling a single canvas. She has always had her pictures perfectly worked out ahead of time, and her imagination assigns them to large and small formats with an easy certainty, as if cracking eggs into a pan.

"It's incredible how much I enjoy my work," she would say. "You can't imagine how happy I am to get up in the morning."

I don't remember ever being happy to get up. Only on Sundays and on vacations was I happy to get up, and that was a long time ago. Those were my student days. But Olga goes across the hall, gobbles up two or three eggs, stands in front of the easel, and paints from morning till night. Some people are lucky. But why get worked up over it.

I had to sign in every morning with a pencil attached to the spine of an attendance book, or punch my card in a time-clock. I wouldn't say that I was bored really — I can become absorbed in my work and it goes well — but somehow it isn't the same. A Marxist would say that I am completely free, because I have understood my necessity. I have understood that I have to make a living. I'm good with numbers, I have a decent spacial sense, and drawing is easy for me. Of course I don't mean to grumble. Being an architect is a good profession, but I haven't been able to cross the border from drudgery to creation. I'm a team player. I carefully complete assigned tasks and I place housing units according to predetermined norms on specified plots of land.

I never managed to realize any of my own projects. There were always too many obstacles between me and the realization, between my project and its construction, and I was unable to overcome them.

There are no obstacles left between me and Olga. That's why I was able to make my decision with such certainty. The only thing between us was time, reminiscent of a continent. That time is behind us — our youth — but right now I have the feeling that the most important time is still ahead of me.

Olga has been present in my imagination from the moment I first saw her. Her image inverted in me. It became fixed in my mind as the landscape of home. By the way, Olga, do you remember that I told you once that you are my landscape, my homeland?

At first there was the prelude, but nothing happened — I was just looking at a landscape a train was passing through. This took place twenty years ago, but nothing really took place — I just saw Olga for the first time. Although it was a clear afternoon, the tow of the blue spectrum of night colors carried me with it like the incoming tide, like the outgoing tide. An intense feeling cast me up onto dry, foreign land, and I've explored it in my mind for two decades; the feeling dragged me to unknown depths, in which my fantasies have been submerged. As the old Czech saying goes: Love is born in the eye and falls into the heart.

The year nineteen forty seven, late summer. I had two years of architecture school behind me. I was still full of enthusiasm, full of hope. Before the beginning of the fall term, I was going to see Štěpán at the Hrádek parsonage.

My mother was a sincere Catholic. I inherited from her the belief that the Lord God is above me and that everything goes according to his plan. With all the naiveté of childhood and all the desire to explore of adolescence, I was happy to keep this inheritance, but eventually I had to part with it. At the moment when I stopped believing, I found a good friend. He was a Catholic priest.

Štěpán did not persuade me, did not challenge my doubts. He took me lovingly from the landscape of childhood, which was biblical and liturgical, to the landscape of adulthood, which is commonplace and aesthetic. It was as if God, from whom I was parting, wanted to reward me for the sincerity of my childhood faith and sent an angel into my path, who said: Don't be afraid to be alone.

Štěpán served in a country parsonage on the southern Bohemian border. I was hitchhiking there. I was sitting on the bed of a truck that was carrying baskets full of apples. The journey through this landscape, enveloped in the scent of apples — this is the prelude.

Warm air flows around me. Indian summer is dominated by the sight of clear, contrasting colors: red, yellow, green, and blue. In vain I try to count the ponds that reflect the sky and the bright white farmhouses. Lanes cross over dams. The occasional horse and carriage ambles slowly through the ponds. A stork — perhaps an angel — glides over a wayside cross at the edge of a field.

When a man is still very young, he enjoys visiting graveyards and thinks of death as of a distant, hopeful prospect for the future. Do you remember? In the south there is a church in a village called Brloh. In a marble slab set in the wall of the church, engraved in empire cursive, are the words:

> Have mercy on me
> at least you, my friends,
> for the hand of God has touched me.

Then, while I was being transported to the south, enveloped in the scent of apples, the warm hand of the landscape was touching me, and the thought of death was attractive. I would like to be buried here someday, here beside this church, or there at the foot of that one, which after hundreds of years has taken on the likeness of a person of both sexes. Slender stone towers, swelling, ever-pregnant cupolas. Czech gothic and Czech baroque, but a twenty-year-old student of architecture thinks: how's that — Czech baroque and Czech gothic? Well yes, but the gothic and the baroque in Bohemia is more like it.

Bodies buried in graves in a landscape with a tradition do not lie in nothingness. They lie in history and are history themselves. The stone walls are overgrown with roses and elderberry; spirea wreathes even the bones of those for whom no one picks flowers anymore. The rain has washed away the names on their tombstones, but I am with you, my friends. Now and forever ours is the kingdom of our landscape, amen. And you see, Olga, this is what we will forsake.

But I still don't even know you, and I am watching the southern Bohemian plain, my dear, from the bed of a moving truck. The scent of apples intoxicates me as incense does a child in church. I want to bless it, but with what words and what gestures? So I watch.

This is the kingdom of my landscape: It governs itself affably and does not encourage the invention of colossal myths. Quietly and imperceptibly, as only trees can, it outgrows its horizon in the shape of solitary lindens, and out of their compressed rings it carves a Madonna in the image of the Mother of God, based on a painting; or the painting of a beloved woman, based on a feeling.

The landscape is peaceful, as if painted once and for always. Her thin lips take on a gentle smile. She lyrically disregards European dogma, by which she is nevertheless defined, but in her own way, with a provincial charm whose flaws are transformed into the mystery of character. She isn't rational, but this doesn't mean she's irrational. Chastely, from under scarlet, cobalt, and gold drapings, which so resemble clouds, and from under clouds, which so resemble the drapings of a gothic statue, she provokes the desire to rest on her hills, with their loving names: Džbány, Libín, Bula, Čihadlo, Klet', Mahelník. I have within me a relief map of my experiences with these oddest of words, to which has fallen the wonderful fate of becoming the proper names of small, unchanging, isolated hills and mountains. I have within me, Olga, a relief map of your body, which at this point I've not yet felt. The ends of my fingers have not desired it. I was passing through the landscape.

And through this landscape runs a train. In the distance it is still small. Won't toys always remain a feature of the way you regard objects? And aren't you yourself like one point of a toy observed from a distance by the driver of the train, who is watching you from the smoking, approaching train? You must cross paths. You will meet. Who and what will go past first? Him and his little train? Me and my little truck?

If the bars by the tracks had fallen a second later, or if the truck driver had got just a little more speed out of that old rattler — and he did try, the whole machine was shaking — we wouldn't have had to stop so violently in front of the bars, and the apples and I would have been on the other side. Perhaps I would have only looked up and waved to the engineer and everything would have been different. I wouldn't be sitting here with you in the studio, intoxicated once again by the scent of evaporating turpentine, poppyseed oil, and paints. I love that scent.

"Olga," I said, "that painting on the easel is upside down."

"You're right," said Olga, and she went over to the easel and turned the painting right side up.

"I look at it upside down and I can see right away if everything's where it belongs."

"I understand that perfectly," I said.

"Why didn't you become a painter?" Olga asked. "You watch and observe like a painter. I think you also experience what you see, the way a painter does. Light, shadow, and patches of color which you add and take away, and that's the miracle — you preserve the round world in a rectangular format. For me there is no greater happiness or freedom. Between the imagination of a painter and the painting there are no obstacles. Between a project and its construction there's an entire mountain."

Between a project and its construction is an entire mountain of bricks and a social regime. Olga, you could also call them the materials and the investor. I would like to level that mountain of bricks a little, and face up to that regime, but I have never been able to do so. Why get worked up over it. Would I like to paint? Yes. Definitely. Perhaps. Maybe. I don't know. I've never believed in my talent. And what is talent without certainty? Useless cultural ambition.

"But I'm glad, Mikuláš, that you are the way you are," said Olga, "that you aren't different. I need a normal person by my side. Two painters under one roof would be a madhouse."

"So you think that I'm a normal person," I said. "A completely normal person. Thanks a lot."

"Be glad!" she said. "After all, it's your greatest talent and art, and my certainty. I'm afraid of people who are always obsessed with something."

That's true, Olga. I haven't been obsessed with anything for a long time, but I don't know if there is any art to it — cutting yourself off, freeing yourself, being alone. I've long since rid myself of any ambitions, and I gave away my talent to thoughts and fantasies. The most important thing for me is to go into the woods, walk on forgotten paths with my hands in my pockets, and observe the architecture of trees and grass. I don't struggle for anything anymore. I live a commonplace life and I only have one requirement — that my life be aesthetic.

The world around me is obviously very ugly. Banality, kitsch, and decay are devouring city, village, and field. Doesn't it seem to you that we are living in a garbage dump? But luckily I know my paths, and I know of vacant places where I feel good, and there are enough of them. Prague's Old Town, Malá Strana, the Castle, architecture spiritualized in gardens. Uninhabited parts of Křivoklátsek. The kingdom of the South Bohemian landscape. A good book, a beautiful painting, a little music and a little wine.

Often on my walks I've thought about whether this found freedom is not tantamount to indifference. Sometimes it has seemed to me that I was merging with the beautiful indifference of the architecture of trees and grass. And the apathy of snow, which rustles when falling heavily — you must know that, too. Often I have wanted to let myself be covered by this musical snow, but because I'm a walker I went back home. Then I would read a book in bed, a love story, which is always the most simple: between the eternal me and the eternal you lies an invincible piece of dying body.

Olga smiled at me. What is more beautiful than this: a

smile you've known for twenty years, that is always equally dear to you? The glow of the evening lamp reflected in her eye, which was now dark blue, like a fleck of amethyst. The rain thrummed on the gutter as if onto a cymbal, and a gust of wind shook the windowpane. The bent corners of sheets of paper trembled on the table. And through her window came the tow of the blue spectrum of night colors, like then, although then it was a clear afternoon.

We are stopping in front of the bars — the truck, the baskets full of apples, and me enveloped in their scent. The truck is still straining and jerking, and one apple nearly rolls onto its oily bed. I catch it and hold it in my hand. Meanwhile, the train is passing between the bars, whistling. It gives three short whistles and one long one; I wave and the engineer salutes. That's how it should be, of course. And just as is routinely reproduced in the world of toys, the stationmaster stands in front of the station in a blue uniform and watches the passing train. He holds a red flag by his side, as is appropriate.

Then, there were still wagons with open platforms. I liked to stand on those platforms and lean over the green railing. I felt as if I were on a balcony that moves through the landscape with you. Now we are already, perhaps forever, shut up in compartments. They say it's safer, considering the higher speed. But why get worked up over it.

Then, the train slowly rattled and knocked along the tracks. On the platform of the last wagon stood Olga. I didn't know her name yet, but she must have long since had a place in my field of vision, like a nearby mountain whose name I didn't know yet.

Although I am happily settled into the abstract landscape of late afternoon, enthused by my observation and intoxicated to the point of concrete bliss by a cloud of apple-scent that is suddenly and carnally coupled with the shadow of the smoke of the passing train, I'm in despair. I'm confused. What should I do? Yell?

Jump from the bed of the truck and stop the train with my body? Run along the tracks after the train, which has already passed?

What do you do in such a desperate, fateful moment? You throw the apple you happen to have in your hand, and you follow its arc.

It could definitely be calculated. The speed of the train and the arc of the apple, but it would have to be a very complex equation, and I have the feeling that someone has long since worked it out.

Olga smiles, maybe at me, maybe at the flying apple, and she catches it with both hands as if it were a ball. From that moment, I will remember her smile, her face, and the purple fleck in her eye forever.

It's still a clear afternoon. The smoke from the locomotive temporarily but thickly covers the entire area. The rippling darkness of the acrid eclipse is penetrated by one ray of sunlight, fixing it vividly in my sight. In the tow of the blue spectrum of night colors, Olga's eye is illuminated for a moment. My memory can add and my memory can take away, but it is certain that this glimpse transported me into that fleck of color just like a painter into his painting.

And then the bars go up. It's so normal. The truck trembles to a start. I jump up and watch the train pulling away. You are standing on the platform in a long white dress. It's so abnormal that the train is taking you away.

If I had been photographed at that moment, naturally my gestures would have been captured. I would like to study them. An outstretched hand? A man starting to run? A figure struck with wonder? A body frozen in surprise? A man kneeling with his ear to the track? Could the resonance of this lifeless matter carry to you, through the wheels and over the rail, the beating of her heart?

It's hopeless. It's already in the distance. Already all that can be seen is a little box in the middle of receding tracks —

now only a point with an elongated pear of smoke behind it. Already it's behind me, even though the glimpse of an object being lost is now and forever before me. And I know that it's the beginning of something, a beginning so perfect it contains its end. And I know that I will keep returning to that beginning and that it will surprise me again and again as an everyday marker of the passing of time: that already it is autumn, time to begin heating; that already it's light and, as you see, I haven't yet fallen asleep; that already the first snow is falling, and the last is also melting; that already I have gray hairs — have you noticed, Olga?

I remained standing on the tracks for a moment longer. I am standing on them to this day, and you are riding to France like Christ in his cart. I beg you, grant my wish, take me with you. Relieve me of these memories and do not lead me into the temptation of loving the image of your receding figure more than your approaching age.

In the gravel on the sides of the tracks, like a tropical chapel, stood the white cube of an electrical transformer. In the hot, trembling air, in the intense sunlight, it appeared to be as unreal as you. The transformer hummed. Even the tracks along which the train had left trembled brightly like strings — seeming to have the granular nature of resin rather than the nature of iron — certainly out of fear that they would take to the air with the parched fragrance of chamomile, which flowed over the ditch from a feebly abundant field of herbs. The sea of flowers was mad with pollination and bees, which invisibly composed an additional accompaniment to the voice of the transformer. The honeyed fragrance was narcotic.

And what did I swear to, my arm probably still reaching southwest? Ave Maria! I said, yes and Ave Maria, I love you and I will never love another and I will love you from this moment on and with all my heart and with all my mind and with all my strength forever and ever, Amen.

A glass shard glistened spectrally in the gravel. A little bell chimed. The monstrance of the sun was setting into a poplar, and white down was falling from it. Something else might come from the opposite direction. It frightened me to realize that my dangerous situation persisted. I surprised myself with the way I was intoning, promising, taking oaths. When I withdrew from the tracks, I had that feeling that I was someone other than the person I had been a few moments before. I had fallen in love and I was surprised at the certainty with which I recognized this. Proudly I realized that it is a beautiful state to be in, and I intended to remain in that state regardless of whether I ever again saw that being who led me into it.

But was it only this one being who passed that led me to this extraordinary, permanently awakened state of mind? Wasn't she part of a picture and wasn't that picture part of an atmosphere, another part of which was me?

It was a picture. A picture I have turned over so many times in my memories, in my consciousness, to keep convincing myself again and again of its perfection. I assure you, Olga, that everything in it is just where it belongs.

Then, there weren't as many cars as there are now. I had to walk several hours on foot. The train that had gone by, the local, was the last one of the day.

My shoes squeaked ridiculously loud. I took them off and went barefoot. A golden evening had already set in above me, and the front of another night was approaching from the east. I've always enjoyed noticing how the periods of the day vary. Each has its own particular sounds.

Somewhere bells are tolling. Somewhere someone is pounding on a scythe with a hammer, and it rings and rings. A duck lands on a pond, scattering water. A field of stubble erupts and shoots water up from sprinklers. A rifle fires twice from beyond a pine forest. On waves of air in which dew is already forming, the echo of the train drifts through the sacred labyrinth of the coming night. It is traveling from somewhere to somewhere on a route that can't be seen. There's a constant clattering out there, and when the whistle sounds, filtered by the velvet of distance, it pierces my heart.

I'm still standing at the wayside cross. Will you permit me to pray here, Our Father, who art in Heaven, in whom I no longer believe? Here, in front of this cross, I would like to intone a few words that spring forth from the tradition of my childhood. Hail, Queen of grace, I am with Thee, blessed among rivers, and blessed is this, the country of Thy life.

I arrived in Hrádek after dark. The parsonage was all lit up. I was looking forward to getting something to eat. As I entered the hall, Olga entered through a side door. She was carrying a plate of apples with both hands. She was carrying the plate of apples gently pressed against her gentle breasts.

I must admit, Olga, that it seemed a matter of course, even inevitable to me, as if somewhere someone had thought it up beforehand and arranged it almost theatrically, and so I wasn't even surprised. I would swear that you weren't astonished either. Except that the little yellow-and-red pyramid of apples shook, and one rolled off.

Once more that day it was necessary for me to catch a falling, rolling apple. I managed to. I put the apple back on the plate and, with my other hand, briefly held the plate from underneath, as if warning it not to shake anymore. Under the edge of the plate I felt your hand.

In the past twenty years I have not been forced by any similar situation to catch something in midair. Not so much as a pencil has chosen to roll off a table. Many times I have walked through fruit orchards and, with thoughts of you, observed the perfect architecture of the ripe fruit. Either they were hanging on branches or they were already lying in the grass. Not one apple has chosen to break off so that I could see it fall. I don't remember ever catching that moment, and yet it is so common. Believe me, I would run and catch it before it hit the ground, even if a fence and an acre of land lay between me and the tree.

Much later, when I told you this in all its details, I was a little embarrassed. Aren't they ridiculous? Aren't they foolish? But you just laughed and said:

"I too could describe in detail the scene of your appearance that evening in the parsonage. I could draw for you the way the shadows broke in the candlelight. I could describe in detail how you approached me and how you caught the apple falling from the plate I was carrying. What you said when Štěpán introduced you to me, and when he was introducing you to Václav. Our portraits appeared reflected in a mirror. If we were to remove the glass surface of the mirror from its frame and dip it in some ideal developing solution, it would be possible even now, after so many years, for us to peel from the glass the silver foil on which we were recorded."

MARTA KADLEČÍKOVÁ
Ode to Joy
Translated by Dana Loewy with Robert Wechsler

When I think about it sometimes, it seems that it has always been this way. I cannot visualize the past. It is as if it were separated from the present — which already has its memories, too — by a hard and impervious shell. My only vivid recollections are of the period of the change that brought me to where I am now.

Back then, we were beginning to get lovely late winter mornings. The days were awakening early and they were filled with bright sunshine. Precisely the way they are now. Perhaps this is why I am recalling it now. But that year we had much more snow; the winter had been long and spring was anticipated more anxiously. The gutters were incessantly spouting water, bits of dirty, icy snow were falling off the roofs, and during the nights beautiful icicles formed on everything, only to melt again, helpless, in the morning sun. Birds started chirping eagerly, the pavement glistened wet from all the melting, and the music of brass bands, deployed all around town, sounded even more festive and cheerful than usual. It strikes me that those town musicians have it pretty hard during the winter months. Maybe they are rotated more frequently then. I don't know. But I suppose that they are aware of their joyous mission to remind people that life is beautiful and cheerful and that they ought to smile all the time.

During those late winter days I occasionally noticed a strange weakening of my right wrist. I remember it very clearly. It somehow felt too loose. This may sound strange, but if the individual parts of the human body were bolted together, I would have said that my right wrist needed adjustment with a screwdriver. A little tightening or something. Of course I did not permit this to ruin my spirits. Only once or twice did I mention it to my cleaning lady.

Old Felicie shook her head with concern, and then she illogically but soothingly proclaimed that spring was coming. She had a point, even if the tree branches were still all bare and black, and the grass, lurking underneath the melting snow, was gray. However, as soon as the sun came up, people would rush outside in the thin light coats they had kept ready in their closets so long, just to prove to themselves that spring was at the gates. And in some windows — despite the dampness — featherbeds appeared in the mornings.

When I was buttoning my coat before leaving for the office on one such delightful morning, the forementioned right hand suddenly refused to obey me. It bent limply at the wrist, then swayed like a broken flower stalk and fell to the ground. Mechanically, I finished buttoning my coat and gazed numbly at my hand lying on the carpet, its fingers helplessly extended. At first I only felt astonishment so powerful it did not leave the least bit of room for shock or any other stirring of the mind. I assume that such an unexpected incident, defying reason, would disconcert anyone, but on top of everything I am a man who detests any kind of change. I bent down and, baffled, inspected the hand for a moment. It had broken off precisely at the wrist joint, which was clean, smoothly sliced. I looked at the stump protruding from my coat. Not a drop of blood was anywhere to be found, nothing. I was reminded of my dear mother, who on Sunday mornings would stand at the kitchen table and, using thread, cut neat slices from freshly cooked loaves of bread dumplings. The hand rested heavily on my palm. It was warm, alive. What to do with it. Such an unexpected, unpleasant complication. The striking of the kitchen clock roused me from my reverie. It was high time I left. I dread arriving late at the office. Not because of the fines that are imposed. It is simply my nature always to appreciate order and the following of rules. I placed the hand in my left pocket and walked out of the house.

The sun was shining splendidly, as if the sky were never to darken again; the birds were jubilant in their song; the melting snow was flowing off the roofs in dirty streams; and like every other day, marches blared out cheerfully. I patted my left pocket and shrugged, annoyed. What to do with it, to be sure. I had planned to take a little carefree walk before work and instead I was unpleasantly forced to take some kind of a stand.

The faces of the passersby were lit up with smiles. Everyone was rushing eagerly to work or to school, everyone was looking forward to his duties, everyone had a jubilant gleam in his eyes; I was the only one shuffling along the street like a sourpuss. I felt a pang of shame for allowing such an unpleasant yet purely private matter to run away with me. I straightened my back, lifted my eyebrows, and extended — not without a certain amount of effort, I must admit — the corners of my mouth. Such a beautiful morning, I reminded myself. I was lucky that no one took any notice of me. If a patrol of the public order squad had seen me, I would have been issued quite a fine for my gloom. And rightly so. Only children up to the age of eight were allowed to cry or lament in public. They do not understand. What does my hand matter to anyone. On top of it all, I had been observing the loosening of my wrist for some time, and it was no one's fault but my own that I had failed to consult a physician. The more I silently reproached myself like this, the harder it was for me to keep a brisk pace and a joyful expression. I began to look for excuses. Although a person like me must be well beyond suspicion, I would hate to make it seem as if by complaining about my wrist I were trying to avoid the work I carry out most zealously and, in a sense, even enjoy. Well, yes, in a sense. By the way, I presume that I'm not an exception. Otherwise we would not be able to live in such a perfect solidarity and rejoice in our existence from morning till night.

Deep in thought, I came to the main thoroughfare and, as

usual, stopped at the newsstand. When it came time to hand the fellow some change, which I carried in my right pocket, I had to reach across for it with my left hand. Very inconvenient. But just a cursory glance at the newspaper headlines helped to improve my mood significantly. Nothing but pleasant items and useful information. As usual. Sometimes it occurs to me that we are being pretty spoiled. We cannot imagine that there were times when many unpleasant things were being published. That must have been awful.

I slipped the paper under my right arm and again harkened to the vigorous, uplifting tune that was floating above the busy morning avenue. My thoughts again wandered to the contents of my left pocket. I had to arrive at some decision before I reached the office. Ah, what a pleasant little walk this might have been. I had only two alternatives. To keep secret the fact that I had lost my right hand would most likely not prove successful, but perhaps I could gloss over the whole matter, say, by adopting a light-hearted, jocular tone and then managing to my work left-handedly, as it were. Had my left hand fallen off instead, it would have been easy, I muttering irritably to myself. Then again, learning to stamp and sign with one's left hand cannot pose such an insurmountable problem, I immediately consoled myself. The second alternative was to go and confide in a doctor. Perhaps a doctor could help me. Given my hitherto impeccable record, suspicions would be minimal. Besides, I intend to assert right from the start, most emphatically, that I will continue working. However, it is conceivable that a visit to a doctor would be pointless. It's rather likely, in fact. Suspicion would be the only consequence of such a visit. So what should I do? I must admit that I was considerably uneasy when I entered the office building.

And rightly so. I don't even want to think about that morning. I was wounded in my softest spot. I found out how little trust I enjoyed in the eyes of my colleagues. At first I attributed their furtive glances to amazement and perhaps even sympathy. After all, pieces of extremities do not simply fall off of people like overripe pears from trees. But no, soon I realized the painful truth. In short, they assumed I wanted to help myself to disability payments. By no means do I want to diminish the respect which we customarily accord, which by law we must accord the disabled, but if it were not for my savings and a small inheritance which I had prudently left untouched, I don't know how I would have resolved my current predicament. And yet my coworkers were such splendid citizens. Surely they rejoice just as I do. I am not talking about sorrow, for which there are no reasons. Of course not. Not even that hand — one can live easily without a hand, I said to myself. After this disappointment, I concluded that, amidst an atmosphere of general mistrust, I am not taking any risks if I consult a doctor. Quite the contrary.

Yet the visit did not cheer me up a great deal. I myself was partly to blame. I should have conceived a plausible accident. I should not have been surprised that the physician mistrustfully shook his head. He put one hand into the pocket of his black overcoat, while his other hand played with a golden watch chain. Only when I repeated for the third time that I would not request any support and intended to continue my work at the office, did he put on a long white lab coat and examine both my wrist and the hand that had been sitting on his desk throughout our conversation. He shrugged and called a colleague. They debated for a while before sending me out in the hall to wait. After a long wait, I was led to a small examining room, where another physician sewed the hand back onto my wrist, supporting it with a small plank and binding it all up with stiff calico. This small operation cheered me up at last. You see, a simple procedure is all it takes for everything to be all right again. At the office I proudly showed off my splint to my colleagues; I think they were impressed. Suspicious looks turned into astonished ones and even those gradually vanished, because I came to the office regularly and promptly as ever before.

Every morning I left the house at the usual hour, feeling

joy at the sight of the trickling eaves and at the sound of the birds' songs and the lively music. But I was not at ease. My hand was in a strange state. Again my colleagues began to turn away from me but this time I could not blame them. My fingertips were turning blue, and the splint was beginning to give off an unbearable odor. Not even the eau de cologne with which I liberally doused my splint relieved its effects on my environment. I would even have to say that it made the odor still worse. At my next visit to the doctor, they removed the bandage; the hand fell off when they removed the plank. Now it looked like a dead extremity. Perplexed, the doctor stared at it and then used large pincers to throw the hand into the wastebasket. Then he questioned whether I still intended to keep up my work at the office. "Yes!" I exclaimed joyfully, and with that we parted.

Slowly, things were getting back to normal again. I learned to sign, stamp, greet, eat, and dress — in short, to do everything — with nothing but my left hand. I got used to it so much that slowly I began to forget that I ever had a right hand. My colleagues were also getting used to it, because the odor was a thing of the past and along with it, thank God, perhaps also the suspicion that I wanted to shirk my duties. In the mornings I rose gaily once again, whistled a tune, fed my canary, watered the flowers, and left the house with a joyful smile on my face. Most of the time, the sun was shining brightly, and on the trees the first tiny greenish-yellow leaves were appearing. If it were not inappropriate, one would have liked to jump for joy. However, I know my limits. A grown man, even more so a clerk with a claim to a pension, must painstakingly avoid disgracing his position. The only thing that somewhat marred my splendid mood was Felicie, the cleaning lady, who could not conceal her sorrow at my loss and from time to time would uninhibitedly lament. I felt ashamed for her, repeatedly admonished her, and was glad that no one heard her. And so life went on in an orderly fashion: working days were punctuated by Sundays and holidays, the weather was warming up, joy all around. Until, unfortunately, one literally fine day, things turned complicated again. Thoroughly. That morning I left the house a little earlier than usual in order to have breakfast at a small dairy bar on the corner, something I like to do every once in a while. Refreshed by the meal and elated after conversing with the genial waitress, I contentedly went on my way again.

The town, glistening in the morning sun with all the shades of gray, was thrusting its many spires into the translucent haze; from wetly shimmering roofs chimneys were sending encouragingly ample puffs of smoke into the sky.

I turned into a short, quiet street, no pedestrians any-where, and I think I was even whistling softly to myself. Suddenly, in my wrist — the other one, my last — I felt that strange loosening, that limpness, which I would have liked to have forgotten forever. Alarmed, I quickened my pace, as if it were possible to elude one's unpleasant sensations. After a few steps, my hand limply swung and fell to the pavement with an embarrassing slap. My first thought was, what will people say! I looked around. Fortunately, the street was completely deserted. I bent down and tried to pick up the hand. However, for an untrained man that is a very difficult task to accomplish, especially if he is upset. To make matters worse, I heard someone approaching. With lightning speed I stood up, stuck my stumps in my pockets and gazed at a faded poster advertising an old theater program. The passerby was a little boy carrying a school bag on his back and, thank goodness, he walked quickly and inattentively. I stared at the worn letters in front of me and gradually it began to dawn on me how nonsensical my under-taking was. Why scramble to pick up the hand if the first one ended up in the trash? As soon as the boy disappeared around the corner, I pushed the ill-fated limb to the gutter with the tip of my shoe. A hand barely measures eight inches from the wrist to the tip of the middle finger. But alas, it was too thick and would not squeeze through the bars of the grate. For a while I used force to try and stuff it between the narrow openings. It did not work. Infuriated, I kicked it hard. The hand filled me with fearsome hatred. More than anything, I would have liked to trample it to bits. Monstrously nonsensical, it was lying contemptibly in the middle of the street where I had propelled it with a vehement kick. At that moment I completely forgot that I was in public, that I was a decent, even-tempered man, and that my behavior was utterly improper. My stumps in my pockets, I ran over to the hand rather clumsily and glared at it for a moment; then I spat on it and, with another kick, dispatched it onto the opposite sidewalk.

Unspeakable dejection overpowered me. This was the end. I would not be able to stamp anything anymore. Theoretically the possibility remained that I could learn to do it with my foot, but in practical terms this was probably not realizable. Could one deal with people barefooted, leg up on the desk, without causing the reputation of the office to suffer? That moment I became a parasite, a loafer, an applicant for assistance. Against my will. But who will believe me? That day, while passing through the gate, I had to exert a great deal of effort to put on a suitably merry smile. In the office I silently held up both my stumps for my colleagues to see. Their joyful work expressions suddenly vanished from their faces. I recognized my impertinence and hid the stumps in my pockets again. My nearest coworker turned to me and inconspicuously sent me out into the hallway. After a moment, he came out after me and, in a whisper, told me to meet him in the men's room. I was starved for any word of encouragement, for a sign of trust, so I waited for him, resigned and patient. But it would have been better had that conversation never taken place. Even today, the memory of it brings me sadness. And that is something I desire least of all. When my colleague finally appeared, he locked himself into a stall with me and in the gurgling of flushing water he confessed to me how much he admired my determination. I looked at him with amazement, and he added with unexpected bitterness that he understood me, that anything was better than this, and his hand circumscribed a sweeping half-circle. At last he wished me good luck and told me to be careful and not to show myself at the office from now on. Man's envy is dangerous, he said. He slapped me on the back and slipped out.

I stood above the toilet bowl comfortably aghast. The gurgling of the water mournfully subsided. No, this man did not belong in the joyful world, filled with smiles and the enjoyment of work well done, in which I had been living until now. I was incapable of admitting that someone would not be proud to be part of our mighty institution, which determined the fate of so many people. I regained control of my emotions. Heaven knows what that man was thinking. Still, I stumbled out of the bathroom as if drugged. The words I had just heard troubled me more perhaps than the loss of my second hand.

This time the doctor examined the stump with a great deal of suspicion, and he demanded to see the lost appendage. After I explained, he hesitated for a moment, then reluctantly scribbled something on a piece of paper and dismissed me with the words, "Submit this with your application."

Never had I walked the street with such an unbecoming expression on my face. My painful feelings were only aggravated by the blaring sound of a jolly march and the happy faces of people rushing past me.

I reached my building, I wanted to go inside. It occurred to me that with those wretched stumps I would not be able to unlock the door to my apartment. Fortunately, a little boy was playing in front of the building. It was very awkward, but finally he understood, reached into my pocket, took out my key, walked upstairs with me, unlocked my door, and left. I was sorry I could not reward him for this favor, but he would have had to reach into the pocket of my coat himself to extract the money, and I did not have anything else on hand — God, what an empty expression. I slammed the door shut and wanted to unbutton my coat. Again I had to come up against the stumps. For the first time in my life I regretted not being married. Then I remembered that Felicie was supposed to come, and I calmed down somewhat. With one stump I lifted my hat and tossed it to the ground. Just as I bent down to try and pick it up — I had to learn to do it, I told myself — my right foot fell off. Including the shoe, naturally. It happened so suddenly, I lost my balance. My left leg, unsupported by its right counterpart, buckled under. It wouldn't have taken much to twist my ankle. I let the hat be and hobbled to the kitchen on my left leg, with the intention of eating a little something. Again, those stumps. The only accessible food was a forgotten piece of bread lying on the table. I took hold of it very clumsily and bit off a piece. But it was too difficult. I dropped the bread and hopped to the bedroom. My bed was still unmade, just as it had been when I rushed out in the morning. With my coat buttoned up — as there was no other option — I rolled onto the bed and lay there exhausted.

Streaks of golden sunlight were falling across my featherbed and my winter coat. From the street came cheerful music, the din of traffic, and the cries of children playing. In my overcoat I was hot, and muddled thoughts were spinning through my head, out of which the same one kept emerging — it would be best if I never rose again. And yet I did not want to think this thought and I refused to accede to it. It kept intruding between memories of a happy life, filled with industrious work and joy, between memories of my quiet pleasures, my childhood, my mother, whom I could see bending over me, taking me to church — I could discern her shape very clearly but, strangely enough, I could not picture her face. I recalled scenes from my school days, images of vacations complete with yellow fields and ponds; my Sunday bachelor outings filed past. All this was interfused with water flushing and a toilet bowl, everything was whirling through my head in extremely rapid succession, incoherent fragments, one image after the next, full of colors, suffused with radiant sunshine. Only the one persistent sentence, out of all the things reeling through my head, had neither color nor shape: it was black, composed of flat, distinct letters, as if someone were relentlessly etching it painfully onto my forehead with a thin, bony finger.

At last, I fell asleep despite the heat. I must have slept for a very long time, because I did not wake up until Felicie's arrival. She reacted as usual when something astounded her. She threw up her hands and shook her head. Then, without having to ask me many questions, she grasped the situation, approached the bed, and proceeded to pull off pieces of my clothing. My left shoe, including my other foot, was lying limply on the featherbed. The rest Felicie shook out of my pant legs and my sleeves, and then she lowered her eyes. "Oh my goodness," she said after a moment of silence, but she uttered it very quietly, knowing I cannot stand whining, and left the room.

Astonished, I surveyed my substantially diminished body. No reason to give in to panic. The essentials, namely my torso, neck, and head, remained, I said to myself, and then I wearily closed my eyelids once more. When I opened my eyes again, I saw Felicie stowing what had fallen from my clothes into her battered, red canvas bag. She glanced at me and, with a self-conscious, apologetic smile, she remarked that anything might come in handy. As she was putting the foot into the bag, she said she'd like to remove the shoe. I observed to her that, from this day on, I would not need shoes any longer. "True," Felicie said as if she were amazed she hadn't thought of it herself. Then she inquired where the other one was. I was so benumbed after my long nap that it took a moment for me to remember that it was lying in the hall. Poor Felicie, how joyful she was about the shoes. And even more so when I told her she could take the other clothes in my closet.

She clapped her gaunt hands joyfully, carried the red bag outside, and returned with a huge laundry basin. It was evident that she had quickly thought things over. My dear Felicie, I would have never guessed that she would become such a great support to me. She lifted me off my bed and set me into the basin. It was as if it had been molded for me. There was —

actually there still is — enough room around my ribcage, and the brim of the basin reached up to my neck, so that the view was sufficient. What am I saying, sufficient — it was downright magnificent. Then Felicie covered me and the basin with a checkered cloth, carefully tucked it in under my chin so that I would not be cold, opened the window, and lifted me onto the sill.

Below, in the tiny park, two little girls were playing with hoops. One of them had pretty blond hair flowing down her back. It was softly waving in the azure air of spring. The birds' songs quivered beneath a translucent sky, and in the corner of the building's small garden forsythias were blooming.

After Felicie made the bed and covered it with a spread embroidered with violets, I dictated to her my application for assistance. She handwrote it in an awkward script, and I had to point out several errors to her, but in the end the result was passable.

That sunny morning my present life began. The days are once again well structured and orderly. In good weather I spend my days in the basin on the window sill. In the morning Felicie brings me the newspaper; before she goes home, she carries me to the bathroom, cleans out the basin, and turns down the bed for me. She feeds me three times a day; she had the rest of the day to attend to her own business. Over time we have come up with some minor improvements: a small reading stand, a board across the brim of the basin with a little bell I can easily hold between my teeth and ring by shaking my head when I need to summon her. The only problem is that, lately, the poor woman is a little hard of hearing, so that the bell may be becoming a mere formality. But this is a minor issue, since I do not need anything anyway most of the time. Of course, she must come every day now, and I have to pay her much more than I did before. However, if I factor in how much money I save on shoes, tailors, cabs, and myriads of other expenditures which now I no longer incur, it is not so bad at all.

Felicie bought me a used baby carriage for my birthday, and she takes me out for a walk on occasion. We undertake such outings at dusk in order to avoid attracting attention. The face of a grown man in a baby carriage looks somewhat bizarre, if not downright comical. But despite the twilight, I derive great pleasure from our excursions. I always display the most joyous expression with utmost spontaneity. I don't have to strive for it, it is always there. In the basin, in the bathroom, in my bed, perhaps even while I'm sleeping. The alarm that I experienced standing over that toilet bowl has been mercifully shrouded by time. Life is joyful, so joyful I sometimes feel sorry I am unable to snap my fingers with good cheer. It doesn't matter. As I said on that first morning after awakening into the present situation — the essential part of me remains. Especially my face, which is unwaveringly able to fulfill its duty, smiling constantly. Cheerfully, by all means cheerfully, I tell Felicie when sometimes she shakes her head at me with concern. Poor old woman, I don't hold it against her. She hasn't learned anything. She is up to her neck in her old ways. Almost as much as I am in my basin.

PAVEL GRYM

from **The Chinese Dragon**

translated by David Powelstock

> The second half of the twentieth century is poor in
> adventures, and when writers have no adventures to
> tell, their words become clichés and lose their meaning.
> —Isaac Bashevis Singer (1904-1991)

It is in the nature of rain to be indifferent in equal measure to both people and things.

It was raining lightly but persistently.

The broad black hat of the shop assistant was wet through, but the water was not enough to wash away all the dirt or diminish the smell of excrement. Fine runnels blazed trails through the venerable dust of the shop windows, forming glinting spider webs on the glass.

The shop assistant turned up the collar of his long overcoat, but even this did not help drive away the feeling of cold and penetrating damp. He shuffled along hesitantly, pushed by a crowd of tired and peevish people trudging, eyes to the ground, past the blank shop windows and lampposts, most of whose lanterns were broken. The glass in many of the windows was broken, too, and covered with crude boards or pasted over with paper, small strips of which had been torn off by wind and water. Pieces of paper, various scraps, and refuse of all sorts fell to the sidewalk from overflowing trash cans and bins. The hatter's window, into which the shop assistant glanced unconsciously in passing, was full of dust; dust lay thickly even on the three or four crumpled hats that rested on heads with the same dull expression that could be discerned on the faces of passersby. The only enticement offered by the tailor's window next door was the despairing nakedness of a dressing dummy, hands raised in a despairing gesture. Its pleas, however, were disregarded.

The shop assistant's immobile face, with the slight depressions of its premature wrinkles, vaguely called to mind a bowl of slushy dough or a pale moon. His long, voluminous coat enveloped a frame that seemed bulky and strong, but its bulk called to mind a balloon that, in spite of its expanse, could easily become a helpless plaything of the wind. His dull, expressionless face, bearing no trace of passion, aversion, or pain, of wonder or disappointment, had caused him difficulties even in his youth; in those who regarded it, this face, whose dull indifference seemed to imply nothing certain, stirred up an almost hysterical fury. The mute queries or misgivings this reticent boy directed, only very rarely, toward those around him were understood as provocation, or at best as awkwardness or a pronounced doltishness, which in spite of its innocence and harmlessness so thoroughly irritated the listener that he felt the urge to use his fist or the object nearest at hand to sow his helpless rage in a deep furrow across the immobile paleness of this doughy face.

The questions he posed now, however, were posed to himself alone. He treaded slowly and heavily, merging with the quietly flowing crowd of silent, expressionless faces. Each person hurried toward his own destination, self-absorbed and heedless of the others, unless someone chanced to be in his way; each anxiously gripped his bag, briefcase, or bundle containing something that might mean nothing special to anyone else, but that had some value for him; the bundle might just as easily be a chunk of bread as a broken doll that, when picked up, would erupt in half-intelligible cries, rolling its sole remaining eye; or else some small device, a hearing aid or music box, so greatly valued by its owner, for whatever reasons, that he could not part with it even on the way to work, or shopping, or some other destination, but to anyone else they are of no interest and have no distinct purpose. After all, there was not a lot that could be bought in the city, and people worked not so much out of necessity as from a certain inertia; it invariably seemed better to occupy oneself with some small matter than to stare at the bare walls and listen to others' indistinct sighs echoing in the building where you just happened to find yourself.

It occasioned a certain animation in the street when, amid the row of closed doors and blank windows of erstwhile stores and workshops, one of a set of shabby double doors opened, a stout woman with disheveled black hair hanging over her swarthy face pushed across the threshold a small cracked table covered with some sort of wares wrapped slapdash in torn paper, and two other women, enough like her to be her sisters, took up agreed-upon positions on either side of her.

One of the women, armed with a broom, began to rain forcible blows on the heads of the zealously clustering interlopers, whose assault threatened to force the table, together with the women, back into the shop's interior. The possibility could not be ruled out that someone might try to grab the goods by force and escape without paying. While the one woman poked and beat back the insolent zealots, the eldest handed the merchandise to the nearest customers, who continuously elbowed, kicked, and punched their way to the table, and the third took their money and, seated expansively on a chair, shoved the bills beneath her massive buttocks, to better defend them against the intrusions of light fingers. From time to time, goods were accepted in exchange; after their value was assessed, she placed these goods behind her, in the shop's gloom.

The division of labor was exemplary; only in this way was it possible to meet the demand of all these people, who bought without thinking what it was they were actually buying or whether they had any use for it, because the opportunity to buy anything at all was so unheard of that they bought more for the sake of the buying itself than out of any urgent need for any particular thing.

The knot of people mumbled, groaned, fussed, and were tossed about as some tried to bore their way through to the table, while others, taking malicious joy in the realization of their intentions, pushed through the crowd in the opposite direction in their struggle to get their captured prey off to a safe distance. Even if a person bought something for which he had no need or use whatsoever, there was always the possibility of selling the thing to someone else, or trading it for something more necessary at that moment.

Despite considerable agitation and sporadic outcries, the struggle by the table proceeded quietly, because too loud a cry would have been too conspicuous and untoward; nevertheless, despite the buyers' assiduous etiquette, loud groans were heard from the crowd whenever the broom came down a little harder, catching someone full on. In spite of all this, the table was soon emptied, and the woman in command grimaced half maliciously, half regretfully, but not by any stretch apologetically, at the remaining interlopers; her comrade-in-arms put down her weapon, and the third woman, the one in charge of the take, backed into the depths of the store under their guard. Behind this woman and her two sisters, if they really were her sisters, the table disappeared, the door closed, the lock rattled, and the store, with its indecipherable sign, its letters long ago erased by the rain, fell quiet again, slipping from the notice of the people trudging by, rejoining the row of silent storefronts, empty windows, and tightly shut doors.

The crowd, momentarily distracted, reconstituted itself into a slowly shifting stream, and the shop assistant was forced to adapt.

Suddenly he felt a sharp pain below his left knee, and before he could open his mouth to let out a voiceless cry he heard a discontented growl from below. He looked down on the upturned, scowling, stubbled, and indignantly wrinkled face of a legless cripple on a low cart, pushing tenaciously with his one remaining arm and with the help of a short, stout stick, edging his way forward through dozens of indifferent legs in an effort to overtake the rushing unimpaired as if his life depended on it, and impatiently swinging his stick against the legs of those who were too slow or indecisive, including the bewildered shop assistant, who now stepped aside to let the grumbling cripple pass him and thus satisfy his desire to reach some undoubtedly important destination.

The shop assistant stopped, withdrew toward the wall of a building, and pressed himself into the nearest recess so as not to be in the way. Puzzled, he rubbed the afflicted spot with the fingers of his right hand.

A high-sided cart clattered by at the end of the street. Garbage women in dirty gray smocks with dusty scarves over their heads were emptying into it the various bins, buckets, boxes, and baskets full of rags, paper, abandoned objects, and broken toys; there had been especially many toys in the trash lately, because the number of children in the city was declining, and those who remained had gradually outgrown their toys and put aside their former pleasures without regret.

When all the bins and baskets in one spot had been emptied, a burly woman with a commanding manner urged the driver in a harsh and somewhat vulgar voice to move on, and when the horses had pulled them away and stopped again, she was the first, cursing, to seize the next container of trash and objects, which, like the toys, had become useless deadweight.

The cart had not yet reached the middle of the street, but was already so full that every jolt of the bumpy pavement with its jutting and sunken cobblestones, caused it to lose some of its cargo. But the women paid no attention to this.

A toy horse fell into the mud at the shop assistant's feet, a horse carved out of wood, with the tattered remains of a string around its neck, a broken leg, and the mournful eyes of one who is going somewhere, driven by the need to leave, escape, and hide out somewhere else, but who has no precise destination and who finds no refuge.

The rain did not stop.

*

The mere sight of this worn wooden horse with a string around its neck and a broken leg sufficed to set the early memories of the man standing over the broken toy flying off far into the past.

Even as a little boy his frame had been bulky by comparison with the other children. They shrank from him; his seemingly cruel indifference and ostensible strength inspired fear in them, until they discovered his weakness, realized their error, and gleefully misapplied their new realization by relentlessly committing misdeeds against the defenseless boy. From that point on, he was the favorite target and victim of insulting and inhumane practical jokes, as if the children were taking revenge on him for the weakness and submissiveness they themselves felt when they realized that his size meant nothing and that his strength was merely a chimera.

At first glance no one would have associated him with the slight and fragile being whose perpetual timidity every so often gave way to the ill-concealed anxiety with which she observed the momentous and barely comprehensible events that unfolded around her. No one would have expected to find the mother of this oddly hypertrophied child in this fearful woman, with her shy and apologetic smile, who performed her wifely duties by the side of her burly husband inconspicuously, quietly, and self-consciously, with a circumspect conscientiousness some would have called flawless.

It was odd to see her slight figure alongside the indifferent-looking doughy giant, whose broad face had space enough for the entire spectrum of emotions, but whose pale surface neither then nor later showed any clear, legible signs of the wonder, pain, joy, disappointment, and defiance typical of children his age.

The child's indifference so greatly irritated the strong,

bearded man who was his father that he conceived an intense dislike for the child from the very first glance at his absent expression, which showed no interest in familiar voices or faces looking down at him — although, for the time being, in the interests of decency, he did not make his feelings very clear.

The father's aversion, unspoken but obvious, worried the mother at first, but eventually she simply came to accept it as fact and adjusted to it, as did the child, who took as compensation for this bearded hulk's disinterest the attention paid him, albeit with a certain reserve, by his mother.

To be sure, with the arrival of further children, even the mother's lukewarm concern waned, without any corresponding decrease in the father's malice. And so the family unit accepted the future shop assistant as an allowable presence, but not a necessary one, something to be conscious of, but nothing to go very far out of one's way for.

By some odd sort of intuition, his siblings divined the boy's odd status in the family and happily exploited the fact that their treacheries went unpunished. They did not include him in their games, or at most as the sacrificial lamb of their caprices; they did not invite him into the kingdom of their childish secrets; and they had no inkling of his desires, ideas, or dreams. He was included among their numbers, but he was ascribed neither meaning nor significance, and the boy aspired to none. While each of the other children excelled at something, or least distinguished himself by some individual habit, taste, or preference, this large boy excelled at nothing. It was not even possible to say whether he was better or worse at a given thing, for he never tried, and he was so irrelevant, dull, and alien that he was factored out of the others' every concern, and he uniformly factored them out until it came to a complete separation.

He never got to experience praise or acknowledgment, but he did meet with countless jeers, pokes, and blows. Nevertheless, he learned to take them without a trace of discomfort or even irritation, without being a tearful, stammering tattle-tale. With fixed expression and without a word, he dodged these rebukes and blows, and showed no sign of anxiety or defiance, or even any pleasure when something unpleasant befell one of his tormentors. Everything that occurred in the normal course of events seemed to reinforce the solidarity of the family or, more precisely, the solidarity of the rest of the family, which excluded and stood against the lonely boy.

Almost as a rule, any wrath provoked by one of the three more fortunate siblings would ultimately be turned against the innocent boy.

It was their father's fancy to compose morally strict, didactic stories and subsequently read them solemnly before the assembled family. The success of these endeavors could be justifiably doubted.

During his slow periods, of which there were unfortunately more than there were periods of successful commerce, the rabbinically thick-bearded father would seat himself at the table by the parlor window, hat on his head, and, uttering an occasional cry of satisfaction at a fortuitous expression or exceptionally witty turn of phrase, compose moral tales about reluctant, erring heroes searching for the painful yet worthy path to virtue or, alternatively, immoral pariahs deservedly plunged into the depths of contempt.

If a work was finished in time, the family's humble supper would be followed by a solemn reading of the new literary gem, during which it was advisable from time to time to smile slightly, thoughtfully nod one's head, and emit cries of amazement and gratification, not unlike those cries of joy emitted by the father during the application of words to paper; it is for God to judge those excessively strict, uncomprehending, and envious publishers whose willful opposition prevented these pearls of the father's soul from ever being anointed with printer's ink, thus violently silencing the earnest efforts of one of world's humble geniuses.

In his home, however, it was necessary to listen attentively and with exemplary gravity, as the children quickly learned to do.

Nevertheless, during one of the father's readings one of the boys, perhaps because he became lost in thought and neglected to pay due attention, perhaps because something truly funny had occurred to him, let out an entirely ill-timed and inappropriate laugh.

The father fell silent, looked up, placed his papers on the table top, silently stood and, red-faced, stepped toward the culprit, raised his mighty mitt, grasped the boy by the scruff of the neck, and in one powerful motion plunged his startled face into a bowl containing the uneaten remains of a mushy salad. The father then released the boy and, as the sobbing miscreant, watched and simultaneously urged on by his mother's imploring gaze, scurried from the room to cry himself out and then wash up, the father, with a silent frown, returned to his place at the head of the table to resume his reading.

More often than not one thing leads to another, and this case was no exception.

After reading a while longer, when the father raised his eyes to ascertain his listeners' level of attention after the foregoing demonstration of crude inconsiderateness, his glance encountered the indifferent gaze of the future shop assistant.

The dull expression on the listener's face was apparently sufficient evidence of his insolent lack of interest.

And while listening to his father's distinguished composition!

Flinging his papers down on the table, the father leapt to his feet, grabbed the boy by the hair, and, accompanied by the others' terrified silence, dragged the taciturn scoundrel through the dark hallway, opened the door to a closet with a single little air vent, and in one motion threw him inside. The boy went reeling and fell face down among the brooms, pails, boxes, and rags used by the mother to keep the household in a state of sparkling perfection and immaculate cleanliness.

Unlike his predecessor, this offender was sentenced to remain confined in the darkness all evening. At first the boy could hear the muffled voices issuing from the parlor, but gradually even these fell silent. Only when all had gone to bed and the father had fallen asleep did his frightened mother, looking anxiously over her shoulder, release him with a quiet sigh and, one finger pressed to her lips, lead him to his bed.

And so things remained.

After this, he was no longer allowed to participate in family events such as the father's readings. He was, however, required to remain within earshot — on this the father insisted — but out of his sight, behind the door into the hallway, which was left open just enough that his father's moralizing sermon could be heard.

Excluded from his siblings' and classmates' games, he would come home after school and sit in a corner, and if his father returned unexpectedly early, with frightened sighs, his mother would lead the boy off to the closet, as if he were serving out a life sentence among the brooms and rags. Once the door was closed behind him it stayed closed, either out of apathy or out of fear of the father, whose vehement indignation would certainly have been aroused by any show of sympathy or even concern.

Whatever preoccupied him, whatever it was he thought about, he confided to no one; in any case, his thoughts would have met with disinterest or lack of sympathy. His siblings, with the accustomed carefree nature of youth, which accepts change as a fait accompli, took the new order of things in stride. The boy's status was a reality requiring no elaboration, and if he was spoken of at all, his name was never used, as if he hadn't any; he was simply the one behind the door, and if the mother asked, "Is he back yet?" or, "Is he home from school?" there was no need whatsoever for naming, because everyone knew who was meant. And if, for example, the father, during the family's preparations for a festive excursion to the park outside the city, said in response to an unspoken question in the mother's eyes, "He is not going," the verdict was clear, and there was no need to ask upon whom it had been passed.

Only in the late evening was the boy allowed to withdraw to his allotted cubbyhole at the other end of the apartment, originally intended as the servant's quarters (for which the not very successful builder had not had enough materials), where he stored his few personal belongings and a single toy, whose poor condition had caused his more rapacious siblings to overlook it: a carved wooden horse with mournful eyes and a broken leg.

The situation was not much different at school, where his inscrutable face, his indifference, and his inability to respond in the usual manner progressively enraged his teachers, until they finally lost interest in him and ceased to notice him at all.

Even grades, supposed to reflect the acquisition of hard-earned knowledge, seemed not to matter much in his case; they did not carry the same weight as for the other students, and they played no role even when the accounts of the children's diligence were reckoned at home.

While, with knitted brow, the father meticulously scrutinized the report cards laid by the others one by one on the table with quivering emotions, here conferring restrained praise, there reproach, he showed no interest in the future shop assistant's grades. Two or three times it happened that the boy stood with his important document completely unnoticed and ignored, and his mother did not dare call attention to his presence; his father would then ostentatiously leave the room or engage in something obviously more important to him. And so the boy ceased to participate in this particular family ceremony, too, and he was not missed, just as he was not missed by the teachers when he left school for good; not one of the educators seemed even to note his departure, and if they had, they would probably have been relieved at being spared the necessity of seeing this unfathomable, taciturn student, who was guilty of nothing and excelled at nothing, but whose quiet, resigned presence irritated them and provoked their anger.

The quiet discussions about what was wrong with the

boy, to which no one except possibly his mother paid much attention, including the boy himself, were interrupted by events that had no small significance for the life of the family; which is not to say, however, that under different circumstances the boy's fate would not have turned out the same.

One night he was awakened by a persistent thirst.

Quietly, so as not to arouse unwanted attention, he crept across the room and past the doors behind which his siblings lay sleeping, and stepped out into the foyer where, in accordance with the father's wishes, a weak light perpetually shone. His unwieldy body swayed awkwardly from side to side in his attempt to tiptoe. He stopped when he heard from his parents' bedroom his father's imperative groans and his mother's loud sighs, like moans of anguish, pain, and fear. He was seized by an oppressive despair. He carefully grasped the knob and opened the door. The weak light fell on the bed and revealed his father lying heavily on his mother's slight, naked body. The father wrestled with all the tenacity and savagery that came naturally to him, and the mother's body writhed impotently beneath his weight. As the father's swaying motions accelerated, the groaning mother dug her fingers into his exposed back and her legs clutched the body of her assailant in a desperate embrace.

Even if the boy had not screamed in fright, the weak light penetrating through the gap of the opened door would have given him away.

The father turned his head toward the door, and his eyes, framed by his bristling hair and beard, glinted maliciously. He disengaged himself from the grasp of his embrace and leapt up with a screech of savage hatred; he froze still for an instant, looking like a wild barbarian, his genitals jutting upward in warning. Then, with a vulgar oath, he ran after the boy, who fled, zigzagging between chairs, into his own little chamber in the foolish notion that he might find sanctuary there.

The blows he met with when the naked man caught him were perhaps not as painful as the loss of that lone toy, which the wild avenger furiously trampled to pieces, mindless of the splinters sticking into the soles of his bare feet; and even more painful was the betrayal that placed a boundary marker of disappointment and distrust between the boy and his mother forever.

Betrayal is worse than open enmity, whose moves can in the best of circumstances be anticipated, because betrayal does injury to trust; it approaches insidiously and picks its contaminated fruit without any warning.

The mother's betrayal, at least as the boy understood it, was proof of the duplicity of her earlier closeness to him. It dispirited him that precisely this fragile being, toward whom he had felt trust, not only submitted to but welcomed the atrocities of this hairy thug, that her slight body lifted its delicate, birdlike breast into this bear's embrace, not just out of duty and resignation, but, as it seemed, happily and with obvious pleasure.

Although he had learned not to surrender to the flow of his emotions, and still less to their ostentatious display, this assent, willingness, and welcoming of violence disturbed him.

With his siblings the distance only grew wider, not that they had ever been close, but with his mother her purity had offered a sanctuary of hope, so that this sudden and violent loss of faith brought with it shock and disappointment, which gave way ultimately to a profound bitterness.

For a little while he still made an effort to encounter her as often as possible, if necessary under false pretenses, in order to obtain some explanation (although he had little hope of one) and some assurance that everything would again be all right (although he put little faith in this). Instead, the mother, without hiding her embarrassment and agitation, would more hesitantly than decisively pull her delicate hand free from the grip of his fleshy one, shake her head no and, silently, without a single word, run off somewhere, leaving behind only the fragrance of lilies-of-the-valley, those flowers so appealing to the eye and nose but in reality poisonous, and leaving the bewildered and dispirited boy standing alone in an empty room, his mouth open in an anguished moan, his hand impotently sinking into the emptiness.

He did not have to dodge his father's heavy fists for long. The next time they met face to face, the future shop assistant found him to be unusually calm and quiet. It is probably for this reason that the reclining man with the cross stuck in his clasped hands struck him as a perfect stranger.

*

Buffeted by the wind and rain, the graying plaster of the buildings, buttressed here and there by thick beams, crumbled and fragmented, came down on the pedestrians' heads in the form of sticky flakes.

The amorphous mass drifting silently past the dusty glass of shop displays, tightly shut doors, and broken windows, many covered by a couple of crossed, weather-beaten boards, gradually disbanded and dissolved.

Some hurried into offices, whose uncertain business hours could never be anticipated, or on some other extremely important mission or appointment; others disappeared into the few rarely open shops or toward some other destination, which they did not bother boasting about and which the others neither knew nor cared about.

Moving along with hesitation and still without a clear purpose, the shop assistant found himself suddenly and unexpectedly alone, and for a moment he was confused, for at least in a crowd it was possible to remain concealed, to avoid unwanted attention, while his solitude rendered him visible and vulnerable.

He was suddenly all by himself in a depopulated expanse, perhaps once some sort of square, with a few tree stumps and a dry, half-excavated fountain. In the middle of this empty space, framed by abandoned buildings, was a structure no doubt once quite tall, but now crumbling, with two towers and two onion-shaped domes covered with rotten shingles.

The building's plaster had crumbled off in places to reveal the reddish brickwork beneath. Its high, narrow windows had been mostly knocked out, and shards of colored glass and fragments of stone littered the green expanse of weeds and moss. Even the steps leading up to the main entrance, with its half-unhinged gates, were strewn with bricks, shards of glass, and splinters of wood. One side of the heavy wooden gate, with its rusting metal inlays, hung drunkenly from its post, while the other side had vanished entirely; the resulting opening seemed to bid the solitary wayfarer to enter.

He decided to obey this summons, more out of confusion than intent.

The broken walls jutting into a tall window in the shape of a pointed oval were marked by numerous slashes, colored smudges, shameless inscriptions and figures, and deeply etched scars. On the walls, in an incomprehensible arrangement, hung a series of empty frames, long ago richly ornamented, but now pitifully worn and abraded, displaying only limply fluttering scraps of canvas.

On the ground, among scraps of wood and brick, lay the scattered ruins of wooden pews and prie-dieus, which had long ago ceased to call anyone to humble genuflection. Among this wreckage were the half-clothed, half-naked bodies of men and women, arms amputated at the elbows, legs pierced by broken arrows, and severed heads with eyes fixed in awe and wonderment at all the destruction, to which they surrendered in their impotence.

He stepped hesitantly through the remains of hope, joy, humility, and glory until he reached the raised area at the far end of the hall.

Seemingly rooted in the floor and leaning against the wall out of some strange whim, an unclothed figure rose from the waist up, head sagging dolefully, arms spread wide, suggesting the outline of the cross to which they had once been nailed. In the steadfast silence, pervasive filth, and desolate solitude, this wretched face above the haggard body, wonderfully preserved despite signs of destruction, personified reproach. However, it was possible to find in it, beyond the clarity of its suffering, a promise of soothing equanimity.

With some emotion, the shop assistant remembered that some time long ago, as a child subjected to the cruel will of the man called his father, he had heard stories about a man whose suffering was supposed to redeem the suffering of others, but this was merely the glimmer of a bygone experience, of which nothing remained after all these years but a vague recollection of the cross in the fingers of his deceased father.

He had the feeling that he was supposed to do something, but he considered in vain what that something might be. However hard he tried, he could call forth only a dull impression, which was immediately pushed to the background by the image of the thick fingers of the hulk in the coffin tenaciously gripping the symbol he now saw life-sized before him.

Finally he sighed heavily, screwed up his mouth when he felt a pain in his chest, and walked out of the dried-up well of hope just as confused and uncertain as when he had entered.

*

The event that shook the family left the boy indifferent, as did the ensuing disorder, in which he played no part. He felt neither sorrow nor relief, and he adapted to the changing state of affairs without any effort. When told to wait, he waited. When ordered to put on his holiday clothes, he put them on, and later, neither recognized nor noticed by the arriving guests, he watched from a distance as men in black suits and women in black dresses came into the dining room that had been transformed into a funeral parlor, as they pressed his ashen mother's hands with sorrowful expressions and delivered ad nauseam the same words of sympathy, squinting at the recent widow and at each other to ascertain the effects of their displays.

When the mummery of condolences was almost complete, and the guests were asked to gather in the front yard for a subdued toast (a break to lighten the mood), the boy, again forgotten, stood up and walked slowly to the table where only recently, without him of course, one of the solemn family readings had taken place and on which the deceased man was now displayed in an open casket, so that the participants in this sad ceremony could gaze one more time into the face of the man who had never aroused much interest — until his sudden death made him the object of a modest curiosity. The cause of his death was as banal as his life had been and is hardly worth mentioning at the expense of other, much more noteworthy occurrences.

The boy looked silently into the face whose kindness he had never known.

When his eyes passed from the yellowed face to the clasped hands, into whose stiff fingers a small wooden cross had been thrust, and a furtive glance had established that he was in the room alone and that no one could see even from the hallway and become the unwelcome witness of his act, he impulsively tore the symbol of sacrifice and love from the defenseless hands of the deceased and, anxiously shielding it from prying eyes, went down to the cellar, placed it deliberately on the last step, and with the pride of an avenger trampled the cross to splinters beneath his heel.

In the general confusion reigning in the period of mourning his quiet rebellion went unnoticed, and if a fleeting sign of satisfaction passed across the boy's face as the coffin was lowered into the grave, it was because he alone knew that the greatest act of his life so far had been to deprive his tormentor of the undeserved consolation that he took the cross in his father's hands to represent.

From the standpoint of the family, their liberation from the father's implacable strictures was inconveniently purchased at the price of uncertainty regarding what to do after the passing of their breadwinner, who had furthermore left little behind. Moving to a more modest apartment and selling a few things would only help temporarily. Above all, the woman, now all alone, had no idea what to do with the growing boy. She convinced herself that she was acting out of helplessness when, with no small relief and with the recommendation of acquaintances as an excuse, she decided to entrust the boy to a distant and inexpensive institution that engaged in the upbringing of children in early adolescence.

The boy took the news of this falteringly delivered decision without apparent emotion. His siblings were already distant to him, and the pain of his mother's betrayal was still too much alive for him to make parting with her unbearable. Ultimately, the reality that the remoteness of the institution, the mother's new worries, and the lack of money for travel would of necessity limit their relations was a certain relief to both of them. There was nothing the boy would not be content to leave behind, and his mother's decision freed him of the need to make any decision of his own.

Their parting in the courtyard of the cheerless gray building standing in the middle of a desolate park littered with fragments of broken benches and sculptures may have seemed poignant, but as soon as his mother was seated in the train headed home, she was delighted by how easily she had relieved herself of the burdensome custody of the taciturn boy, and especially of his quizzical and reproachful looks; and it was no different for the boy, who, at the headmaster's suggestion, calmly and quietly withdrew to his assigned room to acquaint himself with his new duties and his new classmates.

His mother's promised visits never materialized. Although she remarked more than once to friends and acquaintances that she was making plans to visit the boy, and perhaps for a fleeting moment she really intended to, she always put the trip off, alluding to other concerns, the children's sickness, urgent house-work, sleet, the remoteness of the institution, lack of money, atmospheric disruptions, and the long and arduous journey; and each time she arrived at a decision to put the trip off to a more opportune time, she felt, in addition to a slight feeling of shame, a certain relief as well.

It did not seem that it mattered very much to the boy.

He did not bother to write letters describing his feelings and experiences, a task which would have caused him certain difficulties in any case. When he received a letter, which was not very often, he put it aside without reading it. And so he did not even know if he had been invited home for the holidays or vacation, as were most of the institution's charges; instead, like the others who remained there during such times for this or some other reason, he went out at harvest time to help the local farmers gather their meager crops. His mother's dispatches came more and more infrequently, until they stopped coming altogether.

Life at the institution was monotonous, almost unbearably so; the students were supposed to acquire the basic qualifications needed to practice one of several rarely chosen, not very demanding professions, such as wheelbarrow driver, sundial maker, or general assistant. After their lessons the students had to stay within the grounds, surrounded by a high wall with one gate guarded by a strict gatekeeper, and so they varied their days in the institution by means of savage games, in which the future shop assistant was often the victim.

For them he represented an insoluble mystery, and this impotence soon became an annoyance to them. As they quickly realized, he did not confide his thoughts or boyish dreams to anyone, as the others did, and so he remained for all of them an enigmatic traveler without baggage or identity.

His figure towered over the others, motionless and mute as a forbidding rocky massif, and his uncommunicative, unreadable face conspicuously and threateningly distinguished itself from their rowdy boyish faces.

But as soon as the little terrors around him discovered, as had his siblings before them, that his size and apparently threatening expression were not evidence of determination or strength, that he posed no danger, they began to take revenge on him for his inaccessibility and reticence by doing all sorts of mischief. He became the butt of crude jokes and the victim of all sorts of pranks, but he accepted these torments as a reality that simply had to be accepted, and never let himself be provoked into anything imprudent.

So they found a new way of looking out for themselves after their incendiary efforts. Whenever any sort of disruption was being investigated, they cunningly fingered him as its author and, in fact, as the perpetrator of a whole range of misdeeds. And since the boy's responses to the intrusive questions of the investigators and of the headmaster himself seemed evasive, aloof, and indifferent, since he did not defend himself against their accusations, for he considered this pointless, his behavior was perceived as a confession. And so, whether out of impatience or bias, the investigators frequently accused him of wrongdoing and, to the malicious glee of the others, punished him before the entire institution. He accepted even these punishments as something essentially uninteresting, dull, necessary, and utterly normal.

He aroused no special interest among the teachers and custodians as a good, or even particularly bad student; he distinguished himself neither by exemplary virtues nor by misbehavior; he took little interest in what went on around him, nor did those around him take much interest in him. And so it went until one day the headmaster called him in and informed him that his days at the institution were numbered and his training complete. He showed neither enthusiasm nor resistance as he was informed that, with the consent of his mother, about whom he had heard and known nothing for a long time, they were sending him to the city to seek his place in the world.

This is how he became an apprentice, and afterwards a full-fledged shop assistant. His calm disposition aroused trust in employers and customers, but at the same time they were somewhat indignant at the apathy with which he correctly but unenthusiastically filled their orders, obeyed their commands, and did the tasks assigned him.

It is well known that difference alone is often enough to provoke annoyance. He stood rigidly by the shopkeeper's side, behind the counter, and handed over, wrapped, or put away the merchandise just as he was directed. He worked in a succession of shops before he found his way to the place that would have a decisive effect on his fate. He was certainly reliable, but each of the shopkeepers, who in the pursuit of success and profit had to be prompt, compliant, glib, and courteous in order to keep their customers, was bothered in turn, as were some of the customers, by his inability to curry favor and chatter entertainingly, to be courteous and attentive, the bread and butter of shopkeeping. And so the shop assistant, with the help of the sullen bureaucrat whose job it was to attend to such matters, frequently switched cubbyholes, streets, and stores, until he wound up at a clothing and dry goods store called The Chinese Dragon.

Except for a few trifles, he carried out of the past only one vague experience.

The out-of-the-way bookstore, one of the last of its kind, was frequented by a few elderly men in threadbare overcoats, clearly not particularly wealthy. With the shop assistant's unobtrusive complicity, they paged through the much-handled books in evident embarrassment, then with sighs and apologies placed them back on the counter: too expensive and nonessential to the life of an old man.

Among the occasional visitors, there was one who caught the shop assistant's attention in a particular way; it was a pale, unattractive girl who would enter with a shy smile, as if apologizing for her appearance and for how bold she was to enter the store and join the company of the old men silently turning pages — boldness some might have considered unseemly.

Without himself knowing why, the shop assistant welcomed her infrequent visits, but he showed his pleasure so meekly and inconspicuously that the girl probably did not even notice.

He observed with interest as she leafed and read through

the books displayed on the counter and in the dust-covered cabinets. Sometimes she would even point bashfully at a volume beyond her reach, and the shop assistant would hand it to her with unusual readiness.

Women, he was convinced, could be the carriers of the blackest betrayal.

And yet he seemed to find in her pale, freckled face, limp hair, and downcast eyes something he had never noticed in anyone, with the possible exception of his mother, prior to her betrayal.

The girl too hardly ever bought anything, and would leave the store with faltering words of apology, leaving behind only a slight suggestion of cheap perfume, until finally, for whatever reason, she stopping coming altogether. After some time, the shop assistant resigned himself to this as an immutable fact. Not long afterward, the bookstore, deemed entirely superfluous and unprofitable, was closed down; boards were nailed across the emptied display window; and the shop assistant never again saw either the shopkeeper, who went off to a retirement home, or the girl — for the morose bureaucrat in charge of finding work for the wards of the institution brought him to an entirely different part of the city, one in somewhat better repair, to a place with a large hanging signboard, which read A. GRUBER, WIDOW. Over the inscription, the goggling, unseeing eyes of a grotesque Chinese dragon popped out into the street.

When they entered, a girl whose tired face expressed extreme despair and distaste, crept out to meet them from the dark recesses of the shop, utterly shattered by the thought that she would be forced against her will to offer her services to these intruders; and when, after a certain amount of exertion, she reached them, she slowly raised her head, her mouth hanging half open, and with obvious disgust asked them what they wanted.

While the shop assistant remained silent as usual, in his brisk, measured manner the bureaucrat asked her to summon the widow.

Even at this first meeting, the widow, who had taken over

the shop after the death of her husband, came across as coolly observant, inaccessible and strict. Unlike other shopkeepers, who glibly emphasized the high quality of the merchandise, she made some customers uneasy by silently and carefully watching their fingers as they stroked the bolts of cloth laid out on the counter or the fabric of the hanging clothes. Thin, in a long black skirt and a white blouse with frills and pleated collar, her bosom bound up high on her torso, her hair tied tightly in a black bun above her pale face, with its piercing eyes and its skin stretched taut over protruding cheekbones, she stood behind the counter near the old-fashioned register like a hawk awaiting its prey, carefully listening to the rustle of banknotes and the clinking of coins.

Even those in the immediate neighborhood knew little about her, and the information exchanged in confidential whispers relied more on appearances and speculation than on confirmed fact. Except for the door through which customers passed into the shop, the place remained tightly shut, and it was difficult for anyone to recall having ever seen a visitor.

And if little was known about the widow, who even behind the counter was hardly known for being open or voluble, even less was known about her prematurely deceased husband. There were a few furtive stories here and there, telling of shady business, secret meetings, and strange journeys that reportedly brought in significant profits, and there were also tales of the wealth the reticent, distrustful couple had hidden away within.

Few people were moved by the death of this dwarfish man, who walked or rode down the street with a slightly mocking, haughty smile, speaking to no one and greeting no one, as if the success of his trade in clothing and dry goods meant nothing to him; hardly anyone remembered him with any emotion, and even the widow herself showed little reaction, aside from her mourning dress.

The pair did not make use of servants, except for one slightly deranged woman from the neighborhood who occasionally came to clean the shop. Consequently there was no one who could let out the carefully guarded secrets of the building. It was known, however, that its mistress strictly insisted on the careful locking of doors, of how many keys, latches, bolts, bars, chains, and grills protected the place against unwanted visitors; and all of this, together with the couple's silence and lack of sociability, corroborated the conviction of the surrounding quarter's inhabitants that the building concealed God only knew what treasures, the more so since its inhabitants did not use banks.

And they spoke not only of money, but also of expensive furniture, which of course no one had ever seen, of expensive paintings and tapestries, and of rare gems. The imaginations of the tellers and listeners of these stories were exercised most of all by a wondrous golden Chinese dragon, its eyes, arched back, and tail encrusted with precious stones.

That such a dragon actually existed could be confirmed only by two trustworthy witnesses, who had seen it with their own eyes; one was a jeweler who bragged about arranging its purchase from a distant foreign land; the other, a notary, had glimpsed it briefly during the settlement of the estate. According to these witnesses, this jewel, suspended on a golden chain, was magnificent. The jeweler, interrupted in his ecstatic praise of the piece by an intrusive question regarding its cash value, could only raise his eyes to the heavens and wave his hand, as if he hadn't the courage or breath to pronounce such mind-boggling numbers.

No one, of course, could explain the discrepancy between these stories of fairy-tale wealth and the shabby building with its cheerless and poorly maintained shop; there were even those skeptics who dared to express doubts as to the wealth of the strange couple, but there was as little evidence to support these daring protests as there was irrefutable evidence of vast treasure.

It was to this place that the shop assistant was taken by his guardian. Many judged that the widow, in choosing a new helper to replace the forlorn girl who preceded him, was won over by his taciturnity and self-restraint, the traits that best accommodated her own disposition and the order reigning in the shop. There was, however, another hypothesis, no more distant from the truth: that she regarded with delight his bulky frame, which aroused uncertainty, timidity, and anxiety, if not outright fear of its strong, thick-fingered hands, capable, or so it seemed, of crushing almost anything with a single squeeze; the throat of a prospective criminal, it was concluded, would be decidedly defenseless against such a grip.

The new helper suspected none of this. Urged along by his impatient guide, he entered the shop rather hesitantly, but certainly without surprise.

Although his expansive body just barely fit into the space between the counter and the cabinets that contained the bolts of fabric, his seemingly clumsy hands adapted with surprising ease to the wares he now was selling; he threw the proffered fabric on the counter and spread it in such a way that its folds made a very good impression — whenever, that is, there was actually something to sell, for almost all the stores in the city had to contend with sporadic deliveries.

It would even happen that for days at a time there would be nothing to do in the shop; the shelves yawned emptily, and wrapping paper hid the mannequins' nakedness. At such times the widow would go off, lock herself in her boudoir, and occupy herself with some more or less superfluous papers or thoughts, and the shop assistant, left on guard in the store, just in case, loitered out front on the half-empty street, along which entirely unknown people from other parts of town sometimes trudged; the girl he hoped to see, however, never passed this way.

From the very beginning she made unambiguously clear to him his duties and few rights, his standing and his place. He slept in a designated cubbyhole of the apartment, which was decorated in a way that hardly corresponded to the stories told about it. It was a sign of great confidence that he was entrusted with the keys. Unless given some meaningless errand, however, he never went out into the city; after the store closed, if there was no other work to do, he would sit alone and devote himself to thoughts he never confided to anyone, so that he remained an unknown stranger to those around him — until something happened to fundamentally change his position.

*

Now, as he ascended the stairs that led past the back door of the store to the apartment on the second floor, he still had no inkling that out of this confusion would emerge the biggest decision of his life, one he would reach himself and which would, like the proverbial pebble, start an avalanche of urgent decisions.

One evening, as he was putting away and straightening the bolts of cloth after closing, the widow, who had until now behaved toward him with aloofness, looked him over with some interest as if appraising some task that had escaped his attention; and when he looked up to see if there was something he was doing wrong, he noticed that an indication of satisfaction and resolution had settled on her thin lips.

It had gotten dark, the street had emptied, the entrance to the shop had been carefully locked and the security gate closed, when the widow signaled with a nod for him to follow her.

When he did not immediately understand, she repeated the gesture more emphatically and started off herself with a rustle of her long skirt. He followed her hesitantly. He vividly recorded how, as she locked the rear door of the shop with an amused nod of her head before setting out up the stairs, the barrette lodged in her tightly gathered bun reflected the flame of the lamp that burned eternally on the staircase.

As in bewilderment he mounted the stairs to the second floor behind her, right before his eyes, with each step the widow took, the flesh of her small buttocks, tightly bound in clinging satin, swayed provocatively from side to side with the brazenness of a procuress.

He did not know what was expected of him, and his

vague presentiment filled him more with aversion and fear than desire. Adding to his fear was the fact that he always entered the apartment with a certain apprehension, and had set foot in the rooms beyond his own only when, for example, he had to convey some message that could not wait. After passing through the door at the top of the stairs, he almost always turned immediately into his cubbyhole, where, aside from a small bed, there were only a few absolute necessities. Even the widow's invitation to ascend the stairs with her seemed exceptional and meaningful, although its meaning eluded him.

When the woman had led the flustered man to the top of the stairway, she opened the door and nodded for him to enter. His bewilderment became even greater when, with an odd little smile, she opened the door to her bedroom and pushed him inside. He stumbled, staggered, and found himself standing, uncertainly, next to a made-up bed.

The widow shut the door, turned, and again subjected him to a scrutinizing gaze; apparently satisfied, she stepped toward him with a deep sigh and, with an amorous murmur, began to touch him proprietarily, finger him and finally undress him, all the while provoking and caressing him in various ways, until alongside his growing fear and astonishment there arose in him feelings he had never before suspected.

Nevertheless, when he was completely naked, instead of shame and embarrassment he above all felt surprise at what was happening to his body, because, although it had sometimes happened, albeit not very frequently, that his maleness made itself known, it had always been a pale reflection, a flaccid imitation of what arises in similar situations with other men, or of what they wish would happen.

In his bewilderment he did nothing that might have helped the woman in her endeavor. She, for that matter, seemed not to expect him to, and for this reason her hands, lips, and even her teeth worked all the more assiduously, and when she was done undressing him, he looked on with no less confusion as she herself deliberately and carefully undressed, as she carelessly threw her clothes to the floor around her in blatant disregard of the principles that usually governed her strict and exacting notion of order. Finally, she threw off her last shred of underwear, with a shake of her head set free her imprisoned hair, which flowed down in tresses, pushed him toward the bed with a slight twitch of her lips and a suppressed snarl, threw him down on it, and began to attack his helpless and paralyzed body with a passion no one would have expected from this strict shop owner.

He fearfully submitted to her precisely aimed touches and fondling, more frightened than aroused by the unfamiliar and unenticing nakedness of her bony body and the swaying pouches of her aging breasts; with a feeling of shameful defeat he yielded and succumbed to her rough conquest and greedy caresses as, with hoarse cries, with her fingers and her hands and the insistence of her entire body, she aroused him, incited him, and straddled him at last.

However, greater than his efforts or his ability to comply with her demands were his confusion and fear, greater and stronger than the woman had anticipated, and thus the outcome could hardly be called successful.

Despite his timid efforts to comply with her wishes, it was not in the shop assistant's power to help her; even repeated efforts did not lead to the desired goal, and finally a half-woeful, half-angry groan of futility at all this wasted effort escaped from the woman's lips.

She turned away from the dejected giant and sat on the edge of the bed with her head in her hands, stared for a while at the floor between her bare feet, sighed and stood up, and then carelessly, shamelessly, making no effort to hide her nakedness before this man who had so miserably failed her, she gathered her scattered clothing and left the room without looking back.

The shop assistant felt desperately humiliated and disgraced.

Slowly, feeling the weight of enormous transgression, he

gathered his things, crept out of the bedroom and, his throat constricted with anguish, closed himself up in his cubbyhole.

The following days could not improve matters.

With cunning vengeance, the disappointed woman, who understood the shop assistant's failure as a foul betrayal, assigned her helper more and more difficult tasks; even when there appeared to be no work to do in the shop, nothing could satisfy her: she found fault with everything he did and berated him for no reason with glances, words, sighs, contemptuous exclamations, and demeaning remarks; she even took revenge on him to her own detriment by furiously and pointlessly unrolling the bolts of fabric he had moments before neatly rolled and stacked with the greatest of care.

As has been remarked, the first important decision can set off an avalanche whose final outcome no one can predict.

It might have been possible for the shop assistant to bear the woman's capricious cruelty, if it weren't for the humiliating memory of that evening.

It was clear that his domineering mistress would not simply allow him to leave, lest the embarrassing story of her amorous advances toward her employee become known to the outside world. To ask for permission to leave was impossible, so he would have to leave unnoticed, quietly, secretly, avoiding the cries and reproaches that would have otherwise rained down on his head.

And so, as quietly as his clumsy body would allow, he crept out into the hallway, at the end of which was an open window like a gaping hole into the courtyard; he quietly opened the door to his room, slipped inside, gathered his few possessions, the handful of objects he considered important, stuck them in the pockets of his long overcoat, and quietly stepped out into the hall, determined never to return.

The sense of order cultivated in him by years at home and in the institution even now made him take a few steps counter to his intention. Because it was the desire and command of his mistress that all the windows in the house be shut every night, he walked to the end of the hallway and carefully closed the open window. He seemed to hear a muffled sigh from the bedroom or from one of the other rooms. The unapproachable woman had made it explicit that even in moments of sudden grief, which were in any case rare, she did not wish to be comforted by anyone; and so he left her loneliness unanswered and, his face tense with anxiety, passed through the hall on tiptoe, carefully descended the stairs, went out into the deserted street, and headed off in a daze through the gray twilight toward the train station, a path he knew well from his errands. He was firmly resolved to leave behind not only the shop, but the city as well, to hide somewhere, although he could not, even remotely, imagine where he might find such a hiding place, how to get there, or what to do.

*

Sometimes he was visited by dreams.

He saw himself in a snow-white gazebo in the middle of a meadow full of chrysanthemums, engaged in some vague yet unquestionably important activity; it did not matter that in reality he had never seen such a gazebo, but had composed its image from bits of overheard conversations and a hazy picture from some childhood book.

In his dream it is a lofty, white wooden structure, an ethereal tower whose interior is filled with wicker garden furniture. Snow-white columns ending in the heads of benevolently grinning fauns and supporting a graceful dome jut up from its intricately carved railings. All around the gazebo stretches a meadow, flat, fragrant, and strewn with thousands of flowers, ending finally on the horizon in a welcoming forest on a gentle slope, where the bright red roof of a small castle gleams among the trees.

The boy is sitting, occupied with his work, when he is interrupted by the sound of distant voices yelling and calling. He looks up and sees his entire family approaching across the meadow and calling out to him.

The father is running in front, dressed in a white suit and pale green vest, waving to him with his pale straw hat. A little to the side is his mother, waving a parasol; her hat, tied beneath her chin with a muslin scarf, has slipped a little to one side, detracting from her seriousness. Behind them, but not by much, run both his brothers and his sister, the eyes of all three shining with joy.

As they all run, it is odd how as they lift their legs they gently rise off the ground, slowly fly through the air, softly land, and then, with the next step, lift off again. The boy's joy at their approach is prolonged and grows with each slow spring that shortens the distance between them.

They never reach him.

Before the boy could be granted a loving embrace, the dream always shattered and dissolved in a mist, as if he was never meant to experience its conclusion.

When he raised his eyes, it was not a white gazebo that stood before him, but the decrepit train station, its denuded walls stained with black deposits of dust and smoke.

About the Authors

Michal Ajvaz (b. 1949) is a poet, fiction writer, and essayist. His publications include the poetry collection *Vražda v hotelu Intercontinental* (Murder in the Intercontinental Hotel, 1989), the story collection *Návrat starého varana* (Return of the Old Komodo Dragon, 1991), and the novel *Druhé město* (The Other City, 1993; excerpted here).

Alexandra Berková (b. 1949) is the author of a collection of short stories, *Knížka s červeným obalem* (The Book with a Red Cover, 1986), and two novellas, *Magorie* (Magoria, 1991) and *Utrpení oddaného všiváka* (The Sufferings of Devoted Scoundrel, 1994; excerpted here). She also writes plays for radio and television.

Tereza Boučková (b. 1957), the youngest daughter of novelist Pavel Kohout, is the author of the novel *Indiánský běh* (Indian Run, 1992). The novella *Křepelice* (Quail, 1993; included here) is her latest published fiction.

Pavel Brycz (b. 1968) is the youngest contributor to this anthology. He has published a story collection, *Hlava Upanišády* (The Head of the Upanishads, 1993; excerpted here). His stories and poems have appeared in literary magazines, and he has also written lyrics for rock songs.

Daniela Fischerová (b. 1948) was best known before the Velvet Revolution for her plays, radio plays, and screenplays, many of which were translated and staged around the world. She has also written children's literature and fairy tales, most recently *Lenka a Nelka, nebo Aha* (Lenka and Nelka, or Aha, 1994). Her most recent book for adults is the story collection *Prst, který se nikdy nedotkne* (The Finger That Never Touches, 1995; excerpted here).

Pavel Grym (b. 1930) is a theater historian and feuilletonist involved with the Spejlba and Harvínka Theater. He has written for the stage, radio, and television, and is the author of many fairy tales and instructional books for children. Excerpted here is his novella *Čínský drak* (The Chinese Dragon, 1993)

Daniela Hodrová (b. 1946) is a literary scholar as well as a novelist. Her novels include the trilogy *Trýznivé město* (The Suffering City): *Podobojí* (Utraquists, 1991), *Kukly* (Chrysalises, 1991), *Théta* (Theta, 1992); as well as *Perunův den* (Perun's Day, 1994; excerpted here).

Marta Kadlečíková (1935-1996) won the American Writers Fund Short Story Prize for Eastern and Central Europe and was the general secretary of the Czech PEN Club from 1968 until 1990. Her stories were published extensively in literary magazines and collected in *Povídky* (Stories, 1993; excerpted here). She also wrote numerous film scripts.

Alexandr Kliment (b. 1929) is a journalist, screenwriter, and novelist. His work was banned after 1970 and published only abroad; he worked as an ambulance driver and porter. He is best known for his novels *Basic Love* (1981) and *Nuda v Čechách* (Boredom in Bohemia, 1979; excerpted here). His latest book is *Modré pohádky* (Blue Fairy Tales, 1994).

Vašek Koubek (b. 1955) is a musician, poet, and prose writer. He has published a book of poems, *Teď' to je čistý* (Now It's Clean, 1992), and two story collections, *Povídky* (Stories, 1993; excerpted here) and *Vesnické povídky* (Country Stories, 1996).

Jiří Kratochvil (b. 1940) is the author of two collections of short stories, *Orfeus z Kénigu* (The Orpheus of Kénig, 1994; excerpted here) and *Má lasko, Postmoderno* (Postmodern, My Love, 1994). Both collections contain new and old material, because much of his writing was banned. He is also the author of a novel trilogy and a number of radio and theatrical plays.

Ewald Murrer (b. 1964) is a poet and editor as well as a prose writer. *Sny na konci noci* (Dreams at the End of the Night, 1996; excerpted here) is his most recent book of short stories. In addition, he has written *Vyznamenání za prohranou válku* (A Medal for the War That Was Lost, 1992) and *Zápisník pana Pinkého* (Mr. Pinke's Notebook, 1986).

Halina Pawlowská (b. 1955) is the editor of the Czech illustrated magazine *Story*. Her novel *Díky za každé nové ráno* (Thank You for Each New Morning, 1994; excerpted here) was made into an award-winning film of the same name, for which she wrote the screenplay. She is also the author of three recent collections of short stories.

Pavel Řezníček (b. 1942) writes surrealist poetry and prose. His work has been translated into several languages, especially French. His most recent novels are *Alexandr v tramvaji* (Alexandr on the Streetcar, 1994) and *Zvířata* (Animals, 1993; excerpted here).

Jáchym Topol (b. 1962) is a poet, rock lyricist, and founding editor of *Revolver Revue*, an originally samizdat cultural magazine. His first novel, *Sestra* (Sister, 1994; excerpted here), won the Egon Hostovský Prize, and his most recent prose work is the novella *Anděl* (Angel, 1995; excerpted here). He is currently translating Native American poetry into Czech.

Michal Viewegh (b. 1962) is the author of three novels, *Báječná léta pod psa* (The Blissful Years of Lousy Living, 1992), *Výchova dívek v Čechách* (Bringing Up Girls in Bohemia, 1994), and *Účastníci zájezdu* (Sightseers, 1996; excerpted here). He has also written a collection of literary parodies. He will be the first of the writers in this collection to have a book appear in English translation.

About the Translators

Neil Bermel (b. 1965) is Lecturer in Czech Language and Literature at the University of Sheffield (England). Bermel received his Ph.D. in Slavic Languages and Literatures from the University of California, Berkeley in 1994. *I Am Snowing,* his translation of Pavel Kohout's *Sněžím,* was published in 1994 by Farrar, Straus & Giroux. He translated the Fischerová story.

Jonathan Bolton (b. 1968) studied philosophy as an undergraduate at Harvard and is currently working on an M.A. in Czech literature at the University of Texas at Austin. He has studied Czech at Masaryk University in Brno and at Charles University in Prague, and has translated excerpts from the diaries of Jan Zábrana. He translated the Kratochvil story and the Berková excerpt.

Andrée Collier (b. 1967) lives in Boston. After spending five years in Plzeň, she obtained an M.A. in Russian and Eastern European Studies at Harvard University. She frequently writes about Czech literature for *The Prague Post*, and is currently studying and translating the work of Czech women writers of the Sixty-eight generation. She translated the Kliment excerpt.

Caleb Crain (b. 1967) translated *Václav Havel: The Authorized Biography* by Eda Kriseová (St. Martin's Press, 1993). He has written for *American Literature, The New Republic, Newsday,* and *Out.* He's at work on a novel and a Ph.D. in American Literature at Columbia University. He translated the Koubek and Boučková stories.

Tatiana Firkušný (b. 1945) grew up in Czechoslovakia and came to New York in 1965, following her marriage to the concert pianist Rudolf Firkušný. She has a degree from New York University, and has done translations from Czech for a number of publishers and institutions. She co-translated the Ajvaz and Hodrová excerpts.

Veronique Firkušný-Callegari (b. 1966) grew up trilingual in Czech, English, and French. She has a degree from Barnard College, and has collaborated with her mother, Tatiana Firkušný, on a number of translations from Czech. She also translates from French, German, and Italian, and works with opera singers as a Czech-language coach. She co-translated the Ajvaz and Hodrová excerpts.

Julie Hansen (b. 1970) is a doctoral student in Slavic Languages and Literatures at the University of Michigan in Ann Arbor. She is currently translating Josef Škvorecký's collection *Hořkej svět* (A Bitter World). She translated the Murrer and Brycz stories.

Dana Loewy (b. 1960) teaches business writing at California State University, Fullerton and translates from and into Czech and German. Her book-length translation *The Early Poetry of Jaroslav Seifert* (Northwestern Univ. Press) is scheduled for publication in spring 1997. She co-translated the Kadlečíková story.

Jason Pontius (b. 1970) studies Czech linguistics at the University of Chicago; his primary object of study is Czech linguistic purism and language planning in the nineteenth century. He is also the editor of *Mutatis Mutandis*, an occasional journal devoted to the theory and practice of literary translation. He co-translated the Řezníček excerpt.

David Powelstock (b. 1964) is Assistant Professor of Russian and Czech Literatures at the University of Chicago. Among the works of Russian and Czech poetry and prose he has translated are two novels by the Czech writer Iva Pekárková, *Truck Stop Rainbows* and *The World Is Round* (both Farrar, Straus & Giroux). He is currently working on a book about the Russian poet Mikhail Lermontov. He translated the Grym excerpt.

Malynne Sternstein (b. 1966) is Assistant Professor of Slavic Languages and Literatures at the University of Chicago. She is currently working on a comparative study of the Czech and Russian avant-garde movements. She co-translated the Řezníček excerpt.

Lisa Ryoko Wakamiya (b. 1970) is a graduate student in the Department of Slavic Languages and Literatures at the University of California at Los Angeles. Her interests include the Czech literary Baroque and twentieth-century Czech and Russian literature in emigration. She translated the Pawlowská excerpt.

Robert Wechsler (b. 1954) is the publisher at Catbird Press. He edited the translations in this book, and co-translated the Kadlečíková story.

Alex Zucker (b. 1964) is a freelance editor in New York City who has translated a great deal for a number of literary publications and newspapers. He has translated *A Trip to the Train Station* by Jáchym Topol, and is currently translating Topol's novel *Sister*. He translated the Topol and Viewegh excerpts.

Acknowledgments

Michal Ajvaz: Excerpt from *Druhé město* Copyright © 1993 Michal Ajvaz, by permission of the publisher, Mladá Fronta.

Alexandra Berková: Excerpt from *Utrpení oddaného všiváka* © 1994 Alexandra Berková, by permission of the author and of the publisher, Petrov, Brno.

Tereza Boučková: *Křepelice* © 1993 Tereza Boučková, by permission of the author.

Pavel Brycz: "Dance on the Square" from *Hlava Upanišády* © 1993 Pavel Brycz.

Daniela Fischerová: "Letter for President Eisenhower" from *Prst, který se nikdy nedotkne* © 1995 Daniela Fischerová, by permission of the author.

Pavel Grym: Excerpt from *Čínský drak* © 1993 Pavel Grym, by permission of the author.

Daniela Hodrová: Excerpt from *Perunův den* © 1994 Daniela Hodrová, by permission of the author.

Marta Kadlečíková: "Ode to Joy" from *Povídky* © 1993 Marta Kadlečíková, by permission of the publisher, Arca Jimfa, Třebíč.

Alexandr Kliment: Excerpt from *Nuda v Čechách* © 1990 Alexandr Kliment, by permission of the publisher, Český spisovatel.

Vašek Koubek: "The Bottle" and "Hell" from *Povídky* © 1993 Vašek Koubek, by permission of the author.

Jiří Kratochvil: "The Story of King Candaules" from *Orfeus z Kénigu* © 1994 Jiří Kratochvil, by permission of the publisher, Atlantis, Brno.

Ewald Murrer: "The Mask" from *Sny na konci noci* © 1996 Ewald Murrer, by permission of the author and of the publisher, Petrov, Brno.